Jane Linfoot writes fun, flirty fiction  bit of an edge. She lives in a mou... where her family and pets are ... domestic chaos. Jane loves hearts, flowers, happy endings, all things vintage, most things French. When she's not on Facebook, and can't find an excuse for shopping, she'll be walking, or gardening. On days when she wants to be really scared, she rides a tandem.

www.janelinfoot.co.uk

 x.com/Janelinfoot
 instagram.com/Janelinfoot

ALSO BY JANE LINFOOT

The Little Cornish Kitchen Series
The Little Cornish Kitchen
Tea for Two at the Little Cornish Kitchen
A Winter Warmer at the Little Cornish Kitchen
The Little Cornish Beach Hut Café
The Cosy Croissant Café

The Little Wedding Shop by the Sea Series
The Little Wedding Shop by the Sea
Christmas at the Little Wedding Shop
Summer at the Little Wedding Shop
Christmas Promises at the Little Wedding Shop
Love at the Little Wedding Shop by the Sea

Also Set in St Aidan, Cornwall
A Cornish Cottage by the Sea
A Cosy Christmas in Cornwall

Other standalones
How to Win a Guy in 10 Dates
The Right Side of Mr Wrong
High Heels & Bicycle Wheels
The Vintage Cinema Club

THE COSY CROISSANT CAFÉ

JANE LINFOOT

One More Chapter
a division of HarperCollins*Publishers* Ltd
1 London Bridge Street
London SE1 9GF
www.harpercollins.co.uk
HarperCollins*Publishers*
Macken House, 39/40 Mayor Street Upper,
Dublin 1, D01 C9W8, Ireland

This paperback edition 2025

1

First published in Great Britain in ebook format
by HarperCollins*Publishers* 2025
Copyright © Jane Linfoot 2025
Jane Linfoot asserts the moral right to be identified
as the author of this work

A catalogue record of this book is available from the British Library
ISBN: 978-0-00-876600-9

This novel is entirely a work of fiction. The names, characters and incidents portrayed in it are the work of the author's imagination. Any resemblance to actual persons, living or dead, events or localities is entirely coincidental.

Printed and bound in the UK using 100% Renewable Electricity
by CPI Group (UK) Ltd

All rights reserved. No part of this publication may be reproduced, stored in a retrieval system, or transmitted, in any form or by any means, electronic, mechanical, photocopying, recording or otherwise, without the prior permission of the publishers.

Without limiting the author's and publisher's exclusive rights, any unauthorised use of this publication to train generative artificial intelligence (AI) technologies is expressly prohibited. HarperCollins also exercise their rights under Article 4(3) of the Digital Single Market Directive 2019/790 and expressly reserve this publication from the text and data mining exception.

For Eric, Theo, Dahlia and Lyla-Rose – with love. xx

Life shrinks or expands in proportion to one's courage.

ANAÏS NIN

MAY

1

The Harbourside, St Aidan
Window Boxes and New Leaves
Sunday

'A summer by the sea might not be what we'd planned, Pumpkin, but it may turn out to be awesome.'

As I'm talking to a pony, I'm not expecting an answer, and we both know I'm reassuring myself as much as him. Getting Pumpkin all the way from Somerset to Cornwall on a sunny Sunday when the narrow winding streets of St Aidan are heaving with visitors means there's been no time for regrets about the life we're leaving behind.

Arriving on the harbourside with a bright chestnut Shetland pony who shakes his blond mane as he takes his first breaths of sea air means an audience is unavoidable and Pumpkin insists on getting an ear scratch from every group of visitors we pass. His hooves are clattering on the cobbles as we finally leave the brightly coloured boats bobbing in the harbour and head off towards the beach path.

I give a firm tug on his lead rein when he tries to snatch a mouthful of daisies from the window box of the last of the little stone cottages that line the quayside. 'The flowers here might be at nose height, but they're not there for ponies, mister!'

As I hitch up my rucksack of essentials I feel the vibration of my phone in my pocket. I'm guessing it's my big sister, Scarlett, checking in on us.

Me having to move out of the bedsit where I've spent the last few years wasn't ideal, especially when I have a pony in tow, but Scarlett has come to our rescue and offered us the use of her Cornish holiday home while she's away in the States. It's all been a bit rushed and I'm hoping to slip into town quietly so she can bring her other half, Tate, up to speed with the arrangements before he hears it from anyone local.

When it comes to organisation, Scarlett is epic. Within a couple of hours of me jumping at her offer she'd sorted a space by the harbour for me to leave the horse trailer, organised a local parking permit for my car, had a fencer to check that the field her cottage stands in is pony-proof, and a botanist to check there were no poisonous plants. And if this is her now, she'll be ringing from the departure lounge at Heathrow to fill me in on any last-minute instructions.

'Great you're there safely, Betty! What colour is the sea?'

I look out across the bay. 'The water's deep turquoise, the sun is making it shine like fish scales, and there are lines of white breakers racing towards the shore.'

She gives a wistful sigh. 'Tell me some more. I need a last Cornish fix before I fly away.'

I look around. 'The seagulls are calling as they follow a fishing boat, the pink and white cottages look like Lego houses stacked up the hillside behind me. We're walking past that cafe made out of planks, and it's so busy the queue is spilling off the deck and onto the sand.'

She moans. 'I'm *so* going to miss the Surf Shack.'

I catch sight of the painted menu board. 'However delish the ice cream sundaes are here, once you get to New York you'll be all about the cheesecake and the hot dogs...' I always forget she's practically vegan so I add, 'They're bound to have fabulous meat-free versions.'

Scarlett and I are four years apart and other than sharing our surname and our auburn hair tone we couldn't be more different. I try to sidestep the sensible stuff, where she grabs it with both hands. As a child, while I was making flower petal dinners for butterflies she was strutting around in Gran's cast-off high heels, taking shorthand notes and picking out her wedding cake from the Marks and Spencer *Complete Guide to Celebration Icing*.

Her entire childhood was spent trying to fast-forward to adulthood, and at thirty-two she's made a name for herself as a buyer in the fashion industry, she has an architect husband, Tate, and they live in a gigantic house that they built themselves in the coolest suburb in Manchester. Thankfully they stopped short of kids, because much as I love her, I'm not sure Scarlett has the space to add a child into the whirlwind that's her life.

Obviously they had to put their spare energy into something, and the next best thing to a baby was a holiday home, which is how Pumpkin and I ended up here in the picturesque village of St Aidan at the furthest westerly edge of the country.

I'm not implying that Scarlett wouldn't do a wonderful job if she and Tate did choose to have a family. As kids she was like a tigress when it came to defending me – she once flattened an entire bus shelter of lads when they had me in tears calling me ginger-nut – and since we lost our mum she's been there for me without question.

My jaw is on the floor at what she's achieved in her life, but even thinking about the commitments she's made turns my knees to jelly. I've had a string of hot dates and calamities rather than relationships, my jobs since uni have been temporary or freelance, and I'd run a mile before I stepped into the same room as a mortgage leaflet. All the way to twenty-eight my hello-clouds-hello-sky attitude to accommodation has worked like a charm. And then, very abruptly, it's turned around to bite me on the bum, which is how I've landed here. But it's basically all because of Pumpkin.

Most people assume Pumpkin is our childhood pony, but our mum actually rescued him when Scarlett left for uni. As a lifelong single parent, she'd brought us up to be independent and self-reliant, but having given us the tools to fly, she didn't want the thought of us leaving her on her own to hold us back. Ever practical, with the empty nest racing towards her, she jumped in and filled it with the kind of horse-child who would never leave home, and then took him to work with her in her job as an art therapist at the local hospices.

If Mum had had any idea that she was going to develop a brain tumour serious enough to need surgery, she would never have taken Pumpkin on. As it was, her cancer came out of nowhere and galloped at a million miles an hour. One day, she was at the optician with blurry vision, the next we knew, she was packing her hospital bag ready for her operation. She was so upbeat we never took it in that she may not come home again.

When she died the summer after I turned twenty, there was never any question of us not keeping Pumpkin. At first Scarlett and I juggled our lives and shared the pony care between us, but once her career took off it was down to me.

I've spent the last six years rubbing along in deepest Somerset where we grew up, staying in a make-shift room in the stable yard at an animal sanctuary, which came free with Pumpkin's board and lodging in return for me giving a hand around the yard and having a steady nerve with a pitchfork at haymaking time. Thanks to my degree in media studies, I now write freelance pieces for the living-the-rural-dream aspirational blogs and magazines that millennials can't get enough of and which are inhaled like oxygen by city dwellers with burnout. So long as I miss out the bits about freezing my butt off in the winter, and the strawberry fields next door getting decimated by summer drought, I've had the perfect authentic base for me to create the rural content there's so much appetite for.

We always knew the lease on the sanctuary was precarious, but no one imagined how fast plans would be passed for a housing development, or that bulldozers would be moving in to flatten the buildings around the yard within days of them serving notice.

Luckily the other local rescue centre was able to take in most of the animals along with the owner and her ancient caravan. But Pumpkin and I were always slightly on the outside and it was quietly understood that we'd make our own arrangements. Which is how we came to be jumping across to a new county, and arriving at our stop-gap here in Cornwall.

My vegan slip-up has refocused Scarlett, and she's onto her local contacts. 'If you lose your key, Zofia, the cleaning person, has a spare; she comes on Mondays. For cake, coffee and friendly chat there's Clemmie's Little Cornish Kitchen at the end of the beach; Plum's at the gallery up the hill; Floss is at the beach huts before the hotel; Nell delivers free-range eggs and Zach is bringing the hay. Anything else you need, they'll be happy to help; you've met most of them when you've visited.'

I'm pleased I read up on this. 'It's all in the welcome pack you sent?'

'Well done for doing the homework, Betsy.' She stops for a moment. 'You can turn Pumpkin straight out into the field when you get to the cottage. It's so lucky we chose a place with land and an outbuilding that will double as a stable.'

It's that adjoining patch of ground that is the lifesaver here for Pumpkin and me, along with my sister's heading off to be with Tate for five months while he sorts out the expansion of his company's New York office.

The cottage I'm heading to is Scarlett and Tate's refuge, an old boathouse that was lovingly restored, piece by beautiful piece. It's so precious I've never known them to let people stay without them being there themselves; Scarlett wouldn't be doing this for me now if I wasn't desperate, so I won't be letting her down. I'm determined to tiptoe in, and when I leave in October it'll be as if I'd never been there.

I'm walking while we talk, and suddenly I get the first glimpse of the long slate roof nestling into the side of the next cove and my tummy churns with excitement. 'We're almost there, Scarlie. I'm so grateful. Anything you want me to do just say—'

She's straight back on topic. 'The builder's just finished an outdoor shower area. If you could see your way to giving that a test run? ASAP!'

'Of course.'

'No need for a swimsuit, Tate's sited it so it's totally private. With a town full of hot surfers, you're going to have a fun-packed summer!'

As if I'd be disrespectful enough to go naked in someone else's brand-new shower. And despite being renown for my long trail of exes, thanks to one awful experience I've avoided men altogether for the last couple of years. As I've not ever shared that with Scarlett, who doesn't seem to have noticed, it's a relief to keep up the pretence and hide behind the jokes.

Scarlett carries on. 'Oops, looks like we're boarding. I'd better go.'

'Love you, Scarlie, travel safe, talk soon.'

Whenever I've visited here before, I've always been struck by the sense of calm you get when a place has been designed to perfection. As we turn up off the beach and take the grassy path towards the low stone building with its ash-grey window frames, that feeling engulfs me again. There's not a chip of gravel out of place, and the timber gate to the field is perfectly balanced as it swings open.

'Just the kind of short, rough grass that will keep your waistline under control, Pumpkin.' The fence looks as secure as Scarlett promised, with the cottage sitting half in, half out of the field, but I have a quick check around myself because you can't be too careful with a pony. Then I unclip Pumpkin's lead rope, give him a tap on his rump to signal he's free to go, and smile as he canters off, kicking his heels. A few minutes later, when he's grazing quietly, I climb the stile into the hillside cottage garden, and pull out the key Scarlett sent me.

Scarlett knows I'm a scatter brain, and thinks she can overcome that with her forward planning. Obviously I'll try my hardest not to mess up, but I haven't locked my room for six years so I know I'm going to have to up my game here.

I push the door open and step into a long kitchen/living space that could have come straight off the pages of *Elle Decoration*. I ease my bag off my shoulders, marvelling at how such a sleek kitchen can smell of baking even when there's no one here to cook in it. Then, as I wander over to a square window that overlooks the field to check on Pumpkin again, I have two surprises. Not only is the window open, but there's a tray of pastries on the windowsill.

This is Scarlett and her attention to detail. As if it wasn't enough that she's letting me stay here, she's also had one of the friend-slash-helpers she mentioned earlier drop in with a baked-goods welcome gift. When I take a swirly bun and sink my teeth into it it's warm, delicious, and has some kind of delectable toffee pecan thing going on. In fact, it's so moreish it reminds me how ravenous I am, and I eat three more straight off. I'm heading back for a fifth when I notice the trail of flakes I've dropped across the floor, so I leave the rest to have outside with coffee later.

My next stop is the bathroom, which is off the lobby that leads to the bedroom, and described by Scarlett as 'compact and entirely unsuitable for claustrophobics'. I'm grateful to have a bathroom at all, and since it's just me I won't have to close the door. I take three goes to watch the soft-close loo seat shutting, then I'm out again.

As I leave, I notice the recessed shelf above the wash basin is stacked with an array of products that definitely weren't here on my last visit. It's completely out of character for Scarlett, who likes everything tidied away, but I take down a bottle of L'Occitane almond oil shower gel, pop open the top and breathe in the scent. I have to say the Aldi version I have in the car falls a long way shorter than the comparison articles claim.

I'm putting the bottle back on the shelf when my phone pings with a message from Scarlett.

> How is the new drench? Is the thermostatic mixer working?

Another ping.

> There's ten minutes before we take off. Please, please, PLEASE try it then I can tick it off my list.

This level of persistence is why she's come so far in life. But it's warm outside, I'm wearing so many layers that my clothes are sticking to me after the walk, and it's not like I have any other pressing commitments. And if I'm doing this for Scarlett, I can borrow her pricey shower gel.

I grab a towel from the bathroom cupboard, remember the need for speed, and throw off my clothes as I cross the kitchen. By the time I arrive on the raised terrace, and reach for the shower control, I'm stripped down to a T-shirt and some briefs. A second later a waterfall of warm water is cascading over my face and I'm luxuriating as a froth of gorgeous-smelling L'Occitane bubbles washes over me. Taking in the slatted wood side screens and the rectangular bronze shower heads, I add outdoor showers to my mental list of topics to write about over the next few weeks. Buoyed up with excitement, I give a second generous squirt of shower gel. I'm reaching to turn the temperature up a notch, when I hear a cry behind me.

'Hey! This is *not* a public shower!'

So much for Scarlett's privacy claims! Although ... unless the person shouting has come across the field like I did, they'll have had to get through a locked gate to reach the courtyard on the garden side of the house. When I whip round to see who's speaking, I take in tousled dark brown curls and board shorts that are clinging in all the wrong places. Worse still, he's leaning against Scarlett's wall and swinging a towel over his shoulder like he owns the place.

I give a cough. 'Back at you. If you're looking to wash the salt off your Havaianas, you could try the Surf Shack, a short stroll along the beach?'

He's laughing quietly to himself. 'Nice try! Why not dry off, leave quietly, and we'll say no more about it?'

What can I say to someone who's completely wrong but won't admit it, all while wearing a soaking T-shirt that's now entirely transparent and pants that have disappeared right up my bum?

I forget the rest, and launch in. 'Whoever you *think* you are, I'm afraid this place is mine for the next few months. That's even my horse in the field.' That should be more than enough proof for anyone. 'So I suggest you admit you've made the mistake of a lifetime, and get the hell out of here. Like, now!'

He blows out his cheeks. 'Okay. Let's *hypothetically* accept your claims are true.' He frowns as his eyes focus. 'Whose shower gel do you think you're using there, pony girl?'

My eyes snap open and I stare at the bottle in my hand. 'It belongs to my sister, Scarlett, who owns the cottage.'

His nostrils flare as he draws in a breath. 'It's actually *my* gel. And it's in Scarlett's bathroom because *her* husband, Tate, arranged for *me* to look after this place while they're abroad.'

'B-b-b-but...' I seriously doubt Tate would have, because he knows this is Scarlett's sacred space. My heart falters, then it leaps again as I grab my phone from the table. 'I'll talk to Scarlett. She'll sort this out.'

She picks up on the first ring. 'Betty, how's the shower? Does the thermostat work?'

'All good.'

'That's the news I was waiting for.' I imagine her punching the air, laughing. 'It's a double, don't forget to make the most of that. Switching my phone off now, see you on the other side.'

'Scarlett, wait! There's a guy...' Too late. I'm talking to myself.

What the hell do I do now? I'm not used to ordering people around, but my instinct tells me I need to be firm here.

I force my face into a smile. 'Well, Mr Occitane, it's going to be the morning before Scarlett can confirm to you that I'll be the one staying here. You'll need to make alternative arrangements tomorrow, but I'm happy for you to stay until then.'

As a person who just got forced out of their home, I'm reluctant to evict him on the spot, and if he leaves first thing, it's no big deal. With one sizzling hot guy who refuses to accept he's in the wrong, I'm lucky it won't be for longer.

I beam at him again. 'So if that's all okay with you, I'll get back to my shower.'

He laughs. 'It's big enough for two, you know?'

I ignore that and wave the plastic bottle at him. 'I'm done with the gel if you'd like to take it.' I toss it towards the house and he springs and snatches it out of the air in exactly the show-off, athletic way I knew he would, then grins at me.

'Message received, loud and clear. I'll take mine inside.'

I've no idea why my cheeks are burning. Hiccups like this are what keep life interesting; in a few hours' time I'll wave him on his way and get back to my very peaceful summer.

And I've got at least ten minutes to regain my cool before I have to face him again.

2

Boathouse Cottage, St Aidan
Clean sheets and crumbling cliffs
Sunday

'You don't recognise me, do you?'

I was so busy avoiding getting thrown off the property earlier, I was less observant than I should have been. Now I look more closely as I cross the kitchen, there is something familiar about his stubbled jaw, but it's mostly the way his eyes look like he's laughing at some side-cracking private joke in a very superior way. And now he's had a shower and has reappeared with towelled hair, in jeans and a polo shirt, apart from the smirk, he's scrubbed up pretty well.

'Give me a clue?'

He looks even more pleased with himself. 'Scarlett and Tate's wedding party...'

My stomach gives a horrible lurch of shock, then I collect myself and try to act like a normal person would. That was the day minimalism went out of the window and they got married in a country house hotel with a deer park, a lake and a hundred and fifty close friends.

The guy is staring through narrowed, hazel-brown eyes. 'I was one of the three best men.'

I ignore the goosebumps on my arms, and swallow down the nausea in my throat. 'And I was one of the seven bridespeople.'

The bride and groom had equal numbers on their sides, but where Scarlett's team were a happy mix of unpretentious women, some of Tate's crew were up themselves to the point of being obnoxious. *And then there was Mason, my plus one, who I've trained myself never to think about and is the reason why I feel like I'm about to throw up.*

The smile lilting around the corners of this guy's mouth turns to triumph. '*You* were the bridesmaid everyone was looking at!'

I fire a warning shot. 'Be careful where you go with that. These days hasty observations about women can land you in very hot water, if not in court.'

He gives a cough. 'Due to your amazing red hair, obviously.'

He's missed that the bride's is a very similar shade, though in his favour Scarlett is more of a strawberry blonde where I'm copper, and her hair has always been naturally sleek where mine is seriously messy.

I shake what's left of my own hair. 'There's less of it now.' Two years ago it was long and wild, caught up in braids and twists, woven with pearl strings, but I cut it off in an attempt to leave the past behind. Lately I've been rocking an asymmetrical choppy bob that's now grown out and looks a lot like I've got a beech hedge in autumn spreading across my shoulders.

As for the milk-white silk slip dresses Scarlett chose for her attendants, they looked fabulous on the others, because they knew what was coming and had spent the previous six months in the gym, dieting away their hips and getting breasts. Even the one with a seven-month baby bump carried her dress off better than me.

My summer of haymaking in Somerset coupled with a serious apple crumble habit had put more pounds on me than it took off. I also missed out on the group memo about ditching our underwear. Take it from me, leaving my bra on the floor and using tit tape for the first time on the day of the event was never going to end well. Whoever this guy is, if he remembers my neckline sliding all points south, east *and* west the entire day, he has that in common with the other hundred and forty-nine guests.

I come in from outside in my wet T-shirt with a towel wrapped around my chest, and noticing his gaze sliding down to my cleavage, I decide I may as well correct his wrong conclusions. 'My boobs are smaller than they look. They only stick out because my ribcage is big.' I might have flashed them around to get attention once, but I definitely don't do that anymore.

'Thank you for clearing that one up.' His grin breaks fully free at that point and unleashes the kind of slices in his cheeks that would have melted me as a teenager. At the ripe old age of twenty-eight, after a series of dickhead boyfriends and one gut-wrenching incident no one knows about, I'm more discerning. These days it takes a lot more than cute dimples to even raise an eyebrow. No one's come anywhere near the starting blocks, and after what I went through, I can't ever imagine that changing.

My track record suggests I'm crap at appraising men, but as

this guy holds out his hand my internal knobhead alarm explodes into action.

'In case you've forgotten, I'm Miles. Miles Appleton. It's great to run into you again.'

I tuck my phone under one elbow, cling onto my towel, and ease out my spare hand. Our palms meet with a tingle, and when his fingers close around mine, it hits me like a ton of bricks.

Talk about overlaying bad things with worse – I should have known the minute I saw him! His name is laser-cut in my list of men to be avoided until the end of time. Miles Appleton, the best man Scarlett had personally selected as my visual-match slash partner-for-the-day who refused to come anywhere near me. All Scarlett's hopes for elementally composed groups were tossed aside when he glued himself to the pregnant bride attendant half his height, and I ended up partnering Tate's twelve-year-old half-brother who was small for his age. As Miles basically trashed her wedding album single-handedly, I doubt she'll have forgiven him either. Which makes it doubly strange that he's here at the cottage.

Even though I used to be famous for giving people the benefit of the doubt, it's unlikely anyone could make the leap from the total tosser he was to acceptable, which is all the more reason for me to tread very carefully here.

'I'm Betty. Or Beth. Or Eliza. All short for Elizabeth, which no one ever calls me.' I go overboard on the name options so I can skip the 'happy to see you' bit. I'm appalled that he's turned up, and he's just redoubled that. Then it hits me there are other priorities to deal with. 'I should get dressed.'

I stare around the floor, looking for the skirts and cardi I tossed away earlier.

He coughs again, and comes forward with a pile of neatly folded garments. 'You might need these?'

I hide my horror that he must have touched my bra to move things to this stage, and carry on.

'Valet service?' Maybe that's how he clawed his way back into Scarlett's good books. I look into his eyes as I move forward to take back my clothes, but all I get is a rather alarming shiver down my spine and the sense that he's staring over my shoulder. 'Everything okay back there, Miles?'

He pulls a face. 'That very much depends, Eliza Beth Betty, on how you define fine. My plate of fresh bakes by the window has vanished, and in its place I'm looking at ... a donkey?'

As the penny drops I spin around and run the length of the room. 'Jeez, Pumpkin, head *outside the window please!*' I push my way past his bony cheek to peer over the thick stone sill and confirm the worst. I hare outside and leap over the stile into the field, with Miles a breath behind me. We come to a halt by an upturned tray next to Pumpkin's neat front hooves. As I wedge my thigh against Pumpkin's shoulder to shove him backwards, we all look down at the pile of pastries scattered among the grass blades.

Miles frowns. 'Are ponies allowed to eat laminated pastry?'

'Why?' Pumpkin's crumb-free nose suggests we disturbed him before he got that far.

Miles is scrutinising the ground. 'I made a lot more pastries than are here, that's all.'

I can't possibly fess up that I ate my body weight of the things before he even came back, so I move this on. '*You* made them? You have personally nailed the art of croissant dough?' As baking skills go, that's high level! I move on to covering up. 'Isn't puffed crust mostly filled with air? They probably crumbled to nothing as they fell.'

He turns over the tray and pushes the remnants onto it. 'When a horse refuses them, I get the message. My previous attempts weren't edible either.'

As I lean on Pumpkin, I'm cringing with guilt that he has no idea how delicious they were, but it's his fault for crushing my self-esteem so thoroughly at the wedding. He was the one who strutted round all day ignoring the one person he was supposed to be escorting. However bruised I was by that, I still have standards, so I give a sniff. 'I'm sorry these are ruined. I should have closed the window when I put Pumpkin in the field.'

We make our way back to the kitchen, and he drops the pastries into the bin. 'Yet another wild idea I won't be revisiting.' He's talking in riddles, but there's no need to reply because he's picked up my clothes pile again. 'As I was saying, Scarlett and Tate tidy as they go. We might want to do the same?'

Could he be any more condescending? Except that's not the worst part of what he's said. 'We?'

He nods. 'Until tomorrow, I'm afraid that's us.'

I suspend my disbelief at what an arse he sounds, and finally get where he's heading with this. 'You're thinking about arrangements for tonight...' As my pony just demolished his baking, I'm on the back foot here.

Miles raises his eyebrows. 'You take the bedroom. If you give me a few minutes I'll change the sheets.'

His assumption that he's in charge makes me disagree on

principle. 'We women have spent a century fighting for equality. I'll take the sofa, then it saves on laundry.'

He narrows his eyes. 'It's your call. I'm going out shortly, so I won't be in your way. I'll do my best not to wake you when I get back.'

Heading for the bathroom to dress, I make myself beam at him. 'By the time I wake up in the morning, you'll probably be gone.'

There's no reason at all I should be feeling disappointed. If this is about closure, I've pretty much got that. Locking myself in the minuscule bathroom, I give a sigh of relief that after tomorrow I'll have no further need to shut the bathroom door at all. I mean, even with Scarlett's Purdy and Figg lemongrass toilet drops, there's no way I could do a number two with a stranger around.

First thing tomorrow Scarlett will be on the end of the phone to sort this out, and then it'll be Pumpkin and me at Boathouse Cottage, all the way to October!

3

Boathouse Cottage, St Aidan
Rocks and hard places
Monday

Miles might be a world-class plonker, but this time he was as good as his word. By the time I'd walked along the beach to St Aidan and back to get some dinner and a bag of carrots for Pumpkin, Miles had gone and I had Boathouse Cottage to myself. I took a moment to soak in the emptiness of the long kitchen diner, with its high ceiling that follows the sloping planes of the roof and ends with a living area, also known as the tranquillity zone, which is so far away it's literally in the distance. Then I dropped my bags on the floor by the island unit and headed off to eat a sandwich and Hula Hoop tea while I watched the sun set over the bay from the sun lounger on one of the terraces above the end of the cottage. As Pumpkin's coat turned to gold in the fading light in the field below, I had to pinch myself to make sure the sound of the rushing waves in the distance was real. Then I went inside, stretched out on the immense sofa with Pumpkin still in view, jotted down a few lines about today, and put my head on my pillow with my notebook tucked under my cheek.

But instead of closing my eyes and drifting into a deep exhausted sleep, my mind replays the night of Scarlett's wedding. Over and over.

When you look back on life there are watersheds – significant moments that separate the past from the future so decisively, it's not like you've changed valleys, it's more like you've moved to a different country entirely.

Mum dying was awful, but we pulled together afterwards and carried on in a way she'd have been proud of because we knew that was what she wanted.

But Scarlett's wedding marked a different kind of line in the sand for me. Before it I was this ditsy girl with the crazy long list of exes. The one who showed the world how to party and then some. I might have already been slowing down a little by the time I was twenty-six, but after the wedding, I completely left that person behind.

It wasn't *actually* about what happened that day with Miles. That was annoying and confidence-sapping, but what came next was the kind of thing that stopped my life as I knew it and changed how I felt about myself forever.

I've spent the time since trying to erase it from my mind, and I'd imagined I'd succeeded. But yesterday's unexpected collision with Miles has brought it crashing back into my consciousness and in the early hours I can't stop it banging around my brain.

Me and Mason had started out so well. There was no hope of anyone from my own circle reaching Scarlett's lofty requirements for my plus one, then one Saturday a few weeks before the wedding I ran into a guy on the dance floor at a friend's party. I asked the question – do you have a suit? – and instead of rolling on the floor laughing, he told me he had a wardrobe of the things and offered to show me them. True, we were both wasted at the time, but I'd asked every hot guy in Somerset for months with no luck, and meeting him felt like serendipity.

Better still, having the wedding to focus on was like fairy dust for the dates that followed. Instead of yawnsville IT-manager work talk, we focused on exciting things like how to get to deepest Cheshire by seven in the morning, how many suit-hanging hooks his executive Beamer had, how many different sex positions we could manage in his car. Better still, when we had a Zoom call with Scarlett she was so taken with him she sent me three giant thumb emojis on the sisterly WhatsApp chat *while we were still talking*.

As we set off on the day, I was pinching myself that for the first time ever at a wedding, I was going to have a guy of my own to drag onto the floor when the first dance finished. Then, at five in the morning on the way there, we hit traffic on the M5 and Mason got out a hip flask, said *alcohol and sex, there's a lot to like about weddings*, and it went downhill from there. When he fell off his chair during the toasts it took every bridesmaid except the pregnant one to coax him upstairs for a recuperation nap. When I went to check on him later and he was snoring with a bottle of whisky on the pillow and porn on the TV I mostly felt relief that he wouldn't be coming down again.

I went up to bed at midnight, checked he was still breathing then went to sort out my hair. I was pulling out the pins when I saw him in the mirror behind me – belt undone, shirt open. I can still hear my own voice, ringing out across the bedroom.

I don't want to sleep with you, Mason, not tonight.

Then he's spinning me round, trying to kiss me. And I hear his reply.

We'll see about that.

His laugh as he rams me against the wall. The surprise when he takes hold of the milky white satin of my shoulder strap, the shock of how one pull rips the front out of my dress. How my boobs are striped with tit tape.

Me lurching forwards, feeling the spike of my heel embed itself in his foot. Knowing from the flintiness in his eyes that I'd hurt him, then him muttering '*you cockteasing bitch*' and then my face hitting the wall and my cheekbone exploding with pain. Then him yanking my arm so hard it's crunching in its socket, then the floor rushing towards me. Me crashing down against the striped velvet tub chair. The pain shooting up my arm when I put my hand out to break the fall. Him walking away.

And then a long time later, he's looking down at me huddled in the chair.

Girls who get drunk and fall off their heels. You never learn, do you.

He's squatting down, squinting at my cheek.

You can't go down to breakfast looking like that. We need to leave.

Then we're pushing clothes into suitcases, and hurrying through reception.

I know what happened in that hotel room was nothing compared to what some people go through, but it's like a stone that I carry around in my chest that weighs me down. Before it I was light, it was easy to fly, but I took that carefree self for granted. This has tethered me to the ground.

I used to be wafty and ephemeral. I used to live life like nothing mattered, and now I know better. I used to feel invincible, but that certainty and self-belief was shattered in a single second. One crushing blow. My face smashed against a wall, my arm wrenched, the pain exploding as the bone in my wrist splintered.

And the most devastating part is that if I'd been a better, cleverer person it could all have been avoided. And it has always felt it was all my fault.

4

Boathouse Cottage, St Aidan
Less than zero
Monday

I left the blinds open last night, thinking I'd get up at first light and take Pumpkin for a stroll along the sands. But thanks to me only falling asleep hours after dawn broke and my head being buried in my sleeping bag, it's almost eight by the time I'm leading Pumpkin along next to the frothing waves at the water's edge.

I force myself to put the past back in its box and channel my lighter side. I pick up a stick, pause where the sand is still firm and write a thought for this morning. *Waving from the beach.* Then I add one for yesterday. *Life is full of surprises.* I pull out my phone and snap the sea swirling around my curly writing.

I mean, I hate what happened, but if I don't keep it buried, where will that get me? It's like Mason's won every day.

At first I hid myself away and hoped I'd feel better as the

bruises faded. But even when the splints came off and my wrist was stronger, I'd lost all my confidence. For a while I didn't want to leave my room and even a quiet outing to the local pub was an effort. I used to feel big and now I felt small. I hoped it would pass, but it didn't. But I couldn't wreck every single moment by dwelling on it, and over the months I perfected a way of blocking out the bad bits and pretending to be fine, so I could distance myself and get the hell on with things. I grit my teeth, close the shutters in my head, and act airy.

Scarlett! That's my job for today.

I'm about to ring her from the privacy of the beach when it hits me. 'So much for an early morning call, Pumpkin! If New York is five hours behind, they'll be in bed.'

I'm still muttering under my breath about it, standing by the stile later, giving Pumpkin his morning carrots, but when a shout from the kitchen door makes me jump, I'm cursing even more. It was too much to hope Mr Appleton would leave without forcing the issue.

I call across the garden. 'I can't call Scarlett until after three, Miles.'

In two leaps the man is at my elbow, his foot resting next to mine on the bottom fence rail. 'I'm pleased you brought that up, Betty Bets.' He rubs his thumb across his jaw. 'On reflection, we might be better not to bother them with this on their first day.'

This couldn't sound better. 'If you're happy to leave now, I'm good with that!'

He narrows his eyes. 'Has it occurred to you that I could be the one who gets to stay?'

My blood runs cold. 'That definitely won't happen.'

He's completely relaxed and unhurried when he replies.

'There's a fifty-fifty chance it might.' He watches my eyes open wide with horror. 'Or we could just both stay? That way neither of us is disappointed, and we don't embarrass Tate and Scarlett. By the time they find out about their mistake, it'll be old news, and we'll all have moved on.'

The idea is so awful it takes me a moment to grapple with it. 'How would that work?'

He shrugs. 'You must have lived in a houseshare before?'

My mind flashes back to the nightmare of my first ever flat. 'At uni I lived with a metal head, an insomniac archaeologist, two round-the-clock gamers, an acapella group and a shower hog. I come at life from the bright side, but it wasn't my best nine months.'

'We're both old enough to be civilised.' He pulls down the corners of his mouth. 'I assume you won't be bursting into song, and as I never played drums, that only leaves the bathroom to sort.'

I've never acted my age, but if it's this or nothing, I'll meet him halfway. 'I'll shower when you're not here.'

He takes a breath. 'That's easy, then. I'm often out.'

I'm thinking of the size of this place. The utility room alone is bigger than any room I've had since leaving home. The levels of luxury are incomparable. I may never feel comfortable enough to poop again, but it shouldn't be too hard to coexist with someone who's never in.

He's frowning. 'Obviously there'll be the usual house rules – clear up after yourself in the kitchen, and so on.'

Twenty seconds in, my warning bells are ringing again. If he's already trying to take over, I might need to fight for this harder. 'I don't actually have anywhere else to go. That's why Scarlett will definitely say I have priority if we speak to her.'

He blows out his cheeks. 'Unfortunately, I'm the same. And since I've been here some time, I must have been offered it first. I'm confident I'd get the casting vote, but I'm prepared to be generous.'

My heart sinks. 'Right.'

He takes a breath. 'There's only one parking space, and my car needs a charger, so if I take the space here, I'm happy to pay for your parking in town.'

This is outrageous, but he sounds very sure of his ground. 'What if I need to shop or come home in the dark?' We walked in along the beach because I'd never get a horse box down the lane from the St Aidan road, and I have the parking permit Scarlett arranged for the town, but I'd planned to leave the car here the rest of the time.

He pulls a face. 'In those situations I'm happy to pay for taxis. So the only outstanding issue is tidiness.' His eyebrows go up. 'You left some bags in the kitchen?'

'In a very neat pile.'

This time he stares at me sideways. 'Once we find somewhere suitable for you to put your things, you owe it to Scarlett and Tate to keep the place as neat as they would.' He's still staring. 'If you're on board with that, we've covered most areas.'

Which leaves me with more questions than ever. Why would anyone who talks like a company brochure be here in St Aidan where everyone hangs loose? Why isn't he off tidying a boardroom somewhere?

I give a cough. 'Except the bedroom.' It's the last place I want to draw attention to when I can't take my eyes off his bare forearms, but I can't help making fun of his tone. 'We haven't talked about long-term sleeping arrangements yet. Or will your vision for that be circulated in a group email later?'

He takes a step back. 'Sorry. I assumed we'd take a week each, with Sunday as changeover day.'

I stare him straight in the eye. 'In my house share experience clear communication works better than assumptions, Miles.' I pause for a second. 'A bedroom change every two weeks would give us both more continuity.' Damn. That's an extra week before I get my hands on Scarlett's organic hemp sheets and super-king bed, just because I want to disagree with him.

'It's your call.' The stare he sends back is as hard as mine. 'Great point there, Betsy Beth, but if you're going to be picky about every detail, you're going to wreck this before it begins.'

It's a total myth about redheads being hot-headed, because I'm normally three degrees icier than a glacier, but right now I'm blazing. 'And if *you're* going to act like a dictator – well, what you just said.' I don't give him space for a comeback. 'My quip about emails was ironic, but we should swap details. I'll leave mine on a Post-it on the fridge – you *do* know what a Post-it note is?'

'Obviously.' He looks up at the sky. 'Whether Scarlett and Tate would want them plastered over their Fisher and Paykel brushed-zinc American fridge-freezer combo is another question entirely.'

The last time my chin jutted out like this I was six. 'Fine. I'll leave my Post-it in the fruit bowl.' I read the triumphant curl on his lips, and know I've walked into a trap.

'Good luck finding one of those in a minimalist kitchen.'

My jaw drops open in proper horror. 'Where the hell do I put my apples and bananas then?'

He shakes his head as if he were talking to a lesser being. 'In the crisper drawers in the fridge. Bananas in a beeswax bag.'

'*What?*'

'It's all covered in Tate's running manual video. I'll forward it to you once I get your details. There's a right and wrong way to use your veggie drawers, too. If you want to get ahead of the game with your salads, google it.'

Miles and Tate seem to have entirely missed the point of chilling in Cornwall. It's so absurd I'm biting back my laugh. 'So shall I leave the Post-it in the deep freeze with the mega pack of fish fingers I'm going to buy, or would it be better in the bathroom next to your extensive collection of shower products?' He's not exactly keeping the place as Scarlett would in there.

His forehead wrinkles as he considers. 'Either way, be sure to put it in a Ziplock bag.'

I can't believe what I'm hearing. 'Why?'

'So that your message arrives intact. Both are high-moisture environments.'

Now I'm the one chasing the clouds across the sky with my eyes. 'If that's everything…'

'It's not.' There go his eyebrows again. 'You may want to forget the fish fingers. They're pescatarian, and Scarlett's kitchen is strictly veggie.'

Of course. I knew that anyway. I'm only forgetting because he's making my head spin. His brand of save-the-world fakery always makes me desperate for fish finger sandwiches dripping with melted cheese. Close up he's also got this disgustingly delicious scent that's completely at odds with his obnoxious personality. In my current state I should be blind to this. It's a bit unnerving that I'm not.

To round this off I pull out my sweetest smile. 'Is that everything *now*?'

He's looking down on me, and his voice has softened. 'Maybe this isn't the disaster it seems. Tate always said if I got to know you better, I'd like you.'

How condescending can he be? 'Truly, that's *not* going to happen.'

From where I'm standing, it couldn't be any worse, but I'm not going to let this beat me. In the real world I wouldn't go within a country mile of a guy like Miles, and just because we're thrown together, there's no reason for that to change. He's so annoying, we're likely to have awful disagreements, which is why it's vital for me to take control and make sure I'm the one who calls the shots here. And I might as well start now.

'As long as we avoid each other entirely, we'll be all good.' I turn my high wattage smile up to the max and beam at him. 'So what are you waiting for? Off you go! Enjoy the rest of your summer. I promise I'll find you to say goodbye before we leave.'

He pulls a face. 'So long as we agree that we'll let Scarlett and Tate find out about the arrangements from each other rather than us, the rest is up to you.'

A few strides later he's back in the kitchen, and a few seconds after that, I hear the sound of his tyres crunching on the pebbles as he drives away.

I flatten my palm and hold out a last carrot for Pumpkin. 'Not quite what we'd planned, but we won't let this hold us back.' He chomps on his snack while I scratch him on his favourite place above the white star on his forehead, and give his ears a tug. 'Guys like Mr Appleton keep their suits at the office and work really long hours. We have nothing in common, our paths won't cross, he won't be bothering us anymore – so let's get on with our summer.'

In an hour's time Zofia will be here to clean. I'm not getting my hopes up, but she might be able to tell me where Miles has sprung from. I'm not going to let this guy take up any more of my time, but knowing a bit more about him can't do any harm.

5

Boathouse Cottage, St Aidan
Rainbows and designer labels
Monday

'Are you Zofia?'

It's ten on Monday morning, so it's the right time for Scarlett's help to arrive, and the woman by the door has let herself in. But her Rag and Bone jeans and pricey Tod's loafers are throwing me off.

'I *am* Zofia.' A grin spreads across her face. 'You're thinking my white Prada shirt is not right for a cleaner?' Her navy-blue padded velvet hair band is like the one Kate Middleton was wearing on the Woman and Home website, and she catches hair the colour of Pumpkin's winter straw into a scrunchie.

I'm not going to pretend. 'It was more your shoes.'

She stares down at immaculate beige suede toes. 'Those too. I am in a good disguise, yes?' She puts her hands on her hips. 'Long story short, my husband, Aleksy, is the builder here. I clean all his sites when he's finished the dirty work, and this place was too nice to leave so now I'm here every week. But no worries, I'll change my shoes before I begin.'

'Lucky Scarlett.' I grin. 'She's my sister.'

'If you are Betty, I'm very pleased to meet you.' Zofia holds out her hand and laughs as she shakes mine. 'See, my nails are the giveaway, they are not matching the clothes. When I am not cleaning up after builders, I am working in my borders.'

My ears prick up. 'You have a garden?'

Her eyes get even brighter. 'It's my favourite place. I'll show it to you if you ever have time.'

'Yes please!' I'm always happy to visit a garden. Years ago it was to find pretty corners I could include in my freelance work, but now I go for the love of it. 'Do you live nearby?'

'We have a wreck I call the Bird's Nest that we bought for a song a couple of miles along the road to Rosehill. Most builders' homes are never finished, but ten years on ours has barely begun.'

I smile. 'Our next-door neighbour in the village where we lived with Mum was a builder. He'd reconstructed most houses in the area, but his wife still grumbled about the holes in their own walls.'

Zofia rolls her eyes. 'I am always the last in the queue, but as I am mostly outside with my flowers, I don't mind so much.' She smiles. 'Has Scarlett arrived safely?'

I nod. 'I've had a message to say she's landed.'

Zofia sighs. 'Central Park, Macy's, Tiffany's. I know them all from my modelling days.'

This sounds like a good way to prolong our chat. 'You and

Scarlett must have a lot in common with your fashion backgrounds.'

Zofia looks over her shoulder and sniffs. 'We do, but I do not share her love for minimalism.' She comes a step closer and drops her voice. 'Clean lines are good for dusting, but hand on my heart ... for me this kitchen is very bare.'

'For me too!' I glance along the empty monochrome counter tops then look down at my dress with purple, yellow and blue stripes, two sizes too big, layered over my on-show fuchsia bralette and shorts, topped with an oversized green cardi. 'I should probably get a whole new toned-down wardrobe so I fit in better with the architecture.'

Zofia reaches out and pats my hand. 'You are cheering up my day. Your put-together look is dazzling in a good way.'

It's more about grabbing anything from my jumble of a bag than a style, but I'm hoping we have bonded enough for me to slip in a question. 'Do you know much about my housemate, Miles?'

Zofia shrugs. 'Only that he arrived out of nowhere with his foot in a pot while I was away visiting my mother, and has serious good taste in toiletries.'

That's an interesting summing up. 'So when would that have been?'

She frowns, as she slips her feet into some trainers and snaps her hands into plastic gloves. 'Three weeks ago. Maybe four.'

There's the clunk of the side gate closing, then footsteps on the gravel, and when a tall figure appears behind Zofia, we freeze, knowing we've been caught talking about him.

I'm the first to break the silence. 'I thought you'd gone out for the day?'

He pulls a face. 'I left my Ray-Bans on the island, but it could be your lucky morning.' He tucks them into his shirt pocket and turns to Zofia. 'Betsy Beth would like to know, is there a fruit bowl?'

Zofia nods. 'High cupboard in the mud room. Made from iron.'

Miles's eyebrows go up as he backs towards the doorway. 'It's more likely to be hammered steel, but thanks for that. You can knock yourself out buying bananas, Betsy Beth.'

I'm more confused than ever. 'Where the hell is the mud room?'

Miles gives me that 'lesser being' look. 'You might know it as the boot room, or the laundry?'

I'm trying for clarity. 'The utility?'

He's biting back his smile. 'Yes. But no one has those anymore. They're very last century.'

As he heads back out again Zofia chuckles. 'He's a *very* nice boy. Like Henry Cavill on a playful day. He smells good too.' She sees my look of disbelief, and laughs. 'You'll like him once you get to know him better.'

'I definitely won't.' When she's so obviously smitten, there's no point filling her in on the backstory.

She takes out a pile of dusters from the cupboard and rolls up her shirt sleeves. 'I'm guessing you're here on holiday?'

I pull a face. 'If only. I write for holistic lifestyle blogs and publications, which means anything that's pretty, sustainable and original.'

Zofia nods her approval. 'That sounds like a dream job.'

I'm constantly running to keep up, and I only get paid when

I place a piece, but I'm very lucky to have the work, so I agree. 'It's easy when I write about things I love myself.'

Her eyes are shining. 'Flexible working hours too. Except working for yourself, you may end up working all the time.'

That makes me smile. 'My trouble is not working enough. Today I'm reading up on sirens.' Now I'm out in the real world I need to push up my income with speculative pitches. It's not that I'm lazy – I just need to do more writing and less dreaming.

'I'll leave you to your mermaids, then.' Zofia reaches into a tall cupboard and comes out with a vacuum cleaner. 'Scarlett has already given you my number for the spare keys. Call me whenever you'd like to visit; the blooms are at their best now, so don't put it off too long.'

I laugh. 'Thank you. In the meantime, I promise I *won't* be locking myself out.' That's a promise to both of us. I have a sudden thought. 'Do you happen to have an outside shower I could use for some pictures?'

'I wish. I don't even have an indoor one!' She gives a chortle. 'Don't look so disappointed, I do have some very nice marigolds.'

'It's fine.' I should have known better than to get my hopes up. That's the rule about good ideas for pieces, you rarely find them where you expect them.

She waves as she heads towards the bedroom. 'You can bring Miles to see the garden too; he can give you a lift in his racing car. Zooming around country lanes together, you'll be best of friends before you can say hair-pin bend.'

'No, no, and no! To all three!' My protest is loud, but no one hears because it's drowned by the noise of the vacuum cleaner.

As for Miles, I've seen enough of him already to last me a

lifetime. My aim for the rest of the day is to stay out of his way. If I head for the top of the garden, I should be safe there.

6

Boathouse Cottage, St Aidan
Long distance calls and pressing matters
Tuesday

Who knew there was so much to find out about sea nymphs? I spent the rest of Monday on the sun lounger and was so absorbed by sprites and water kelpies I emptied two cans of Garnier Ambre Solaire dry mist without even noticing. At this rate I may spend more on sun products than I earn from selling pieces, but as I wrote in one of my lines in the sand yesterday, *Every long road has a beginning*. Scarlett would argue that's not strictly true, but I'm embracing the sentiment not the facts.

When Pumpkin and I head out for this morning's walk I take my writing stick again. With the width of the bay stretching out beside us as we amble towards St Aidan, I'm running things past him. 'I'll write something for you first.'

I work my bum off to make sure Pumpkin wants for nothing, but whether you're a pony or a person, happiness is all about the small things. 'How about *I heart carrots?*' He has to wait a few minutes until I draw a bunch of the things too. 'And I could do *This is my lucky day*. If you walk across the bottom of the writing, I'll take a photo of horseshoe prints in the sand going past it.'

It takes four attempts to master, but we persevere and the results are fab.

As Pumpkin falls back into step beside me again, I can't help smiling. 'After so long getting that right, my next phrase has to be *Never give up*.'

There's something all-embracing and positive about writing in the sand. The noise of the waves pounding further along the beach gives it a power all its own, and for someone like me, who finds commitment hard, it's deliciously impermanent. There's always the thought that in no time the sea will rush in to obliterate what you've written, so you can put yourself out there, and push yourself to be even more daring.

With that in mind, I move on to a *Kick ass*, a *Get off your butt*, an *I am, I can, I will*, and as an afterthought I add in *Dream BIG!* By the time I've snapped all those, my stomach is aching for breakfast, so I'm more than thankful when we get to the harbourside.

As I pass Seaspray Cottage at the end of the beach, I see The Little Cornish Kitchen sign by the low wall to the beach and look up to see Scarlett's friend Clemmie is on the balcony with a toddler in her arms. She points down and waves at Pumpkin, and I wave back with extra warmth because even though we're all different shades of auburn, it's still rare to find four redheads together. Then I head to the bakery up the hill where they are happy to serve me while I stand with Pumpkin at the door.

The carrier in my hand is fully loaded as we make our way back along the beach, and I'm still talking to Pumpkin. 'The weight of this lot, my next message in the sand should be, *Never visit a cake shop when you're hungry.*'

Pumpkin's look tells me he'd rather press on and get back to his field.

I give his side a nudge with my thigh. 'You were bred to be sturdy, *you're* the one who should be carrying the cakes here, not me.'

He ignores that, but as we turn towards Boathouse Cottage I'm feeling so upbeat that I take my phone out. Before I know it I'm surfing my can-do wave and tapping out an email to the editor of my favourite magazine.

> Morning, Fenna, writing from the beach with a pocket full of shells and the waves breaking over my toes. Staying in a gorgeous Cornish cottage with views of the ocean, all the way to October. If you'd like me to send you and the readers a first-hand taste of Cornwall, you know where I am.
>
> Waving from St Aidan, with the wind in my hair,
> Betty xxx

I add my mobile number and the full Boathouse Cottage address for authenticity, and that's it.

When I read it back, it sounds a lot more like something Scarlett would send than me, but it's too late – it's gone.

I turn Pumpkin out in the field and fill up his water bucket. When I get back inside and put the kettle on for coffee, the first surprise is that it's already midday. The second surprise is that Miles is in the house rather than out somewhere, and the third is what he's doing.

'You're *ironing*?' *Without a shirt on!* Don't you just hate it when unpleasant guys strip off and they're disgustingly tanned, toned and attractive under their clothes?

He looks up at me. 'You'll find the board and iron in the end cupboard in the mud room when you need them. If you'd like me to leave them out for you, I'm only doing a couple of T-shirts.'

Though stunned by the half-naked man in the kitchen, I was still able to wonder why would anyone iron those?

I threw on three different sheer cotton dresses earlier, nipped a belt around my waist, and topped it with a cropped sweater that's falling off one shoulder. Far from needing a press, the whole outfit works *because of* the creases.

I point at my crumpled skirt. 'Do I look as if I iron?' I take in Miles's bemused stare. 'Thanks for asking, I'll get the iron out myself if I need it.' I already know I won't!

I sound a lot more chilled than I feel. As for Miles, I'd be happier if he weren't around at all, because I get a weird adrenalin rush every time I have to even look at the hollows in his cheeks or the stubble shadow on his face. Add in the flashes of muscled torso, and my whole body is thrumming.

With what I'm trying to put behind me, I'm shocked that I'm actually reacting to a man. I can only think it's my subconscious kicking in to let me run the hell away from those pecs and that gently etched six pack and the arrogant prat they're attached to who is parading them like nothing's going on.

I know I'm a libertarian, but for the sake of my pounding heart, maybe we should be making some house rules on exposure. I mean, how would he feel if he came in to find me ironing in a bralette?

I give a cough. 'For the record, isn't ironing semi-nude a health and safety issue?'

He laughs. 'I'll be careful not to burn myself.'

'Even so...' I open my mouth to argue this, but as my phone rings all I can think is, if this is New York calling they must have got up before they went to bed.

I jump and press accept. 'Scarlett! You've started early! How are you getting on?' Somehow I've also accidentally switched on speakerphone, because my voice is echoing back at me.

When she replies her voice is so loud it's bouncing off the ceiling. 'Super busy. I've been doing calls since six.'

There's no hope of privacy, so I'll keep this simple. 'And how's Tate?'

Miles is shaking his head, mouthing 'not now' at me across the kitchen.

Scarlett sniffs. 'Straight off the plane and into the office.'

I'm so dismayed for her I blurt out more than I should. 'What happened to taking time for the two of you? That's why you wanted to go!'

She ignores that and moves straight on. 'I've organised a hay delivery. They're dropping it in the outhouse later in the week.' She turns the spotlight back onto me. 'Since when did you play Britpop, Betty?'

I'm pointing at the mini speaker further along the island unit, making cut throat actions to Miles but Scarlett's on to us. 'I distinctly heard a line from Champagne Supernova just before. *Is someone there with you?*'

I'm stamping on the ember before it bursts into flames. 'Alexa's gone rogue, or maybe Zofia left it on.'

'Zofia came yesterday, Betty.' She has a point there, but the music is off now. 'I meant to warn you – I bumped into Miles Appleton last time we were down.'

I take a gulp.

'You know, he's the one who—'

I need to stop her! 'Sorry, you're breaking up. I can't hear you, talk again soon...' I end the call with a shout, and turn to Miles.

His eyes are wide with curiosity and laughter. 'I'm the one who what? *What did I do?*'

I move on quickly. 'I'm not comfortable lying to Scarlett.'

That distracts him. 'There's no point making unnecessary problems. Tate and Scarlett are bound to compare notes soon.'

I watch him make meticulous folds in his T-shirts, then glance at my own clothes tumbling out of my bag beyond the sofas. 'Why aren't you at your office?'

He hesitates then he grins. 'Working from home today.'

My phone rings again. 'If this is Scarlett calling back, I might be best just to tell her now.'

When I look, it's not her number, but I answer it anyway.

'If you just sent me an email from Cornwall, you must be Betty? This is Fenna Weaver, editor of *Inspire* magazine.'

She actually rang me! My mouth falls open with shock, then it hits me I need to get my shit together. 'I am. I did. How can I help?'

'How wonderful that you'll be holidaying for so long! I'm looking for six hundred lyrical words on the theme of "Garden". I recall you write well about fairies?' She sounds as confident, well-spoken and pleased with herself as Miles.

'I have done.' My mind is racing. 'I could do some tips on how to attract them – a bit like you would do for blackbirds or bees? By Friday?'

'By four this afternoon would be better. And after that, if you could make me a list of local makers and their specialities. You know the kind of people we like to spotlight?'

Inspire's submissions requirements are imprinted on my brain and I rattle them off. '*Ordinary yet remarkable, simultaneously relatable, interesting and photogenic.*'

'That's it. We'll see how they fit with future themes, and take it from there.'

'Fabulous...' I'm pondering how many thank yous would be too many, but I'm saved the trouble, because she's already gone.

Miles is unplugging the iron. 'Looks like you're working from home too.' He pulls a face. 'I couldn't help overhearing. Maybe take your phone off speaker next time.'

The way Fenna and Miles come across, I can't begin to imagine what it must be like to feel *that* entitled! It's seriously not the kind of club I'd ever want to join. But if Fenna needs bulletins from the real world, that's something I can do. I have three short hours to prove to her that I'm up to the job.

7

The upper terrace, Boathouse Cottage, St Aidan
Making it up as you go along
Tuesday

As soon as I've made some coffee, I grab the bakery bag, tuck my laptop under my arm and head off up the garden.

Once I've installed myself on the top terrace lounger, I check out a few blogs about how to fill gardens with wildlife, then I channel my inner fairy, and three strawberry tarts later my mind is working faster than my fingers can type.

It's funny when I write. Sometimes it's painful, then other times, like today, it's effortless. A couple of hours later I'm reading through what I hope is a final draft.

The first clue I have that I'm not alone is the shadow falling across my keyboard, and a second later Miles's shorts appear by my shoulder.

'You're really writing about fairies?'

I sigh. 'With so little time to turn this around, I could do without the interruptions. But, yes.'

He holds out the drink he's carrying. 'Brains work better when they're hydrated. I thought elderflower cordial with fizzy water might help.'

The ice chinks as I take the glass from him. 'That's very thoughtful. I didn't have you down as an elderflower kind of a guy.'

He looks guilty. 'I'm not. I used yours. I hope that's okay?' He frowns. 'I have another question too – how do you write about the habitat of something that doesn't exist?'

I take in a breath. 'There are two kinds of people, Miles: those who don't believe and those who keep an open mind. That's the difference between us. It's why I got the call, not you.'

'So what have you said?'

I shrug. 'Never light a bonfire without checking for fairies first, grow pollen-rich plants, there's a list of flowers suitable for fairy crowns... I also said to encourage spiders because fairies use their webs to spin cloth for fairy dresses.'

'Put like that, it almost sounds real.'

I laugh. 'People like you might read it as parody. It's a bit of fun, but deftly done, what's not to like?'

'So it's escapism?'

He's one of those irritating people who want a definition for everything.

I roll my eyes. 'If you think, on balance, if life is better with fairy wings in it or without, I know what most of my friends would say.'

He shrugs. 'When you put it like that...'

I give up. 'If something makes you feel better, why knock it?'

'And you get paid for this?'

Now I'm the one smiling. 'I'm hoping so, if they like what I've written. I won't be sending them anything if I talk to you all afternoon though, so if you don't mind, I'll get on.'

He's still standing there.

'Why are you looking at me like I'm a rare species?'

He's blinking. 'Is it my eyes, or are you wearing three dresses all at once?'

I blow out a breath. 'Miles, I can't go there now. Please just eff off back to your laptop.' He still hasn't moved. 'Okay, I have loads of clothes I love and this way I get to wear them all. A lot of them are transparent, and doubling up minimises the shock to the public.'

He picks himself up after that. 'Your laundry pile must be vast.'

I can't believe we're still going. 'The thin fabrics dry in no time. So long as I don't iron it's manageable.' I'm trying to wind this up now. 'So are we done here?'

'There is one more thing...' He hesitates. 'If you need an eye for detail, I can have this checked through for you?'

I draw in a breath. 'A lot of people claim they're fabulous proofreaders when they're not.'

'But I have to do it all the time, for board meetings and company stuff.' He's standing his ground. 'Try me. It won't take long. You don't *have* to include the corrections if you don't want to.'

It goes with the territory. An arrogant guy, confident in his own abilities, happy to blow his own trumpet. But he has picked up what I hadn't even thought about; a second pair of eyes are good for spotting blunders, and I haven't got anyone else lined up to help.

I try to sound as gracious as I can, while protecting myself at the same time. 'Thank you. But only on the condition that you keep your judgemental comments on content entirely to yourself.'

'It's a deal. You never did leave me your details on a Post-it note, so I didn't leave you mine.'

I'm shaking my head. 'I'm still looking for the fruit bowl.'

'Miles dot Appleton at Gmail dot com.'

'Thanks Miles dot Appleton, check your inbox in ten.'

When I look up again, he's gone. So much for him hanging around.

8

In Pumpkin's field, Boathouse Cottage, St Aidan
Flying without a licence
Thursday

'What the hell are you doing with that bucket?'

It's two days later, and since Tuesday, when Miles did an unexpectedly good job of looking through the piece I finally called 'The secret lives of fairies – how to make yours the garden they choose', I've been silently congratulating myself on avoiding him.

I spent yesterday and this morning wandering round the cobbled streets of St Aidan where the shopfronts are a patchwork of colour, each with a whole new personality opening onto the pavement. I came across everything from rails of surfer T-shirts flapping in the wind gusts, to curated homewares with beautifully styled candlesticks, and plump gingham cushions piled artfully on hand-hewn tables.

By this afternoon my phone was filled with pictures, and my

longhand notebook was bursting, so I came back to the sun lounger to look at what I'd gathered. But due to a seating issue I had to suspend my plans, which was why I decided that as Pumpkin's field needed a tidy, now was as good a time as any to sort it.

I drop the latest scoopful of dung balls into my bucket and straighten up to look at Miles, who's on the other side of the fence, blinking in the afternoon sunlight.

I bite back my smile. 'No need to panic, I'm collecting Pumpkin's poop.'

His face screws up in a look of total disgust. 'You're telling me that picking up pony shit is an actual thing?'

I need to explain this one syllable at a time. 'Horses eat grass so it's not *that* offensive, it's only like mucking out a stable. If I put all Pumpkin's dung in one corner it keeps the field clean, which is good for the pony's health and good for the ground too.'

He couldn't look any more appalled. 'Well, thanks for sharing that.'

'You're welcome.' He isn't. I don't know what he's doing here at all when he should be at work, but his face is such a picture I'm going to milk this to the max. 'Horse droppings make great fertiliser, but only when they're well-rotted.'

He's giving his usual know-it-all smirk. 'You have no idea how much better my day is for knowing that.'

I can't believe he's sarcastic even over this. 'What kind of job allows you to head home at two in the afternoon, anyway?'

He's straight back at me. 'The kind where I'm the boss.'

'Of course.' I walked into that one.

My seating problem earlier? When I came back from St Aidan, desperate to flop down and put my feet up, Scarlett's lounger was already taken. Which is why I ended up out in the field with sweat running down my spine in a river, rather than doing the job later when the sun was down.

Scarlett isn't the kind of person to deprive herself, but she only has one lounger because Tate isn't the type to sit still, and there's no point in wasting precious terrace space. He's far more likely to be striding around talking on his phone, which is why it comes as a bit of a surprise that I'm having to fight his friend for the lounger.

I can't leave it at that.

'So when you're bossing it, what are you in charge of?'

He shifts his foot onto the fence. 'I grew a clothes company from a market stall to a global operation.' He's reacting to my blank look with a sardonic grin. 'Now it's worldwide, I mostly work remotely.'

It's all remote from me. 'So you'd *really* rather be on Scarlett's chaise in St Aidan than in your executive suites in random capitals?'

'Something like that.' He hesitates. 'Even multi-national tycoons face bumps in the road sometimes.'

His answer throws me. 'Aren't those super-expensive cars you drive designed to float over the potholes? Surely people like you can't have ordinary problems like the rest of us?'

'You'd be surprised.'

The twang of sympathy in my chest is unexpected. 'Should my heart be bleeding for you?'

'Definitely not that. I'm just less hands-on than I was. And slightly in between projects.' Miles leans forward and rests his elbows on the fence. 'So how's *your* work going? Did that Fenella person like what you sent her? Have you uncovered lots of locals making incredible earth-friendly products that no one has heard of before?'

What's unbelievable is that *whatever* he talks about, his voice always has the same mocking edge.

'It's Fenna not Fenella, and she *is* using the piece.' As he helped, I owe it to him to tell him that much at least. She actually used the word 'delightful', but unlike Miles, I'd rather play my achievements down than boast about them from the rooftops. 'I'm still compiling the list of local craftspeople.' I haven't uncovered as many stand-out shops as I'd hoped for, but I'm not about to share that with him.

Miles tilts his head to one side. 'Did you see the Deck Gallery up above the bakers? That might be worth a visit.'

Funny he should say that. I walked in there twice, hoping to say 'hi' to Scarlett's friend Plum who's the owner, and came straight back out again both times when I saw him lounging with a coffee cup in front of him.

I can't help asking. 'Do you have an interest in local crafts?'

He gives a shrug. 'I'm in business; for me, anything that turns a profit is worth a closer look.'

I throw a freebie out for him. 'There's a vegan ice cream parlour selling home-made ice cream for dogs. If you're looking for a takeover, they do it in six delicious flavours.'

He sniffs. 'I'd be looking for wider distribution deals, rather than making the stuff myself.'

Typical. Guys like him, who do nothing but cream off the profits, are everything I despise.

He clears his throat. 'Talking of freezers, I think you dropped some stuff in the utility?'

Let's get this right. 'You mean the mud room?'

He nods.

If he's picking on this, he's picked on the wrong person. 'If you're talking about the patch of floor in front of the washing machine that was full of *your* clothes earlier when I went to put *mine* in – yes, that's down to me.'

Come to think of it, that was my third attempt to use the washer, and every other time I tried it was in use too, which was why I finally gave up and dumped my own load on the limestone tiles instead.

He blows out his cheeks. 'We can't afford student squalor this early in the game. We'll both get more out of this if we keep our standards high.'

I give a sniff. 'My pile of clothes and damp towels isn't squalor. It's actually holding my place in the queue for the washing machine you're hogging.' He's not the only one who can talk like he's reading an effing thesaurus either. 'For one small human, you do a ginormous number of wash cycles. Would you care to enlighten me with what's going on there?'

He shrugs. 'It's not complicated. If I have washing, I put the washer on. It's two loads a day, three maximum. Watch and learn, here, Betty Beth – that's the way to avoid trip hazards spilling out across the kitchen.'

I'm staring at him. 'You can't be serious? Even with an eco-washer, that's a terrible waste of water *and* power. Haven't you ever heard of a laundry basket?'

Miles stares at me through narrowed eyes. 'Every good business model actions things as they occur, and I extend that to my daily tasks too. This way I'm ready to move on to the next big thing the minute it comes up.'

It would be sensible to do our washing together, but however much I want to save the world, I've found the limit of my commitment here. I'm still making detours to the boat-dwellers shower block at the end of the harbour, whenever I need to 'properly' use the loo, so I'm not ready to risk getting my Brazilians tangled in his chinos.

He's so up himself I despair. 'You're not the only housemate on this beach, mate. And I'm certain I left my laundry in a neat little heap.'

His voice rises. 'Neat? It's more like a volcanic eruption! The lava flow spreads right across the tranquillity zone and out to the French doors beyond the sofa.'

I roll my eyes. 'Let's not overreact, it's only a few items.'

He's shaking his head. 'It's total anarchy in there. It's the same with the vegetables.'

'Excuse me?' I'm blinking, trying to keep up.

He drags in a very deep breath. 'Is there a reason why they're next to the sink and not in the fridge?'

I make up the first excuse I think of. 'I thought it would be good to have a veggie patch on the work surface – for vegetables we want at room temperature.'

He's straight back at me. 'Not on my watch! This is complete disrespect for Scarlett and Tate.'

My voice rises. 'It's three carrots and a cucumber, Miles! I was actually intending to put them in a salad box, but if you're being this anal, I'm definitely not. It'll do you a world of good to live with them where they are.'

He pulls his know-it-all face. 'I'm trying to have an open and honest discussion here, Bethy Bets. There's no need to be obtuse.'

Whatever that means, I may as well be honest. 'I'm trying to be as tidy as I can here, Miles. I'm a naturally messy person, if you want to see proper chaos, I can easily arrange that. You'd be surprised how far a backpack of tulle can spread once it's unleashed. I still have four more in the car on the harbourside.'

He holds up his hand. 'No, no! I'll take your word for that. I just hoped we could resolve our issues calmly, without an argument, that's all.'

We both know that means I should shut the eff up and do everything he says, where I suggest he should back the eff off and stop being an arse. I'm opening my mouth to tell him exactly that when he breaks in.

'Is your horse giving me side eye?'

I wouldn't blame him if he were. 'That's his natural way of looking, Miles. An eye on each cheek lets Pumpkin see all around him.'

'Three hundred and sixty degree vision?' He sounds incredulous.

As Miles likes things precise, I carry on to give him the full picture. 'Pumpkin can see everywhere except for a narrow blind spot the width of his tail at the back and another at the front directly in front of his nose.'

'You're joking?'

'If you don't want to know, don't ask.' I sigh, because it's impossible to talk about Pumpkin without softening. 'You're right though; you *can* read a lot about his mood from the expression in his eyes. He's everyone's friend, but he's also very shrewd. He can be disapproving, disbelieving or suspicious as well as happy.'

Miles glances at Pumpkin, who is chewing on a mouthful of

grass a few feet away. 'If you can read him so well, what's he thinking now?'

I take a few moments to study him. 'He's got his ears pointing towards us, so he's been listening. And you might have been right the first time – from that look you're getting now, I'd say he's decided you're a bit of a dickhead.'

Miles takes a step backwards. 'You're making it up!'

I'm laughing, because I'm not. 'The first rule of horse management: if you want to stay in a pony's good books, don't diss the owner.' I laugh more. 'He's a Leo; he's fiercely loyal and hugely charismatic. He actually shares a birthday with Yves St Laurent.'

As Miles turns and heads for the house he's muttering, 'What the actual…? Now I've heard it all!'

It's very hard to get the same impact and satisfaction of roaring away up the road when your car is silent and electric, but from the spin of Miles's car tyres on the gravel as he leaves, Pumpkin and I get the drift.

At least that hasty exit solves my problem of where to sit to work. Two minutes later, I'm fully installed on the lounger, checking through my research notes.

9

In Pumpkin's field, Boathouse Cottage, St Aidan
Buckets, spades and transatlantic fantasies
Wednesday

I couldn't risk another day like Thursday afternoon. I hate conflict, but I refuse to let myself be pushed around, so in the hope of getting away from Boathouse Cottage and staying out of trouble, I throw myself into my work. But things don't always work out the way you hope.

Six days later, I'm lying on a rug on the grass near Pumpkin, on the phone to Scarlett, explaining why I *still* haven't landed a commission to write a Cornish piece, and silently cursing myself for ever thinking that this would be easy.

'All Fenna says is "keep on with the legwork, Betty, you're bound to bring me a gem soon."'

The other major change is that I've also made a permanent relocation to the field for my outdoor working because it's the one place where I can guarantee Miles isn't going to turn up. I'd never usually bore Scarlett with descriptions of my life, but if I fill every space in our conversation with me, at least I avoid having to lie about the outrageous and unbearable housemate she still doesn't know is living here.

I carry on without a pause. 'I'm desperate for unique selling points, but whenever I come across the right amount of "unusual" there's always a downside. The company making knicker fabric from abandoned fishing nets sounded fabulous, but their range was far too racy for the target audience.'

This is Scarlett's territory so she forces her way in with a laugh. 'I imagine *Inspire* readers will wear undies made from organic cotton, not recycled polyester.'

I let out a groan, because this is exactly what I'm up against. 'I've trawled the towns and villages right along the coast, I've sent hundreds of pictures to Fenna in bite-sized batches to tempt her, so I'm not sure where to go next.'

Scarlett butts in again as I tail off. 'You've been chatting so fast I haven't had a chance to ask – how's the house?'

'Wonderful.' I'm kicking myself for letting that question through at all, because it's not just awful: it's gone from bad to horrendous.

When Miles isn't doing laundry, he spreads himself all over the sun terrace, which I thought I'd bagged for myself. Worse still, he makes a kind of pretence of asking me if I mind if he sits there, and is down before I can reply. Once there he appears to do zero work, but manages a maximum amount of exposure of hot male body parts that are completely distracting.

Back in the kitchen we clash on everything from how to slice lemons to how much salt chips need. Every time I eat a pastry he follows me around with a mini vacuum picking up the crumbs. The other day he asked me if I knew my shirt didn't have a back in it. How has he missed the bare midriff trend if he's got a clothes company? As if the hot naked glimpses aren't bad enough, even worse is him insisting that floors and furnishings are kept entirely clear (of my clothes), and he's also got this obsession with playing powerful motivational classics. If I walk in one more time on his speaker blasting the Marriage of Figaro Overture at full volume from the top of the microwave while simultaneously getting a view of his rippling back muscles as he leans into the fridge, I may have to move out.

As things stand, I'm making the most of a bad situation; my clothes are rammed into a couple of rucksacks beyond the sofa where I also sleep, and I go in and out to Pumpkin and my new outdoor field-office through the French doors that open from the living room. If I'm honest, it's very close to how I've lived for years, but with the addition of luxury limestone flooring instead of lino with the pattern scuffed off.

The devastating part of the equation is a hundred per cent down to Miles; add him in and it's like the world has turned upside down and been shaken very hard. I'm really not a grumbler, and I know these are very much first-world problems, but none of it is good. If anyone had told me one small man could be this annoying to live with, I'd never have believed them. So much for me imagining life with a housemate would be seamless and trouble-free.

Scarlett's butting in again. 'Have you seen Miles at all?'

'What does he do – for a job?' I've blurted it out before I can stop myself.

She sounds slightly awestruck. 'Miles actually founded *the* Dedication label.'

Even I've heard of that. 'Jeans and sweatshirts for rich people? That cost arms and legs?'

'That's the one.' She hesitates. 'I'm not sure about now. Tate's friends jump in and out of companies so fast it's hard to keep up. Why?'

With that explained, I'm going to handle this with a true statement rather than a direct answer. 'If I came across *that man* on the edge of a huge hole that someone had very thoughtfully dug in the sand, I'd have to push him in. That's all.' That expresses exactly how I feel without giving away our actual situation. And him owning a label that well known explains the attitude.

I push this back to her. 'How about you – ten days on, have you even seen Tate yet?'

She draws in a breath. 'Let's just say, if I saw Tate next to a hole on the beach, I'm afraid I'd be very tempted to do the same.'

It takes a moment to grasp the magnitude of what she's implying there.

'Scarlie, you can't mean that?' With a whole Atlantic Ocean between us, it's hard to tell.

'Obviously, I'd have to locate him first.' She finally laughs. 'I'm sure he'll come home before midnight one day soon, but it's not stopping my enjoyment any, thanks for asking. You were right: the cheesecake here is fabulous.'

I'm wiping the sweat off my brow in mock relief. 'Phew, at least you're having the time of your life.'

'I totally am. We'll talk again soon, love you lots.' There's a second of silence. 'I'm not telling you how to live your life, but with your pieces, Betsy … you might find what you're looking for more easily if you stop trying so hard.'

And then she's gone.

I roll my eyes up to the cornflower blue sky, then look at Pumpkin nuzzling at a patch of grass. 'That's just the kind of useless advice a successful person like Scarlett would pass on.' I blow out a breath. 'What I need are tips for failures.'

I've used up the wave of optimism I arrived on, my attempt to find sensational ideas for Fenna has fizzled to nothing and I'm completely stuffing up being a housemate. Maybe Scarlett is right; I really do have nothing to lose by putting work stress to one side and doing something for me for the afternoon.

I reach for my phone and call Zofia.

10

Zofia's cottage, Rosehill
Blooms and bad judgement
Wednesday

When I reached Zofia, not only was she free for a mid-afternoon visit to her garden, she was also about to pass the end of the lane, so in no time at all she arrived to pick me up. Now we're flying inland towards the village of Rosehill along narrow country lanes with endless high hedges. Unlike Miles, Zofia doesn't have the problem of a car that is silent.

She yells across to where I'm sitting on the weathered blue leather of the passenger seat. 'Don't you just love my trusty old Alpha? It's the only car that roars louder than Status Quo.' She crashes through the gears. 'It's terrible for guzzling the gas, but Aleksy has electric vans, so our carbon footprint is not so bad.' She slews into a sliding skid around the next corner, and as we drift to a halt in front of a monumental gateway flanked by high stone walls, some ancient timber gates swing open.

'Automatic gates were Aleksy's first job when we arrived ten years ago.'

As she pulls into a broad gravelled area, I'm frowning at the long house built of fudge-coloured stone and mentally waving goodbye to the cottage garden photos I've secretly been hoping for.

'Welcome to Bird's Nest Hall.' Zofia rolls her eyes. 'If ever I say small, I'm being ironic. When you see the roof, you will understand why the name is a joke too.'

I look up at the prickly straw of the eaves. 'A thatched house so big it could belong to the beanstalk giant.'

As we climb out of the Alpha, Zofia waves her hand towards the wall. 'We came down from London to work on the Cornish gold rush and ended up here. I will show you the inside after the work is done.' She beckons me to follow. 'The house is not important, I bought it for what is on the other side.'

We make our way around the house gable, and when we emerge into the splash of sunlight on the front of the house I gasp. 'A walled garden!'

Zofia's voice has softened. 'That's what I fell in love with. It's a physic garden!'

I've heard of these before. 'Is that where the plants have to be medicinal, herbal, or edible?'

She nods. 'The oldest ones date back to the sixteen hundreds, which was probably when this house originated, although the box hedges are newly planted in the old pattern.'

The grass between the beds is soft under our feet, and there is a central path, with bushes bursting into bloom along each side, and beyond that there are borders. There are so many long views and close-up shots to take as I reach for my phone I hardly know where to begin.

'Lavender plants always look so beautiful when they're in a line.' I crush a sprig between my fingers, then breathe in the deep, oily scent. 'You have all my favourites here – bay, feverfew, viola, lemon balm, rosemary, jasmine, evening primrose.' They're arranged in groups, repeating further along the borders, which are bursting. 'Everywhere I look there's another favourite.'

Zofia raises her eyebrows. 'It's nice to meet someone who knows their plants!'

I wrinkle my nose. 'I learned the names from my mum. I'm definitely not a gardener myself, I'm more of a fan girl.'

Zofia smiles. 'Did you know there are three hundred different types of thyme? It's my challenge to have as many different varieties as I can. And it's not limited to herbs – we have roses and perennial geraniums and apple and pear trees, and a rhubarb area.'

'Do you grow plants from seed?'

She nods. 'I do, but I propagate from cuttings too. We have restored the greenhouses in the old kitchen garden on the other side of the wall. The bigger borders are there, with beds for growing on.' Her eyes are shining as she leads me to a wide door and a whole new view beyond. 'I pour the money into the garden, not the house. I tell Aleksy, a garden takes longer to make; his building work can be done at the end, and that way we will finish together.'

I'm pointing at a long border bursting with yellow and orange flowers. 'Your marigolds?'

'I love those especially. A friend harvests and dries the

flowers to use in her healing pomades.' She leads the way to a series of tables by the garden edge covered with hundreds of small pots, each containing a tiny plant. 'So far I've grown new plants to fill the garden as *it* grew, but my true dream is to have my physic garden open to the public with a plant nursery alongside.'

There's so much excitement surging through me I'm flapping my hands. 'Zofia, you're ticking every box for a feature piece in the magazine!' I'm tugging at her sleeve. 'An ancient restored walled garden where the owner propagates all her own stock, growing plants for self-healing *and* aspiring to have her own nursery business? Tell me I can run it past my boss, Fenna?'

'Of course! I'd be honoured!'

I'm leaning against her, collapsing with relief at what I've stumbled across. 'Cosmos and zinnias and nasturtiums and cornflowers and love-in-a-mist. There's something amazing about a sea of mixed flowers...' I break off mid-sentence, but someone takes my thought and runs on with it.

'The way they sway, and rustle like water in the wind...'

I turn to smile at Zofia for getting it so right, but then I realise the voice is deeper than hers and she's not moving her lips.

There's a laugh on the other side of the wall, and a second later, Miles comes sauntering through the doorway, cool as a courgette that's been in the chiller tray.

As usual, he gets in first. 'I thought I'd find you in the second garden. It's exactly as you said, Zofia.' He raises one eyebrow. 'Sorry for creeping up on you. It's so wonderful I had to join in with your visit, Betty Beth.'

'Forget about the creeping, why are you here at all, Miles? You're hijacking my tour!'

I know that when I'm so close to solving my immediate career and cashflow problem I should let this go, but as my main reason to come was to stay out of Miles's way, I can't stay quiet.

Zofia shakes her head. 'This is down to me. When I met Miles in town on my way to pick you up he asked if he could come too, so I thought two birds with one stone – my Boathouse Cottage people can enjoy it together.' She's looking from Miles to me and back again. 'And I am right. You do love it; it touches *both* your hearts in the way I knew it would.'

I'm organising my reply to that when I see that Miles is staring down at my leg.

'Is there a rip in your dress?'

I give up. 'It's not a dress, Miles, it's a skirt – at least the top layer you're talking about is.' I carry on. 'It is slightly torn, yes, but I mended it as best I could, and the fabric is so pretty I couldn't bear to throw it away.'

He's squinting down. 'I thought maybe you'd caught it on a rose thorn.'

I shake my head. 'No, it's a hole that was already there when I bought it in the charity shop. I may not choose it if I were going for an afternoon at the palace, but for a last-minute outing three mins up the road I decided Zofia might like the daisy print so much she'd overlook the flaw. Can the fashion police forgive that blunder?'

Miles is staring at the sky. 'I was being concerned, not picky.'

'Great! In that case, thank you.' I clap my hands and take a jump towards the most distant corner of the garden. 'Espalier pears! My mum loved those too. I must take a closer look!'

Miles grins. 'Anything that interesting I have to see. Shall we all go?'

I frown. 'As it's personal to me, you'll probably get more out of watching the wind on the marigolds.'

He's still looking hopeful. 'That's a hard "no" then, Bethy?'

I nod. 'I won't be long.'

I'm not sure what it is about Miles that makes me so agitated when I don't give a toss about him or what he thinks about me. Before he arrived, I was calm, and now every nerve in my body is on edge.

It's exactly the same at the cottage. Even if I'm way down Pumpkin's patch of grass, the moment Miles strolls out onto the terraces, my eyes are drawn to him, and however hard I try, I can't look away. The only way I can rationalise this is that my sixth sense sees him as a rival rather than a housemate. You wouldn't turn your back on a shark, would you? If he were a tiger, it would make perfect sense to watch every graceful, beautiful, hungry move, so you could save yourself before he went in to eat you.

At least walking across to the other end of the garden gives me a little distance. He's this awful blend of super critical and insanely distant, while seriously looking straight down his nose at me at the same time. It's as if every interaction we have has to end in a verbal scuffle. Every time we see each other, we fight.

As I reach the far wall with its neat lines of fruit tree branches and dangling pears spreading across the stonework I turn and see Zofia's walking two steps behind me.

I sigh and smile. 'Mum's espalier pear was up against our kitchen wall, but it wasn't ever neat like yours. She'd seen them growing against walls in the National Trust gardens and was determined to try for herself at home.'

Zofia considers. 'Espaliers need a firm hand with their pruning. Scarlett told me you don't have your mum anymore.'

I sigh again. 'She would have loved it here. Whenever I'm anywhere especially lovely, it breaks my heart that she can't be with me to share it. But she wanted us to live happy lives, so I try to make the most of every moment and not dwell on the sad bits.'

Zofia catches hold of my hand. 'It means a lot to me that you feel that here. This place is very special, but I am simply a very lucky custodian taking care of it for a while.'

My smile widens. 'And doing a very good job of it.'

She points further along the wall. 'See, next to the pears, there's a medlar tree. They're very old fashioned; you don't see them very often.'

I'm remembering GCSE English. 'There was one of those in *Romeo and Juliet*.'

'We must mention that to Miles.' Zofia comes in closer and lowers her voice. 'You have noticed that he can't keep his eyes off you?'

I roll my eyes. 'We all know how straight guys are with women's chests. That's how we don't die out as a species.'

'It's not your boobs, it's your face. You do know what it means when a man stares at your mouth?'

I have to put a stop to this. 'I honestly haven't seen that. And I also absolutely know he never would.'

I'd never planned to share my total humiliation at Scarlett's wedding, but if Zofia needs an explanation to stop her imagination from running away with this, so be it.

'Zofia, Miles and I have more history than you realise. A few years ago, at a family event, Miles went out of his way to avoid me, and upset other people a lot more than me with what he did.' I give Zofia a moment to take that in. 'That's how I know – you're not just wildly off the mark, you're *categorically and absolutely*, completely mistaken.'

Zofia frowns. 'Believe me, I'm old enough to have seen it all before. I'm almost never wrong.'

I laugh. 'I'm going to be the exception to your rule. I've never met anyone I argue with so much.'

She laughs. 'You can't deny he *is* very pretty.'

I sniff. 'Not on the inside. They're the worst kind.'

She's looking at me through half closed eyes. 'Let's wait and see, shall we?'

If Zofia's this instinctive, I may need to go a little further to make my point.

I make my smile bright. 'I've actually given up on men, but that's a story for another day.'

Zofia's eyebrows go up. 'Or you could save time and tell me now...'

It's incredible how often I have to justify that I'm on my own. I'm actually terrified that if I don't and lower my guard the truth might slip out accidentally. If anyone knew that I'm the kind of weak person who let a situation get so out of control that someone broke my wrist, I'd never hold my head up again. I mean, if I still feel like it was all my fault, everyone else would too. It's still a bit beyond me, how I willingly walked into a room with someone who turned on me like that.

It's always good to start off with the truth. 'Our dad left when Scarlett and I were small, and after that my mum never had another long-term partner.'

Zofia's eyebrows shoot upwards. '*What?!* No one at all?'

I shrug. 'She always had dates, but she never met anyone she liked enough to be a keeper.' I wrinkle my nose as I remember the reasons she'd give for moving on. Not putting butter all the way to the edge of their toast. The 'a' in bath being too long. Mustard yellow socks. Not buying free range eggs. As a teenager I found her pickiness as off-the-scale annoying as it was absurd. It actually drove me round the bend more than Scarlett and her seamless line of 'steady boyfriends'. I look for a way to sum up. 'I suppose Mum was an idealist who didn't want to settle for anything less than perfect.'

Zofia nods. 'And do you have the same high standards?'

It comes out as a snort. 'Hell no! After how that worked out for her, I went for all the fun and none of the judgement.'

Zofia's eyes light up. 'More boyfriends than hot pasties?'

'That's the one.' I pull a face, because it's still all true, but out loud it sounds a bit much. 'Lines of the things. More names than you'd fit on an A4 sheet if you wrote in teensy writing. And I had a ball along the way. But now I've left all that behind.'

I'm winding my way around to the speech I've polished that covers the truth like an invisibility cloak.

I blow out my cheeks. 'A new boyfriend every week sounds great, but one day it hit me that I was wasting my energy on wasters. That the fun wasn't fun anymore. That without the guys and the parties, I'd achieve so much more. So I moved on to better things, and here we are.'

When I add in a ta-da twirl this usually works like a dream to give my non-negotiable-single state a positive shine, and I'm desperately hoping Zofia will buy into it the same way everyone else does.

She watches me come out of my final spin. 'And how's this workaholic celibacy working out for you?'

I give her a wink. 'I prefer to call it professional focus. And since it re-booted my writing work, it has a lot going for it.'

I link my arm through hers and we make our way back across the garden, stopping for photos as we go. By the time we get back to where Miles is standing, I've got all the shots I need for now.

I smile across at her. 'If you don't mind taking me back to the cottage, Zofia, I'll get onto Fenna straight away and see if we can get the go-ahead on the idea. Then I can come back for longer to do the piece itself.'

Zofia gives me another searching stare. 'Are you sure you won't stay for tea?'

Miles steps towards us. 'I need to go now too. We can save you the drive, and go together.'

My heart sinks. 'I'll walk back.' I take in his doubtful expression and know I need a better excuse. 'I travel in the slow lane, Miles. Zofia mentioned you drive like you're in "Need for Speed".'

Miles shakes his head. 'Zofia is legendary in St Aidan for how many times she's put her car in hedges. If you survived the journey here, driving back with me will be like falling off a wall – in the best possible way.' He's still looking at me. 'It's five minutes at ten miles an hour. Put your big girl hat on, Betsy Beth, and live dangerously for once.'

Zofia is beaming at me. 'Well, that's settled then! Off you both go, and come back very soon!'

And just like that I'm overruled.

11

In Mile's car, on the way back to Boathouse Cottage
Wild winds and edible knickers
Wednesday

'Enough fairytales for you in that garden?'

Even though I've got the window of Miles's car down (full marks to me for managing that technicality), now we're in here his scent is making my head spin. And in spite of his car being the size of a lorry on the outside, once I slide into the passenger seat and we both close our doors I'm practically sitting on his lap. Being near enough to see the creases on his knuckles as he taps his fingers on the steering wheel is way too much for me.

I cross my own legs, then uncross them again fast when my entire upper thigh unexpectedly slides into view. I'm also regretting the outfit choice that means I'm somehow looking down on an expanse of my own bare stomach. How the hell does that happen when I'm wearing four outfits? And as if the situation wasn't bad enough already, now Miles is taking the piss by going on about fairies. There's another thing I need to sort out while we're here.

'You told me to put my big girl pants on back there.'

'Not "pants".' He gives me a sideways glance as he swings the car around in a circle, and eases it out between the gateposts and out onto the road. 'I actually said "hat".'

I could have done without making that slip, but that's not what's important. 'Are you implying I need to grow up?'

If he is, it's seriously insulting, and he needs to explain himself.

He pulls a face. 'Growing up means different things to different people.'

He's not getting out of it like that.

'Are you implying I'm in any way like a child?'

He blows out his cheeks and his finger tapping rate doubles. 'Child-like qualities aren't necessarily bad, Betsy Bets. They *can* be refreshing and endearing.'

This teasing refusal to ever give a straight answer is another thing about him that drives me wild.

'Stop dodging the issue, Miles. I'm either like a baby or I'm not.' He got himself into this corner, I'm not letting him off the hook.

He drags in a breath. 'Okay. Don't take this the wrong way. But sometimes you do appear to be over-reliant on Scarlett's opinions.'

'Rather than what?'

He's looking at me full in the face. 'Rather than having confidence in your own.'

'Fuck, Miles.' I want to yell at him for the rest of time for that. 'Look at the road, before you kill us both.'

He's still talking but at least he's looking forwards now. 'Obviously you're the expert on little things like piskies. It's the bigger stuff I'm talking about.'

I'm picking my jaw off the floor. '*Piskies?*'

He nods. 'They're the Cornish version of pixies. If Fennel's readers like fairies, they're going to love those.'

This is so unbelievable I shake my head in silence.

There's some more tapping on the steering wheel, then he's looking at me again. 'Zofia and her garden sound perfect for those features you've been struggling to find. Well done for that.'

He never fails to astonish me. 'What the hell has any of this got to do with you?'

He shrugs. 'Just being a supportive housemate.' He pulls a face. 'I don't deliberately listen in, but when you take your calls in the kitchen and tell the horse everything right next to the fence, it's hard not to feel included.'

I can't believe what I'm hearing. 'Is there anything else you'd like to bring to the table while we're here?'

I'm obviously being ironic, but he turns to me again. 'If Zofia's going to make good copy, you might like the lot down Saltings Lane.'

I can't believe he's talking like he's a local. 'How long have you actually been here?'

He hesitates. 'A couple of years. Just while I step back from the business. It's definitely temporary.'

I put that shock to one side for now and get back to what's important. 'Where the hell is Saltings Lane? And what's down it?'

'We just passed it. There was a sign saying Shepherds Huts, and there are barns with local makers. I'm surprised you haven't been there already.'

I open my mouth and let out the yell that's been waiting since we set off. 'Stop! STOP! STOP!'

Miles jumps on the brakes. 'What do you want me to do now?'

I'm shaking my head that he even needs to ask. 'Turn around, please, so we can have a look!'

'This is Cornwall, Betty Beth, there's no space for turning.' He grins across at me. 'I'll reverse.'

Three hundred yards going backwards at top speed? On balance, I'd rather have waited and come back on my own later.

12

The Barnyard, Saltings Lane, St Aidan
Chocolate chips and lucky breaks
Friday

It turns out that suitable subjects for pieces are like buses. I've waited the best part of two weeks to find any, then three come along on the same afternoon. At the end of Saltings Lane, Miles and I found a field with a view of the sea filled with shepherd huts and garden rooms, all decorated in different styles and colourways, and enough swinging fairy lights for me to know this is my kind of heaven. There's also a barn full of carefully chosen quirky accessories and second-hand furniture that is ready for painting, so customers can create designs that are completely unique to them, and do as much or as little of the work as they choose. The best part for me was that every single corner was so beautifully arranged and presented, even Miles couldn't find anything to be sarcastic about.

In ten minutes flat I'd taken enough photos to persuade

Fenna to commit to a long piece on decorative themes for huts and garden rooms, and some step-by-step features on individual up-cycling projects, as well as the big spread on Zofia. The speed Fenna emailed back, she must be as excited as I am.

The assistant at the shepherd's hut company is called Edie, and she said to come back again today to take in the Friday market that's here for smaller traders too. So now I'm here exploring the bit they call the barnyard, which has smaller units in some converted buildings around a courtyard that is bursting with makers and doers.

When I set off from the cottage forty minutes ago there was a stiff breeze blowing the clouds across a bright blue sky. The solid indigo of the sea was streaked with foam, and the early weekend visitors were scattered in groups across the sand huddling behind their windbreaks. I walked along the beach to the harbour, only stopping to write *Make my day* and *Blue, blue, blue*, then wound my way up the twisty road to the top of the village and on towards Rosehill. Turning into Saltings Lane I can already hear the sound of voices a hundred yards further down the lane.

I hurry along and join the crowd milling around the courtyard, buy a coffee from the side of a wonderfully weathered camper van with a stack of vintage surf boards on the roof, and then I catch sight of an open stable door and, beyond it, shelves stacked with rainbow-coloured felt slippers with curly toes, and I know I'm onto a winner.

The handmade felt bags and open baskets stacked high on the shelves inside the converted, white-washed building are the kind of wonderful that make me think for a second that maybe one day I *would* like a home after all. It's the strangest feeling, and for a fleeting moment it's as if I'm in someone else's body, not mine. But then I come to my senses, fan my face with relief, and treat myself to a garland of tiny, felted pom poms the size of marbles that are small enough to fit in my pocket.

The woman gives me my change and smiles. 'There's lanterns, candles and recycled metalwork next door. And then there's the soap factory, the patchwork store, and vintage clothes and at the end there's a bicycle shop with books. And don't miss the "anything goes" produce boxes outside; you mostly put your money in the jars for the things you buy from those. Everyone's talking about the sweet pea posies. And the Little Cornish Kitchen have a muffin table in the unit next door.'

A moment later I'm back outside, helping myself to the last two bunches of flowers complete with their own jam jar vases. I'm not sure what happens in the next hour, because I'm definitely not used to having cash to splash around, but today I'm suddenly surrounded by things that are both beautiful and such great buys they're crying out to be mine. With Fenna's three pieces coming up, I feel rich enough to rush around like a shopaholic. What makes things even more moreish than the vibrant colours are the items I find in unexpected places. I'm gasping at the rainbow stack of patchwork quilts in the fabric stable, when I come across the kind of china bowl I've been waiting for all my life.

I'm already carrying way too many packages, but I take it down from the shelf anyway to sigh over its bright floral design.

I dip into my purse for a ten-pound note, then smile when I recognise the familiar red hair of the woman in a flowery tea dress who is taking the money.

Her face lights up as I arrive at the table. 'Hi, I'm Clemmie.

We've waved at you from our balcony. My daughter Bud is smitten with your pony.'

As the woman I recognise from the gallery comes in with a tray of cakes, Clemmie calls her over. 'Plum, look, I'm finally face to face with Scarlett's sister.'

Plum swishes her dark ponytail, puts the tray down and pulls me into a hug against her paint-splashed dungarees. 'Lovely to meet you, you must be Betty?'

I hug her back. 'That's right.'

Plum jumps across to the door. 'Wait a moment, and you can meet Nell, too.'

Clemmie laughs. 'Meeting three mermaids in three minutes, that has to be a record.'

A woman in a checked shirt and a gilet comes in pushing a buggy, holding out her hand. 'I'm Nell, we're out without our tails today. Due to Plum's chamber of commerce initiative, and the rest of us being inundated with babies, Clemmie's having a Little Cornish Kitchen stall in Loella's fabric shop.' She gives me a hearty slap on the back. 'If ever you need eggs, I deliver to your door.'

Clemmie laughs. 'Don't worry if you can't keep up!' She takes the bowl from me and wraps it in paper. 'This is a Villeroy and Bosch; it's not that old, but you've bagged yourself a bargain.'

I grin back at her. 'I'm hoping to use it for fruit – if that's not *too* controversial for my housemate.'

I'm not sure why I'm sharing this, other than the feeling that if we knew each other better she'd understand.

'If you're arguing over where to store the bananas, things *are* bad!' Her smile is warm. 'Apart from your grumpy housemate, how are you settling into Scarlett's place?'

I pull a face. 'I'm crossing my fingers I'll last the summer.'

'Good luck with that!' She searches through a pile of patchwork pieces, and then hands me the card she finds. 'In case it doesn't work out, this might be useful.'

I'm staring at the words above the phone number. 'A studio space at the Net Loft?'

She's still beaming at me. 'A shop space with a sleeping gallery, small but perfectly formed, free until at least October, and currently crying out for an occupant. A friend of ours was about to sign the lease, but her dad was taken ill and now she's in St Andrews not St Aidan.'

With holiday rentals round here at thousands a week, I hadn't thought of looking for anywhere else to stay. I mean, swanning into a rental agent just isn't who I am. I prefer to live in the kind of places that happen without me realising they have, where it's easy to slip in and even easier to slip out again.

I wave the card at her. 'Thank you, I'll definitely give this some thought.'

She laughs at me. 'You probably think you won't, but if you're already scrapping over where to put the apples, you might be glad of it.'

Plum leans over and drops a paper bag into the midst of my shopping. 'There's a muffin there to brighten your day. Now all you need is someone to take you and your parcels back to Boathouse Cottage.'

Nell lets out a loud guffaw. 'You're quite a local celebrity. The woman who walks on the beach with a pony the same colour as her hair, people will be fighting to give you a lift.'

Plum joins in. 'A very hunky housemate you've got there. What a shame his personality doesn't match his looks.'

I load my bags onto my arms. 'Actually, I'm good to walk.'

As Clemmie finally ushers me out into the afternoon wind she nods at the card in my cardigan pocket. 'When you do call the number, tell them Clemmie said to ring.'

13

The Barnyard, Saltings Lane, St Aidan
Big bites and loud noises
Friday

Dropping my parcels in a pile on the ground, I'm still asking myself what just happened there. I sit down on some low stone steps, but before I work out which bag my cake is in, I hear my ringtone drifting upwards from my pocket.

'Scarlett! What time is it with you?' I kick myself for starting with a question and rush to fill in the gaps that I haven't told her about in messages. 'I'm at the Saltings Lane barnyard, shopping for England if not the world...'

Scarlett cuts in. 'Time? It could be time to tell me what the hell is going on at Boathouse Cottage, Betsy!'

I knew it was coming, but my heart drops like a stone. 'At the cottage?' I sound a lot like a strangled hedgehog, but Scarlett's voice is steely.

'It's the first day of our long weekend, after two whole weeks

I finally come face to face with Tate, and over breakfast he tells me Miles has been at the cottage – *for months!* Why didn't you say something?'

'Honestly, Scarlie, he's rarely there, it's not a problem.'

Her voice rises. 'It is for me! What the hell was Tate thinking going behind my back? He should have let me know!'

And she should have told him about me, too, but I'm glossing over that. 'Truly, Scarlett, the first time Miles and I coincided, we decided it was so insignificant there was no point mentioning it.' I think what else I can add to make it sound plausible. 'And since then, I've barely seen him.'

Scarlett is straight back in. 'But you hate him! If he's even there for a second with you and Pumpkin, it's too long. I'm so sorry, this is such a cock-up! Lately my life's been one bloody cock-up after another.'

She sounds so unlike her cool, capable, high-achieving self, I'm pleased we didn't force them to argue this out earlier.

I try to sound as soothing as I can. 'If it's ever a problem, I'll let you know. I'm just really, *really* grateful to be staying here at all.' Instead of telling her how obsessive Miles is with the antibac spray on the surfaces, I keep it simple. 'You and Tate need to forget about this. Find some delicious cheesecake to share for lunch and have a glorious day.'

She gives a sigh. 'Tate's already left for the office. I'm going to see an exhibition.'

I'm on this. 'At the Andy Warhol Museum?'

At least that made her laugh. 'That's in Pittsburgh. I'm going to see some Gustav Klimt landscapes. But I'll find some cheesecake. And well done on those pieces.'

Then she ends the call, and I'm back searching for my

muffin. Three bags later, I find it in with the flowers, and it's almost the size of a football. I tease off the paper case, open my mouth wide, and I'm about to sink my teeth in when someone calls.

'Betty Beth! At last! I thought I was never going to find you.'

'Miles!' My tummy clenches. I take a huge bite of my muffin while I still can, then mumble, 'Why are you here?'

His mouth twists into a smile that's even more sardonic than usual. 'There's no need to ask *you* that. If you've been buying for a candle-lit dinner with floral decorations and a choice of new outfits, count me in. What's with the giant folding screen?' He knocks on it as if it were a door. 'Is this yours?'

I roll my eyes. 'No, it just snuck up on me while I was looking the other way.' I take in his wide-eyed look, and give in. 'Of course it's mine. It's for privacy in the sofa area.' It's not just that. I'm actually planning to drape my clothes over it to save me packing things into bags every night.

He's peering into the bags. 'Cushions too!'

I'm as shocked as he is that I bought those. 'Two weeks of Scarlett's empty spaces and I'm desperate for comfort and embellishments.' That's the only way I can rationalise it to myself.

He gives a cough. 'This weekend is when we change over. It's your turn to take the bedroom.'

'Actually…' I can't believe what I'm leading up to here. But when I wake in the morning Pumpkin's muzzle is already misting the glass of the living room French windows, as he waits to say hello. In the evening, I can lounge and watch him silhouetted against the smoky purple of the sky, as the sun slides down behind the sea. When the moon comes out, I sometimes wake and catch him standing quietly in the half-light. However comfy the bed might be, I'm simply not ready to move to the opposite end of the building and give all that up. I send Miles a smile. 'I'm fine to leave things as they are – for now, anyway.'

Miles tilts his head. 'Any time you change your mind, just shout. In the meantime, hide those cushions from Scarlett and Tate.' His expression turns serious, and he bangs his head with his fist. 'That's what I came to tell you. Tate called, they've had the convo, and Scarlett was ... pretty cross.'

'She rang me, too.' I narrow my eyes. 'I'd say she's apoplectic. For the record, if we'd told them that first day, I *know* Pumpkin and I would have been the ones who got to stay.'

Miles frowns. 'If we'd done that the first day, Scarlett may have come straight back. At least we saved them from that.'

It's typical of Miles to breeze in and take the credit for averting the disaster he caused in the first place.

'Honestly, Miles, that would never have happened. They're the most solid couple I know.'

He gives a shrug. 'Every relationship has rocky times.'

I've no idea how the hell we've got here, but I'm leaping in to defend them. 'They don't. I'm Scarlett's sister, I should know.'

'If you're the expert, I'll take your word on that.' He gives my arm a squeeze. 'It hasn't been so bad sharing. I found out about fairies and pony droppings.'

My voice is high with indignation. 'You *would* say that, you grabbed all the good bits for yourself. As for your music – I mean, Greig's Rigaudon from his Holberg suite? At breakfast?'

He looks surprised. 'That's a bit harsh.'

I put my nose in the air. 'Harsh maybe, but also true.'

He blows out his cheeks, then turns to me with his smile

turned on full. 'By way of a thank you for letting me keep the bedroom, and as an apology for *maybe* taking more than my share of time on the sun lounger – how about I cook that dinner to go with your candles later?'

I'm looking down at the petrol blue wax, and however much that look of his is making my resolve give way, I'm determined not to be bought. 'Those candles are way too pretty to burn.'

He shakes his head. 'The candle shop is only there. I'll buy some more.'

I drag in a breath. 'There's a hundred other reasons I can't.'

It's one thing me getting all home-centred and cosy, but that doesn't extend to other areas of my life. I had a moment of holiday-type madness back there, not a personality transplant. When I've given up on guys for the sake of my wellbeing, I'm not about to dabble in meals for two, however great the dine-in deal is. More importantly, actual proper dinner parties for people who get their kicks from formality and pretension simply don't figure in my universe. People bigging up their aspirations, then parading them around a table is everything I despise. I'd actually rather eat my own head than go to one.

Miles stares at me. 'Keep going...'

I'm not sure it's any of his business, but there's no point hiding who I am. 'I don't do dinners, I hate to eat in front of strangers, I'm super picky about what I put in my mouth, and I refuse to do small talk. Is that enough for you?'

'I'm always up for a challenge.' The corners of his eyes crinkle as he smiles. 'Nothing I've heard there has put me off.'

I can't believe he's still pushing this. 'So now I'm a game you use to prove how macho you are? Excuse me for stepping away from that.'

He gives a sniff. 'It's your call. I can't force you to enjoy yourself.' He looks down at the bags. 'How about a lift home? Unless you've already lined up Pickfords.'

'I haven't.' I have to give him this one. 'A lift would be great, thanks.'

He tilts the screen, and hoists it under one arm. 'Days like today are when I'm pleased I ordered the long wheelbase model with the opening panoramic roof.' He gives a sheepish grin. 'When the salesman told me I would be, I didn't believe him.'

Another thing to call him out on. 'That's bullshit, Miles. Guys like you don't need persuading; you want every bell and whistle going.' I stuff the remains of my muffin in my mouth, pick up my bags, and follow him out of the barnyard to the car. It has to be said. 'For this one time only, I concede – it's a good thing you grabbed yourself the cottage parking space.'

The car is parked in the field by the shepherd huts and as we reach it a few minutes later, Miles takes a paper bag from his jacket pocket. He brings out a pastry, breaks it in two, and hands me half.

'Before we get in, tell me what you think of this.'

I'm staring at him. 'Let me guess – you don't want crumbs in the car?' He'd have a fit if he saw mine on a normal day. If he saw it after I've had a hay bale in the back, he'd expire.

He rolls his eyes. 'I often drive company cars. Keeping other people's things clean is a basic courtesy.'

As I push the pastry into my mouth and chew, he's watching me so intently I respond straight away. 'It's an apricot turnover.'

He nods. 'But how good is it?'

I'm confused. 'What's this sudden interest in pastry?'

He pulls a face. 'Nothing important. It's good to do product analysis occasionally, that's all. So be honest.'

'Product analysis of baking? You've picked the right woman for *that* job.' I smile remembering that first day at the cottage when I couldn't eat those croissant things fast enough. Then I look at the last piece of apricot slice in my hand. 'Honestly – I've had better.' Because truly, compared to those, I wouldn't give this the time of day. And then I finish it, clap my hands and swirl my skirts in the wind to get every last crumb off. 'Shall we get going? If it's all the same to you, I'd like to get my screen up.'

Did I really say that? If I did, it's only because I'm excited about having something to hang my dresses over. And possibly because when Miles sees this idea in action, I know it's going to drive him around the bend.

Between us, I can't wait.

14

Boathouse Cottage, St Aidan
Inhale, exhale
Saturday

'What *the hell* happened here?'
It's Saturday morning, and since I put my newly acquired screen into position Pumpkin and I have spent the morning ambling between the cottage and the harbour, bringing more of my clothes from the car. The sun has come out, and so have the visitors, but as Pumpkin was feeling especially sociable, we've only managed two trips so far.

With the screen's four sections zigzagging across the floor between the kitchen island and the sofa, it's given me a surprisingly useful amount of draping and hanging room, and once things are up there, they'll be easily visible, which is a feat in itself. No more digging in rucksacks for lost tulle skirts or vintage flowery tea dresses or silky hot pant shorts – they're all out on glorious show. Not only that, but I can also get to them from both sides.

As expected, it took approximately five seconds for Miles to walk in, take in the changes at my end of the tranquillity zone and kick off with his complaints.

He's so predictable, I'm ready for him. 'I know the screen has patina, but if I cover it with vintage wallpaper, I'm hoping it will make a pretty signature piece slash room divider.'

He's shaking his head. 'It's not the screen, it's what's on it – it's like your laundry trail has gained a fourth dimension.'

I look through the open square window and exchange what the eff? glances with Pumpkin who is out in the field, nibbling grass. Then I turn back to Miles. 'Thank you for making the room so tidy, Betty, and don't the sweet peas on the kitchen island look gorgeous … might be nice, Miles.' Then I have another thought. 'If you're thinking of folding up my clothes, don't you dare!'

He blows out his cheeks. 'Fine, I give in. Take the bedroom. Permanently.'

I'm laughing. 'I don't want the bedroom. I like it in this bit.' I tilt my head towards the riot of colour cascading over the screen. 'This isn't a wind-up, this is just who I am. I've never had this much space before. It's actually amazing.'

He pulls a face. 'Stars above, you're not even joking?'

'I'm not.'

As I confirm that, his despair is so real I go past the point of hilarity, through amusement, and reach a place where there's a twang in my chest. Truly, I never *ever* saw myself getting to the point of feeling sorry for Miles Appleton, but for a fleeting second I do. Obviously it's completely misplaced, because at the end of it all he's still the same knob he's always been.

He's staring at me intently. 'Not wanting to force you to overshare, but if this place is big, where were you before?'

I take a breath. 'I was at uni in Bristol, and after that I mostly stayed at an animal sanctuary in Somerset and paid my rent with jobs around the yard.'

'Totally rocking the *Country Living* dream, then?'

I blow out a breath. 'A room the size of a cupboard in a clapped-out porta cabin wouldn't be for everyone, but I enjoyed the animals. And the rural pieces I wrote when I was there came straight from the heart, and the readers seemed to like that.'

He nods. 'That's why you're all over the pisky stuff.'

I smile. 'I can write all day about hay meadows and Morris dancers, and I've blown a few rural myths out of the water in my time – there's no such thing as micro pigs.'

His eyes are wide. 'I'll take your word on that.'

I hesitate for a moment, but it's only polite to ask. 'I landed here when the refuge was evicted by a property developer. How did you end up in St Aidan?'

He shakes his head. 'I came down to Cornwall to help someone, and when she unexpectedly found she could manage without me, Tate suggested I stay here.'

Well, that's cleared that up. There's no ambiguity with the pronouns there. He definitely came here because of a woman, and there's no reason at all I should feel like I've had a pony kick in my stomach knowing that.

He looks down. 'I had my foot in a pot at the time, too.'

I remember Zofia mentioned this. 'A broken ankle and a shattered heart. No wonder Tate caved.'

He rolls his eyes. 'It wasn't quite like that.'

It never is. This is guys all over. They never truly open up; they'd always rather leave you guessing.

If you think that the card Clemmie gave me yesterday has been on my mind, you'd be right. During my first trip into town this morning I actually dismissed it entirely as I waved up at her on her balcony. Then I walked back into the cottage to find Beethoven's 9th symphony bouncing off the kitchen roof, so the second time in town I got directions to the Net Loft, and found I was looking at a simple whitewashed building just off the end of the harbourside which had been split up into small shop units. The end one looked empty, but since I'm looking for a bedroom not a retail space, I put it in the too difficult pile, went back to my car and got on with the rest of my life. So that's the end of that.

Miles is frowning now. 'Excuse me, but what exactly are you wearing there?'

What was I saying about him being an arse? Flipping the attention back onto me to avoid being straight himself. I look down to remind myself. 'Paper bag shorts in floral cotton, a bra top, two silk kimonos and some fairy wings.' I take in his grimace. 'They were under the front seat of my car, I put them on to carry them back.'

I dress to please myself, and I always have, and I love seeing Miles wince at my combinations because it's like me waving a finger at his boring conventionality. If Miles were selecting a woman's outfit, I imagine he'd choose a short, strong-coloured satin cocktail dress, with eff-me heels, and bare shoulders. My point is, it would be very obvious, but even more, it would be a million miles from the pale satin bridesmaid's slip I was flopping about in at Scarlett's wedding two years ago.

In the interest of keeping this balanced, I bat the conversation straight back to him again. 'Would you like to tell me about your clothes?'

He gives me a strange look then looks down at himself. 'Jeans and T-shirt. A stylist sends me a selection from the company collection, and I put them on. Does that answer your question?'

I'm picking my jaw up off the floor. 'That's as much input as you have? And what happens to the surplus when this woman sends the next batch?'

He gives a cough. 'It's actually a guy, and any input from me would have happened earlier when the ranges were being designed. Whatever I don't wear to destruction is responsibly handed on.'

How can anyone make clothes sound this boring? Especially when they're supposed to have a hand in making them and they're the kind that cost shedloads. But I shouldn't be surprised, because it all goes with the territory. And like everything else with me and Miles, we couldn't be further apart if we tried.

Men who leave their choice of anything as individual as T-shirts in the hands of someone else must be more interested in money than what they actually put on their back. At least it's good news on the repurposing and the gender of the stylist. My tummy drops again, and then I recap and reassure myself, because that wasn't ever an issue; I'm pretty certain that Miles likes women not men. And it's no concern of mine anyway. Definitely no shits are given in that direction from here.

As for what Miles's life looks like beyond the boundaries of Boathouse Cottage, if it includes boardrooms, free clothes, fancy cars and friends like Tate's wedding crew, I can only imagine it's light years away from the places I've inhabited or the life I've lived. Which is why we have absolutely nothing in common and even less to talk about unless we're disagreeing – which we are amazeballs at.

Obviously, the pricey kit is the reason his bum looks so hot. The upside of expensive gear is that it makes the most of every asset. And leaves poorer mortals like me struggling to keep my (mental) hands off them. At least that's that problem explained to me.

'How exactly would you describe your style?'

His voice cuts into my thoughts, and I have to say he's got me there. I think about earlier, doing twirls along the beach singing at the top of my voice with 'Prada' in my ear bud, Pumpkin trotting beside me.

'Each outfit I choose is thrown on in a multilayered way so it's easy to move in, but with unexpected gaps.' I know he loves a definition. 'If you insist on giving it a name, I'd say it's pre-loved stratification. Or it could even be retro-surprise-lamination.'

He lets out a slightly bitter laugh. 'A bit like that damned laminated pastry, which proved so impossible to make.'

My heart sinks again because this is another thing that's been playing on my mind since yesterday. I know Miles isn't my favourite person, and I know I was sizing him up and couldn't afford to appear weak, which is why I was economical with the truth when the situation came up that first day. But as a person, overall I like to think I'm honest and would treat people as I'd like to be treated myself. And since the question of the pastry came up again yesterday, much as I disapprove of and dislike Miles, I'm going to have to come clean on this.

I remind myself of the way he opened the roof of his car and swung my battered old screen into the space without any more hesitation than a quick dust down with his jacket sleeve. Then I screw up my courage, and launch.

'You'd made a tray of pastries the day we arrived.'

He pulls a face. 'Every one ended up on the ground in the field. Not that it mattered – the bin was the best place for them.'

I'm wrinkling my nose. 'Why do you say that?'

He gives a shrug. 'I'm not chef-trained, but coming down here sparked an interest in artisan baking. As an on-trend growth area it's a no brainer. The entrepreneur in me had this warped idea that muffin shaped croissants would be the perfect base for hundreds of different fillings.'

Something in the intensity of his gaze has caught my interest. 'Go on.'

He pulls a face. 'I had time on my hands, so I studied the YouTube videos, and began to experiment for myself. My idea was to short-cut the croissant dough process to speed up production. I'd been trying to perfect the bake for weeks and every batch had been like rock.' He takes a breath. 'I'd made one final change with the method, but I seriously doubt it had made any difference. That one final disaster felt like a subliminal message, so I took the hint to leave baking to the bakers, and moved on with my life.'

I'm screwing up my courage. 'The bin might *not* have been the best destination for those buns.'

He looks at me. 'What do you mean?'

'I ate one before they fell.'

His eyes narrow. 'And?'

'They tasted good enough for you to bake more.'

He looks like he can't believe what he's hearing. 'So they were edible!?'

'More than that.' Damn, now I've come this far, I might as well go all the way. 'They were delicious. Beyond delicious. I actually ate four.' Thinking back to the crusty outsides giving way to the soft, doughy centres, I remember the taste of the toffee pecan and I'm practically drooling. 'I only stopped at four due to dropping too many flakes on the kitchen floor, and because Scarlett rang to ask me to test the shower.'

Miles is nodding. 'Now you mention it, I wondered where all the mess had come from.'

I have to protest here. 'There weren't *that* many crumbs.'

He refocuses and looks at me again. 'So two weeks down the line, what do you suggest I do with this information?'

I might as well give my honest opinion. 'I wouldn't waste any more time. I'd say go and bake your ass off. ASAP!'

There's a smile around the edge of his lips. 'And if I do, would you be around to assist with some analysis?'

'Hell yes.' A housemate who bakes croissants could turn out to be a dream houseshare after all, except he hasn't moved yet. 'So what are you waiting for? Go and do baking!'

He raises one eyebrow. 'To get in the zone, I'm going to need Figaro...'

I let out a groan. 'Please tell me you're not going to make the ceiling shudder again?'

He nods. 'It only works when it's extra loud.'

I brighten. 'So you won't be using the sun terrace?'

He holds my gaze. 'Only in between rolling sessions, while

the dough is resting.' Then he blinks. 'If you'd like to use it, don't let me stop you.'

There are clouds with silver linings, and there are no-win situations, and I already know which this is.

I make my smile extra bright. 'Lucky for me I won't be here this afternoon. I'm going out to research my pieces.'

Any other time or person, I might have been prevaricating. The awful reality of life with Miles means I'd rather go to work.

He turns his attention to the kitchen. 'I won't disrupt the chiller trays in here, I'll take over the fridge in the mud room.'

I just hope there are some decent bakes to show for the inconvenience.

15

Boathouse Cottage, St Aidan
Snap decisions and incredible crunch
Sunday

When I come back to the cottage later on Saturday there's no sign of Miles (hurrah!) nor (boo!) his baking. I make the most of his absence, watch the sun slip down behind the horizon from the lounger, then when the sky darkens, I move inside and fall asleep a long time later watching my fifty-fourth viewing of *Gilmore Girls*.

Next morning, I nip to the bathroom early to avoid any unnecessary meetings in the hallway. As I slip back onto the sofa at 5.45am I hear Miles call softly from the far end of the kitchen, 'Don't mind me, I'm making an early start I won't disturb you.'

Too right he won't. I pull the covers over my head, snooze for another hour, then I grab some clothes and a backpack and slip out through the French windows and into the field where Pumpkin is standing waiting for me.

If ever I mention my best friend is a pony, people think I'm joking. But Pumpkin is always up for an outing. Better still, he's empathetic, constant and dependable, he has a good sense of humour, and mostly he doesn't argue with me. When I stop to think about it, I probably spend more time with Pumpkin than I do with any person. He's less than delighted to find I've come out without my morning carrot treat, but he soon cheers up when I clip his lead rope onto his head collar and we set off along the beach towards the town.

Pumpkin doesn't understand everything I say, but he's adept at picking up cues and reading wider situations. When I mention we're on our way to buy carrots from the shop, his walk speeds up.

It's shortly after seven, and we almost have the beach to ourselves. As usual, I'm stopping every couple of paces to pick up shells or stones, but as there's no one to chat to we make good progress, striding along the firm damp sand over the wavy ridges left behind by the outgoing tide. It wouldn't be a morning walk around the bay if I didn't find a stick and stop to write and photograph a message to myself and/or the world.

Today, in anticipation of what might (or might not) be coming later, I write *Taste the difference?* A bit further along the beach I stop again to do an anticipatory *Yum yum*. When I stop later to look how many white streaks there are on the sea, for some unfathomable reason when I look down at my feet, I find a sign looking up at me that says *Nice bum*.

As I'm wearing ripped denim cut-offs with cycling shorts and a lace-over dress, I must subliminally be complimenting myself, or possibly Pumpkin's lovely round rump. For the record, I definitely wouldn't be writing that about anyone else I know. Certainly not about Miles, however much I find it hard to take my eyes off his butt, which I shouldn't even be noticing.

It's amazing how time passes when you're wandering along the shore. Near the end of the beach we wave at Clemmie who's sitting quietly on the balcony with a child on her knee, then carry on across the harbour and up the winding street to the Spar shop where I buy a bag of carrots for Pumpkin. Then I go to grab a takeaway coffee from the van next to the doughnut stall, which is opening up in anticipation of a busy Sunday.

I take a sip of my coffee and mutter to Pumpkin. 'When I smelled those sugary doughnuts, I was *this* close to buying a box. I hope Miles comes through for us.'

I can tell by the way Pumpkin blinks he's recognised the name.

I nudge his flank. 'Miles needs to do a lot of baking to make the leap from being the knobhead you decided he was last week.' Looking up from checking the time on my phone, I see Clemmie standing on the balcony beckoning.

By the time we've walked along to the balcony, she's coming out of the front door underneath.

I smile at her. 'Someone else up bright and early?'

'Two babies mean we always are.' She grins. 'The Little Cornish Kitchen will be opening soon. You're both very welcome any time, the apple trees give plenty of shade.'

I look at Pumpkin. 'Could you decimate an orchard in the time it takes me to eat a muffin?' I smile back at Clemmie. 'We're not eating today. We're out walking while Miles bakes. It's a fine line. We don't want to get back too early but if we wait too long, I might expire.'

Clemmie wiggles her eyebrows. 'It sounds like someone is upping their game.'

'There's still a long way to go, isn't there, Pumpkin?' I take another sip of coffee even though it's making my hunger pangs worse not better. 'We're walking towards Oyster Point while the magic happens.'

'We came down so Bud could see Pumpkin close up.' Clemmie looks at the child in her arms. 'Would you like to stroke him, Bud?'

Bud has the same auburn curls as her mum, but she wrinkles her nose, pulls away and scrunches her hands into fists.

'Maybe another day?' I walk Pumpkin through a half circle so we're facing the harbour again.

'Don't forget to look out for sirens by the sea pool.' Clemmie's smile widens as she steps back onto the doorstep. 'Plum, Nell, Sophie and I are known locally as the mermaids, but you, me, Bud and Pumpkin are like a little auburn sub-group.'

'I'll take that,' I call over my shoulder as we set off. 'We're heading back for ten, so we'll give you gingernut piskies a wave on our way past.'

When I'm out with Pumpkin, even just for a walk, things always take longer than I expect because along the route there might be a hundred conversations. By the time we've seen the sea pool and we're on our way back, the harbourside is as busy as I've ever seen it. Far from being alarmed, Pumpkin is in his element. The more people there to pat his head and tug on his mane, the better he likes it. My timing goes out of the window, and it's gone eleven by the time Pumpkin trots off across his field again.

As I push my way in through the French windows, the smell

of hot pastry immediately makes me drool. I'm scanning the island unit and empty work surfaces, looking for even a teensy plate when Miles appears in the doorway.

'Sorry I'm late. We got caught up in the crowds.'

'It's fine. You're here now.'

I swallow. 'If you've already eaten the bakes, I can make a sandwich.'

He jumps forward. 'Please don't. They're in the mud room. Sit down and I'll get them.'

By the time I'm climbing onto my high stool, Miles is already pushing a wide platter of pastries in front of me.

'You've made different types?' Remembering how they tasted last time, I'm melting in anticipation.

'Almond and raspberry, double chocolate, pecan and salt caramel, and apricot.' He points to each as he names them, then slices them into quarters. 'Try them all and tell me what you think. Once I've seen your reaction, you can eat as many as you like.'

Considering how many I ate last time he might regret saying that.

'Almond and raspberry – with white chocolate icing...' I take a bite, then another straight away because it tastes like heaven. Then I remember what I'm here for, and find some words. 'Flakey, delicious, I love the way you've got ground almonds in the centre, and the flakes on the outside, all shot through with raspberry coulis. And the fresh raspberries on the top are the cherry on the cake.'

Miles watches me move onto the next. 'Double chocolate has dark chocolate slices, and cocoa in the dough too.'

I pop a piece into my mouth and let the cocoa explode on

my tongue. 'I've never tasted anything quite like it before. It's incredible.'

He smiles. 'I should be serving you spoonfuls of cucumber sorbet to clean your palate between flavours.'

For one time only I forgive him for being the kind of guy who hangs out in places where they have fancy shit like that, and grin at him. 'I'm good without the greens, but I bet these would be amazing with herby cream cheese, or spinach and ricotta.'

He holds up his finger. 'Thanks for that. It's noted in my memory bank.'

I reach out for my next piece. 'Apricot – aha! Let's see how these compare to yesterday's pastries.' I'm chewing and waving my hands at the same time. 'No comparison. They've blown the others out of St Aidan bay.'

'And the last one. Basically it's pecan nut with toffee drizzle.'

I go straight in for a whole one. 'If these are what I had last time, I already know.' This time around I'm not even trying to keep the flakes under control. I take the bun in my hand, open my mouth as wide as I can, and go for it. I'm still grinning as I wipe the crumbs off my cheeks when it's all disappeared a few moments later.

He raises an eyebrow. 'Not so bad then?'

I have to be honest. 'If I could only eat one thing for the rest of my life, these would be up there.' I stop for a second. 'Have you got any more? Last time I ate four, but I could easily have eaten eight.'

Surprisingly there's no judgement on Miles's side. He

laughs, and looks secretly proud. 'If every potential customer felt like that, I'd definitely be onto a winner.'

I'm sitting up straight in my seat. 'So they *are* a commercial venture for you?'

He sniffs. 'It's very early days. I've never baked before, let alone sold food. But my mum's dad was a baker, so if it works out, I'll be following the family tradition.'

He's caught my attention. 'So what are you going to call them?' I pick up a chocolate one. 'If croissants crossed with doughnuts are cro-nuts, shaped like muffins ... they'd be cruffins.'

He pulls a face. 'I'll certainly run that past my marketing teams.'

I roll my eyes that he's got one of those to hand. 'I'm afraid I'm an instant person, I can't possibly wait for them. For now, I'm going to call them boathouse buns.' I try it for size. 'How many boathouse buns have you made today?'

He gives a shamefaced grin. 'There's another sixty in the mud room.'

I'm making it up as I go along, but I might as well state the obvious. 'Even if we save a dozen for immediate consumption, that still leaves forty-eight more than we can't eat ourselves, so we may as well use them as testers.'

He's looking at me through narrowed eyes. 'Any research will need to be meticulously devised and targeted.'

I can't believe what he's missing. 'You've got a beach full of people who'd be very happy to give their opinions. It's baking not rocket science, why waste the audience?' I'm not usually a bossy person, but I can't hold back on this. 'Miles, this is

St Aidan, not London. It's free for the taking. Look, I'll do the talking. Stop prevaricating and fetch the goods before everyone goes home.'

His jaw drops, but a second later he slides off the stool and three minutes later Miles and I are down on the beach with a platter of his boathouse buns.

16

The beach by Boathouse Cottage, St Aidan
Big guns and belly laughs
Sunday

'We're about to launch a new pastry range, would you like to taste some preview samples? There's no charge.'

Heaven knows what I look like with my hair caught up in a scrunchie and my flowery shirt flapping wildly around my purple satin shorts, but as we approach the first group we come to on the sand, I put on my brightest smile and cross my fingers tightly behind my back.

As Miles steps up with the platter of samples, they help themselves, fill their mouths with bun fragments, and hold their thumbs up in appreciation, before going in again for more.

I'm trying to gather as much information as I can. 'Any particular favourite?'

There's a chorus. 'Apricot!' 'Toffee!' 'Chocolate every time!' 'Raspberry all the way!'

Then someone calls, 'They'd be amazing with cinnamon, too.'

Another chimes in, 'Or vanilla custard.'

I grin. 'I'll mention that to the baker.'

Miles finally breaks his silence. 'I hope you don't mind people you don't know disturbing your afternoon?'

One girl laughs. 'With baking this delicious, feel free to disturb us every Sunday.'

As they lick their fingers, one of the women looks up at me. 'We've met already. You're the one we saw with your pony earlier?'

I smile. 'I am.'

A guy carrying a surfboard comes to join the group. 'I saw you and your pony outside the Surf Shack.' He nods at the platter. 'If you're selling those chocolate ones, I'll take four.'

Selling? I hadn't actually thought any further than extending the reactions beyond mine, and maybe making an order of flavour preference, but if the chance is there, my instinct is to jump at it.

'We could do you a special introductory price of three pounds each.' I'm thinking they must use shedloads of butter. 'Is that okay with you, Miles?'

He raises his eyebrows. 'You're our boss on the beach, Betsy.'

I'm used to fundraising for the animal rescue, so what happens next is like second nature. 'We can do six for fifteen?' I laugh. 'They're very moreish. I just ate four and they didn't touch the sides.'

There's another chorus, of 'Great!'

'We'll have some too.'

'And us!'

Before Miles has finished collecting the notes, the girls beyond the next windbreak are calling us over. 'Did you say pastries?'

'Where's the pony gone?'

'Can I have a selfie with the horse?'

I laugh and wander over. 'Sorry, Pumpkin's back at home, but we do have some slices of boathouse buns here for anyone who would like to taste them...'

The people call across the sand. 'Once you've tried them you'll want more.'

I laugh. 'I certainly did.'

That's the thing. When I believe in what I'm offering people, it's like sharing the good news with friends, especially when I've already broken the ice with Pumpkin earlier in the day. If Miles had any doubts about the quality of his baking, the next half hour chases them away for good. We move from group to group along the beach, often drawing our own crowd, and long before we draw level with the Surf Shack the buns run out.

Miles taps the crumbs off the platter and drops the knife into the bag he'd been carrying the baking in. 'I guess this is where we turn for home?'

I fall into step beside him as we head back towards the cottage. 'Whatever your fancy team does down the line, St Aidan says "yes" to boathouse buns.'

He gives a shrug. 'It's good to have that reassurance when I'm ready to take this forward. As I already have the contacts, I'll be leapfrogging the baby steps on this one.'

Whatever comes up, Miles and I have entirely opposite

approaches. It's as if a large part of the world I inhabit is invisible to him.

I stoop, pick up a shell and cup it in the palm of my hand. 'Small is beautiful. I would apply that to growing a business too.'

He stops for a moment and looks at me. 'How come you're such a natural with the selling?'

I frown and remember the struggles. 'The sanctuary where I lived always needed money, and I used to man their weekly cake stall. If I didn't sell the goods the animals didn't eat, so I learned fast.'

I take a breath as I remember. When my arm was mending, cakes were lighter to lift than hay bales and mucking-out forks, so I swapped my Saturdays on the yard and worked the market instead.

Miles is looking at me as we stomp along, our feet sinking in the soft sand. With the wind in his hair and his cheekbones etched in the bright afternoon sun, he looks so at one with the shore, for a few seconds it's hard to think of him as the big noise with the fancy car. For a moment, with all his high-flying trappings stripped away, he's just a human like all the rest of us.

He clears his throat. 'A lot of people mentioned the pony. He obviously makes a big impression.'

I grin. 'What can I say. Pumpkin and I both love meeting new people. We try to believe the world is a sunny place and that comes through.' I hesitate. 'But don't be fooled for a second into thinking that means we're pushovers. If someone wrongs us, it takes a lot for us to forgive them.'

He looks at me with a half-smile. 'Hint taken, understood and duly noted. I'll do my best not to upset you.'

I give him a cold stare because there's no point in pretending. 'Unless, of course, it's already too late.' Two years too late, with me. 'You already stuffed up with Pumpkin, remember.'

He looks hurt. 'Now I'm really kicking myself that I stayed in the outdoor shower too long.'

The man is driving me to distraction with his annoying habits, but I hadn't noticed that one.

'Occasionally Pumpkin can be bought off with carrots. I'm less easily persuaded.' I'm laughing at him because he thinks I'm joking. 'So what about these boathouse buns? They're too good to keep to yourself.'

He rubs his chin. 'We're still at the prototype stage.'

I hate things that take an age. 'If you leave it another twenty years, by then people might only be eating protein pills.'

He stops and puts his hands on his hips. 'What's this child-like craving for immediacy?'

Even when I pull myself up to my full height to make myself appear like a fully-fledged adult, I'm still a lot shorter than him. 'It's for your benefit not mine.' I don't usually bullshit, but sometimes it's necessary. 'I'm your first platform tester, I'm available, and I'm obviously an expert in my field. I mean, I got the last lot spot on, didn't I? You can probably extrapolate my results and predict the taste of every person under thirty in the UK.'

His voice is high with surprise. 'You're not even thirty? That probably explains why your opinions are fluid and your tastes tend towards the juvenile.'

For eff's sake. I am this close to giving up on him. I actually would if I weren't so desperate for another taste of pecan and toffee. 'Do you want your buns taste-tested, or not? How about vanilla custard and Nutella for next time?'

'What about cinnamon?'

I wrinkle my nose. 'It's too grown up. I've never taken to it.'

I swear I can hear him laughing as he turns away.

'Have you ever had a relationship, Betsy Eliza?'

I'm picking my jaw up off the floor at the intrusion. 'Why would you ask a question like that?'

He shrugs. 'Just checking out where you'd fit in a demographic profile if we're thinking about trend building.'

As a reason it's a bit of a shit answer, but as usual, there's no point pretending about my life before I was twenty-six. 'My dating history is the stuff of stand-up routines, but I'd have to know you a lot better before I treated you to that one.'

'I'll look forward to that down the line, then.'

'Miles, truly, it's never going to happen.'

'Never say never.' He gives a laugh. 'So is there anyone in the frame currently?'

Obviously I have no plans to include a partner in my life now or at any time in the future, but I'm not about to share that with Miles. As for the years before Mason, I never looked for anything beyond a good night out. Me and my friends from sixth form made the most of our after-exam parties, because none of us could bear the thought of hitting freshers week as virgins, and it took off from there. As my line of ex's shows, their ability to crack me up while drinking twenty Jägerbombs didn't translate into other areas, like dependability or longevity.

'What's with the post-pastry interrogation?' I roll my eyes so he knows he's overstepping. 'With Pumpkin as my gatekeeper, it's pretty hard for any guy to get past the radar. As you saw, he's great at spotting tossers.'

Miles laughs. 'Maybe he should be widening his assessment to include baking skills?'

I'm shaking my head at how unbelievable Miles is. 'You're telling me you'd bake to climb up Pumpkin's approval ladder?'

Miles pulls a face. 'Did you see how he looked at me?'

'Why would you even care?' One glance at Miles and I answer my own question. 'You have to win at everything don't you?'

He pulls down the corners of his mouth. 'Pretty much.'

There's no point letting his misdirected ambition go to waste. 'In that case, let's try custard, Nutella, and apple buns next, and a few more pecan and toffee just to be sure they're working. Whenever you're ready. Tonight, if you like.'

He hesitates. 'Sorry, I'm committed elsewhere this evening. But definitely tomorrow.' Then Miles slips the roll of notes into my hand. 'As the super salesperson and research chief, I think this belongs to you.'

And a moment later I'm through the gate and back in Pumpkin's field, and Miles is off up the lane getting into his car.

17

The beach by Boathouse Cottage, St Aidan
Usherettes and green bananas
Monday

When Pumpkin and I get back from our amble along the beach next morning, there's no sign of Miles, but Zofia is hard at work in the kitchen in her yellow rubber gloves.

I get in first with my apology. 'I'm so sorry about the crumbs! Miles has been trialling laminated pastry and I've been devouring the results. Not even Miles managed to capture all the escaping flakes.'

Zofia's eyebrows go up. 'Lots of layers and rolling, great for those biceps of his.' She laughs. 'I'll forgive you both for the mess.'

I smile my thanks. 'The sweet peas I bought from the makers market on Friday were lovely, but they're finished now.'

She watches while I collect the jam jars from the island and sweep the dried-up petals into my hand. 'You are welcome to go to my garden if you'd like to pick flowers and take photographs for your magazine. The light is very clear this morning.'

An offer like that has me rushing to the Villeroy and Bosch fruit bowl, which is where I keep my rarely-used car keys. 'If you really don't mind, I'd love to. That's the wonderful thing about gardens, they change all the time, especially with the mercurial weather we get around here.'

Zofia smiles. 'I am whizzing round today because I'm off to Plymouth to the theatre later. Pick as many flowers as you want, and go wherever you like in the garden.'

I beam. 'So long as I can find it again. I've been back several times since that first day, but Cornish lanes are narrower and more samey than any in Somerset.' Picking up my bag, I laugh. 'If I do lose my way, at least I know I'll always end up somewhere interesting.'

She gives me a nudge on my way to the door. 'As the summer traffic builds it takes longer and longer to get to places, but you'll get used to it. I'll tell Miles to send out a search party if you're not back by nightfall.'

It's not only the roads that are different here – I swear that there are Cornish time slips, too. When I leave Boathouse Cottage shortly after ten, I'm joking about failing to reach my destination but it's five hours later by the time I arrive back in St Aidan again.

There are so many reasons to get sidetracked. My phone is filled with photos from my visit to Zofia's garden, but I also stopped every time I saw an honesty box shop at the end of a farm track or by a garden gate.

Even though it's a Monday, as I climb out of my car in the area beyond the jetties the public car park by the harbourside is rammed with cars, and I'm thanking my lucky stars that Scarlett organised a parking permit for me for the boat owners' end.

I'm clutching an armful of brightly coloured zinnias from Zofia's garden, and my head is so full with images of the gorgeous garden-gate shops I've seen that I nearly walk into a set of steps that are propped on the pavement in front of the Net Loft. When I blink and look again, I see someone on the inside with a squeegee cleaning the windows of the studio I looked into the other day.

Before I know what I'm doing, I've stepped into the doorway. 'I take it this is the vacant studio. Have you found a tenant already?' I've no idea why my heart's dropped like a stone when I'm not thinking about the place for myself.

The man in overalls dips into a bucket of water and wrings out a cloth. 'No tenant yet. That's why I'm giving it a spruce-up. One person was interested but it was too small.'

'Clemmie gave me a card when I was up at the barnyard.' My voice is operating with no input on my part. 'It's probably too big and I definitely don't need a shop.'

'You may as well look now you're here.'

I laugh. 'I probably can't afford it.'

'You never know.' The man laughs. 'The building is run by a cooperative, so the rent is low and all-inclusive. It's the kind of deal you can't walk away from.'

I'm already looking at a high gallery on one side of a double-height space. With the whitewashed walls and the light splashing down from high level roof lights, it reminds me of a rustic version of Boathouse Cottage.

The man is not holding back with the persuasion. 'It's very quiet, just the sound of the waves crashing in the distance on stormy days and the jangle of the rigging on the masts of the boats in the harbour. With tourists and fishermen passing the door, it's a good spot for footfall.'

I turn to look through the window. 'You can't beat a view of lobster pots with the sea beyond.' I look at the pale turquoise shimmer in the distance. 'It changes colour all the time. It was aquamarine this morning.'

'However long I'm here, I never get tired of that.' The man laughs then holds out his hand to shake mine. 'I'm Malcolm, by the way. My Beth does the lanterns at the barnyard, and I live at Periwinkle Cottage, just along the lane from there, with Edie's Aunty Jo.'

'Lovely to meet you, Malcolm.' I might as well introduce myself too. 'I'm Betty, staying at Boathouse Cottage while my sister's abroad.'

His grin widens. 'You're the one who walks that ginger-haired pony called Pumpkin.'

However many descriptions I hear, there are always new ones to make me smile. I take in the twang of guitars coming from an ancient CD player. 'Is that Razorlight you're playing there?'

A whole new smile spreads across Malcolm's face. 'It's on the Dad's Juke Box compilation CD Beth made for me for Father's Day four years ago. Are you a fellow fan?'

I let out a sigh. 'Let's just say, if my housemate played Razorlight more often I might not be here.' That's not quite true. With Miles it's a lot more than our musical differences; it's our entire attitude to life.

Malcolm points to the staircase. 'Well, your living and

sleeping space is up top, kitchen and bathroom are under the gallery. The rest is for whatever you want to use it for.'

'Is the postcard rack staying?' Of all the ridiculous things to ask. I peep into an unexpectedly spacious kitchen with a range cooker and tall fridge already in place. Then I glance into a bathroom large enough for the double-ended freestanding bath, and my heart is well and truly lost.

Malcolm nods. 'It's everything you see. Washing machine in the porch. There's a tiny sitting area opening off the bedroom level, with space for a washing line when it's not too windy.'

I slip upstairs and take in a wide low bed, a door opening onto a balcony, and even better views across the double-height space below and through the roof windows out to the sea. As I hurry down again, and head towards the door for some inexplicable reason I'm watching a mental slideshow of all the garden-gate shops I saw this afternoon.

'Thank you for showing me round, Malcolm.' I have to be honest. 'It's lovely, but it's out of my league.'

'You might want to hear the details before you write it off.' Malcolm's got his hands in the pockets of his painting overalls. 'This blank canvas is a snip at five hundred a month.'

That's less than a lot of my friends pay for a room! When I do the maths and think I already have enough savings to cover that until the autumn, my heart skips a beat. This could be my ticket to freedom – my own space, my own bed, my own bath. I could do laundry whenever I wanted to. I could even fit my own small sun lounger on that balcony.

'You're right, Malcolm. That does sound … *very interesting.*' I'm hoarse with excitement.

He nods, beaming. 'I told you it was worth hearing me out.'

My mind is racing faster than my heart. 'So what would the arrangements be?'

He leans forward and points along the harbourside. 'George at Trenowden, Trenowden and Trenowden solicitors has drawn up a contract you'd sign, and you'd pay two months' rent upfront. After that, you could be in as quick as you like.'

'A contract?' It comes out as a strangled squeak.

As it's always just been me, I've always tried to keep my needs minimal. The times we signed for shared houses at uni, I was carried along with the group. If this is down to me on my own, it's so much more stressful. If I'd had the same ambitions as some of my other friends, I'd have aimed higher years ago and had a more luxurious life to show for it. The reason I'm footloose and totally without ties is because I've always avoided responsibility like the plague, with work and with housing. I might have been uncomfortable, but at least I've been my own person and kept my integrity.

The more money you have, the more you buy and the more money you need. It's the classic consumer spiral that I've always refused to buy into. It would be a complete mistake to go back on my principles now.

Malcolm shrugs. 'It's quite straightforward. Everyone else has signed without any problem.'

However annoying Miles is, the thought of putting my signature on a formal document is taking every bit of breath out of my lungs. I fan my face to get some air, aware of a river of sweat running down my spine inside my crop top, my dress and my two overlapping cardigans.

If it's a choice between acting like a fifty-year-old, or arguing over where we keep the cornflakes, I'll stick with the aggravation because once I sign my life away there's no going back.

'Actually...' I'm backing out of the door and out onto the cobbles. 'I was probably right the first time.'

Malcolm's face has fallen. 'It's standard stuff, nothing untoward.'

'I'm just not that kind of a person.' I catch my foot in a pile of fishing nets, stumble, and my flower bunches skid across the pavement. I struggle back to my feet again. 'Thanks all the same. But it's not for me.'

And then I pick up what's left of my bruised zinnias, and hurry off towards the beach.

18

Boathouse Cottage, St Aidan
Crash mats and slim pickings
Monday

My walk back to the cottage is more of a half-run. I should be jubilant for dodging the Net Loft bullet, but there's a tiny voice in my head that's telling me I might be disappointed I walked away.

I give Pumpkin a wave as I slip in through the gate and head for the French window which I usually leave off the latch, but when I get there, it's locked. I jump the style and head to the door that leads through to the kitchen and is always open when there's someone in, but that's locked too. It's only as I dig in the pocket of my shorts for my door key that it hits me: I did a last-minute change before I rushed out to Zofia's this morning, and I've come out without it.

I've gone two entire weeks without getting locked out or losing my key. I'd meant to hide an emergency key in Pumpkin's outhouse, and I'm kicking myself for not. I put down my carriers, pull out my phone, and cringe at the thought of asking Zofia to bring the spare. Then I remember she's gone to Plymouth.

I head through the gate and out on to the lane. Miles's car in the parking area means he's off on foot, but if he knew I'd come out without a key he'd have a field day. I'd rather sit on the grass for a few hours with Pumpkin than have Miles rip into me for my immature behaviour.

I scan the windows along the lane and when I have no luck there, I go back through to the garden and check each opening meticulously. I'm about to give up and sit on the sun lounger, but as I climb the steps to the terrace, the height lets me see a crack at the bottom of a higher window towards the end of the house, which must open into the bedroom.

If I shove the outdoor table along, and put one of the benches on the tabletop, I might just be able to slide in through the window. I take two seconds to consider if it's too great an invasion of Miles's privacy to land in his bedroom, then I go for it anyway.

Scarlett having hewn oak outdoor furniture rather than Argos plastic means the job takes fifteen minutes rather than two. I wrench my stomach lifting the bench up into place but at least when I spring up onto the table my furniture stack is solid. I get onto the bench, reach across to the window ledge, and give a silent hurrah when the frame slips upwards far enough for me to climb through.

I throw my bag in ahead of me. Take a second to think head first or feet first, see a mental picture of myself in a neck brace, and opt for feet.

My thighs are in all the way to my bottom before I realise it's going to be a squeeze. By the time my bum's slipped over the inner sill, I'm committed. Then, thanks mostly to my shiny satin shorts, gravity takes over and I drop downwards. There's a terrible moment when my boobs are so compressed by the frame I hear the fabric of my bra rip. Then something gives, and I'm arching down through the air, and landing in a heap of splayed knees on Scarlett's hand-knotted bedside rug.

I'm checking all my limbs have come in with me, reminding myself this is a legitimate chance to take in the details of Miles's bedroom when I hear a cough. My blood runs cold and when I slowly raise my head the face I'm looking up into is Miles's.

'What the hell happened here, Betty Eliza? I'd have come to the door if you'd knocked.'

It's so like Miles to turn this on to me.

'Since when do we lock the door when we're home?' One of the reasons Scarlett loves it here is because people can go out and leave their doors and windows wide open, and come back to find things exactly as they left them. It's so refreshing to be able to trust people, and have neighbours who look out for you. Not that there's much here to take, due to the empty look. Then my heart misses a beat. Of course Miles would lock the door if he was with someone and didn't want me walking in on them.

I start to back track. 'It's completely understandable to lock the door if you were ... entertaining people.' The immediate stab in my chest is engulfed by a wave of relief for whatever scene I just avoided parachuting into here.

I pull my eyes into focus and see he's naked except for a pair of jeans, which have the fly unbuttoned far enough to see there's nothing underneath.

My throat is dry as I take in the view all the way down to his bare toes and back up again. Then my voice rises to a shriek.

'What if I'd dropped through the window into the middle of a bonk fest? I'd have literally expired with embarrassment.'

There's a twist to Miles's lips. 'It's fine, you were nowhere near, she left ten minutes ago.'

'What the hell?'

He's biting his lip, holding back his grin. 'I'm joking. I went for a shower, and decided if someone came and stole your clothes collection while I had my head under the rainforest spray you'd never forgive me.'

'So there was no visitor?'

His eyes are dancing with amusement. 'Nope. And no sex fest, either.'

I'm still on the rug where I landed, staring straight ahead at the shadow that's pushing against the denim to one side of his fly buttons. Truly, this is not the time to remember how much I like sex or how much I've missed it since I gave up dating. I mean, I've often had that thought whispering at the back of my mind when I've seen him stretched out on the sun lounger, but this is the first time my brain has yelled and ordered me to do something about it. Considering who I'm staring at here, I'm out of order on every level.

When I finally force my gaze upwards to meet his, I find his eyes are locked on my chest. I brush an invisible speck off my dress, and stare down to find an extra-large expanse of cleavage where a button has ripped off my top.

As I clear my throat, Miles leaps forward and holds out his hand. 'Let me help you up.'

I'm about to rearrange my legs so I can get to get to my feet when I hear my ringtone. As 'I'm a believer' echoes around the bedroom, Miles picks up my bag and hands it to me.

'A call for you, Betty.'

I pull out my phone and lean my shoulder on the side of the huge double bed. 'It's Scarlett. I'll take it down here.'

I watch Miles whisk around, and when he turns back around to face me again his jeans are done up and he's pulling on a T-shirt. Then he heads off towards the bathroom and I accept the call.

'Scarlett?'

'Just checking in to see how you and your unexpected housemate are getting along?'

I aim for something that hides that we *aren't* getting along. 'Pumpkin is yet to be convinced, but I'm helping Miles with his latest project – giving him a youth insight.'

'Really?' Scarlett sounds surprised. 'I hope he's paying you well. He can certainly afford to.'

I swallow back my drool, remembering the toffee pastry melting on my tongue. 'We have a mutually beneficial arrangement.' I'm certainly not complaining, but I throw another thought in to move this on. 'Miles is pretty upbeat considering his heart has been shattered.'

Scarlett sounds puzzled. 'Tate never mentioned that.'

I give a shrug. 'It must have been when you were super busy.' Scarlett's the one who usually worries about me, but for once I have to ask. 'You and Tate *are* talking again now?'

Scarlett sighs. 'Not exactly. So much has changed with the move, it's hard to pinpoint what's wrong.'

'Too many hot dogs?' I am not the right person to give relationship counselling, especially when it's transatlantic.

She sounds hesitant. 'It could be stress? He has a lot of responsibility with the expansion.'

There's no point her asking me, but if we're talking about people behaving oddly, this is very unlike Scarlett too. I've never known her stop to question before.

She carries on. 'So long as you're okay. That's what I rang for. Give my love to Pumpkin.'

And then she's gone, and as I scramble to my feet, Miles wanders back in.

He grins from behind the towel he's rubbing his hair with. 'It's great you mentioned our collaboration. What did Scarlett think?'

I laugh. 'She hoped my salary was adequate considering how loaded you are.' I give a cough. 'Feel free to listen in.'

'You were talking so loudly I couldn't help it, even from the bathroom!' Miles frowns. 'And why did you say I'm broken-hearted when I'm not.'

I roll my eyes. 'Whatever. It's typically male to be in emotional denial.'

He frowns. 'As there's no way out of that, how are Scarlett and Tate?'

My loyalty is to Scarlett, but I don't close him down entirely. 'I don't want to talk behind their backs ... but I sense they've been better.'

Miles is close enough to reach out and squeeze my wrist. 'We both want the best for them – and I'd say that's a good summing up.'

Now I've got this far, I may as well go one further. 'Scarlett knows there's a problem, but she hasn't put her finger on it yet.'

With my thoughts out there, I'm aching to see if Miles comes back with an explanation.

Miles raises his eyebrows. 'Nailing things down is one of Scarlett's super-powers. I'm sure she'll sort it.'

'Let's hope you're right, Miles.' That isn't what I was looking for, but I'm thinking back to his promise to bake today. 'Have you been busy in the kitchen?'

He pulls a face, then looks at his watch. 'I'm afraid I got called away. If you're hoping to tap the tourist tasters, we're probably too late for today.'

Damn.

He must have read my mind. 'If you're *that* disappointed, let me bake you a quiche for tonight? Or a homemade pizza? I can do both of those.'

I'm remembering the bag I left outside. 'I've already shopped for dinner.' Green beans and carrots with tops on, and a cheese omelette with freshly laid eggs will be less stressful than anything eaten with Miles.

'Great!' Miles sounds a lot less bouncy than he should, then he brightens. 'I'll bake tomorrow. That's a definite commitment!'

I'm putting my own needs to one side here. 'Or you could do it closer to the weekend when the beach will be busier?'

'Good thinking, Eliza Bets. I'll confirm later.' He tilts his head to one side and stares up above my head. 'How about the window? Can I close that now? But if ever you're planning a midnight entrance, let me know, and I'll open it again.'

As I march off to drag Scarlett's outdoor furniture back into place, I wave a finger at Miles to tell him where to stick his last comment. It's only as I get back to the kitchen I suddenly realise:

I was so caught up staring at the guy himself, I didn't scrutinise his room at all.

19

Boathouse Cottage, St Aidan
Starfish and Caribbean cruises
Thursday

The best lessons in life are learned the hard way. Let's face it, if anything can teach me to take better care of my key, Monday afternoon is already up there with the stuff of nightmares, even without the view of Miles halfway into his jeans, that pops into my head approximately sixty times a minute.

In the end it's Thursday before I hear from Miles about the baking, which is fine by me, because in the meantime I send off my piece about Zofia's garden to Fenna, who likes it so much that she's up for more.

This morning I've been up to see Edie at the barnyard first thing, to take some 'before' photos of some bits of furniture that she's about to paint, which will make ideal pieces for DIY furniture transformation projects, then I come straight back and do a beach walk with Pumpkin. We've got as far as the harbourside when I get a text from Miles.

> First batch of baking red when you are

I've noticed Miles talks into his phone a lot – annoying habit number five hundred and forty-three – and I assume his voice app wrote this and that he actually means baking is ready, not red.

We'd actually done a bit of a detour to walk past the Net Loft. My brutally honest inner self must have decided that me mentally undressing my housemate three thousand times an hour is not a healthy way to coexist. At least Miles's text means I'm saved the embarrassment of standing outside the empty studio with my nose pressed against the glass.

I give Pumpkin a firm nudge away from the harbourside window boxes and lead him back towards the sand. 'Sorry to cut your walk short today, but this is our cue to hurry home, okay?'

It obviously isn't. The sun has come out, and there are groups of people settling in for a day along the beach, and I have to coax Pumpkin into a trot to get him past them. By the time I put him into his field, I'm swiping the sweat off my forehead, and flapping the open front of my button-through dress to fan my midriff.

Since Monday I've made a point of leaving the French windows by the sofa unlocked as a precaution, and when I slip into the living room a wall of hot pastry scent hits my nose.

I blink away the image of Miles's naked six-pack and focus on him pushing his dark brown curls off his forehead behind the island unit.

'Betty Bradwell, ravenous and reporting for duty, what have you got for me, Miles?'

He laughs. 'I came across a Cornish palm tree yesterday along by the beach huts, so I thought we'd go tropical. Hot banana, hot banana with chocolate, and banoffee.'

'You know banoffee pie was invented in Essex not the Caribbean?' I am terrible at pub quizzes, but this is my star useless-knowledge fact, and I'm not going to waste it.

Miles raises an eyebrow. 'I'm all about the taste, not the geography, Betsy Bets.'

I take the plates and knives that are waiting and spread them out. 'I haven't had any breakfast, so let's try first, and argue the details later.' As he turns to load up his platter I can't help adding, 'Squirty cream might work with this.'

I can't believe I've been here almost three weeks without buying any, but now I mention it, it's not the kind of thing Scarlett would have in her cupboards. It's more the kind of item she'd ban from the house.

Miles laughs. 'Great minds! I've made my own.' He opens the fridge and pulls out a bulging piping bag and puts it in front of me on the island next to his baking. 'Go ahead, dive in!'

I push up my sleeves. 'Right, I'll start with the plain banana and work my way up. And stuff messing about, I'm going for the full buns.'

As I close my teeth on the crust it snaps and crumbles, then gives way to the soft chewy dough in the centre, all still warm with strips of hot banana.

I wave the bun in the air. 'I have to give it to you, Milo-pie, this pastry couldn't be better.' I sink my teeth in for the second bite and sigh. 'Cooked banana is an inspired idea.'

Miles looks like he's holding his breath when I go in for the next. 'This one has a swirl of chocolate spread in the dough spiral and chocolate chips in with the banana.'

I take my time to chew. 'If this were the only one you'd given me, I'd be deliriously happy.'

'And now for your favourite.' He takes a breath. 'This is a croissant swirl, with cooked banana strips and caramel in a hollowed-out centre, topped with grated chocolate spirals. In the real world, it would be sold with a swirl of cream on top, but for now, I'll let you help yourself.'

I pick up a banoffee bun, squeeze on a dollop of cream, take a taste and let out a groan. 'That is orgasmic!' I choke as it hits me what I've said. 'It's delectable. Luscious. Heavenly even. And very moreish.' I squirt on more cream and demolish the rest.

His smile widens. 'No one's ever compared my baking to sex before, but that ultimate pleasure explosion is what I was aiming for. So thanks for that.'

I'm kicking myself for being so careless with my compliments. 'I'll finish these, and we'll see if St Aidan agrees with me.'

Miles has his finger in the air. 'For the record...'

'Yes?'

He gives a cough. 'The kitchen and I already have a five-star local authority hygiene rating.'

'When did you get that?'

He shrugs. 'As soon as I got here. A few weeks before you arrived.'

His timeline at Boathouse Cottage is getting longer and longer.

He carries on. 'And I've sorted out a street trading permit, too, with permissions to make sales on all the nearby beaches.' He nods. 'If you were worried about everything being legal and above board – now it is.'

'Well, thanks for looking out for me. I'd probably have winged it for a bit longer myself, but that's just me.' This is so typically Miles. If selling buns is *this* official, all the joy goes out of it.

He rubs his hands together. 'The rest of the buns are in bags, whenever you're ready.'

I'm thinking how I can make this fun again. 'I might bring Pumpkin. If we're short of custom, he'll pull in a crowd.'

'Oka-a-a-y.'

I can tell by Miles's tone that it isn't. 'If you're worried about his dirty look, I'm sure he's moved on.'

'It's not that.'

While I'm waiting for Miles to come out with objection number six hundred and forty-eight, I'm testing myself. I want to see if the mesmerising attraction I feel towards him reduces when he's being a complete tool. Are his super-charged testosterone levels easier to block out when he's boring the pants off me with his obsession with rules and red tape? Nope, there's no change at all. I could still happily rip the T-shirt off his disgustingly honed pecs, morning, noon and all bloody night.

Miles gives a cough. 'Now we're operating within the law, it would be a shame to wreck that with an animal running amok on the beach.'

I can't believe what I'm hearing. '*Pumpkin doesn't run wild!*' Miles is rolling his eyes harder than me. 'It's entirely possible he could stamp on peoples' sandcastles. Or their children. *Or even them.* I'd rather not pick up the tab for that.'

What the actual eff? 'Pumpkin has his own insurance. It covers vet's bills, and public liability. Scarlett looks after the direct debit, but I've got the paperwork.'

Miles's eyebrows go up. 'If he's insured, that's different.'

I'm shaking my head in despair. 'He needs to be well covered the way he looks at those quayside window boxes. The plants in there could run to thousands.'

I look at Miles again, to see how I feel when he's being mean about Pumpkin, and – no surprise – when he turns, his bum is still as delectable as his pecan toffee croissants.

I've never experienced feelings like this around a man before. With the guys before Mason the catastrophes were each very different, but they all followed a reassuringly similar pattern. We'd start with friendly banter. If we made it as far as bed and the sex was okay, it was game on. And then sometime later it would all unravel – usually spectacularly.

There was the guy who hit on me when he really wanted my flatmate instead, and the one who was still so hung up on his ex he rang her every evening, and the gay vet who wanted to parade me for his mum.

But my skin feeling like it's scorching when someone's in the room, or my stomach doing cartwheels when someone appears is a whole new ball game. And however much I'm zoning out what happened with Mason, the vestiges of that should be enough to block my nerve pathways forever. I shouldn't be feeling like this – end of story.

I turn to Miles. 'So Pumpkin's allowed to come?' I take his eye roll as a 'yes'.

Even though I look up at the living room ceiling all the way to the top of the roof, my own eye roll still isn't enough to express my despair.

20

The beach by Boathouse Cottage, St Aidan
Every day is a Saturday
Thursday

By the time we reach the beach, Pumpkin's speed picks up to a fast walk and he races over to the first couple we come to sitting in their matching folding canvas seats.

I take a breath and begin the pony part of my speech. 'This is Pumpkin...'

The woman puts her hand out and tickles Pumpkin's nose. 'There's no need for introductions, we've done this before. This is your favourite place for a rub, isn't it, laddie?'

I'm kicking myself for not taking more notice. 'Of course, didn't we see you by the harbour a couple of weeks ago?'

The woman smiles at me. 'We're Carol and Martin, from The Crow's Nest, next door but two to Plum's gallery. We've often seen you since from a distance.' She looks back at Pumpkin. 'You've got pompoms on your head collar today! How smart is that?'

They're the ones I bought last Friday, which I'd hung to brighten up Scarlett's minimalist living room shelf, and grabbed today hoping they'd add some pizazz for the beach.

The woman leans towards me. 'We heard you were out selling cakes on the beach last weekend. Is that right?'

Her husband joins in. 'We were over in Truro. The Yellow Canary was buzzing with it when we got back.'

I'm taken aback. 'I didn't think people would recognise me when I wasn't with Pumpkin.'

Carol smiles. 'Everybody knows! You're the one with the pink and orange skirts who twirls along the shoreline and writes notices in the sand.' She smiles. 'Our cottage looks straight out down the beach. We often watch you, as we have breakfast.'

Their cottage must be one of hundreds that look down on the bay. As I remember how many windows there are with a direct view of the sand, I feel queasy. All this time I've considered the beach as my own private space where I was entirely alone with my thoughts, and now it turns out a lot of the village has been there with me. It just shows how wrong you can be.

Her husband nods. 'It's been the highlight of our morning walks the last few weeks, looking out for the messages you've left.'

My tummy had tensed, but when the full realisation of what they're saying hits me, it goes in full spasm.

Miles gives me a nudge. 'Nice to know that Pumpkin isn't the only local celebrity.'

The woman's looking up at me. 'I hope you don't mind me asking, but why are you writing them and who are they for?'

I'm opening my mouth to reply, but Miles gets in first.

'Some of those thoughts in the sand have been very profound, so if you're not comfortable answering that, Betsy, we'll all understand.'

I turn to Miles. 'You, too?'

If the thought of two random strangers seeing into my head was unnerving, this is ten thousand times worse. I didn't even know he walked on the beach.

He shrugs. 'Like they said, once I noticed, it became compulsive. I didn't want to miss any.'

What can I say? It's not as if we're on a desert island. In fact, these beaches are often rammed, but the thought was they were rammed with strangers who I'd never coincide with again, not locals who would start quizzing me about every nuance. They weren't ever private, so I might as well explain. 'They were me writing whatever came into my head in the moment, first for myself, and then as an open message to the world.' I'm pondering. 'They were always going to be temporary, but I had a feeling that once they'd been washed away by the sea, that would somehow make them last forever.'

Carol nods. 'That's a lovely way of putting it. What was it you wrote yesterday – "Make spray while the sun shines!"'

I'm relieved that she hasn't picked anything more personal. 'It was my beach-y take on the old "make hay while the sun shines" saying. However sweaty, exhausting and prickly it used to be throwing bales about, I had a sudden pang for the haymaking I'll be missing this summer.'

Miles chips in. 'Betsy Bets comes from Somerset, that's why she's all about the maypoles and the fairy rings.'

I roll my eyes. 'I also cover cow pats and pig driving.'

Carol laughs. 'That quirky humour of yours might be why we enjoy them so much. They're all refreshingly different, but they're very uplifting too. Like the place where they're written.'

Martin nods too. 'It's not only us! All our friends look out for them. They're a favourite discussion point for everyone in the Yellow Canary. And the Hungry Shark.'

I consider shrivelling up on the spot, but if it's gone this far, I might as well roll with it. 'I suppose they're my way of telling my story for the summer. I have photos of them all, they're my project while I'm in St Aidan.'

Carol pats my hand. 'Thanks for sharing that, Betsy.' Then her smile fades. 'You won't stop because we've mentioned it? You are going to carry on?'

'Of course.' A tiny idea is growing in my head. 'The cakes you mentioned just before are a new range of bakes which Miles is working on. Tell all your friends, we'll be leaving messages on the beach about any new flavours that are coming out.'

Miles grins beside me. 'Totally flawless. As a marketing strategy, that's next level.'

However uncomfortable I was earlier, I'm happy at how this is turning itself around. 'As for the boathouse buns, if you'd like to try them, Miles is carrying lots of free samples in his bag.'

Martin is on this. 'I was told we could buy them?'

I beam at them as Miles dips into his carrier. 'You probably heard already, the bakes are what croissants would be like if they were made in heaven. Today we have three banana-based variations.' I pause to let them help themselves to the slices Miles is holding out on his platter. 'If you like what you taste, we do have some for sale.'

Martin's pushing flakes into his mouth. 'We'll take six.'

I laugh. 'Finish tasting first, then you can decide which you'd like.'

Martin holds up his hand. 'Six of each! If this is another limited edition, our friends at the Yellow Canary wouldn't forgive us if we didn't take some for them too.' Martin is licking his flingers. 'Once we get to the pub, they'll disappear in seconds.'

I'm pushing the result here. 'I take it you like them?'

Martin considers. 'On a scale of one to ten...' Then he slaps his knee with his hand. 'No! These actually blow scales into oblivion. They're extraordinary.'

'He's right.' Carol's sucking her finger. 'Except I'd call them sensational. I'm just thinking – we'd hate to miss out on these a second time. Could you take our details, and let us know when you're next coming out?'

Miles passes her a small brown paper bag and a pen. 'Write your name and number on there, then Betsy can text you. If you'd like to be on our mailing list, add your email too.' He beams. 'You can unsubscribe at any time.'

I look at Miles again. 'You bought bags?'

He gives a shrug. 'I also have tissue paper squares for eat as you go, and boxes for the larger orders. Talking of which...' He pulls out three rectangular cartons, and hands them to Carol. 'Betsy Bets tells me fifteen pounds for six is our introductory deal, how about we call that forty for eighteen?'

Martin pulls some notes out of his pocket, and that's a third of our stock gone already. Easy as that.

'Thank you, enjoy, we'll be in touch.' I give a small pull on Pumpkin's lead rein. 'Come on, mister, time to meet some more customers.' I grin over my shoulder. 'They might not tickle you as well as Carol, but we'll see her again soon.'

As we walk off, I'm tempted to do wide-armed spins of joy along the high tide mark, but one look at Miles's office-on-a-Thursday-afternoon expression and I rein myself in.

Instead I look at the people scattered across the beach, with gaps of sand between them and think aloud to Miles. 'You might want to make the most of the crowds over the weekend. If the sun shines, every inch of the beach will be covered, but it'll thin out again on Monday.'

Miles nods at me. 'Good thinking. We'll look at flavour lists when we get back.' He's talking softly behind me as we walk. 'If we carry on at this rate, we'll be done before lunch.'

There's no time to say more because Pumpkin has been met by the advance guard from the next family and his neck is already covered in small sticky hands.

And that is pretty much the pattern along the beach. Thanks to Pumpkin's triple stack of cuteness, charm and love of attention, there's more focus on ponies than baking. But the second we move on to the bun samples they're snapped up faster than you can say chocolate croissant, and along the way they're compared to everything from cannonballs to angel wings.

This is the wonderful thing about real, live people: give them the freedom to express themselves and the chances are they'll be a hundred times more creative than any marketing team Miles has squirrelled away in some pretentious office, pouring over their laptops.

And in line with his very annoying tendency, Miles is right about the timing. The sun is still high in the sky when we sell the last of the buns and come back along the beach.

By the time I've turned Pumpkin out in the field, Miles is folding up his carrier bags and putting the left-over boxes and bags into the mud room cupboard.

He joins me in the kitchen and grins. 'You were certainly on fire today. Limited editions, croissants made in heaven, and a mailing list!'

I shake my head and remember what he said. '"You can unsubscribe at any time!" How hilarious was that?'

His expression goes all serious again. 'It wasn't a joke. It's an essential requirement that mailing list databases comply with all current regulations – one of which is offering the on-going opportunity to opt out.'

I need to get this straight. 'So can I create a WhatsApp group of Pumpkin's mates who get advance warning of pastry sales? Or do you have a data protection policy that forbids that?'

His frown lines deepen. 'In the longer term I'll need to run it past my legal team.' He must sense I'm about to shriek, because he hurries on. 'If you keep it to a small circle of close, personal friends, I'm sure that will be fine for now.'

It's easy to tell he's been blinding me with jargon, because I've completely missed that he's heading towards the door.

He stops for a second and rests his shoulder on the frame. 'Great work there, Betty Eliza, thanks for your help. The cash by the fruit bowl is yours.'

When I blink again, he's gone, and a few moments later I hear the scrunch of his car tyres on the lane.

Why the hell would I be disappointed to have the rest of the day to myself? Me and Miles pouring over future plans for the bakes was literally said in the moment and meant slightly less than zero – which is exactly how I understood it at the time. My afternoon is going to be so rammed with work, I wouldn't have fitted that in anyway.

21

The Barnyard, Saltings Lane, St Aidan
Double espresso and interruptions
Friday

The next day is Friday, and my first job for this blue-skied, blustery morning is to take pictures of all the furniture pieces that Edie painted yesterday at the barnyard. Even in their new muted undercoat shades, the shelves, bedside cabinets, chests of drawers and little dressers are already looking like newly invented versions of their former selves.

While I'm there I drop into the maker's market. I nip into the felters' and invest in enough felted pompom garlands to make Pumpkin stand out from the crowds on what promises to be a busy weekend on the beach. Then I load up with garden posies from the outdoor stalls to pretty up the cottage, and spend a long time taking photos because there are so many gorgeous displays. Honestly, I wasn't hanging around just so I'd bump into Scarlett's friends from last week, but when Clemmie bobs out of the doorway and waves me over, my heart skips a beat.

As I step into the stable she beams at me from behind her tray bake piles, pushes a chocolate flapjack into my hand and whispers in my ear, 'the Net Loft is still there. If living with Miles and his film-star good looks gets too arduous, you know where we are.'

I take it she hasn't heard about my very embarrassing anti-materialism freak-out the day I had my impromptu tour. 'You obviously haven't spoken to Beth's dad, Malcolm?'

Clemmie's face twists into a grin. 'Actually I did. He said how much you loved it.' She laughs. 'You aren't the first person in St Aidan to be bricking it at the thought of responsibility. We've all been there.'

'*You have?*'

She nods. 'It's scary the first time, worse if you're doing it by yourself, but it gets easier. That's why everyone in St Aidan tries to help each other. I've only got my stall up here because I'm covering for Loella who does the patchwork, while she's away.'

It's a relief to know that I'm not completely on my own. 'The studio is different because it has the living space too.'

Clemmie nods. 'Maybe you need a partner to share the downstairs. Did I hear you and Miles had been out selling pastries?'

I'm looking at Clemmie's stacks of tray bakes and my stomach clenches. 'I hope we weren't treading on your toes – or anyone else's?'

Clemmie shakes her head. 'There's always room for pastries in St Aidan, especially something a little bit different like yours.'

There's a deep throaty laugh, and Nell appears from behind

a shelf unit filled with scarves clutching a baby and a nappy bag. 'Us mermaids are fully tied up with babies and toddlers. Even our friend Sophie is having one.'

Clemmie nods. 'They're babies for such a short time, we'd hate to miss a moment, so we've scaled the Little Cornish Kitchen back for this year.' Her smile widens. 'It's great there's something delicious to fill that gap.'

As for Miles, he's the one I'm trying to get away from. He's the last person I'd team up with, so I'll be honest about that too. 'The buns are Miles's project, and if he ever does get as far as a start-up, they'll be in the buzziest, on-trend urban locations. Didsbury. Clifton. Notting Hill. Hampstead. Between us, he's got his sights set on high-flying hedge fund managers, not Cornish day trippers.'

Clemmie watches me step back outside. 'People have a habit of surprising themselves, especially in St Aidan. I haven't given up on either of you yet.'

I arrive back from the barnyard fifteen minutes later to find the cottage kitchen smelling deliciously of baking, stacks of pastries on their cooling trays, but no sign of Miles.

I'm leaning in to examine them, talking quietly to myself. 'Vanilla custard swirls – apple and sultanas crisscrossed with zigzags of white glacé icing – and cinnamon – which I will happily leave for everyone else.'

There's an orange Post-it note under the foot of the end tray, next to a pile of the new boxes.

Betsee B, buns 4 U 2 sell, TY, Miles.

Okay, it's a bit cryptic, but as it's giving me the green light to get out there on the beach with the latest set of goods, I'm on my way.

I look through my messages, find the people from yesterday who would like a text alert, and send them off. Carol messages straight back, and I agree to meet her and a lot of her friends in half an hour on the sands just down from the harbour. Since Pumpkin hasn't been out yet he'll be up for an outing too, so we'll walk straight to the harbour then hopefully sell what's left on our way back.

I take a couple of minutes to eat one, a moment to be amazed at how wonderfully the silky sweet vanilla of the custard goes with the crisp of the flakes, then I get straight to work making up the boxes.

It's a little bit like what Clemmie was saying earlier. Going out with the pastries last weekend for the first time was a huge adventure, but almost a week later the fear is less.

Today it's the same as both the previous times; we run out of buns a long time before we run out of customers. But at least that gives me time to write a few messages in the sand. This afternoon I take my inspiration from Clemmie, and write *Surprise yourself!* Then I do a *Didsbury, Clifton, Notting Hill, Hampstead, St Aidan.* Just to keep them guessing. Then I write, *I'm done adulting, let's be mermaids, Girls just want to have sun,* and *Blustery and blue* to describe today.

And after that, I head back, pull the sun lounger out of the wind, and get to work sorting out my photos and writing some words.

It's one of those days without any interruptions when I lose myself in the job. No one comes home to turf me off the lounger, and no one turns on the inspirational classical tunes so they boom out from the kitchen. For one glorious late afternoon and early evening, I have the place to myself, and it's heaven. Sure, from time to time I stop and strain my ears to see if I can pick up the bump of tyres on the stones down the lane. The sound of the handbrake as a car pulls to a stop in the parking area. But however many times I listen, it's never there.

The first sound to slice through my concentration is my ringtone, and as the twangy notes of 'I'm a believer' bounce around the terrace, I'm surprised to see the sun is already slipping towards the horizon. The second surprise is that it's Scarlett. By rights she should be gearing up for a Friday night on the town in New York.

'Hey, Scarlie, do you want me to test the outside shower again before it goes out of warranty?'

There's a moment of hesitation. 'It's a lot more serious than plumbing today, Bets.'

'Keep going...'

'I chose you because you're the one person I know who won't judge.' She sighs. 'Tate was supposed to be meeting me for cocktails an hour ago, and he hasn't come.'

I'm trying to get a handle on how serious this is. 'Is he running late? Can't find a yellow cab? Caught at the office?'

She lets out a hollow laugh. 'Now there's a thing. We come halfway round the world, and last night I go to drinks at Tate's work, and finally come face to face with the reason we're here.'

There's something chilling in her tone. 'What's the matter? Who did you meet?'

'Virginia Kemp. Five foot ten, slender, greener than Greta, with a PhD to match. So much for the office expansion – she pulled Tate out here to land him and he's eighty per cent reeled in. One more sharp tug on the line, he'll be hers.'

'Shit.'

Scarlie blows down the phone. 'We can't talk about this without alcohol. I'm downing Manhattans. You need to match me drink for drink or I won't make any sense.'

'The strongest I've got here is lemongrass and elderflower.'

Scarlett's straight back at me. 'In that case, you're going to have to run along to Jaggers Bar. I'll FaceTime you once you're there, and we'll talk this through one cocktail at a time.'

Only Scarlett would be this prescriptive. 'Remind me which it is?'

Scarlett's sigh is impatient. 'The place I've got a tab, past the harbour, down by the beach, with purple plastic chairs and the twenty-four-seven happy hour. If you run, you'll be there in ten. Go to the bar, ask for Paul, and he'll charge it all to me.' Scarlett sniffs. 'Quick as you can, please. My life is teetering on the edge.'

My chest contracts. 'I'm on it, Scarlie. I'll call you when I'm there.'

She's still organised enough to snap back. 'I'll ring ahead and get your drinks in. Just go as fast as you can.'

22

Jaggers Bar, St Aidan
Sunsets, big calls and high perches
Friday

Even though it's not especially warm, when I sprint up from the beach, the harbourside is as busy as you'd expect for a Friday evening in late May, with weekend visitors thronging the streets. As I reach the part of the beach where Jaggers Bar runs out onto the sands, the groups milling on the terrace outside look a lot like I did when I was eighteen and hell-bent on a party. I slide between them, ask myself where the heck the last ten years have gone, then ease my way into the large open building and pick my way past the crowds. When I finally make it to the bar, a barman catches my eye.

'Hi, I'm Paul. You must be Betty?' He holds out his hand and grasps mine for a second. 'When Scarlett said look out for net skirts and hot pants, she was bang on.'

I wipe the sweat off my forehead and gasp to get my breath back. 'I came straight off the sofa, Scarlett said it was urgent.'

Paul smiles. 'She wanted you to have Manhattans, but they're a bit grown up for us, so we settled on tequila sunrises.'

'Good choice. Retro but cool.' It was Mum's favourite drink from the seventies. Better still, they're easy to drink.

Paul is busy with ice and mixers. 'We usually serve in jugs, but Scarlett asked for glasses. She's insisting I line you up four to begin with?'

As I scramble onto a red velvet stool he's obviously waiting for my input. 'Two tequilas and two mojitos might work better – just to ring the changes.' The buns were the last thing I had to eat, but that was so long ago my stomach is growling with hunger. 'Do you have a food menu?'

Paul shrugs. 'We're liquid only, I'm afraid.'

I watch Paul put down a highball tumbler full of rosy, orange liquid and ice, and balance an umbrella on top, then explain. 'I've done enough drinking to know – I'm a lightweight if I'm hungry.'

He's trying to be helpful. 'We can Deliveroo you some chips?'

'Great idea.' My mouth is already watering then my phone begins to ring. 'It's Scarlett. I'll leave the food for now.'

A second later she's staring out at me from my phone screen.

'Bets! Where are your cocktails?'

I panne around with my phone to show her the full glasses arriving on the stainless-steel bar top, then pick up the first and take a long drink.

On the lopsided view her own row is mostly finished. '*We are going to get off our faces...*'

I cut in. 'Before we do, tell me about Tate.'

From the way she pushes her hair back and blows up her fringe I know she's already tipsy. 'He kept me away from the office until the party yesterday. You know when something slams you right in the face?' Her hand flies down in front of the screen. '*Splat!* It was a complete "eyes wide open" moment.'

I'm thinking aloud. 'Wasn't the movie *Eyes Wide Shut*?'

Scarlett blinks. 'What movie?'

I'm frowning, trying to remember. 'The one with Tom Cruise and Nicole Kidman.'

'What the hell have Nicole and Tom got to do with Tate hooking up with a woman who has tennis balls for butt cheeks?' Scarlett's voice rings out again. 'Drink your next drink, you're falling behind.'

I'm aware that the person I'm obeying is five thousand miles away, but I pick up my mojito and slug it back. Its minty fizz is so refreshing that I empty the glass. Then I think, *what the hell, I need calories from somewhere*, and finish the next one, too.

'If Tate's crossed the Atlantic for this tennis player, it must be serious.'

Scarlett nods as she swigs. 'Thank you for acknowledging that, Bets!'

I'm swirling the ice round in my next to last glass with my straw, watching the grenadine rise through the orange juice. 'There's one flaw in this. If Tate was seriously pursuing a transatlantic office crush, why did he take you?'

Scarlett lets out a groan. 'Me adding myself in was a last-minute impulse. By the time I decided to leap on the love train, there wasn't time for him to stop me.'

Paul wanders over and picks up my empty glasses. 'Same again? Maybe a jug this time?'

With what Scarlett has thrown at me a bucket might be better than a jug, but I know drinking's not an answer, so I offer a token protest. 'I've already had four.'

Paul laughs. 'The trick is to stop counting after one.'

Scarlett fills my screen again. 'Tell Paul jugs are good.'

At one time bottomless cocktails were my idea of the best night ever. I'm guessing they went with the heady days of student finance when I'd survive on a pack of crisps a day all week and save the cash for a blow-out of weekend clubbing instead. Good nights out were harder to find back in Somerset, but there were still some blinders at local fetes and county shows. Then, when I hurt my arm I swapped late nights for early mornings and Saturdays on the market stall, which neatly fitted with me never wanting to go out anyway, and that was the final part of my transformation to the country mouse who sat on my bed watching *Bridgerton* and *The Crown*.

As Paul fills up my glass, I haven't completely let go of my hope for a decent ending for Tate and Scarlett.

I'm sucking a cherry off its stick. 'Aren't workplace attachments frowned upon now?'

Scarlett blows up her fringe again. 'They still happen. Proximity and power are a heady mix.'

I pull a face. 'It could be Tate's mid-life crisis kicking in?'

Scarlett sighs. 'If only. The truth is, Virginia is warm and smart, and her Long Island accent is gorgeous. I feel like a very small nothing beside her.'

She's being so unfair on herself, I have to shout. 'Don't ever say that! You're the most determined, together, clever, attractive, captivating, high-achieving person I know, Scarlie.'

She gives a rueful grimace. 'And I'm also wise enough to know when I'm beaten.' The breath she blows out makes her look even smaller. 'We had our worst fight ever last night after the reception. When Tate suggested we meet up this afternoon I hoped it was to clear the air. But as he's not here, I read that wrong too.'

Giving up is so unlike her. If she's about to toss away everything she's worked for since she was seven, it's up to me to fire her up. 'Promise me you won't go down without a fight.'

She rubs her nose. 'I do have *some* pride left. I refuse to go through his messages.'

As the gravity of the situation hits me, filling my glass to overflowing feels like the best support I can offer. I abandon the straw, tip back my head, let the sweet liquid flow down my throat, and only put my glass down again when it's drained. But instead of the sensation of the proverbial sun climbing the sky inside my chest and raising my spirits, all I feel is blurry.

As Scarlett shouts at me from my screen she's sliding out of the frame. 'Bottoms up, Bets. I refuse to allow a guy to define who I am or wreck my happiness.'

It's like she's reading me my own private mantra.

I'm not sure, but it always felt like Scarlett and Tate totally defined each other, so I add another thought. 'I refuse to let a guy take you down, Scarlie.'

There's a momentary blanking of the screen, a view of what looks like the ceiling, then I hear a guy.

'Scarlett, what are you doing? How many cocktails have you had?'

I recognise Tate's voice, wave at the screen, and leap in to explain why Scarlett is sitting on a bar stool in Manhattan completely rat-arsed.

'Scarlett and I are going drink for drink while we discuss you.' There's no point in sugar-coating this. 'Shagging your counterpart in New York? What were you thinking, Tate?'

Tate gives a cough, which is worrying, because I'd rather have had a hard denial.

'It's not how it looks, Betsy. I'll make it right. I mean, I'm here now, aren't I?'

He's talking to Scarlett. 'Now might be a good time to make a run for home. What do you think, Scarl?'

Scarlett's face is diagonally across the screen. 'We can't leave Bets in Jaggers on her own with six cocktails to finish.'

My tummy clenches as I hear that.

Tate's voice comes in. 'Sit tight, Bets. We're right here with you.'

I refill my glass, and putting the jug down I send a splash across the bar. I'm mopping it up with my sleeve, thinking of the walk back along the beach. How far it will stretch in the dark with the alcohol expanding my perceptions. The way the room is going in and out of focus, even a visit to the Ladies could be out of my reach if I don't go soon.

I prop my phone up against the cocktail jug. 'Talk to Paul while I go to the bathroom. I won't be long.' I slither down from my stool and try not to leave any skirts behind as I land.

Paul's calling directions after me. 'Straight across, Betty, then left at the end.'

It feels like I'm walking on a cross-channel ferry in a

Force 10 gale using someone else's legs, but once I grab hold of the chair backs it gets easier.

It's so long since I've been out that I've forgotten how loudly the toilet doors bang when you forget to close them quietly. Then there's that moment of calm while I pee and hold my head in my hands. Then the door slams again as I open it, and when I wash my hands, the person I'm staring at in the mirror looks like a different version of me. Then the lobby door is closing behind me, and I'm back to steadying myself on the chairs.

It hits me that I used to do this in five-inch heels rather than Converse high tops, and I'm impressed by my past self. In fact, the lack of height might explain why I'm finding it such hard work here. When I get back to the bar, push off on the polished foot rail and try to scramble back onto my stool, it feels less achievable than climbing the north face of the Eiger. I'm halfway up, when a low, resonating male voice cuts through my head and ruins my concentration.

'Betsy, are you okay?'

There's a thud as I land back where I started. Then I look up and there's a moment of recognition and I let out a shout.

'Miles, what the hell? You didn't tell me you drank in Jaggers!'

He pulls a face. 'This is my first time.'

Paul laughs from behind the bar. 'You might like to try our sex-on-the-beach summer offer, three for the price of one, every night in June.'

I reach for my phone, miss, watch it slide along the bar, then shout for the benefit of those in New York. 'Scarlett and Tate, guess what? Miles is here!'

Miles stares down at my screen as it slides to a halt in front of him. 'Okay, guys, I've got the St Aidan end of the party. You two go and enjoy the rest of your evening.' He looks at me. 'Would you like more cocktails, Betsy Bets, or are you ready to head home?'

'Home how?'

There's that twitch to his lips. 'My car is on the harbourside, if you'd like a lift.'

There's a sudden pang in my chest. 'Have you come specially...? In which case what about your real date?'

'Tate rang to say you needed a lift, I'm sure she understood.'

I'm not sure I would have. I feel suddenly defiant. 'I don't need rescuing!'

'No one is saying you do.' He eyes me levelly. 'If we're heading in the same direction, it makes sense to go together, that's all.'

With that query covered, I move on to the next.

'Could we have chips?'

'To eat on the harbourside or to take away?' His arm slides around me, and I lean in as we weave our way towards the door. Then we move outside and the wind from the sea hits me in the face and blows my hair off my head. By the time I get to think, *what the actual eff?* we're already halfway across quayside.

23

Boathouse Cottage, St Aidan
Wet wet wet
Friday

The whole evening seems to have passed like a time slip. All I know is that it's a whole lot later when I make it across the kitchen at Boathouse Cottage, crash down onto the sofa still in most of my clothes and tap out my message to Scarlett.

> Home safe, thanks for sending Miles

As the keys blur, I press send and murmur the rest of what I wanted to say to myself. *Good luck with Tate, let me know how you go,* and blow it into the ether with a kiss from my finger ends.

As my head eases onto the pillow and the room starts to spin like a fairground waltzer it hits me how drunk I am. My last thought before I black out is how lucky I am to have made it back.

When I wake again the sky is lightening with the first pale streaks of dawn, and I'm jolted out of a dream where Miles is snogging my face off. As if that wasn't bad enough, I have the classic combo of a mouth like a desert and an axe embedded in my skull, and despite the dehydration, I'm bursting to pee. Then I remember that Scarlett and Tate might actually be breaking up as I wake, and the world seems to tilt again.

Those two have been such a constant when other things in my life have crumbled. If it's hard for me to think of them not being together, I can't imagine how it must be for them.

I roll off the sofa, untangle the tulle from around my legs, then make a dash through the half-light to the bathroom. Living with Miles, I'm grateful every day that Tate designed a bathroom with an ultra-quiet toilet flush, but at four in the morning my silent thank yous are coming out ten times faster than usual, and there's a second wave of gratitude when I turn on the sink tap and manage to drench my whole head with cold water too. I towel my hair dry in more grateful silence, then ease the door open, step softly out and hurry back to the living room.

I'm two steps along the corridor when I crash into something that feels immovable and approximately the size of a dinosaur. Except when I put the palm of my hand on the object, there are no scales. There's just an expanse of warm skin with supertoned muscle beneath it. Trying to disentangle my arms and legs and still keep my balance and stand up in the darkness is slightly harder than the time I fell backwards into a hawthorn hedge as a kid.

'Betsy? Are you okay?'

Miles's low voice resonates through his chest and against my cheek, and as his arms encircle my body, I stop flapping mine. It takes me a full minute to realise I'm holding on to him too. We stand there, motionless in the dark, and rather than stepping gracefully back and going on my way, I stay. I have no excuse or explanation for what I'm doing other than that I must still be trolleyed – fully intoxicated to the point that I've lost control of my normal physical and emotional functions. Because instead of pulling away, there's a hot rush of desire surging up in the pit of my stomach, and I crush my body against his. The instant thrum of electricity that crackles between us tells me he's as up for this as I am. And now I've got my hands on him I am literally gasping for all the sex I haven't had for as long as I can remember.

I'm grinding my hips against his, stretching my hands up to run my fingers through his hair. Pulling his head down towards me. I'm parting my lips, breathing in the scent of his skin, anticipating how sweet he's going to taste when our mouths fuse. Then, from some very distant universe my override button kicks in to save me, and instead of brushing my tongue against his, I'm slamming my hand over my face, and jumping backwards so fast that when I land no part of my body is touching his.

I bite my lip, gather my skirts around me and try to stop myself shaking. Order myself *not* to go back in again for more.

I flatten myself against the side wall so he can come past me without touching, and clear my throat. 'All good, thanks, Miles. Just nipped to the bathroom for a drink.'

'Is your hair wet?'

Even in the dark I can hear he's doing that puzzled frown of his.

I smile and think of a better reason for drenching my head than having a blinder of a hangover. 'Just rinsing out the smell of the chippy. I'll shower properly in the morning.'

'The citrus and verbena shampoo in there might work for that. Or the almond. Help yourself to whatever you like.'

'Thanks, I will.'

An open invitation to use his shower products, I should be whooping. But all I'm seeing on repeat in my head is me grinding my pelvis against his. As for how incredible it felt, that's a whole other story, which is totally eclipsed by the shame that any of it happened at all. There are other questions too. How am I ever going to live this down? How will I ever face Miles in the daylight? Like, truly, I will never be able to look at him across the kitchen island, knowing that he knows I wasn't just trying to steal a quick kiss. I was a hundred per cent desperate to jump the man's bones.

Pecan and toffee boathouse buns won't ever taste the same after this. Just saying. For the record. I thought I was in a mess when I arrived in St Aidan, but that was nothing. My life as I know it is over. I'll have two more hours of sleep, and then I'll sort myself out. Bring on Operation Total Disaster – I have a mahoosive incident to manage.

24

Boathouse Cottage, St Aidan
Waving and dotted lines
Saturday

Our mum always told us, in the face of catastrophe keep a cool head and keep on going. I'm guessing she based that on our dad leaving us when we were too small to remember, and her having to be both mum and dad to us afterwards. Or it may have been how she stayed so chilled when she dumped all those supremely suitable boyfriends of hers for the most insubstantial reasons, always at the point when Scarlett and I were just getting to know them. Whatever, I'm happy to live it myself now.

When I hear Pumpkin gently rubbing his forehead against the French windows shortly after six later that morning, I make sure that when I think back to two hours earlier and get up and run around the place shrieking *what the actual eff have I done?* it's only in my head. In reality, I tiptoe around the living room, pull on some different shorts and a new combination of skirts and cropped T-shirts, slip on Pumpkin's lead rope, and quietly make my way down to the beach.

I'd hoped a blast of pure salt air off the sea would blow away the pain in my head, but instead the noise of the breakers is so loud I'm holding my fists over my ears. But like everything, a few yards in I get used to it and start to walk normally.

Once we hit the expanse of flat, damp sand left by the retreating tide, I resist the immediate impulse to stop and write 'hands on...' or 'hands off...' anything, and limit myself to a brief *Keep calm and dot dot dot*.

My plan to stay out on the beach until Miles leaves the cottage works like a dream. When we get back the only sign of him is a jug of freshly squeezed orange juice sitting on a Post-it note on the kitchen island, saying *4U B B* in fat black Sharpie next to a pack of paracetamol. And just like that, with a half pint of OJ on board I'm getting on with the rest of my day and heading off to Saltings Lane to take pictures of the next stage of the various items that Edie is in the process of painting.

The readers of Fenna's magazine want inspiration for projects that are pretty but achievable, so I'm mainly concentrating on smaller bits and pieces that don't look too daunting and that could easily be done in a few leisurely sessions over the course of a weekend. There's a small pair of petrol-blue coffee tables, a pink child's chair, a simple cornflower blue bookshelf, and four olive green stools. Once I've taken pictures of the items on their own from all angles, I go on to style them with different accessories. At least it takes my mind off my pounding head, which hopefully will pass, and my other giant problem, which unfortunately never will.

By the time I have a full set of photos, give Edie a hug, and wander back up the lane, the Saturday market in the barnyard is in full swing, and as I go past the entrance the smell from the coffee van draws me in.

I'm standing sipping my Americano, when an arm flops around my shoulder.

'Would you like a chocolate muffin?' It's Clemmie, and she pulls me towards her stall in the stable. 'I've almost sold out. How's your head this afternoon?'

'You know about my hangover?' Of course she does. 'Don't tell me – your cousin works the bar at Jaggers? Or your mum peels potatoes in the chippy?'

She raises one eyebrow. 'Beth's dad, Malcolm, was at the Hungry Shark quiz night when Miles got the call to pick you up. Sounds like you pushed happy hour to the max!'

The second I hear Miles's name, my early morning trip to the bathroom comes rushing back like a rockfall. What the hell was I thinking? The truth is ... I wasn't. It was the middle of the night, I was off my face and half asleep. But excuses won't help me. Keeping calm and carrying on is total bullshit. If I can't even bear to think of Miles as an abstract idea, I can't possibly be in the same cottage as him, let alone put myself in a place where I may lock eyes with him across the kitchen. It's only now when I come to imagine the horror of the situation that it sinks in: I need to avoid seeing Miles ever again. There's no time for hanging about on this; I need to act fast, and I need to act now!

I drag in a breath, pull every last scrap of my courage together, and go for broke. 'Actually, Clemmie, the place we were talking about yesterday...'

Clemmie carries on. 'The Net Loft studio?'

'I'll take it.'

There, now I've said it, there's no going back, but I could be pulling myself out of the biggest hole of my life.

Clemmie's eyes light up. 'I can't wait to tell Plum and Nell. We knew you'd be perfect the first day we saw you. Well done for being brave!'

I'm opening and closing my mouth in shock at what I've said.

She's carrying on seamlessly. 'Let's make this as easy as we can. Malcolm's only next door, he'll be able to run off a copy of the lease for you to take away.' She's looking at my face, reading my expression. 'Or if you'd rather sign it now, that's not a problem either.'

So much has changed. When we talked about the Net Loft yesterday, me moving there was the kind of pie-in-the-sky fantasy that might happen to someone else, but I was ninety-nine per cent certain that would never be me. Twenty-four hours on, I've embarrassed myself so completely, this is the only sensible option I have, and I'm frankly lucky it's there at all.

It's not only me messing up big time by grabbing Miles. Scarlett's situation has changed too. If the unthinkable happens and she splits from Tate, she may well run for home. With their main house in Manchester properly let for their entire stay in New York, Boathouse Cottage would be the natural place for her to come back to. So the studio at the Net Loft is the proverbial port in the storms that are powering in from all directions. The sooner I clinch the deal, the better.

My mouth is dry. 'I'll sign straight away.' My mind is racing, and as I add up the figures there's really nothing left to lose here.

'If I transfer you three months' rent and the deposit, when could I have the key?'

If I pull this off, I never have to see Miles again.

If Clemmie's surprised by my sea-change she doesn't react. 'We'll have to run this past Malcolm, but it could be pretty quick.' She gives me a nudge. 'Just think, no more arguments over fruit or tussles for the bathroom.'

I die silently, replaying that last phrase in my head. I clutch at my throat where my heart is pounding. 'Okay, let's do this before I start hyperventilating.'

And two minutes later, as we speed across the gravel towards Malcolm's cottage next door, I'm ready to sign away my life.

JUNE

25

The Net Loft, St Aidan
Sweet dreams and ulterior motives
Sunday

When I wake up in the Net Loft early on Sunday morning, for the first few minutes I lie listening to the calls of the seagulls as they swoop across the quayside and the ring of the rigging on the boats that are lined up across the harbour. After that I look up through the roof light directly above the pillows and watch the peach pink of the dawn sky as it turns through pale aqua to deeper blue. I lie on my back, stretch out my arms and legs, and for the first time in three weeks I starfish across a bed.

When I first left my shoebox-sized room at the sanctuary, I doubted I'd ever get used to the lofty ceilings and wide open spaces of Boathouse Cottage. I was surprised how easily their expanses began to feel normal and now I've come to the studio, it's another jump again.

After Malcolm gave me the keys and my welcome tour yesterday, I waited until dusk then made a dash along the beach to rub Pumpkin's ears and check his water, and as Miles was out, I grabbed a few bits to bring back. Despite my full rucksack, it still feels like me and a postcard rack rattling around in a warehouse. And however sparse Boathouse Cottage felt when I arrived, this is a new level of empty.

On the upside I have my bathroom and the luxury of being able to visit exactly when I want rather than planning my loo stops for days ahead. I jump out of bed, bound downstairs, and perch on the toilet seat in my skimpy vest, with my see-through pyjama micro shorts around my knees without bothering to shut the door. It's only when I reach for the paper that it hits me that I'm looking straight across the studio and out across the harbour beyond that.

I scream, kick the door closed, finish and flush the gloriously loud flush. Then I wash my hands, nip into the kitchen to get a can of Coke, an almond and blueberry breakfast bar, and the box of Malteser truffles I bought yesterday to celebrate having a home of my own. Once my arms are full, I jump back up the stairs two at a time and vow this will be the last time I'll be flashing my bum at the harbourside car park, which is already full of people.

I open my laptop and spend the next few hours decadently lounging on my pillows, with Radio One Sunday morning bangers bouncing off the ceiling while I write the copy for the pieces for each of the relaxing weekend paint jobs, and eat chocolates.

By the time I send them off to Fenna, I'm pushing my word count record for a morning, and I'm seriously wondering what is going on with Scarlett. I don't want to butt in at a sensitive time for her and Tate, but if I message to tell her I've found somewhere to move to, that leaves the way clear for her to come back if she wants.

After all her generosity with the cottage, telling her I've already moved out seems too abrupt, so I ease in.

> Scarlett, hope you're okay??? There's a place coming up by the harbour I can go to if you need me to move out quickly. Sending huge hugs xx

I take another truffle and start to think about a bath and a walk with Pumpkin, but before I've even scrunched up my sweet paper, my 'I'm a believer' ringtone is echoing across the studio.

I accept the call, and Scarlett's straight in.

'Please don't move anywhere else, Betty! Tate and I have had a huge bust-up. He's moved out of the apartment. I'm staying on as planned, but I've talked to my lawyer in Manchester, and it's vital you don't leave the cottage.'

'You've already taken legal advice?' My jaw is sagging at how fast things have moved.

'It's over. There's no point hanging around.' She sounds strangely detached. 'Tate and I spent the whole of Friday night ripping each other to pieces, and I spoke to Kiera, the hot-shot barrister, yesterday.'

The name rings a lot of bells. 'Kiera who lost her shit in Revolución de Cuba on your hen do?' She was also the main mover on the choice of the milky silk bridesmaids' dresses.

Scarlett sighs. 'That's the one. She says it's imperative I

don't allow Tate's representatives to take possession of the St Aidan property, so I'm counting on you to stay exactly where you are. Every single night if you can.'

My heart is sinking, for all the reasons, but I can't add to Scarlett's load. My problems are so insignificant compared to hers, and I have to support her.

Her voice breaks. 'It's hell on earth here, and very surreal. The one thing keeping me going is knowing you're there to keep the cottage safe for me.'

'It's that bad already?'

'Separation is a war zone. A second of weakness, and I'll pay for it ten times over later.' She sniffs. 'And bear in mind, if Tate starts playing dirty, Miles will be trying to force you out too. You're going to need to keep your wits about you, but I'm confident you'll win.'

After that, there's only one thing I can say.

'No worries, Scarlett, I've got this.'

Then she rings off and leaves me sitting on the edge of the bed, staring past the wrought iron balustrade of the balcony and out to where the sea is shimmering all the way to the horizon.

The truth is, I haven't got this at all. I have no idea how the hell I'm going to handle any of it. I mean, the studio has taken my savings, but that's only money. If it was uncomfortable to coexist with Miles before, after my early hours grope it was already going to be a nightmare. Add in Scarlett's fears, and who knows what might happen?

I'm so deep in my despair I miss the first knock on the shop door. By the time the second comes, I've had time to pull on a sloppy T-shirt and get halfway down the stairs but then the door opens, and a voice calls in.

'Betsy Bets? I've been looking for you all morning!'

'Miles!' I leap down the last three steps, tugging my T-shirt down to cover my shorts. 'How did you know where to find me?'

He smiles. 'My old mate Malcolm from the Yellow Canary told me you were here.'

I'm blinking. 'You actually know Malcolm?'

He nods. 'Before he moved in with his girlfriend up at Periwinkle Cottage he had a bungalow three doors along from my mum, down by B&Q.'

I can't hide my surprise. 'Since when have you had a mother in St Aidan?'

He shrugs. 'She's lived here for years. She was the one who found Tate and Scarlett their cottage.' He runs his fingers through his hair. 'Enough about her. Tell me what you're doing with this place?'

He has no idea how ironic that question is. I can't tell him the real reason, and as it's all changed anyway, I'm going to have to wing it. I seize on the first thing I see in the empty expanse of the ground floor where we're standing, which is the revolving rack.

'I thought I'd have a postcard shop.' I'm making it up as I go along. 'I'm going to make them from the photos of the lines I write in the sand.' I'm still going. 'The extra income will help with the freelancing.'

That's complete rubbish. Added on to my Net Loft lease, it would be a fast way to run my savings to nothing, but he doesn't need to know that.

Miles's eyebrows shoot upwards. 'Genius! A retail outlet is a great way to get a second income stream.'

I'm nodding furiously. 'The best bit is I'll be able to write while I look after the shop.' I can't see myself being tied up here all day every day, but this is make-believe after all.

He tilts his head on one side. 'You'll be able to stock boathouse buns!' His smile widens. 'That's what I came to tell you. There's another load ready for you to sell. Banana custard, and blueberry and white chocolate.'

I swallow hard, my mouth watering. I need to decide how I'm going to play this.

He carries on. 'There are more pecan and toffee too.' He looks at me more closely. 'They *are* your favourites, aren't they? They're to say sorry.'

I'm bemused. 'What is there to apologise for?'

He's frowning. 'You must know?' His frown deepens. 'Okay, as you obviously don't, I'm going to have to tell you. The very inappropriate clinch in the corridor yesterday morning... I'm extremely contrite. It was way too long, and I promise it won't happen again.'

'Excuse me?' My jaw is on the floor, because as I saw it, all he did was to stop me falling over.

He shakes his head. 'I wanted to clear the air as soon as I could.' He rolls his eyes. 'Hopefully this way we can avoid any excruciatingly embarrassing moments when our eyes meet across the mud room.'

I can't quite believe what I'm hearing, but he's got more courage than I have. In his place I'd have rather sofa-surfed at the parental bungalow than bring this out in the open and talk about it. Myself, I was so mortified, I found a place to rent rather than face him out, but that's a whole other story.

Then my heart skips a beat. This could all be part of Tate's dirty tricks campaign. Who knows what they're planning with that, or what depths they'd stoop to. All I know is, I'm going to need to be super vigilant from now on. I can't take anything relating to Tate *or* Miles at face value.

So one impossible situation slides into another.

And to make matters worse, Miles still looks disgracefully shaggable. Considering my history, that's puzzling *and* disturbing.

'Consider it done, Miles, and let's move on.' I make my smile very bright, and ignore the flutters in the pit of my stomach. 'How many buns have you made to sell?'

He gives a shamefaced grin. 'Only sixty.'

I beam and put my hands on my hips. 'Lucky for you, St Aidan's heaving, and Pumpkin needs a walk. What are we waiting for?'

Miles gives a cough and wrenches his eyes away from my hem. 'Maybe for you to put on some shorts that aren't see through?'

I cough back at him. 'Good point well made, Mr Appleton. Give me a minute. *And no looking up my T-shirt as I go upstairs.*'

If this is the start of their campaign, whatever it is, they're already playing a blinder.

I can't take this lying down. I'm going to have to up my own game to expert level. Starting from now!

26

Boathouse Cottage, St Aidan
Angels, fish and seahorse tails
Monday

Once Miles and I came back yesterday afternoon, I took charge of the buns which he'd already boxed, and sent him off to get on with his day. That left Pumpkin and me heading for the beach to meet the crowds and sell our wares. We came back a couple of hours later with empty bags and a pocket full of cash.

With that job done, I spent the evening going through my photos to see if any of my sand-writing quotes *would* work as postcards. I start by thinking there won't be any, but in the end there are so many it's hard to narrow it down. By the time I remember it's not supposed to be real, I've already found a fabulous online deal, and I'm too invested to pull back. When I get to the checkout, I'm so impatient to see the results, I sod the expense and chose the fast-track delivery option. And while I hold my breath for Wednesday, I'm trying to make up for my rash spend by chasing down other ideas for magazine pieces.

Monday is the day Zofia comes. She likes to have the place to herself, so I make sure Pumpkin and I are out when she arrives. When we get back a couple of hours later she's already back in her beige suede loafers and is in the kitchen chatting to Miles.

She rushes over, drops a kiss on my cheek, and steers me towards a row of plants lined up on the work surface.

'Betty Beth, I've brought you some living herbs to liven up your summer salads.' She stops and points. 'Curled parsley, flat-leaf parsley, chives, thyme, oregano, basil and summer savoury.'

I'm despairing that she's followed Miles's lead and doubled up my name, but I'm smiling at the mass of bushy green leaves and terracotta pots. 'Thank you, Zofia, they're way too pretty to eat, but I bet Fenna would love herb growing too!'

Zofia's eyes light up. 'I can see it now! Readers filling pots with compost, readers planting seeds, readers with watering cans. You must come and take pictures this afternoon!'

I'm beaming. 'Those herbs definitely make the kitchen a happier place.' I catch sight of Miles looking at the ceiling. 'Don't knock it, Miles, anything this feel-good has to be positive.'

As I think of Scarlett and Tate, who may never enjoy this place together again, there's a pang in my chest.

Miles raises his finger. 'Have you told Zofia your news?'

'My news?' As he and I haven't acknowledged Scarlett and Tate's rift, I'm surprised he's talking about it now. 'I was hoping to keep that on the back burner until it's more public.'

Zofia laughs. 'Nothing is secret in St Aidan! I'm sorry, a little bird already told me – you've taken a workspace at the Net Loft!'

'*That* news!'

Miles nods. 'Betsy Bets is opening a postcard shop. How brilliant is that?'

Seeing Zofia reminds me of all the honesty box outlets in her village, and before I know I'm extending my make-believe mission statement. 'It's very early days, but I'd love to bring a garden-gate vibe into town too if I can find the right things to sell.'

Zofia looks thoughtful. 'It's very a big space to fill if you're *only* doing postcards.'

I'm looking at the deep green of her parsley and remembering her greenhouses and cold frames full of cuttings. 'If you'd like to sell some of your plants, I could try those? And your cut flowers would fit in too.'

She beams at me. 'Magnificent! I'll give you my very best price!' Her smile widens. 'And the same little bird said you've been selling those pastries you make too, but I also know that from my vacuuming.' She laughs. 'So pastries, flowers, plants and postcards? That sounds like a good mix.'

I hold up my hand. 'The pastries aren't for the shop. They're Miles's personal business project. He's taking those straight to national franchise level.'

Zofia frowns at him. 'Are you sure?'

I might as well explain. 'There's small business, like I would be, then there's big business like B&Q, then there's Miles.' I pull a face. 'We're galaxies apart in our ethos.'

Miles gives a cough. 'It's not that bad, Betsy Eliza.'

It is. In fact it's probably worse, which reminds me. 'Yesterday's takings from the beach are in the fruit bowl under the apples, Miles.'

Miles holds up a finger. 'While I'm working on my product development, all my costs will be absorbed down the line.'

Zofia winks at me. 'So many big words, you're right to say he's ready to take over the world.'

I'm yawning at the office talk. 'And I need to know this because...?'

He's blinking at me. 'I should have made this clear before. Any money you collect from sales is yours to keep.' He shrugs. 'That way it leaves me free to concentrate on the range. You'll be doing me a favour.'

I can't quite believe my luck, and I'm not about to refuse, so I offer the best I can from my side. 'In return I promise to bring you every scrap of feedback.'

'That's good enough for me.' He's rubbing his hands. 'So the next important thing – what about fittings for the Net Loft?'

Zofia sends me another look. 'His ethos might be up the spout, but we can't fault his enthusiasm.'

'I've already got the postcard stand.' I'm thinking of the village shop boxes. 'The rest will be freestanding. I'll start with a couple of tables for the plants and add more if I need them.'

Zofia nods. 'I'll see what I have in the outhouses at the Manor.'

Miles is nodding too. 'My mum has planks in her garage. I can knock together any shelving you want.'

I can't believe how far this has come in five minutes. 'Well, thank you both for your help.' I'm summarising. 'I'll see what's at yours, Zofia, when I come to take pictures for the herb growing. If it's okay with you, I'll quiz you about the fruit trees while I'm there.' Fenna's given me an open order for pieces featuring apples. Pies, crumbles, cider makers, picking, growing them – apples are so versatile and universal, readers can't get enough of them.

Zofia is collecting her cloths and putting them into her buckets, then she looks up. 'Before I go ... is Scarlett okay?' She hesitates. 'It's just that I had a message last night saying she and Tate were splitting up, but to carry on with my cleans as normal.'

My intake of breath is so big, I'm still grasping to find the right words when Miles steps in.

'Let's not jump to conclusions. I'm sure if we give them space, they'll sort this out.'

Zofia pulls down the corners of her mouth. 'Let's hope so.' Then she sighs and smiles again. 'Call by whenever you want, Betsy Beths. I'm in all afternoon.'

By the time I look up again, Miles has followed her out too. And I'm left wondering how a simple card rack expanded to a full-blown shop – and more to the point, how the hell I'm going to handle it!

27

The Net Loft, St Aidan
Lemon sorbets and promises for the future
Wednesday

It's funny how my mind plays tricks on me. As I stand in the Net Loft clutching my postcard package to my chest, the studio space around me has expanded. What seemed so manageable in my head when I was making those reckless comments to Miles and Zofia on Monday is now a huge, gaping, empty void. And the tables and shelves that Zofia's husband, Aleksy, dropped off yesterday only make it worse.

On a wet windy morning when the quayside is deserted the whole idea of selling anything at all feels impossible.

'What the hell was I thinking?' As I spill the postcards over the table nearest to me, every scrap of optimism I had has left the building. I pull my cardi around my freezing midriff and feel as empowered as a butterfly in a wind tunnel. Then I start to spread the cards out, the door opens and Miles pushes his way in.

He props a dripping umbrella against the wall and grins. 'It's torrential enough to drown out there! How's St Aidan's newest entrepreneur?'

Honestly? I could do without the interruption, especially from him, especially now.

'Shouldn't you be somewhere else?'

He looks hopeful. 'I thought maybe I could help – moving furniture, running out for coffee, filling your postcard rack?'

'That's very kind, but there's been a development.' I may as well stop pretending. 'I can't do this after all.'

His voice rises. 'Can't do what?'

I pull a face. 'I can't do any of it. I'm scared, I'm a million miles out of my comfort zone. I just need to lock up, get the hell out of here, and go back to doing what I was doing before.'

I can't blame all this on what happened with Mason, but I don't ever remember having so many doubts before that night. It's as if ever since then the stuffing has gone out of me. I can give a fair imitation of being okay day to day, but when anything more challenging comes along I crumple. It's not that I strutted around being super sure of myself before, but I wasn't a pushover and I wasn't a quitter, and I certainly wasn't the wet and weedy washout I feel like now.

Miles narrows his eyes. 'What happened to Betsy Eliza, the sparky creative dynamo salesperson who knows her under-thirties inside out?'

I shrug. 'That was easy. It was for you not me.'

He blows out a breath of frustration. 'You are hugely

talented and very capable, it's time you used that for yourself rather than everyone else.' His stern face softens as he looks down at me. 'Would a hug help?'

I leap three feet, then recover myself. 'Thanks all the same, but I'm better without.'

He drags in a breath. 'In that case, let's look at those life-affirming cards of yours.' He shuffles through some then picks one up. '*I am, I can, I will.*'

I carry on reading them. '*Climb every mountain. Be brave.*'

His eyes narrow. 'It might be a good time to take your own advice?'

I give a rueful smile. 'Those were me psyching myself up after I arrived.'

Miles is still watching me. 'It's not that long ago, and it seems to me you've come a long way since then.'

I'd rather he hadn't been appraising me, but whatever. 'When I look at the cards spread out it's a bit like reading my diary. I must have been feeling dreamy the day I wrote *Where the spindrift meets the stars...*'

Miles lets out a splutter. '*Nice bum*! If this is a record of your time here, what's *that* about?'

I choke into my fist. 'No one you know.'

His eyebrows go upwards. 'Even so, I bet it's a best-seller.'

It's pouring out before I know it. 'I never used to be a wimp, but there was this thing, and ever since I've been a bit of a ... scaredy cat.'

Miles tilts his head and looks at me. 'The bigger your fears, the better you feel when you face them and come out the other side.'

I'm looking at his grave expression. 'You say that like it came from the heart.'

He shakes his head. 'I told you before, and you might not believe it, but I've had my struggles which is how I know.' He pulls a face. 'The best way to regain your power is to hold your head high, believe in yourself, and move on to better things.'

I bite my lip. 'Thanks for the advice.'

'You're not on your own here.' He reaches out and gives my hand a squeeze. 'If you don't try the shop, you'll never know, but we're all here to support you.'

I try to stamp out the tingles that zither down my spine, and give the man credit for being there. 'Thank you for saying that, too.'

He's the last person I'd have expected to be helping me but here it is. Whatever makes me feel better, I'll take it where I can.

He releases my fingers and grins at me. 'I'm not giving orders, but if you put the postcards out, I can move the tables to where you'd like them, and we'll get this show on the road.'

I laugh. 'Before I have any more wobbles, you mean?'

'I didn't say that.' He holds his expression. 'But yes.'

I'm asking myself how he's so strategic. 'Do you have sisters?'

He smiles. 'Nope, but I've been very well trained by a female.'

'Your girlfriend again.' It's a statement not a question, and there's a twang in my chest as I say it.

'Something like that.' He raises one eyebrow. 'She's more of a woman than a girl.'

Kerching. 'Good point well made, Milo. We all are these days.' I pick up some cards, cross to the rack and begin to slide them in. 'If you're serious about the tables, one by the window and the others across the centre, please, and the shelf units against the left-hand wall.'

'I appreciate a decisive boss.' When he moves into action, flipping the furniture, it's hard to take my eyes off him.

I give a cough. 'Just making sure you're getting things in the right place.'

He sends me a wicked grin. 'Here's me thinking you're checking out my six pack so you can go and write about it on the beach.'

Now I've heard it all. 'You are so up yourself, Miles Appleton.'

His smile spreads. 'I'll be walking back along there later to check, just so you know, Betsy Beth Bradwell.'

I roll my eyes. 'I can see your car from here, so I know that's not true.'

His smile fades. 'Wind-ups really aren't my style. But there could actually be another surprise coming your way that you may find challenging.'

I shake my head. 'Now you sound like Mystic Meg. Please just move the furniture, then go and get on with your proper job.' I watch him pick up the next table. 'If you want a drink before you go, help yourself. The kitchen's under the overhang, and there are cans in the fridge. They're Scarlett and Tate's, but they're almost out of the date, so we may as well drink them.'

Miles swings the two shelf units into place. 'With my current interest in baking, I never pass up a chance to check out the facilities.' As he passes me he picks up a card and squints at it. 'What the heck are pony raids?'

I laugh. '"Pony *rides* this way", not raids.' I give him a nudge.

'Should have gone to Specsavers. In case you miss it, the fridge is the big silver thing.'

I watch his spectacular rear disappear into the distance, then give myself a telling off. At this rate of progress, I'll still be sorting postcards when it's dark.

28

The Net Loft, St Aidan
Snowdrops and daffodils
Wednesday

I may have momentarily got past running for the hills, but the more I look around the Net Loft, the less hope I have of making the place feel like a shop. Even with the cash injection from the bun sales I made, if I did find something I'd like to sell here, I'd only be able to buy a teensy amount of stock.

I only turn around again when I hear the door open and find Zofia shouldering her way in, carrying a wide wooden crate filled with herbs.

I jump into action. 'Plants! They're wonderful, thank you, Zofia! Put them wherever you think.'

Zofia coughs. 'Anywhere *except* near your postcards, which look amazing!' She puts down the box on the next table and picks up a card. '*Today is Tuesday all day.* This is mine, for my days when I'm especially forgetful.'

I lean over to see the plants. 'Let me put these out, and I'll get more of a feel for how it's all going to look in here.'

Zofia heads for the door again. 'Just off for another load.' A few minutes later she's back again, pausing to let me see what she's brought in.

'Violas! These can have a table to themselves.' My heart melts as I'm looking at the mass of vibrantly coloured, small flowers. 'These were my mum's favourite.'

Zofia turns to Miles who's sauntering out from the shade of the gallery. 'Betty Beth isn't lucky like you, she hasn't had her mum for some years now.'

His face tenses. 'I remember that from the wedding. I'm sorry.'

I move on to the other side of the crate. 'She'd have especially loved these orange and purple ones.' Then I find another section of smaller pots. 'You've brought succulents too, Zofia! These are so small and sweet they'll be best on the shelves.'

Zofia is back by the cards again. 'My hands are clean, so I'll start filling the card rack for you while you do the plants.'

I take the mints, bays and thymes and space them out in a line along the table in the window. I'm just coming to the last one when I spot Clemmie hurrying past the pile of lobster pots waving at me from behind her double pushchair, so I open the door again and she squeezes her way in. She drops a kiss on my cheek and pushes a bag into my hands. 'A little housewarming present for you; it's a scented candle from the barnyard.' She pulls a second bag out from behind her back. 'And some Little Cornish Kitchen flapjack specials.'

Miles chimes in. 'The kitchen here is great, but it's definitely a retail outlet not a house.'

Clemmie looks at me very hard.

I beam at Miles. 'If you could possibly go and grab some cans for everyone, I'll bring Clemmie up to speed on our latest ideas.' I wait until his bum slides out of view, then lower my voice. 'Due to unforeseen circumstances, this studio will now be opening as a venue selling postcards, plants and anything else I come across, and Miles and I will still be sharing Boathouse Cottage.'

Clemmie puts an arm around my shoulder. 'That's a pity, but it's a great chance for you to try something new.' Her smile widens. 'Better still, it's a fabulous excuse for a launch party!'

My insides shrivel. 'Absolutely not. I've got so little here, I'll open as quietly as I can.'

As Miles comes back from the kitchen Clemmie jumps in. 'Whatever you're carrying there, they look seriously cool.'

Miles stares at his load. 'I think they're sparkling waters.'

I leap in to explain. 'They're Scarlett's, so they're fashion forward, organic and sustainably sourced. Let's see how they taste.'

I help myself from the tray, pop the can, and take a swig. 'This is mango! And it's delish.'

Clemmie sips at her raspberry one. 'No one in town is selling anything quite like this, but I'd buy it if they were!'

I glance at the ones that are left. 'The designs are so pretty I may have to put the rest on the shelf to sell rather than drinking them myself.'

Miles holds his can up. 'I imagine these are the kind of things your readers would go for, Betty B.'

That makes me smile, because it's not often we agree on anything. 'Maybe I should focus on the magazine readers when

I choose what to sell in here.' I'm thinking out loud. 'I can't compete with any of the fabulous shops in St Aidan, so it makes sense to sell things you can't buy elsewhere.'

The more I run with the idea, the more appealing it is. 'If the shop had the same uncluttered feel as the magazine, I wouldn't *need* to fill it.' I can feel my excitement rising. 'Small and simple, ordinary but beautiful. That's how I need to make it here. I might just be able to do this after all.'

Miles has been listening intently. 'So where are you going to source items that are completely individual?'

Clemmie looks at me. 'If you're looking for small numbers of lovely bits and pieces, the makers at the barnyard should be able to come through for you. I'm sure Plum will help out by asking them.' She's grinning at me. 'I could get Edie to open up the barnyard for you later, then Plum and I could come up with you while the babies have their afternoon nap if you'd like to take a look.'

Miles is looking at me intently. 'I have Zoom meetings later, but if you need me to help, I could always move them?'

I'm fingering my *what the actual eff?* card. 'You carry on with your meetings, Miles. You can definitely help later by picking up orders.'

Zofia grasps my hand. 'Your mum would be very proud of you for doing this.'

My heart swells in my chest, then I swallow the lump in my throat and smile. 'She'd be flabbergasted more like! Scarlett's the dynamic one. Nothing I've done before ever suggested I'd do anything this out there!'

I'm painfully aware, if it hadn't been for a monumental mess up, I'd never have grabbed the studio, let alone thought of selling things.

Zofia nods. 'Like it says on your cards: *Time to astonish yourself!*'

Clemmie picks up another. 'What I want to know is whose is the "rear of the year" on the *Nice Bum* card?' She gives me another wink. 'We could run an opening week competition on the St Aidan Village Facebook page, asking for nominations. That'll raise your profile and get customers flocking to your shop.'

Miles laughs. 'The level of interest that card's generated already, you'd better get more printed.'

And just like that, there's no going back.

29

The Barnyard, Saltings Lane, St Aidan
No doubt?
Wednesday

'It must be hard living with a guy who looks like a *Vogue* model?'

It's mid-afternoon when Clemmie and I push open the stable door of the first unit at the barnyard to find Plum already inside, and she's a long way off-topic here.

She carries on. 'I mean, it's like David Gandy and Chris Hemsworth had a triplet brother. Not that that's possible, but you get my drift.'

I may as well tell it like it is. 'When I bolted down my lunchtime sandwich, it was so I could look at fabulous products, not so we could talk about Miles.'

Clemmie wrinkles her nose. 'Plum was at mine ringing round the barnyard makers, and this question was in my head the whole time she was doing it, so I thought I'd get it out of the way.'

I can see there's no getting out of this. 'Textbook irresistible – is that a good way of putting it?' I shrug. 'He's so far out of reach that it never crossed my mind to think of Miles as anything other than the guy who empties the bins on the days I don't.'

Plum hitches up her dungarees and swishes her ponytail. 'I'd say you're seriously underrating yourself if you think that.'

I bring out my usual excuse. 'I focus on my career rather than guys these days.'

Plum laughs. 'I was exactly the same, Betsy, then someone unexpectedly came along and changed my mind.'

I wrinkle my nose. 'If that did happen to me, it wouldn't be with Miles. He's not just out of my league, ladies, he's in a league from a different universe. When he's in the real world rather than St Aidan, Miles hangs out with super-humans.'

Clemmie grins. 'I don't accept that either. Even so, it must be difficult to stay hands-off when that's paraded in front of you when you're eating your avocado dips for breakfast.'

I laugh. 'It's more likely to be Nutella on toast, and I haven't succumbed to covering him in chocolate spread yet.'

'I assume that the *Nice bum* postcard was about him?'

So that's where this is heading.

As this is Clemmie, I might as well be open. 'It may have been.'

Plum laughs. 'We both noticed this morning he's very eager to help you.'

I don't see a significant connection. 'That's how he is. Any chance to show off his superior skills and knowledge, he's straight in there. It's nothing more than that.'

Clemmie's still staring at me hard. 'If you say so.'

'I absolutely do.'

She grins at me. 'That's Aunty Clemmie's awareness-raising chat out of the way. Would you like to see what Plum's found for you?'

I grin back. 'I thought you'd never ask.'

Plum points to some cushions lined up along the table edge. 'These are an example of the kind of items you get with individual makers. Malcolm's partner, Jo, who also happens to be Edie's aunty, made these up as samples for someone ordering for their conservatory.'

The cushions I'm looking at are striped, with a gathered gingham ruffle round the edge, in lilac, yellow, green, pink, cerise and aqua.

Plum picks one up. 'These are all available for you to buy immediately at a great price, and Jo could make as many more as you wanted in any of the colours.'

I'm fingering the labels. 'Cotton, with removable covers, and fully washable.'

Plum nods. 'Next are scented candles, in recycled glass jars, in a range of nature-inspired summer scents. The person making them has changed the shape of the jars since these.'

I'm picking them up, smelling each in turn. 'They're lovely.'

Plum's nodding. 'They're not too large, so the price point is good too. Obviously everything will be at cost price for you as a fellow local trader.'

I swallow my panic and look at what's next on the table. 'And the lanterns?'

Plum smiles. 'Those are made by Malcolm's daughter. This design is very simple so they're not too expensive. She'll let you have all the ones she has like that, if you want to be unique.'

'This is so kind of everyone.' I'm looking to where she's pointing next at four tall, narrow, wooden shelf units painted in pistachio green. 'CD racks and a hat stand?'

She nods. 'Edie brought those in. People don't use them as much now, but they'll be good for displaying individual items, or you could use them for the scarves I have over here.'

She takes one of the folded squares and flaps it open. 'These are Loella's. Some are cotton, some are silk, some are cheesecloth, but the fabrics are all really soft and light and no two are the same.'

I'm sighing at how beautiful the colours are. 'I love using scarves as belts, but they're also perfect for people who want to buy something small to remind them of their holiday.'

She points to a box. 'These are some odds and ends of vases and glasses that Edie sorted out for you too. And some framed retro cactus pictures, which are quirky and cool.'

'This will be an amazing start. I don't know how to begin to thank you.'

'People are grateful that you'll take small amounts of items, so they'll do you a good deal. What hangs around on the shelves up here may well fly down in town.'

Clemmie's fingering a scarf. 'Plum sells cards at the gallery, but her shelf space is limited, and otherwise she tends to go for pricier pictures or jewellery.'

Plum nods. 'There are more than enough customers to go round in summer, but we still try to have our own specialist area.' She passes me a piece of paper with a list of the prices. 'Once you see what sells, we'll organise some more.'

I can't stop smiling either. 'One of the first pieces I did for Fenna was about a woman who started her linen company with a single tea towel design and a snappy quote about making Prosecco disappear.'

Clemmie nods. 'That's the way to do it. A catchy idea, start small and grow.' Her smile broadens. 'It's hard to believe, but The Little Cornish Kitchen began with a singles sorbet evening.'

Plum is gathering the cushions into a bag. 'We'll put this lot in my car, and I'll run you back to the harbour.'

She pops her head out of the door, and when she comes back in her grin is even wider. 'Tyres on gravel with no engine noise? That might just be your proverbial knight arriving on his charger now.' She laughs. 'Don't knock it. We business owners need all the help we can get!'

My stomach drops at the thought. 'And just like that, I'm in the club.'

Clemmie laughs. 'There's no need to look so terrified. When are you planning to open?'

'I can't imagine I'll ever feel ready.' I don't know if I'm excited or paralysed with fear.

She's laughing more. 'Thursday's a good day to start, there will be people but not too many. I'll give Nell a shout. We'll drop by at twelve tomorrow and be your first customers.'

My voice has shrunk to a whisper. 'There's no putting this off is there?'

As I peep out along the barnyard we all know – I've boarded the train, and there's no getting off. As sure as Miles is striding towards the door now, this is happening!

Clemmie looks out, catches sight of Miles and lowers her voice. 'When someone works out what you need and gives it to you without you asking, that's a sign they care.'

I have to laugh. 'Or else it's a sign they can't bear to be left out.'

I'm really grateful for how kind he was earlier, but this time round I know which one I'd put my money on.

The Net Loft, St Aidan
Pop stars and cheese sandwiches
Thursday

'What's up the stairs?'

The next morning I'm up even earlier than usual so I can sort out Pumpkin and head to the Net Loft. I'd unpacked most things yesterday afternoon, so once I arrived, I spent the next hour moving things from one table to another and the hour after that taking them back to where they'd started. We hadn't arranged for Miles to come, but he pushes through the door at nine and dumps a stack of boxes in the kitchen, then shuttles in and out another four times. By the time he stops and stares at the staircase like he only just noticed it, I'm well past telling him he shouldn't be here.

I search for an answer to his question that has nothing to do with bed. 'Up there it's the roof. And a storage area.'

He looks down at the load in his arms. 'I've got the rest of Scarlett's cans here. I'll take them up, shall I?'

'*Noooooo!*' I leap in front of him and throw my arms out sideways. 'There's plenty of space in the kitchen.' I make a mental note to get a 'no entry' sign and a rope ASAP.

'The kitchen is actually pretty full.'

I'm blinking at him. 'Full with what?'

'My baking stuff.' He frowns. 'What did you think I was putting in there?'

I'm not admitting I was too stressed to notice. 'Why would you bring that here?'

He gives a shrug. 'You didn't have breakfast, and you can't open the shop on an empty stomach. I hoped a few boathouse buns might help fill the gap.'

'Can they be pecan and toffee ones?'

He smiles. 'I thought you might say that. I made the dough before I came so there won't be too long to wait.'

I'm working out how long it usually takes him, and counting back. 'You must have been up as early as I was?'

He gives a shrug. 'Pretty much, but it's all good research. My first time using a different oven, it may yet be a disaster.'

I'm one step ahead. 'Please can it be without the inspiring music?'

He points to his ear bud. 'For one day only, I'll keep it to myself.'

I'm suddenly ravenous. 'I'll get back to tidying and leave you to get on.'

He points to another box by the table. 'There are some large frames in there, and some blown-up prints of your cards I picked up in case you'd like something more punchy for the walls.'

'Thanks for that, it's a great idea.'

He gives a sniff. 'I have an extensive background in retail, so I may as well use it.'

My heart sinks. 'Not *Nice bum*?'

'Like I'd choose that if it's not about mine.' He rolls his eyes. 'I kept it simple, like your concept. *SEA SAND SALT*. And *SAND SALT SURF*.'

As I look at the rolls of paper in the box, I'm grateful for his foresight rather than cross about the intrusion. 'We could sell posters!'

'That too.' His smile widens. 'Forget the worrying, you could be about to have the most fun you've had in years.'

There's a pang of hunger in my stomach. 'You'll call me when the buns are ready?'

He nods. 'And you call me if you need me to hammer in the nails and hang the frames in the meantime.'

With all this agreement, it's a relief he's finally said something I can argue with. 'Milo, it's the twenty twenties. Women use tools.'

He shakes his head. 'I'll try that again. Call me if you need me to hold the frames up to decide the position.' He's staring at the stairs again. 'That's a very big staircase to only lead to a cupboard. With all this height, you'd think they'd have made a room up there.'

My jaw drops, but I go for the double bluff. 'If Malcolm would consider a loft conversion, I could sublet to you.'

That stops him in his tracks. 'There's something I need to tell you.'

'Go on.'

He gives a sheepish glance. 'Tate has asked me to stay on at the cottage definitively, to safeguard his stake in the property.' He hesitates. 'As his loyal friend, *whatever* other accommodation I'm offered, I won't be taking it.'

I give a sniff. 'Funny you should say that. I've had the same from Scarlett. Only stronger.'

He blows out his cheeks. 'At least we both know where we stand now.'

I let out a wail. 'Locked in the houseshare from hell due to someone else's property wrangle!'

'It's surely not that bad?' He sounds hurt.

I pull a face. 'If you say so.' If I'm fighting Scarlett's corner, I may as well be open. 'Just so you know, I will not be taking this lying down.'

The corners of his mouth are twitching. 'I'm pleased to hear that. If the attack was horizontal, I'm not sure I'd resist.'

I give that the eye roll it deserves, and go again. 'I will be maximising every opportunity to get ahead on Scarlett's behalf.'

He nods enthusiastically. 'Okay, I've got that. Shall I get on with the buns?'

My eyes flash open as it hits me. 'The baking's strategic! It's part of your grand plot to get me out of the cottage! I'm right, aren't I?'

He stops again. 'No, Betsy B, the baking is simply me wanting to help out a friend.'

I wince. 'I'm not sure I'd go as far as calling me that. Especially with our new battle lines. But okay, carry on.'

He finally heads off, and a few seconds later I hear the clatter of tins and the thud of dough on the work surface.

When I thought the shop would be the hard part, I was seriously underestimating Miles's capacity to add complications. It also looks like we've started a whole new war. To think I was looking forward to a nice quiet afternoon selling postcards.

31

The Net Loft, St Aidan
Crowded houses and a lot of sparkles
Thursday

Whatever negativity I have felt about Miles, his picture hanging suggestions are bang on, and I can't fault his pecan and toffee bun intervention either. By half past ten the studio is filled with the scent of vanilla and hot pastry and I'm sipping coffee and working my way through my own personal bun stack. I'm biting into my third when Zofia arrives, carrying a galvanised bucket of blooms in each hand.

She comes over, drops a kiss on my cheek, and stares at me hard. 'Not too nervous for your first day?' Then her worried expression moves into a beaming smile. 'For the cut flowers I have begun with mixed bunches, and I also have boxes of garden produce in the car.'

I'm looking down into buckets bursting with yellow and orange marigolds and the bluest cornflowers. 'They're lovely,

Zofia, it's going to feel a lot like your garden. Fresh produce will be great for the garden gate vibe.'

She nods. 'I have so much rhubarb, I am picking it in my sleep.'

Miles's head appears around the edge of the kitchen door frame. 'Zofia gave me some yesterday. You'll be able to give me your verdict shortly.'

I'm frowning. 'On what?'

Miles disappears and emerges from the kitchen seconds later carrying two large trays. 'Boathouse buns with fresh rhubarb, and boathouse buns with rhubarb-and-ginger jam I made earlier.' He puts the trays down on one of the empty tables near the back and picks up a bun and waves it around. 'Same arrangement as usual, Eliza Betty. Tell me how they taste, then these are all yours.'

It's so like Miles to crash into our day without a thought, but it will be quicker for Zofia and me to stop and taste than to argue.

'Try not to drop crumbs.' He hands us a serviette each.

As I close my teeth around the pastry the rhubarb is tart yet sweet on my tongue. I put both thumbs up and push the last flakes into my mouth. 'Yes, amazing, what do you think, Zofia?'

She's waving a bun in each hand. 'Delicious and delicious.' She turns to me. 'I'll finish these and get the rest from the car.'

I go back to the buckets and call to Miles. 'If that's everything, I'll get these flowers into the Kilner jars I have waiting.'

He throws a tea towel over his shoulder. 'There are another four trays of buns baking as we speak.' He takes in my hesitation. 'I've got my hands on a new kitchen, I'm going for broke here.'

I do the maths and put up my finger. 'Before you bake any more, just remember – if I'm stuck in here with my postcards composing rhyming couplets about mythical sea creatures, there definitely won't be time for me to sell buns on the beach today.'

I haven't quite got my head around having to man the shop in person all day every day, but like everything, I'll just have to see how it goes.

Miles is blinking. 'What are you writing?'

I'm going back to basics. 'Fenna emailed to ask for some last-minute lines about mermaids to put out on socials as a taster for this month's magazine. With writing and looking after the shop, I'll be tied up here for the rest of the day.' He still hasn't reacted so I obviously need to be more specific. 'If you make more buns than Zofia and I can eat now, unless you go out and sell them yourself, they'll go to waste.'

Zofia comes back in with another box and joins the conversation again. 'I can always take some home for Aleksy.'

I send her a grateful smile.

Miles gives a cough. 'I know my endgame aim has always been to market through large commercial outlets in on-trend locations, but as you're starting out and the buns are here, I'm happy for you to sell some today.'

However generous the offer, we're really not on the same page here. 'Miles, you're talking upwards of a hundred and twenty pastries. As a fledgling shop, I'm likely to have only a handful of customers today.'

He's narrowing his eyes. 'But if you tell your WhatsApp group there are buns at the Net Loft, they'll all come here to snap up the baking, and see the shop at the same time.' A smile spreads across his face. 'It's cross-brand marketing at its finest!'

I'm seized by a wave of terror. 'I was hoping to ease in with three customers, not a stampede of thirty.' I turn around. 'What do you think, Zofia?'

She looks at the buckets. 'It will be good to sell the flowers when they're fresh. More people will help you do that.'

I have another misgiving. 'The buns are your brainchild, Miles. I shouldn't be relying on those for my launch.'

He takes a deep breath. 'The buns were my idea to start with, but you're the one who sold them to St Aidan.' He looks around. 'As they're only one table in a much bigger shop, I reckon you've got more right than anyone to sell them.'

When he puts it like that, I'm feeling less guilty. 'In that case, thank you, Miles.' I pick up my phone. 'What other flavours shall I tell the group you're doing?'

He grins. 'I thought we'd go with some crowd-pleasers. Double chocolate chip, banoffee, cinnamon, and vanilla custard.'

'You planned this all along?'

He looks around him. 'When you've created a place this cool, you can't keep it a secret!'

Clemmie comes through the door. 'A big-bang opening? That's exactly what I said, too!'

'Okay, I'll message the group now.' It's only what I've done before, but when I press send my hand is shaking with nerves.

Miles hands me a sheaf of cards from his back pocket. 'Here you go. You do the price tickets, and there are boxes and bags in the kitchen to wrap them for takeaway, and I'll go back to my baking.'

I push the plate towards Clemmie. 'Try one of these, they're pecan and toffee.'

She picks one up 'A real, live boathouse bun! I've heard a lot about these but they've always been devoured before I could get anywhere close.'

Zofia and I take another one each and I groan. 'As someone who shares a house with the baker, I despair at how easy they are to eat.'

'I can see why they're legendary.' Clemmie toasts the air with her bun then looks around at the tables. 'Having so little in here actually makes things stand out more! The postcards are amazing, but the real icing on the cake is you joining forces with Miles. That is inspired, well done for that.'

I can't believe how wrong this has gone. First, my random comment about a postcard rack gets so out of control that I end up with a shop, and I *still* don't have a bed to call my own. But more importantly, this should have been me cutting ties with Miles for good and forever – and look how it's ended up! Far from a separation, it's turned into a public coming together.

I blow out a breath. 'It's only for today.' I look at Clemmie. 'I'm truly not planning to steal your customers.'

After that, I promise myself I'll be standing on my own.

32

The Net Loft, St Aidan
Sandcastles and deep blue oceans
Thursday

Plum finishes her bun, picks up a posy and a bay plant, then crosses to the postcard stand and pulls out a card.

She grins at me over her shoulder. 'I'm glad I came early, I reckon this card is going to sell out very fast.'

Before I have a chance to reply the door opens and Carol and Paul from The Crow's Nest come in, followed by three more of their friends from the Yellow Canary, then Malcolm, and Edie's Aunty Jo. What happens next is crazier than anything I could have imagined.

There must be something attractive about a crowded shop, because before I know it the place is full of people who aren't regular customers, and that's how it is for the rest of the day. The buns are decimated, and there are so many people to serve that Zofia stays to help until mid-afternoon, when she goes to get more plants. And when I finally shut the door and leave at four, rather than going back to the cottage, Plum meets me at the barnyard so I can pick up more supplies. While I'm there, Edie's Aunty Jo pops over and offers to run up some calico cushions with appliqué letters saying *SURF, SAND, SEA, SUN and SALT* to tie in with the wall posters, and the first thing I do when I finally get back to the cottage is to order more postcards.

Then I flop down on the sofa with a glass of elderflower cordial, open my laptop and try to pull together some lines for Fenna. After the afternoon I've just lived through, writing's not a chore. It's a relief to dive in, to imagine myself with shimmering scales parting the seaweed fronds to swim with the deepest fish shoals. Then I rise and break the water surface. I'm just shaking my shell-encrusted hair in the starlight when a huge crash in the kitchen drops me back into the Boathouse Cottage living room.

I whip round to see three of the stools by the island unit slam onto the stone floor one after the other. Haring away from them there's what looks like a flying fur rug, and staggering after it, picking up the furniture in his path, is Miles. At some stage the rug must reach the end of the kitchen and turn, because it appears again, careering past the other side of the island unit, leaps up towards the sofa end, flies past my shoulder, and lands in a heap sprawled across my shins.

I grab a cushion for defence, clamp my laptop to my chest, and go in for a closer look. There's a lolling pink tongue, a light brown nose, and a mass of curly hair a very similar colour to my own.

'You're a dog!'

Miles pushes the last stool back into place. 'This is the surprise I mentioned yesterday.'

'It's less a surprise, more a tornado.'

Miles shuffles. 'There was an emergency. I've offered to look after him.'

If this is part of the tactics to get me to leave, however effective it is, I'm not going to rise.

'Well, that's nice.' I think of myself as a mermaid, unhurried and unbothered, gliding thorough the waves. 'Anything else I need to know?'

There are deep furrows in Miles's forehead. 'I'm hoping it won't be for long. You're not allergic?'

I have to say it. 'A considerate housemate asks that question *before* they bring in a dog, not *after* he's here.'

'Right. I'll remember that for next time. As you specialised in sanctuary animals, I assumed you'd like dogs.'

I'm despairing that he thinks we'll be around long enough for it to happen again. 'It depends on the individual dog and how they are with Pumpkin. Not all dogs like horses; some will chase them.'

'Shit.' Miles's face is white.

I'm not going to sugar-coat this. 'With the wrong dog, the outcome could be fatal. Until we know differently, you'll need to be extra vigilant.'

'Would it help if I cut back on my music?'

I can't believe I'm passing up this chance. 'If we're talking about a dog's reaction towards a horse, I'm not sure where your music comes in.'

He shakes his head. 'By way of apology. As a gesture. For the whole situation.'

I'm picking my jaw up off the floor. 'But people like you never say sorry?'

I see his eyes go wide with disbelief, so I jump in to nail this before he takes it back. 'Thank you, not being regularly shaken to my core would help. Does the dog have a name?'

'Fudge.' Miles is nodding. 'Because of his colour.'

'Great. Hello, Fudge. I hope my legs are comfy enough for you to lie on.'

Miles is carrying on. 'I thought with his toffee-coloured hair, he'd be part of the family.'

'Excuse me?'

He must know he's talking out of his bum, because he carries on. 'He also prefers women to men. Due to his past.'

'Was he a rescue?' I'm ready to soften.

He shakes his head. 'No, just a puppy. Brought up by—'

I harden again. 'Your woman-friend.'

He nods. 'And he likes to sleep on the sofa at night.'

This isn't normal warfare, it's a full-blown targeted attack. 'So you're saying I'm going to have to share my bed that's not a bed with your woman-friend's dog?' I imagine I'm a mermaid, heading out of the bay and never coming back and make my smile very wide. 'What's not to like?'

To show how unbothered I am, I tickle Fudge behind his left ear. A second later, he lunges forward and lands on my chest.

I'm being ironic. 'Who knew what was missing from my life was a dog to lick my chin?'

Miles's eyes are like saucers. 'In my wildest dreams, I never thought it would go this well.'

I'm curious. 'How long have you been building up to this?'

'For about a month.' He hesitates. 'Maybe a little longer.'

'Since before I arrived then.' Even more unbelievable. I should try to take back more ground here. 'As he's your responsibility, shouldn't he sleep with you?'

Miles rubs his chin. 'It's probably best to keep him out of the bedroom – for Scarlett's sake.'

It has to be said. 'If you were really considering Scarlett, Fudge wouldn't be here at all.'

As Miles shakes his head, he looks like he's caught between a rock and a hard place. 'If there's any damage, I'll make everything good before we leave.' He smiles. 'On a different note, it would save a lot of running about if you had a fridge with a glass door, so you could keep your cans in the shop.'

Even though it's come from left field, I have to agree. 'You're right but buying more postcards might be my priority.'

'I'll look after the fridge. As a thank you. In advance.'

'For the chaos that's about to rain down on me?' Why is my heart dropping like a stone? 'Is there anything else you need to tell me?'

Miles pulls a face. 'It's probably best if we meet things as they come up.' He takes a breath. 'Think of the fridge as a loan. If ever you're finished with it, I'll take it back.' His smile widens. 'And as soon as you've done your work for Fenna, we can talk about syncing.'

Syncing? When my heart sinks this time it's slowly and sadly. 'I'm not sure I'll have time to go on the sun lounger anymore, consider it yours.'

He laughs. 'No one's going to have time for the terrace. I'm talking about baking and dog walks.'

And I thought that Miles and a shop was as bad as it could get.

33

Boathouse Cottage, St Aidan
Seagulls, light years and thermostats
Sunday

Don't ask me how it happens, but it's actually Sunday morning before I see Miles again. On Friday and Saturday nights, I curl up on the sofa while Miles is still out, and wake in the small hours to find Fudge wedged between my thigh and the sofa cushions. When I get up in the mornings Fudge gets up too, then when I go through the French windows and out into the field he takes himself back to the sofa again. I haven't introduced Fudge to Pumpkin yet, but Fudge has glimpsed Pumpkin beyond the door, and hasn't thrown himself at the window, which I'm taking as a positive sign.

As for the promised fridge, Miles delivered on that quicker than you could say 'chiller unit'. Late Friday afternoon a van arrived from Falmouth. The guys placed and plugged in a very sleek appliance (to turn on twelve hours later once the coolant had settled) and took away the packaging too. Far from being reassuring, it was the kind of complete service that makes me wonder what's waiting for me down the line.

And in the meantime, I spent two days on my own at the shop, which was another eye opener, because compared to Thursday's whirlwind, trade was non-existent. I sold a handful of cards, a cushion, three sage plants and a succulent, but at least that took away the pressure to restock.

Spending time doing nothing but wait for customers in the centre of St Aidan wasn't my favourite thing, but at least it gave me a new view on what else I could offer Fenna. After a morning staring out at the row of harbourside cottages, with their colourful front doors and profusion of planters, I made a dash to take pictures. As the afternoon began to drag, I scribbled a 'Back in ten minutes' sign and nipped along the side streets and alleyways further up the hill to do the same. It's amazing how many frames you can capture and how far you can get in a short time if you hurry. After every outing I came back and edited the pictures, and so long as the sun stays out, by Monday I should have enough to tempt Fenna with a few new angles. I know as a shopper I hate to find a 'Back in ten' sign, and I really don't want to become the shop that's closed more than it's open, but now I have bills, I have to be realistic about finding ways to pay them.

When I wake shortly after dawn on Sunday and hurry back from the bathroom, I'm so busy thinking about capturing the village in pixels, that at first I miss that I'm not alone in the kitchen. It's only when Fudge's cold nose nudges my bare knee that it hits me that Miles is up too and standing by the kettle.

He holds up a mug. 'Can I pour you a coffee?'

'Milk, no sugar, please.' There's probably a catch, but for once I don't care. 'You're up early.' Unlike me, at least he's made the effort to pull on some jeans and a T-shirt.

He pushes the mug towards me. 'I was hoping Fudge and I could join you for your morning beach walk.'

The feeling of my heart sinking is getting horribly familiar, but I force my face into a smile. 'It's not that complicated to do for yourself. You stand on the sand with the dog beside you, and then you move your legs.'

His frown deepens. 'You're so comfortable with animals, and I'm struggling here.' He looks up hopefully. 'It would be a chance for Fudge to spend time getting used to Pumpkin?'

'For someone who claims they have no idea about animals that's an unnervingly sensible suggestion.'

Miles tilts his head. 'So, we can come?'

I take a swig from my mug. 'Give me five minutes to get dressed and drink this, and I'll be with you.' I look at Fudge, who is staring at me equally expectantly. 'If there's a choice of leads, bring the longest one.'

And just like that, a proverbial hammer smashes through my sacred Sunday morning walk, along with everything else.

However much Miles and Tate are trying to wreck my life, I refuse to let it bring me down. By the time Pumpkin and I are wandering along the water's edge, watching the foam frills rush towards us across the shine of the wet sand, I've breathed in enough cool salty air to feel calm again.

Miles calls from a couple of yards away. 'I'll stay on the drier sand.' He gives a head shake. 'Fudge is supposed to be fifty per cent French water dog, but he hasn't embraced his wet side. He doesn't like getting his paws damp.'

I smile. 'Lucky for Scarlett he's not fully immersive! What's his other half?'

Miles wrinkles his nose. 'Poodle and golden retriever, with a dash of hound. So I'm told.' As Fudge yanks and pulls Miles almost horizontal, he shakes his head. 'Any useful tips from St Aidan's most famous pony walker?'

Pumpkin and I pick up our pace and fall into step beside Miles and Fudge. 'Encourage him to walk next to you rather than tugging, keep him on the lead until you're sure he's not going to disappear over the horizon, always carry poop bags, and have fresh water for longer walks.' I take a few more strides then ask a question of my own. 'Does Tate know he's at the cottage?'

Miles pulls a face. 'Tate sees strength in numbers.'

I blow out a breath. 'Those two really are up shit creek, aren't they?'

Miles winces. 'Everything Tate has is because he worked his arse off for it. I can't understand why he'd jeopardise that.' He kicks a stone and sends it bouncing across the sand. 'Me being Team Tate doesn't mean I condone his behaviour.'

I'm hiding my shock. 'I'm a hundred per cent Team Scarlett. But thanks for saying that.'

Miles picks up a stone and hurls it into the water. 'A lot of us would give anything to have a relationship half as strong as theirs. It's infuriating to see him throw it away.' He shakes his head. 'Anyway, how are things at the shop? Do you want any more of my buns?'

I'm so shocked that I stop walking and he crashes into my shoulder. 'I thought Thursday was a one-off?'

He purses his lips. 'There may be more to learn from regular small-batch baking than I'd first thought.'

'What about your national roll out?'

He gives a shrug. 'The other day reminded me a lot of when I first started out as a green sixteen-year-old.'

I'm puzzled. 'Was that when you left school?'

He shakes his head. 'Not exactly. My education was a bit patchy. I probably left when I was twelve. Or maybe nine.' He pushes that aside and carries on. 'I'd forgotten about the adrenalin rush of a raw start-up, the thrill of running on your wits and gut instinct.'

I roll my eyes. 'The freedom to be so small you can change from day to day. Isn't that what I said all along?'

He gives a rueful grin. 'Back then I was still thinking of the real world. If I stop fighting it and accept that I'm living beyond the end of nowhere, in a place where everything is minute, small scale makes sense.'

I'm trying not to let my mouth drop open. 'You *do* have regrets about the past?'

He stares at me. 'You didn't believe me?'

I frown. 'It's the way you exude confidence. You just give the impression that life couldn't be any better.'

'Don't be taken in by the jeans and the car.' He thinks again. 'Don't be fooled by any of it, not for a second.'

He walks a few more paces, then slows. 'I wouldn't have come anywhere near Cornwall if it hadn't been for some catastrophic problems.'

'You wouldn't?' I look at him again because it's hard to take this in.

He shakes his head. 'It's the last place I'd have chosen, but there wasn't a choice, so I made the best of it.' He gives a rueful smile. 'If you pretend things are great when they couldn't be worse, very often great things do happen.'

I'm not even trying to hide my shock. 'And have they?'

'What do you think?' His eyes are dancing with self-mockery. 'Still waiting. It's a good thing I'm patient, but each new day could be the one.'

'Give me time to catch up. Is this the real Miles or the pretend version?'

He laughs. 'While you work that out, let's deal with the logistics for the shop and the baking. You do want to carry on selling with Pumpkin?'

I jump at that for Pumpkin as much as for me. 'That's the fun part for us.'

I'm racking my brain trying to work out an hour-by-hour list of who goes where and who does what to make this work. Just as my head feels like it's about to explode it hits me – Miles is craving a plan. If I want the fastest way to drive him round the bend, I only need to think back to my vegetable pile on the side the first week. I know he's trying to help me, but with all the body blows I'm taking from Team Tate, I may as well pile in as many as I can from my side with this.

'And the rest?' Miles is staring at me expectantly.

I give a cough. 'We're going to stay true to the ethos of small-scale start-ups ... and wing it.'

His jaw drops. 'We're going to what?'

I laugh. 'Make it up as we go along. Be truly flexible. Until we see how it all pans out, we'll do what we want on the day.'

He lets out a howl. 'That's never going to work!'

I'm trying not to smile. 'We won't know until we try it, will we?' In the interests of the shop, I make a concession. 'We might need to decide the night before, so we know what time we need to get up.'

From the way Miles kicks the sand, I take it he's not happy.

I look at him. 'Are you in or out?'

He gives a sniff. 'We'll try it for a week, and revisit.'

I'm not sure exactly what I've won, but it feels significant. I have to admit his buns could be the saviour for the shop. On the downside, it's going to mean working with Miles most days, which on current form promises self-destruction within minutes rather than hours. As for all these new complications and revelations, I'm more confused than ever.

I grin at him. 'You'll have to work out how much you're going to charge me for the pastries.'

He gives me a nudge. 'And you'll have to say how much you're going to charge me for using your kitchen.'

I look at Pumpkin and Fudge, their lead ropes loosened, wandering a stride ahead of us.

'We'll have to work out where the animals fit in too.'

Miles's head is tilted as he watches them. 'I'm no expert ... but does Fudge think Pumpkin's a dog?'

I shake my head. 'Dogs rely on their noses, and Pumpkin definitely smells like a horse.' I run forwards, bury my face in his neck and take a deep breath. 'It's very distinctive. Like a cross between a farmyard and a hay field.'

Miles gives a shudder. 'I'll take your word on that.'

I laugh and drop back to walk beside him again. 'So are you good to take Fudge out by yourself from now on?'

'Hell no!' He looks even more appalled. 'I don't mind beach

walking on my own, but if I add in a dog, I feel like everyone knows I'm faking.'

I bite back my smile. 'So how is our master businessman going to troubleshoot this one?'

His face relaxes. 'That's easy. We're going to keep walking with you and Pumpkin.'

If I write anything in the sand today, it's got to be *fml*.

Every time I chalk up a point for Team Scarlett, within seconds he gets me back.

There's one thing he may be overlooking. 'How is your woman friend going to feel about all these walks along the beach without her?'

He gives his usual exasperated sigh. 'Okay, let's clear this up. I don't have a woman friend in that way. It's just a terrible mess. The reason I'm running and holed up here.'

'Miles?'

'I'll shut up now. That's already too much for my confidentiality clauses.'

'So who owns Fudge?' If I'm spending so much time with the dog, it's best to know.

Miles sends me a shamefaced glance. 'He belongs to my mum.'

'Your mother?' My mouth is hanging open again.

Miles closes his eyes. 'Another situation, another restricted area, another black hole information exclusion zone.'

I make my voice light. 'Another day with the Appleton family in St Aidan.' And the shocks just keep on coming. I'm staring at the horizon trying to play this down. 'That's fine by me. With so many no-go areas, I'm looking forward to some very peaceful walks.'

Except it's not fine. None of this is fine at all. And with every new twist it gets worse. I'm going to have to push forward and try to find a way to pull myself out of the mess.

34

The Net Loft, St Aidan
Picture frames and shopaholics
Wednesday

Miles needn't have worried. Sometimes the reality isn't as bad as whatever you're dreading, and ten days into our improvising we haven't had any major disasters to take him out of his comfort zone. So far, he's making the dough for the pastries at the cottage and doing the shaping and cooking at the Net Loft, while simultaneously negotiating with the council to get the hygiene rating there fast-tracked.

Once the trays with new glass domes on the Net Loft table are filled with pastries and the next batch has been made, he looks after the shop, while I drive back to the cottage with boxes of pastries and take Pumpkin out to find custom along the beach. When those buns are gone, Pumpkin goes back to his field and I go back to take over at the Net Loft.

Since Monday Pumpkin has been wearing his saddle with

two gingham bags-for-life made by Edie's Aunty Jo slung across, so rather than me carrying the buns, Pumpkin carries them for me. I also bought some mini bunting from the barnyard to hang around his neck and stretch along his flanks to his tail. I haven't actually shared with him that with his bulging bags and colourful flags he looks like a walking country fair, but there's no mistaking what we're out for – visitors definitely see us coming!

In the shop I'm holding to my vision, and when an item runs out, I'm bringing in whatever else rare and beautiful I can get my hands on. The hat stand now has some small, vibrant, jewel-coloured felted bags hanging from it, and for the last couple of days Zofia's brought courgettes in instead of rhubarb, and next week she's promising bunches of cut herbs.

From my side, the beach walks with Miles haven't been anything like as bad as I'd feared either. So far, we've mainly focused on Fudge. As his recall is non-existent we had so much work to do with him, that there's been no time for conversation to drift to more difficult areas.

If anyone had told me when I first arrived here that I'd not only be spending time with Miles, but would also be working with him, I'd have laughed them out of town. He's still just as up himself and he still looks down on the rest of the world from his lofty, boardroom perch – especially on me – but five weeks on it's less jarring. I've seen his entitled attitude paraded so often that I no longer want to splatter custard pies in his face every time he opens his mouth. I probably wouldn't even rush to push him into that proverbial hole in the sand Scarlett and I used to fantasise about. He's still just as infuriating, sometimes even more so, but somewhere along the way I've learned to distance myself. Stay chilled. Keep my cool.

Then sometimes, just sometimes, he's so kind and warm and understanding. And that's when things get most confusing of all.

As for the way he snubbed me at the wedding, it's ironic that Tate and Scarlett aren't even together anymore. I could take that as a sign that perhaps it's time for me to forget it and move on, but weirdly, rather than making me not want to work with Miles, what he did that day is spurring me on. If his skills enable me to get the shop off the ground, it's like tipping the scales back in my favour. If this is a chance to get my own back in some small way, or better still, to feel better about myself, then I'd be mad not to take the opportunity. And strangest of all, it's his throwaway interventions – a sentence here, a confession there, a candid disclosure – that are really helpful. The kind of thing that when I look back and dwell on it, makes the light of confidence inside me grow.

You'd hope that so much rational thought would spread to other areas too – that the guy would have lost his fairy dust when it came to the lust stuff. In fact, the opposite has happened, but you can't win them all. I'm sure my sensible brain and my out-of-control sex drive will realign eventually, and he'll just become another ordinary mortal who happens to be quite good-looking, but who I have no interest in slamming against a wall whatsoever. All I can say is, roll on that day.

This afternoon, I'm about to close the shop door after the last customer so we can go home when I see Clemmie, Plum, and a crowd of children hurrying across the harbourside, all of them carrying boxes.

Clemmie comes in with her double buggy, puts her box by the hat stand and directs the others to add to the pile. 'We're doing the school run for our very pregnant friend Sophie today, so the kids are helping bring a few more bits from the barnyard that had come as far as Plum's gallery.'

Zofia is close behind her, with a bag of plants in one hand and a Henry vacuum in the other. 'If I drop these in now rather than first thing, I'll give the place a quick going over while it's empty.'

She's barely finished her sentence when Miles arrives too and puts a stack of boxes of Scarlett's pretty canned drinks down next to the fridge.

I watch the kids cross to pet Fudge where his long lead is tied to a table leg over by the succulent shelves, then turn to see Miles. 'I thought you'd gone to Falmouth?'

He nods. 'I called in my favourite upmarket cash-and-carry while I was there.' He waves a bag. 'As a thank you for looking after Fudge this afternoon there are some new drinks for you to try, all picked for their pretty labels.'

Me, dog-sitting? I'm as shocked about that as anyone, but it was the same as letting Fudge on my sofa at night. I hadn't meant to, but when it comes to that toffee-coloured nose and a tail that won't stop waving, it's hard to say 'no'.

I smile at the women. 'Vanilla cola rather than Pepsi, and more exotic water.' I dip further into the bag 'Hibiscus, watermelon, cherry blossom and key lime! And fruit-infused teas too. Those are perfect!'

Zofia gives Miles a pat on his arm. 'We'll send you shopping again!'

I nod in agreement. 'We've learned a lot the last ten days. The pastries are what pull the customers in, and as most people will want a drink to go with them, they may as well buy those from us. And after that, we hope they'll be tempted by the rest.'

Plum is grinning. 'Two weeks in and you're already talking like an old hand.'

'I'll take that.' I grin back at her. 'Fruit tea is a great alternative to cans because it only needs hot water, but I refuse to do washing up and single use cups are wasteful, so we're a bit stuck.'

For once Miles's self-satisfied smile is justified, but it cranks up a notch. 'That's where these come in!' He whips a stack of cups out of his pocket. 'Reusable cups with lids, that people buy alongside the tea if they don't have their own mugs with them.'

Zofia punches his shoulder. 'You are shooting from your big guns today, Miles!'

His smile widens again. 'Better still, for a tiny amount more you can include a company logo and have free publicity forever.'

I laugh. 'Logo? We don't even have a name!'

Clemmie is straight back at me. 'So choose one!'

I pull a face. 'If I'm wearing four dresses because I couldn't choose between them, how will I ever decide on a name?'

Zofia gives me a nudge. 'Let *us* help you!'

Clemmie's eyes light up. 'Keep it simple. How about Betty's?'

Zofia purses her lips. 'There are already Betty's in Yorkshire. It needs to be new.'

Plum's stare is hard. 'I bet there's never been a Betsy and Miles?'

I hate it. I mean, when have I ever wanted to be associated with Miles in any form, in public or in private? I give a cough. 'It would need to be Milo and Betsy because Milo sounds more playful, and Miles's buns are what are making it work.' Then I think again. 'Or better still, Milo, Zofia, Betsy, and friends.'

Zofia pulls a face. 'Listing everyone is inclusive, but it loses the punch.'

Miles is looking at me, his eyes half closed. 'Betsy and Milo! It's simple and unique – like the shop.'

I'm trying it out for size. '*Betsy and Milo – the shop with nothing in.* With a curly "and" not the word.'

Miles gives a cough. 'I'm confident you can improve on the tag line.'

Plum looks around. 'It's like the gallery. The empty bits make the stock that *is* here pop.'

I'm forcing myself to find a way to accept this. 'The name's not a big deal. It's only for a few weeks, after all.'

Plum turns to me. 'Edie does signs on planks that won't break the bank. She can do you a couple for the walls, and one to hang in the window.'

When they're helping so much, it's only fair I join in. 'I'll go up to see her later and talk about sizes and colours.'

Miles jumps in. 'And I can put up the fixings for the rope to hang the sign.' He backs off. 'Unless you'd like to screw some hooks in yourself.' His voice rises hopefully. 'Or we could do it together?'

Clemmie gives me a smile. 'This way it's so temporary you can take it down in seconds if you change your mind.'

'That's good by me!' I need to make up for that by being the most enthusiastic I've sounded since they got here. 'I'll get a "Betsy & Milo" Facebook page up and running tonight and put something on Insta.' That way I can have my nervous breakdowns in private on the sofa later.

Zofia is pulling out the cord of her Henry. 'If that's everything, off you all go and leave me to my cleaning.'

Miles unties Fudge from his table leg, Clemmie turns her buggy, and I follow them all out onto the quayside. With the wind whipping my skirts against my legs, it's so cold I'm thankful for all four layers.

Plum calls back over her shoulder. 'I almost forgot! Edie has found some more postcard racks for you. Have a look when you call in for the signs, and if you want them, I'll drop them down tomorrow.'

It's not lost on me. Without that postcard rack none of this would have started.

As I pause to sigh, Fudge runs past with Miles hanging on to his lead.

'Would you like a lift back to the cottage, Betsy Eliza?'

I know I should be independent and walk, and probably take Fudge, too, but for one time only I give in, and a moment after I say 'yes' I'm climbing into Miles's car. And the moment after that he turns to me with the kind of smile that sends my insides into free fall.

'For a cold start-up this is pulling together remarkably well.'

Miles is looking across at me as I settle into the comfy leather seat of his car and slot in my seat belt.

'Considering we're making things up as we go along?' As our eyes meet properly my stomach drops so far it practically hits the road and I drag in a breath to steady myself. 'The stuff you brought from Falmouth earlier was very useful.'

He laughs. 'I buy my butter from that place. With the number of buns we're shifting I'll be going there a lot.'

'Anything I can do as a thank you, let me know.' I want to make it clear I'm not taking any of this for granted, but I already know I'm safe.

He's holding his fingers in mid-air over the steering wheel. 'I may take you up on that.'

I narrow my eyes. 'Apart from helping with Fudge, I have absolutely nothing to offer you.'

'That's not completely true.' He gives me that sideways look of total disapproval, then there's a lilt of a smile at the corners of his mouth. 'I'd like you to do some baking.'

My eyebrows shoot upwards. 'If this is you and Tate trying to humiliate me...'

His tone is quiet. 'It's not.'

My voice rises. 'My superpower is eating, not cooking!'

He holds up his hand. 'No discussion, no explanations, no skills necessary on your part. You need to come to this completely un-prepped or it won't work.'

I'm still wriggling. 'You have to give me more than that.'

He blows out his cheeks. 'It's nothing complicated. Just you and me, for a couple of hours in the Boathouse Cottage kitchen.'

How is it that every time I reach rock bottom I manage to sink to a lower level.

'In any case...' I'm not going down without a fight. 'Tonight and tomorrow I'll be doing the Facebook page, then it's the weekend, and Mondays are usually really busy too.'

Miles lifts an eyebrow. 'And before we know it, it'll be September?'

I sit up and borrow a phrase from him. 'Are you saying we should park it?'

His face breaks into a grin. 'Let's not overthink this. How about we do it when we get a minute to spare?'

Which is the worst of all worlds, because I'll never know when it's coming.

'Saturday? But absolutely none of your music.'

'Understood.' His grin widens. 'Unless you get a better offer.' He gives me a nudge. 'No pressure to do dinner afterwards either.'

That should be doable, even for me. It's slightly worrying that he knows me well enough to swing this.

The kitchen at Boathouse Cottage, St Aidan
New tricks and old dogs
Saturday

'So what's this about then?'

If Miles knows my limitations – which he does because I've told him – I'm still not sure why we're standing in the Boathouse Cottage kitchen next to an island spread with utensils and ingredients on a Saturday evening when there are a thousand more important things we could be doing.

He clears his throat. 'I'm consolidating.'

That confirms it for me. 'We're working towards your world ambitions here?'

'Indirectly.' He hands me a bag with dusky blue fabric folded inside. 'I got you a customised apron, from Edie and Aunty Jo. It's made from organic hemp.'

'That's a little over-the-top, but I'm pleased you shopped locally.' I shake it open, and read the words printed down the right hand front as I put it on. '*Betsy & Milo Sun Sand Sea Surf.* Thank you, that's very smart.' Since Friday, when we hung Edie's signs in the shop, I've been banging on non-stop about how scary it all feels now it's real. Faced with it again, I'm momentarily lost for another variation.

There's another flap of fabric. 'I grabbed one for myself too.'

I watch him tying himself into an identical one and let out a shriek. 'Our names? On matching pinnies?'

One more time, and he's biting back his smile. 'No need to panic, Betty B. It's not only us, there are eighteen more to sell in the shop.' His eyebrows go up. 'Aprons have a lot of longevity. They're like an everlasting advert. I jumped on the free publicity bus while it was passing.'

I'm flapping mine in front of my face to fan away my flush of panic. That's less alarming. And more alarming. And I can't see why we'd be hung up on adverts for something that isn't going to last more than a few weeks. I blow air up over my face. 'Shall we just get on?'

He shakes flour across the work surface then takes the plastic film off two blocks of pastry, puts one down in front of me, hands me a rolling pin and pushes me a flour sifter. 'Now I've nailed the buns myself, the next step is to see if other people can make them, too.'

I'm squaring up my pastry block like he's doing with his. 'So you're aiming for countrywide hand-made mass-production!' The significance is sinking in. 'Isn't that an oxymoron?'

He's smiling to himself. 'Forget the long words, let's see how you do with the dough.' He's already started rolling his own block. 'This is some I've just defrosted, we've got to keep it cool and work quickly so it doesn't get too sticky. Aim for firm, smooth, even strokes, we're heading for a rectangle the size of that silicone mat, and it should be the same thickness all the way across.'

It takes me back to when we used to bake jam tarts with mum as kids. Scarlett and I had our own mini rolling pins, but obviously my sister refused to use her childish one and insisted on using Mum's.

'So when did you get into baking?' I pause to catch my breath.

Miles keeps up his tempo, rolling as he speaks. 'When I first moved here I was keeping a low profile, and everything fell so far short of what I'd had in Manchester I stayed home and worked. Then a couple of months before you arrived someone minor from Bake Off did an over-sixties fund-raiser at Plum's gallery and I got dragged along. I saw them make laminated pastry, had my lightbulb moment, and the rest is history.'

'So had you cooked before?'

He shrugs. 'I knew enough to throw a tasty meal together, but this was different. I was very focused, I had a vision of what I needed, and I went for it.'

I'm puffing as I roll. 'It's harder work than you'd think. I can see why you're ripped.' I'm moving on quickly from that slip. 'When did you come down here?'

He laughs. 'Shortly after Tate and Scarlett's wedding. I haven't had a Saturday night out since.'

'Me neither.' I'm not joking, but I take it he is.

He narrows his eyes. 'So you lost your "plus one" pretty quickly after the reception then?' He doesn't wait for an answer. 'Smart move, you definitely deserve better than him.'

It comes out of nowhere and hits me so hard I feel winded.

This is the worst thing about hanging around with someone who was there that night. There was always a possibility the conversation would swing round to Mason, but now it has I hit out with the first thing that comes into my head.

'Tate had no right to judge!'

Mason was the lowest of the low, but I'd hate other people to know anything about what happened. Especially Scarlett.

She always rolled her eyes about the guys I dated because we had such different tastes in men. Her guys were so permanent, she had to take the whole thing more seriously. With my throwaway attitude, I missed the long service medals, but the guys I saw were more exciting. Before Mason, I used to see the best in people because I had no reason not to. My instinct told me that anyone who could make me laugh was probably a decent human being, and as that had always proved to be true, I'd never doubted my judgement. The world is a much sadder place now that belief has been shattered. I've changed my life to keep myself safe for the future, but no one can ever know how wrong I got it. Scarlett revelled in being my protector, and she'd be devastated if she knew she'd failed with that.

Miles pulls a face. 'It wasn't Tate. *I* came across your date drinking neat vodka at ten in the morning and drew my own conclusions.'

Even thinking of Mason now makes me feel sick inside.

But I have to acknowledge the bad bits that everyone else saw. 'Passing out during the speeches was not a good look.' I attempt an excuse to save face myself. 'It's always awkward for partners whose other halves are stuck with the wedding party, and drinking all day, it's hard to keep track.'

It wasn't as if I were teetotal myself.

Before Mason got out his hip flask and announced his mission statement on the M5, I had no idea his intention for the day was to get as drunk as possible as fast as possible. Don't get me wrong, we all liked to party. Just not that ferociously. And he wasn't even hiding it. If we'd had the conversation in advance I'd have known, which is why I'm so much at fault. And alcohol makes every tendency worse. I'm not even sure he knew he was going to flip as he did. But if I'd only looked more closely at the start, I might have spotted the undercurrents.

I need to move this on, so I go in with a teaser. 'None of those other dating disasters I mentioned included unconscious people.'

Miles gives me a hard stare. 'I'm pleased to hear it.'

Here come my secrets, I just hope they distract Miles from the wedding. 'There was one guy who dated me because he fancied my housemate, another, who was *really* scary, who bought me flowers and proposed the second time I saw him, the one running three girlfriends at the same time, someone who couldn't make a second date because he moved to Australia...'

Miles is staring at me like I'm some kind of rare species. 'How did you not learn from your mistakes?'

I'm puzzled that he's implying it's down to me. 'None of it was planned; they all resulted from random collisions, mostly on dance floors.'

If he knew this is only the tip of the iceberg, he'd have a fit. Worse still, if this is his reaction to a few innocuous dating stuff-ups, I can only imagine how badly he'd think of me if he knew how the night ended for me at the wedding.

He's shaking his head. 'This is why it pays to check out a person's palmarès *before* you commit to a date.'

At least this turns the tables on him. As I get a mental picture of Miles measuring his potential girlfriends' suitability against his required tick list months in advance, I let out a howl of laughter. Then it hits me that it's probably true. 'So how does anyone get to have a date with Miles Appleton? It's probably easier getting into MI5.'

His eyes narrow. 'Why? Are you asking?' The prodding challenge in that glint flips my tummy over.

I could never argue about his looks or how chemically charged he is, but I've never actually considered how he'd be to have on my arm, and I'm both appalled and filled with horror that I'd go there, even for a nano-second. As for that secret adrenalin rush that's pulsing through the pit of my stomach and flushing my skin all the way to my ears, that's the kind of excitement I equate with the kind of terrifying things that I know I'd never do personally, because when I think of them, they scare the crap out of me and they're out of my league/price bracket anyway. Like roller coasters or going over Niagara Falls in a barrel. Or being a paying passenger on Elon Musk's next space trip.

As for the awful time I had with Mason – that was the kind of degrading, depressing and desperate incident that left me with the kind of self-disgust and inner fear that I've tried to bury ever since but that are still perilously close to the surface.

The sooner I shut this down entirely the better, because quite apart from everything else, as we already know, men like Miles don't look at women like me. If it wasn't for me being in his face every day by Scarlett's toaster, he wouldn't even know I existed.

He waits for an answer to his question, his head cocked and his eyes full of curiosity.

I roll my eyes. 'I've already made it clear I'd rather eat my own head than have dinner with you.' I pick up his suggestion, and another gale of compensatory laughter bursts out of me. 'Advance vetting partners isn't exactly spontaneous, is it?'

He shrugs. 'No, but at least I'm well prepared and I avoid disappointment.'

Then I stop and look at him hard. 'And how is this working out for you? I mean, it's Saturday night and you're in sleepy St Aidan in someone else's kitchen, baking with a loser.'

'That's a bit harsh, Betsy. My current issues are down to something else entirely.' He drags in a breath. 'All I'm saying is, you might want to consider forward selection in future. Choice is power, remember.'

And oh how I know that now, but I'm shaking my head in disbelief. It feels like there's so much office-type rationale being applied here, it's like we're stuck in an Appleton company boardroom, not talking about emotive subjects like fun and partners.

At the same time it resonates in the most chilling kind of way, because it holds so true. If I'd followed Miles's guidelines, that one awful night might never have happened. It's just a relief that Miles doesn't know the worst about Mason, because if he did, I wouldn't be able to hold my head up in St Aidan. 'Well, thanks for your input, but that's not a mistake I'll be making again. I've given up dating.'

Miles frowns. 'You can't mean that? If you limit your life because of one bad guy, it means they win.'

I pull in a breath, because he's so close to the truth here, and although it's insignificant compared to what came later, Miles was the bad guy that day too because of the way he snubbed me.

I rub my nose with my fist, catch sight of the tangle of curls bobbing around on my shoulder and try move this on. 'We were so busy barricading Fudge in the sofa area with bar stools, I forgot to tie my hair back.'

Miles springs to the sink, rinses the flour off his hands, and when he turns back to me, one of my scrunchies is hanging from his finger. 'It's a good job I gave up protesting about hair elastics in the fruit bowl. My hands are clean, shall I tie it up for you?'

As he stands behind me, I shiver at the thought of him touching me.

'Would you like a braid or a ponytail?'

Then I come to my senses. 'Thanks all the same, but I prefer a messy up-do, or a French twist secured with a pencil, both of which are much too hard for a beginner. I'll wash my hands and do it myself.'

I'm about to step forward to the sink, but his fingers are already sliding through my hair, pulling it upwards.

His smile widens. 'I've got this! Lucky for you my first job was as a junior in a salon.' He gathers my curls into a bunch. 'I probably had more teenage jobs than you had love interests.'

As the rainbow shivers on my scalp subside it has to be said. 'None of them were about love.'

He laughs. 'We've got that in common too.'

'Excuse me?'

He sighs. 'I told you when we were talking about Tate and Scarlett – that's not a thing I've had myself.'

He sounds so easy, it's out of my mouth before I know it's

coming. 'So what happened at their wedding – why did you mess with Scarlett's choice of bridal party partners?'

There's a beat of silence. 'I'm afraid that day I was dealing with a monumentally tricky situation that was outside my control.' He blows out a breath. 'I scoured the place for you next morning to apologise but I couldn't find you.' I open my mouth to say the words but he holds his finger up. 'Before you jump in with your "people like you never explain or say sorry" line – that's not who I am.'

I'm staring at him. 'What sort of person are you then?'

He narrows his eyes. 'The kind that worried when reception told me you'd already checked out.'

I catch my breath. 'You didn't tell anyone?'

He gives a half-shake of his head and stares into my eyes. 'Were you okay?'

I hold my nerve. 'You know what animal sanctuaries are like with emergencies.' It's a statement rather than a lie.

His brows knit into a frown. 'I don't, so I'll have to take your word on that one.'

He gives me another hard stare and I crumble. 'Fine, I wasn't called away. We left because we had an argument.' I make my smile bright. 'It wasn't going to be possible to make small talk over breakfast, so we slipped away instead, and for the record we didn't see each other again.'

'Good decision.' His grip tightens on my hair again. There's another pull or two, and he steps back, his eyes scrutinising my hairline. 'That's caught most of it, I hope that's messy enough for you.'

It's certainly messed up my insides. When I agreed to bake with Miles, I was grudging rather than enthusiastic, but I'd completely underestimated how hard it would be, or how close we'd be standing or where the conversation would end up. The worst bit about tonight is that when I'm not in control I have no idea what's coming next.

He's back to the sink, then back at my elbow. 'Excellent rolling there, Betty Eliza! Ready to move on to the next stage?'

I'd actually like to run as far away as I could, find a friendly local hill and roll down it, but I'd rather die than admit defeat. 'Bring it on, Milo.'

'For our next trick we're going to cut this sheet of dough into sixteen equal strips.'

Miles hands me a knife and a metal ruler, does one strip himself then leans in close to show me how wide to make the first one, and puts his hand firmly over the top of mine to steady it as I make the cut along the ruler's edge.

I'm biting my lip as I concentrate but all I can think of is how good he smells up close. 'I might cut straighter if I did it on my own.'

He laughs. 'I'll leave you to do yours then and get on with mine.'

As we stand side by side making our cuts I relent. 'Talk me through what happens next.'

He looks at me sideways. 'We'll give each strip a little stretch, then spread them with the fillings you choose, roll them up, put them on their baking trays and leave them to expand in the proving drawer.'

My heart sinks at how long it all sounds. I'm looking at the jars lined up on the island. 'For the fillings I'll have four apricot jam, four raspberry jam and white chocolate chips, four dark chocolate chips, and the rest will be Nutella.' I look up at him. 'I don't see any pecan and toffee?'

He laughs. 'I'm keeping those a secret in case I need them for persuasion later.'

I let out a cry. 'That's not fair! What have I got to bribe you with?'

As he turns to me again for a second his eyes are smouldering, then he blinks and when I catch his eye again the look has cleared. 'I'm always happy when you take Fudge for walks.'

I try to detach myself from what's going on in the moment and concentrate on what we're working towards.

He eases a slice of dough off the side. 'This is how you stretch the strips.'

I groan. 'You make it look easy and you work like the wind.' I watch his tanned hands, with their long fingers and broad knuckles, then go back to my own.

In no time his baking tray is filled with a regular pattern of identical spirals. By the time I add the fillings, roll them up, and get them into the tin, it's such a mess I let out a wail. 'Mine looks like an explosion in a jam factory!'

Miles gives me a nudge. 'It's great for a first try. You'll get better with practice.'

I'm frowning at him. 'You think I'll be doing this again?'

He raises one eyebrow. 'If you're free on Saturday evenings, I'd appreciate the help.' He hesitates then begins again. 'Most people find it easier to learn from a video rather than from written instructions. So I'm hoping to film a step-by-step guide to use as a manual.'

I'm still catching up. 'For your national chain?'

When he laughs his voice is so low it makes my nipples stand out. 'That's the one.' He picks up the trays. 'While these are rising, you could open your latest postcard package?'

36

The kitchen at Boathouse Cottage, St Aidan
Rude words and heavy loads
Saturday

When we share an address and a bathroom it's hard to keep anything under wraps, so Miles could hardly miss the huge box when he was the one who signed for the delivery. That's how busy today has been – my parcel arrived and I haven't had time to open it.

He swings in from the mud room with the box and hesitates by the island. 'Here or on the coffee table?'

If it's been hard brushing elbows by the workstation, I'm not up for clamping my thigh next to his as we pour over postcards, so I make my excuse watertight. 'It's a shame to disturb Fudge when he's quiet.'

Miles frowns. 'He's settled really well this evening. He's usually a lot more in your face.'

I'm looking to where Fudge is lying on the sofa end, his head propped on his paws. He's got one eye on Pumpkin in the field, who is swishing his tail beyond the windows as the evening sky turns smoky purple.

Miles slides the box onto the end of the island and pulls out a couple of stools. 'It feels like a big order, but with three postcard stands to fill, it needs to be.' He turns to me and grins. 'Was I right about the card that sold out first?' He hasn't taken much notice of the cards, beyond the one that *wasn't* about him.

'Different cards sold well on different days.' I think back. 'A lot of people love the *It's my lucky day* one with the horseshoe prints, and the edgy ones have been so popular Clemmie was joking that if I find a fourth card rack I should do a sweary range.'

What Miles doesn't know is that with two extra card stands to fill, I was just about to rush off to the beach with my writing stick when a customer asked if we had any cards with local views and sent me in a whole new direction.

Miles holds up the scissors. 'Will I be overstepping if I open the box?'

I laugh. 'Seeing you've asked, not at all.'

He folds the flaps back and takes out some packing. 'I'll let you take it from here.'

I unwrap the first small package, pull out the cards, smile to myself, and push the top one across for him to see.

His eyes widen. 'It's the sea of flowers in Zofia's garden!' He looks at me. 'What happened to the sand writing?'

I laugh and think how he might put it. 'I've diversified.' I take a few more cards out, look at them myself, then pass them over.

He's flicking through them. 'Front doors, doorstep flower tubs, Zofia's espalier pear tree, boat names from the harbour.'

I hand over the next ones. 'My favourite garden gate jam shop, Pumpkin's favourite geraniums down on the harbourside, and some St Aidan shop windows.'

As fast as I'm unwrapping them, he's taking them from me. Eventually as we come to the end he looks up at me. 'You're a dark horse, Betsy Eliza. They're stunning. I told you you'd be having fun.'

I give a shrug. 'Let's see how they sell first.' Then I give him a smile. 'You are right, I had a great time taking them.'

Miles picks up another card and squints at it. 'What's that about then?'

I lean over to look, and try not to rest my boob on his forearm. 'That's the graffiti on the wall by the end of the residents' car park where the silver surfers group rest their boards. It says *carpe diem* – seize the day. It's Latin.'

Miles wrinkles his nose. 'Thanks for sorting that, I'm not the best at deciphering words.' He blows out his cheeks. 'It's not only Latin – it's all reading. I'm okay with three letter words and short sentences, but if I'm faced with anything as long as a page I give up.' He pauses for a second. 'You must have noticed my cryptic writing?'

I'm finding this hard to take in, then it hits me. 'But you checked my work? That day with the fairy piece, you found every typo.'

Miles's head shaking starts again. 'No, I sent it off to head office and they did it. I'm told the team there are very good.'

I'm still finding this hard to grasp. 'But you knew what I'd written?'

At last he nods. 'That was text to voice software. It's very good now. It wasn't always. But I've had my whole life to find ways to get around the problem, I've never let it hold me back.'

I'm the one shaking my head now. 'I'm sorry if I sound rude, but it's just very unexpected ... considering how successful you are.'

He stops to think. 'My business instincts and vision were good. My enthusiasm and an eye for detail made up for what I lacked.'

I'm thinking back to my own small country village infants' school and literacy hour, and decide there's no point holding back. 'I'm not sure I've ever met anyone who couldn't read before. How did it actually happen?'

Miles pulls a face. 'I was a bit dyslexic, missed some school and never caught up. I simply fell through the cracks. It wouldn't happen these days. It's not exactly a secret but I don't broadcast it either.'

I drag in a breath. 'Well, thanks for sharing with me.'

'It's the least I can do.'

I'm curious again. 'What? Because I'm being your roll-out guinea pig?'

He looks slightly bemused. 'No, because you let me in on your very exhaustive bad-boyfriend list.'

I stare at him. 'That wasn't all of it.' The second that's out, I'm kicking myself. 'Shit. There was no need for me to say that.'

'I look forward to the next instalment.' He's looking at me through half closed eyes. 'This is why you should never make assumptions. People are a lot more complicated than you'd ever imagine, which is why it's best to get to know them more before you put your trust in them.'

I'm certainly having my eyes opened here, but I suspect he is too, and not in a good way.

I push my sinking heart to one side. 'On the bright side, if all these Saturdays go to plan, at least you'll get your one-way ticket out of Cornwall.'

He bites his lip. 'How about you? Are you pleased with how the shop is going?'

There's not often the time, but when I do stop to think about it, I'm astonished at what's come out of nothing in a very short time.

'We have a name, we're on Facebook and Insta, we have tag lines, an ever-expanding WhatsApp group, and after tonight we have aprons, too. We also have money rolling in so fast, I'm surprised you aren't scouring the coast for more places to pop up.' I laugh. 'All we need now is for Fudge to come back when we call him, and we'll have nailed it.'

He blinks at me. 'Say that again?'

I need to keep this real. 'I'm being ironic. Realistically it could be years before Fudge can run free on the beach.'

He frowns. 'Not Fudge, the bit about the pop-ups?'

I laugh again. 'Shops all along the coast, staffed by Zofia's relations and builders' wife friends. It was a joke, Miles.' The look in his eye tells me I need to move on and fast. 'Do you ever dance in the kitchen? It could be time to try. While the buns are baking. Have they risen yet?'

I'm waiting to see his reaction, but he's looking past me and out to the sofa.

'Fudge is eating something. Did you give him bone biscuits?' He jumps down from his stool, clears the barricades, and a nanosecond later, he's at the sofa's end holding something high in the air. 'Bad boy, Fudge! It's a pink jelly shoe, and it's totally demolished. That's why he's been so silent.'

I don't have any jelly shoes, so I don't rush.

Miles is staring at something in his hand. 'All that's left of the top is a gold badge with an orb with a cross on.'

My chest contracts and I feel sick. 'Those aren't jelly, they're my Vivienne Westwood pumps.' I hate making a fuss. I don't put a lot of value on material possessions, but these were very precious. My throat is so dry my voice is a whisper. 'They were a gift from Scarlett when I graduated.' As suggested by mum before she died.

Miles is shaking his head. 'I'm so sorry. It's unforgivable. They're irreplaceable.'

I blow out a breath. 'They were under the sofa. I should have put them away.' I'm trying to work out what's gone wrong here. 'I've never seen Fudge do destructive chewing or I'd have taken more care.'

Miles's face is white. 'He doesn't. Hardly ever. He once put teeth marks in my mum's best leopard loafers when she got a new boyfriend. But nothing before or since.'

I sniff. 'A dog who senses the most heartfelt shoes.' I'm on my hands and knees, my hand sweeping around under the couch. When I find the other one, I pull it out and hold it up. 'At least I still have one.'

Miles drops the first one into my open hand. 'I can never put this right.' He tilts his head on one side. 'Dinner, jewellery, more shoes, weekends away in a spa hotel – I respect you enough to know my usual go-tos aren't going to work here.'

I can't help hearing Tate cheering in the background, but I

need to be firm here. 'I don't want anything, Miles. It was an accident.'

His voice is very low. 'Whatever I do won't be enough, but leave it with me.'

Which is worse than nothing at all, because now it's going to hang over me, and I'll never know what he's going to spring on me.

'What about the pastries? Will they be ready?'

His eyes come back into focus. 'I'll check now. We need to brush them with an egg and milk glaze, and then they'll go into the oven, which I've already pre-heated.'

I zip my pumps into the side pocket of the nearest rucksack, and push my flip flops in there too, just in case.

I sigh. 'You may as well put your music on.'

He watches me as he walks to the proving drawer. 'Are you sure?'

I pull a face. 'Why not? My head is shot to pieces anyway.' All these weeks I've fought against Miles's noise, but tonight it feels like it would be blissful to have a wall of sound that pulses through my body and blasts into my ears so there isn't room for anything else.

He brings the baking trays across to the island. 'We could play yours?'

I wrinkle my nose. 'For once Taylor Swift isn't going to cut it. Just obliterate me with the best you've got.'

'Gustav Holst's Jupiter?'

'That should do the job.' At least it'll take away the need for conversation.

I sense he's about to open his arms, so I get in first. 'A hug is not going to help here. Thanks all the same.'

As the first notes of Miles's favourite tune bounce off the ceiling I have no idea what the hell is wrong with me, but the idea of burying my face in his chest feels a million times less hideous than it did the last time I thought about it.

Then the vibration of my phone reminds me that however big my problems are, they're nothing compared to what's going on across the Atlantic.

37

The kitchen at Boathouse Cottage, St Aidan
Classic fml
Saturday

'Scarlett!'

'Betsy, how's it going?'

As Miles kills his music and my voice echoes around Tate and Scarlett's kitchen my loyalties feel strangely compromised. If Tate hasn't told Scarlett about Fudge being here, I don't want to be the one who dobs them in. And if she doesn't know about Fudge, telling her about my ruined shoes is off the table.

Then I see Miles giving me a thumbs up as he takes the baking trays out of the proving drawer, and I leap into action. 'Miles and I are having an evening at the cottage working on his pastry development.'

Her voice goes high. 'You're spending Saturday night hanging out with the enemy?'

I'm trying to speak in code. 'There's more than one way to crack an egg, Scarlett.'

There's a moment's silence, then she gets it. 'While simultaneously gaining an insight into the other side and their tactics!' She sounds falsely bright. 'I've said this before, I hope Miles isn't taking advantage.'

It's my turn to shriek. 'I have absolutely nothing he could want or make use of.'

She sniffs. 'Seriously, you wouldn't be there if you hadn't.' She has every reason to be bitter, but it's a shock to hear her *this* cynical. 'I rang to tell you I've pulled in my Ground Force team to overhaul the exterior spaces at the cottage.'

I'm shocked at that too. 'I thought the garden was maintenance free?'

'With what's coming next, I need to ensure every asset is at its best. The team is flat out, but they've agreed to fit me in some time this coming week as a special favour.'

'Fine. I'll look out for them.' I expect her to ring off immediately, but when she doesn't, I tiptoe in with a question. 'How are things with you?'

'I couldn't be better. The singles scene here is buzzing, and I've got dates queuing up around the block.'

'Well, good for you.' Of everything I wanted to hear, it wasn't that. 'You don't think it might be better to wait?'

'I haven't had loads of wild and wonderful sex like you have, Betsy. I've been with the same person since the second week at uni.'

I'm trying to put it gently. 'People say when you come out of a long relationship, it's best not to jump into another.'

She lets out a cry. 'But I can't be on my own! I haven't been single for more than four days since I was eleven!'

I wouldn't be borrowing from Miles, but I'm desperate. 'If you're seriously looking for a long-term partner, sleeping your way around New York might not be the best idea. You need to be more ... strategic.' I'm thinking back to what I was told. 'If you rely on chance encounters, you'll waste time. It pays to do your research and plan your selections carefully.'

I can hear her interest sharpen. 'You might be on to something there, Betsy.'

I feel guilty for taking any credit when they're not my ideas. 'It's also a great time to focus on the advantages of not being part of a couple.'

She groans. 'I can't think past how tiny the mortgage would be if I applied as a single person.'

At times she makes me want to give up. 'But think of the upsides! When you're on your own there are no arguments and no fitting in with someone else. You simply decide what's going to make you happy ... and do it.'

There's silence, and then a murmur. 'You've really thought about this.'

I'll go a bit further. 'A lot of people find pleasing themselves is a revelation. Once they get a taste for it, they don't want to give it up.'

'If it truly is that great, what's the catch?'

I pull a face. 'You'll miss the support of a partner at first, but in time you'll get to know which of your friends you can lean on. When you learn to rely on yourself that makes you a stronger person.' I pause to think. 'That's why you shouldn't rush into a new relationship. The recovery will change you, your priorities will be different.'

She sighs. 'I'm certainly wanting different things in a partner than I did when I was eighteen.'

I have to ask. 'What did you look for back then?'

There's no hesitation. 'Good jeans, wheels, a term-time job with some kind of perks, a course with a decent career at the end, and a shared love for Snow Patrol and the Kaiser Chiefs. Tate was way ahead of the field – he did shifts at the Union bar *and* he had use of his granny's Lupo.' She stops. 'And *I* reminded *him* of Florence and the Machine. That was it.'

'You're nothing like Florence.'

Scarlett's laugh is more sour than sweet. 'Fourteen years on it hits Tate I wasn't what he'd ordered, and here we are.' She blows into the phone. 'When did you get so wise?'

I can't help laughing. 'My hundred and nineteen relationship disasters haven't all been a waste of time.'

She almost laughs too. 'I'll let you know how my dates go. I'm seeing an art director, an orthoptist, and a company president next week.' There's a pause for breath. 'All friends of friends, all pre-approved, all scorching, straight, available and loaded.'

'Let's hope they like Snow Patrol.' It's as if the last five minutes never happened.

'I'll settle for them sitting through Puccini's La Bohème.'

This is the point when I give up all hope. 'I'll report back when the garden guys come. Good luck with your week.'

'Back at ya, as they say here.' Her smile passes straight into her voice. There's a moment when I think she's ended the call, then she starts again. 'Thank you, Betsy.'

This time she does go, and I wipe my forehead with my apron and turn to Miles. 'That was Scarlett, calling about gardeners.'

Miles pulls down the corners of his mouth. 'And sleeping her way around New York?' He gives a shrug. 'I'm sorry. I couldn't help overhearing. I wanted to tell you I had.'

I hold out my hands. 'She's a free agent. All we can do is hope she finds her happy place before she self-destructs.'

He frowns. 'Does Scarlett know about the shop?'

'Not yet.' I haven't found the courage to tell her. 'With everything going on over there, it hasn't come up.' I may as well go for it. 'She doesn't know about Fudge yet either.'

'I'll talk to Tate.' He raises one eyebrow. 'Back to the loud music?'

I nod. 'Knock me out, Miles.'

38

The garden at Boathouse Cottage, St Aidan
Chestnuts and five-star reviews
Tuesday

On Tuesday evening when Miles, Fudge and I draw up outside Boathouse Cottage after we've left the shop, there's a snazzy double-cab pickup filling the parking space.

Miles pulls in behind it on the lane. 'I'm sure Ground Force St Aidan won't mind if we double park.'

As we let ourselves in through the open garden gate I'm in awe that they're here at all. 'Scarlett's personal life may be in pieces, but she still has superpowers when it comes to getting workmen to turn up.'

Miles gives me one of his long slow glances. 'It's not a superpower, Bets. It's because she scares the bejesus out of everyone.' He leans his shoulder up against the wall. 'All Tate's friends are the same. We're terrified of her.'

When I first arrived, I imagined Miles rode roughshod over

everybody, but as I spend more time with him and the layers are getting peeled back, he's less like that than I thought. Then it hits me. That opinion didn't come out of nowhere.

'Like I said before, you didn't seem to have any trouble going against what Scarlett asked you to do at the wedding.'

He blows out his cheeks. 'And as I explained, that was due to very extreme circumstances which I'm afraid I can't talk about, and it was only the once.'

'Thanks for that very illuminating explanation.'

He gives me another sideways glance. 'You know Scarlett better than anyone – have you ever stood up to her?'

I take a second to consider. 'I'm usually steamrollered before I have time to argue.'

He nods. 'That's her tactic. Given how she is, it must have taken a lot of courage for Tate to do what he's done.'

I'm pondering. 'I assumed that as a couple they took turns to decide, with Tate taking the lead with the design stuff. But if Scarlett is as scary as you say, that could explain why Tate wanted to leave.'

Maybe falling for someone else was his only means of getting away. As I saw for myself last Saturday, Scarlett simply closes down other people's ideas and carries on with her own. I've always thought she was like that with me because I was her younger sister, so it's a surprise to find she's like that with other people too. The trouble is, there's a fine line between being so brilliant that everyone agrees with you, and being an absolute pain in the butt. And if you do end up on the wrong side of that line, then it's also very hard for people to let you know.

There's a noise from higher up the garden, and I look up to

see four guys in Ground Force vests carrying various machines across the sun lounger terrace.

One of them gives a wave. 'We're just finishing.'

I call up to them. 'Scarlett will appreciate that you came so fast. The place looks immaculate.'

They spring down the steps, and a second later, Zofia comes in through the gate too.

She gives me a nudge. 'Even though I see them every day, I never tire of work boots and tanned calves.'

I shake my head at Miles. 'Here's me thinking she'd be all about the gilets and the arm definition.'

The first guy grins at me. 'I'm Zach, working with Jake, Mark and Tom. If you had another three loungers we'd have stayed on and topped up our tans.'

Zofia laughs. 'I hope you gave the outdoor shower a good going over.'

Jake joins in. 'We've cleaned and oiled the furniture, washed the gravel and hard surfaces, and got every piece of hay off the pebbles.' He looks over at Pumpkin who is grazing in the far corner of the field. 'When we put gravel in, we weren't expecting a pony.'

Zach has sun-streaked blond hair and a warm smile. He winks at me, then smiles a bit more. 'I dropped the hay off as the pony got here. Let me know when you need more.'

Jake laughs. 'When Zach's not doing his landscape work, he moonlights as a farmer.'

I smile at Zach. 'Small bales are hard to find, there's a big place in my heart for any farmer who makes them.'

When Zach's eyes lock with mine again, they're the colour of the sea. 'You're so hidden away along here. I'm guessing that's why we don't see you in town?' He carries on. 'If you fancy getting out, there's a fund-raiser disco at the Surf Shack most weekends, a different good cause every time. We already know you dance.'

I'm getting more used to this now. 'Don't tell me – you've seen me out walking with Pumpkin?'

His smile widens. 'Most of the gardens we work in have great views of the beach.'

Miles gives a cough. 'Betsy is busy on Saturdays.'

I roll my eyes at him. 'You said unless I had a better offer, Miles.'

'Great.' From his tone it obviously isn't. 'In that case, thanks for the tidying, guys, we'll see you at the Surf Shack.'

We watch as they make their way out of the gate, and I smile at Zofia.

'They were nice.'

Miles sends me a look. 'If it doesn't bother you that Zach has a different woman in his ute most days of the week, he's fine. For anyone wanting to improve on their negative dating history, he's not ideal.'

I don't actually believe what I'm hearing. Just as I decide the man might not be as bad as I thought, he wades in and throws the clock back a hundred years. 'Thanks for that, Miles. Now you've given us that hugely positive input, you might need to move your car.'

'Shit, I do!'

As he runs off I shake my head at Zofia. 'What the hell was that about?'

She's laughing as if she's heard a very funny private joke. 'I think that was our Miles being super-protective of someone he cares about very much.' She frowns. 'Listen to their car horns, those men are marking their territory.'

I think for a second and then it hits me. 'No, Zofia, you came in last so you've blocked all of them in.'

'So I have. It will do them good to wait for once.' She laughs even harder. 'I'm only here for a quick word with Miles, so I'll see you in the morning.' She turns as she reaches the gate. 'You've got your door key?'

Now it's my turn to smile. 'Yes, thanks, I have.' I also left the French windows off the latch, as a second line of defence.

As she disappears back onto the lane it's not lost on me. Since I left home at eighteen I've locked myself out of my room several times a week and more. Landing in Miles's bedroom was hideous, but since that awful day I haven't locked myself out once. If it's been enough to shock me into looking after my own key, it was worth the pain.

39

Boathouse Cottage, St Aidan
Last in, first out
Friday

Whatever I thought of Scarlett's dates, I've been holding my breath all week to find out how she got on. But this is Scarlett, not me; two dates down and there aren't any horror stories unless you count nights at the opera, which I probably do. There aren't any success stories either. She's now seamlessly added a music producer, a hedge fund manager and a real estate professional to her list of upcoming meet-ups, so I'm assuming her search is still live rather than on hold because she's met someone she wants to get to know better.

Back in St Aidan, since Saturday there has been no more mention of the chewed shoes, so all the way to Friday I assume Miles has forgotten about them. But this morning when I arrive back in the kitchen after my walk with Fudge and Pumpkin, I'm met by the familiar scent of hot pastry and vanilla, and the island unit is covered in cooling trays stacked high with buns.

As Miles usually does his baking at the shop, I assume today's change in routine must be because he has to go out on some of his other business, and as he packs the buns into boxes and gives me a lift into town, he doesn't tell me anything different.

It's only when we get to the shop to find the lights already on and Zofia with a cup of fruit tea in her hand that I start to question.

'Zofia, you've already restocked the plant tables and now you're dusting the shelves you dusted yesterday afternoon?'

As Zofia nods at me her eyes are shining. 'If you want a job done well, ask a busy person.'

Miles is piling buns under glass domes at the speed of light, then he takes the empty boxes to the kitchen, comes back through and turns to me. 'Right, Zofia's here for the day. Are you ready to go, Betsy Eliza?'

I'm sinking my teeth into a raspberry bun I've just grabbed. 'Me? Go where?'

He's already by the door. 'We're calling on your favourite jam seller first, and then there's a makers' market over in Stoneybridge to check out.'

I hold up my bun. 'Plain ones of these would work really well with baby pots of jam.'

He looks at me. 'Great idea, we'll try that tomorrow. What about this morning? You won't grow your business sitting in the shop.'

My feet feel like they're welded to the floor. 'If I'd known I was going out…'

He laughs. 'You'd have taken all morning to get ready?' His smile widens. 'What you're wearing today looks great. I like it when I see flashes of your shorts.'

It's bad luck all three dresses have splits up the front, but what I'm fighting most is the voice in my head that's telling me I want to look amazing, because I really don't.

Miles senses my hesitation. 'I can take you back if you'd like to change?'

I blow out a breath. 'I'll manage without my fairy wings, just for today.'

Zofia puts her arm around me. 'You look lovely, same as always.'

'Fudge!' I'm still holding on to the lead and I give a whistle. 'He *is* coming too?'

If this is about Miles saying sorry for the shoes Fudge ruined, it makes it less of a thing if he's with us. Better still, keeping to dog-friendly areas means we'll avoid going anywhere too starchy.

I catch Miles's nod of agreement and wave my bun at him. 'If we're out over lunchtime you do know I don't do restaurants, or meat, or rapeseed oil...'

He's looking completely unruffled. 'All your restrictions, likes and dislikes are fully logged in the system. If in doubt, just say "no".'

When it's so insignificant, I've no idea why my tummy is whirling.

I turn to Zofia. 'You're sure you'll be okay?'

She's already pushing her cordless vacuum towards the trail of crumbs I've dropped. 'Couldn't be better. Have a good time, I'll see you tomorrow.'

It's a lot later when the significance of that comment sinks in.

I pass Fudge's lead to Miles and pick up my rucksack and my vintage velvet jacket. 'Shall we go?'

40

The Market Place, Stoneybridge
Winding roads and signature dishes
Friday

'So what do you think?'

It's two hours later, I'm standing at the edge of the marketplace in Stoneybridge, a town forty minutes down the coast from St Aidan, and I have no idea what I'm supposed to be reacting to.

Our first stop on today's excursion was at the garden-gate jam shop featured on my postcard, where Miles had arranged for us to meet the maker, Maddie, in her own country cottage kitchen. Then we sat in the garden in the shade of her apple tree and while the humans tucked into fat, light, homemade scones and strawberry conserve Fudge sniffed in the hedge for invisible rabbits. By the time we left an hour later Maddie had agreed to supply her jams to the shop at a very fair price.

With that in the bag Miles carried on driving along the coast until he finally wound his way down from the hills and along the side of an estuary dotted with sailing boats towards the town of Stoneybridge which spreads up across the hills either side of the river. We parked then made our way through some municipal gardens, past some tall harbourside houses, and ended up in a bustling market square surrounded by buildings on three sides and the estuary road on the other, which is where we are now.

I hitch up my shoulder bag, look across at the hillside beyond the river and try to give Miles a proper answer. 'I love the houses nestled among the trees and the lines of pink and yellow cottages. It's exciting that there's a car ferry to cross the river but the queue looks quite long.'

Miles blinks. 'All very true, but I meant what's in front of us not behind us.'

I turn towards the buildings. 'Which bit am I looking at?'

'All of it.' He's looking at me not the buildings. 'The excellent central position, the town with thousands of visitors every week, the idyllic location.'

I might as well tell it how it is. 'It's funny. When we look at the same thing, I react like a tourist and you sound like you're addressing the directors.'

'I often have been.' He pulls a face. 'Our different backgrounds mean we bring different things to the table. That's why we make a great team.'

I choke into my hand. 'And probably why we argue nonstop.'

He gives a shamefaced shrug. 'Putting my business hat back on again...'

I grin at him and fake a yawn. 'Yes?'

'The shop in front of us has been vacant since last year. It's ours for the rest of the season if we want to take it.'

It comes out so fast I'm still trying to catch up. 'Why would *we* want it?'

'As you were the one who came up with the "pop-up" idea to begin with, I assumed *you'd* tell *me*.' Miles's voice is light and airy. 'It might be fun to see if Betsy & Milo is only a thing in St Aidan, or if works somewhere else, too.'

I want to scream 'noooooooo', but for a second I hold it in. 'Okay. So what happened to "small is beautiful"?'

Miles is smiling. 'Two shops isn't big, and there's no huge commitment; we'd be in and out by October.'

I'm staring at him. 'You're making this up as you go along again?'

He laughs. 'You're the one who said to wing it. We're just flying a little further here.' He's pulled a key from his jacket pocket, and he's unlocking the door. 'If you'd like to take a look, it's open?'

My feet are walking with no input from me, and the space I'm looking around is less scary than it could be. 'It's a lot smaller than the Net Loft, there's no kitchen, but the shelves are already there, and there are even some for cards. If we brought in hat stands and simple tables, we'd get the same feel.' My surge of enthusiasm dips. 'We can't be in two places at once, who would serve?'

'Zofia has friends here. We've already checked – they'd be willing to share the hours between them for the summer.' The way he's standing, he's looking like he already owns the place. 'A quick coat of paint, some of Edie's best *Betsy & Milo* signs, a few carefully selected items and a postcard order – it'll be ready to go in no time.'

I'm not just out of my depth here, I feel like I'm being carried out to sea. Miles has no idea about my limitations. People like him never do. I'm not ashamed of being different, but I need to remind him before it's too late.

I look him straight in the eye. 'Miles. I'm not like you. I don't have money to spare or financial backers. When I barely know where my next coffee is coming from, I can't take on another shop. I simply can't afford this.'

He tilts his head on one side. 'I'd put up the money. Your input would be entirely limited to styling and deciding what we sold.' He's watching my reaction. 'And wherever it goes, we'd be equal partners at the end.'

I shake my head. 'I'm still looking for the catch.'

He shrugs. 'There isn't one. You're the one who created Betsy & Milo. I've done enough start-ups to sense it has lift. It doesn't happen very often, but when it does it makes sense to push it as far as you can as fast as you can.'

'You're happy to do that?'

He smiles. 'I'm ready to give it a go. Ready enough to have lined up two more empty places further around the coast too.'

My mouth drops open. '*Four shops* – all temporary, all with nothing in?'

He laughs. 'That's the bit that makes them special. It's very quirky but very now.'

I'm closing my eyes. 'Okay, still talking hypothetically – tell me how it's going to work.'

He's still smiling. 'Much as it is now, except we have reliable people to look after the Net Loft while we source the stock, deliver it and set it out in the new premises. We'd make sure you still did your beach sales with Pumpkin.' He's watching me closely. 'It would mean a couple of months of hard work and long hours, but we get to do the fun bits. And if that's not enough of an incentive, you'd be sure to find opportunities for new pieces for Fenna along the way.'

I'm being as grounded as I can be in the face of something that feels improbable. 'It's only for a few weeks, but...'

Miles's hand drops onto my shoulder. 'You don't have to decide now. Wait until you've seen more.'

I stare around and my heart is faltering. 'There's an awful lot of shelving to fill.' Last time the shop was a series of accidents. This time I'm walking into it with my eyes wide open.

Miles laughs. 'That's the beauty of Betsy & Milo, a lot of those shelves will be bare.' His arm is guiding me towards the door. 'Let's go and see what we can find on the market.'

It's not lost on me. I walked into here as myself, and even though it's still hanging, I'm walking out as someone else entirely. Not only that. The first shop began with me trying to get some distance from Miles and ended up with me spending more time with him than ever. What he's suggesting here would take that to another level.

And I'm not sure I can handle that.

41

The Market Place, Stoneybridge
Ice cream vans and pushy parents
Friday

The afternoon sun is so warm that I'm happy to linger in the shade of the green and white striped awnings as we make our way around the market stalls. It's no surprise to find that Miles and I approach browsing in the same way we do the rest of our lives – from opposite directions.

Three moments after arriving he says, 'I'll make sure we don't miss anything', then races off and covers the whole area line by line, stopping in front of each stall for two seconds.

I know this because I pause my wandering from one bright object to the next to see what he's doing. I murmur to Fudge, 'For your dad this is a military operation at a million miles an hour.'

By the time he comes back from his whole market tour, I'm deep in concentration at my fifth stall.

He comes up behind me. 'How can you be so haphazard, Eliza B? You're like a molecule in a gas making random collisions.'

I hide my laugh in my fist. 'I've been watching you, too. Have you taken photos and picked up calling cards from them all?'

'Back to the drawing board.' He rushes off again.

By the time he comes back the next time, I've found six definite choices and three possibles and had chats with the makers of all of them.

He sidles up to the stall Fudge and I are leaving. 'Any immediate reactions?'

I smile. 'Fudge has had so many treats he's not going to want his tea. And for now I'm not looking at lampshades, art prints, clothes or cakes, and I'm ignoring anything truly pricey like silver jewellery and leather bags.'

He frowns. 'That rules out most stalls.'

'You think?' I laugh. 'There are beautiful miniature mermaids made from reclaimed fabrics, some coloured bowls, all the same shape but with different painted designs, some hand-printed coasters, two lots of soaps, and some lovely books that would be perfect for journalling or scrapbooking. Oh, and a knitter, and some bright wooden bead jewellery.'

His eyes blur. 'This is why you're buying and I'm backing.' When he raises his eyebrows, I know there's something good coming. 'I found a hand-made ice cream stall. Would you like one?'

I grin. 'I saw that too, I couldn't decide between elderflower and gooseberry, or rhubarb and custard.'

He looks down at me. 'Have a scoop of each. With a white chocolate flake?'

I try not to drool. 'I'll be over there by the stripy mugs.'

I call Fudge, who follows me, and then goes straight in to greet the mug seller.

I'm taking my time, looking along the stall, taking photos of my favourite mugs, when there's a sharp tug on the lead.

'Fudge, don't pull, or I'll drop things!' There's another tug and I warn him again, this time louder. 'Fudge!'

'*Fudge?*' It's like an echo behind me.

As I turn there's enough time to see a dark-haired woman with a well-cut bob standing with a handsome grey-haired man. Then Fudge throws himself at them, bouncing on the spot on his hind legs, leaping up to lick the woman's face until eventually she catches his front paws in her arms.

I'm still hanging on to his lead but as I've completely lost Fudge's attention I have to say something. 'I take it you two know each other?'

The woman's got crinkles at the corners of her eyes when she smiles. 'We do. I'm Jackie, Fudge's mum. I'm also Miles's mum. And this is my friend Harry.'

She smiles up at the guy, then she looks back at me. 'You're the girl with the auburn hair and the horse who came to stay with Miles. I've often seen you from a distance.'

There's a cough behind me and Miles arrives at my side. 'Betty is a woman, and Pumpkin is a pony. Apart from that you're on the nail, Mother.'

I smile and will my hair to be less tangled. 'Miles is staying with me, not the other way round. For the record. Scarlett is the boss.' If there's a chance to get this story straight around the village, I may as well take it.

Jackie beams. 'I'm pleased we've got that sorted out. It's very kind of you to have Miles to stay, and we very much appreciate you taking Fudge, too.' She gives Harry a nudge. 'Don't we, Harry?'

Miles hands me my ice cream and turns to his mum. 'I didn't expect to see you two here?'

Jackie has the same long legs as Miles and the creases in her chinos are a lot like his too. 'You know us – another day, another market. It makes a change from garden centres.' She turns to me. 'We didn't expect to see you here either. Have you managed to leave the shop? You do know he's banned us, but if you ever need a hand, you only have to say.'

Miles steps in. 'Zofia is there today.'

His mum looks at me. 'Miles's first curly croissants were a lot like cricket balls, but all our friends buy them and they're very impressed.'

I laugh. 'The ones he bakes now are surprisingly delicious.' My heart goes out to her for getting so left out. 'I don't want to cause a family rift, but it's a shame not to see the shop when it's only going to be there a few weeks. You're welcome to pop in any time when I'm there, Jackie.'

Miles takes the dog lead from me and hands me his ice cream to hold instead. 'I'll take Fudge back before Harry starts sneezing, and we'll let you get on with your day.'

As a drip runs down the side of my cone I catch it with my tongue. 'The ice cream is yummy, if you're thinking of having one.'

A second later Fudge is on the ground again. Jackie stoops to get a last goodbye lick on her nose, then she links arms with Harry and they wander off.

Miles takes his cone back from me. 'Shall we find somewhere to sit and eat these before they melt to nothing?'

We head to the first bench we find on the edge of the gardens, sit with a decent distance between us with Fudge at our feet, and deal with our collapsing ice creams.

When I get over how delicious it is to taste the tang of rhubarb against the sweet vanilla of ice-cold custard, I go in for the biggie.

'Lovely to meet your mum at last. Her boyfriend with allergies is why Fudge is with us?'

'Correct.' Miles studies his apple pie sorbet. 'It's quite a new relationship and I wanted to give it the best chance to work, which is why I've given them space. When I came here two years ago it was because she'd just lost my stepdad.'

I mull this over for a few licks before I reply. 'Considering how kind of you that was, it's a bit harsh banning her from the shop.'

Miles takes a bite of his sugar cone and crunches it. 'Don't think it's because I don't love her. It's *because* we're such good friends that I'm able to do it.' He turns to me. 'If we let Mum in once, she won't ever leave. Same with the cottage. I didn't want to lay that on you before you'd got established.'

I'm hiding my surprise. 'How bad can it be?'

He gives a half shake of his head. 'She and her friends are all the same. They haven't slowed down to retirement speed yet. They're traipsing round Cornwall, bored out of their skulls because they've got too much time on their hands. If she came to the shop to help, she'd probably bring half of the over-sixties with her and stay until Christmas. But she's got to sort that out for herself – I came to support her. I'm not here to babysit her. She's too young to live vicariously through me. She has to make her own life.'

'I imagined you only worked or watched box sets?'

He rolls his eyes. 'You know what I mean.'

I'm pushing the gooseberry ice further down into the cone with every lick. 'It's nice that you're close enough to take a realistic view of each other.' I think of what he's sacrificed. 'It's also very good of you to have put your own life on hold to come to be with your mum.'

He sighs. 'It was less of a sacrifice than you'd think. A bungalow on a cul-de-sac miles away from anywhere gave me the level of invisibility I needed at the time.'

'Those bumps in the road you're always banging on about?'

'That's the one.' He blows out his cheeks. 'My mum and I have always been close because my dad walked out when I was nine, and we had a few tough years on our own.'

I blow out a breath. 'My dad left us, too, but from what my mum said things got easier once he had.'

He shrugs. 'My mum was better off too. But she had cancer, and I had to look after her because there wasn't anyone else.'

My heart goes out to him when I think of how young he was. 'That was when you missed school?'

He sighs again. 'I was never a big fan. It was fine in the end, because my mum pulled through, and after that nothing else really mattered, but I didn't ever properly go back.' He pulls a face. 'I'd do a few days here and there, to keep them off my back. Not enough to pass any exams, but I learned different things –

skills for life, the importance of money, how to seize an opportunity.'

I smile. 'How to tie a ponytail?'

He nods. 'At sixteen I went to sweep up in my mum's friend's hair salon, and I didn't look back. You'd be amazed at the contacts I built up shampooing hair. By that time my mum had met someone else. Eventually they moved down here together, then I came down to be with her when he died.'

'She's had a rough time. But at least you still have each other.'

Miles looks at the end of his cornet. 'I know I'm lucky. That's why I always try to put her first. But she's very resilient. She almost lost her life all those years ago. Since then she sees it as her duty to make the most of every day. She and Harry met at the Over-sixties. Those half price lunches at the Yellow Canary are like Tinder on rocket fuel. They fell for each other pretty quickly.'

I push the last of the cone into my mouth and lick my finger ends. 'I admire anyone who makes a go of a relationship, regardless of how it happens.'

It's not lost on me how strange life is. If we hadn't bumped into Jackie and Harry none of this would have come up. But now it has I'm leaving this bench with a very different impression of Miles than the one I had when I sat down. Remembering the old saying that men are who their mothers made them, meeting the parent, even for a few minutes, gives a great insight. But I also need to remember that this meeting was accidental.

Miles has taken every precaution to keep his mum away from me, and the other way around, too. I take it he'd rather I was still that auburn girl glimpsed in the distance. And he'd certainly rather have kept his past under wraps.

'You're wondering why I've kept all this to myself?'

I laugh. 'You read minds *and* make croissants?' I sigh. 'It feels a teensy bit secretive. I mean, within days of me arriving everyone knew where I lived and what I had for breakfast, but even now no one seems to know you.'

'Pumpkin's orange, you stand out.' He blows out a breath. 'No, you're right. Trying not to sound even more weird, but I made a permanent move here from Manchester because I had a stalker.'

My eyes open wide. 'What – the obsessive-who-pursues-you-relentlessly sort?'

He nods. 'That's the one.'

I gasp. 'That's not a bump in the road. That's a mountain.'

He pulls a face. 'St Aidan was the ideal place to hide away, but the drawback was the locals know everything about everything.'

I'm with him on that. 'Every seagull that squawks, every message in the sand.'

He laughs. 'For the first few months I went into stealth mode, because it was the only way, but I caught the habit.' His lips twist into a grin. 'When my problem eased, it became a bit of a challenge to see how long I could stay under the radar.'

I grin at him. 'If you went to the over-sixties baking evening and you've been spotted drinking in the Yellow Canary, I guess your incognito days are over.'

He shakes his head. 'It was a lucky break for both of us I went out to that.' Miles is chewing the last of his ice cream, rubbing his hands together, and standing up.

I stand up too. 'So what's next?'

He narrows his eyes. 'We could walk past your favourite stalls, and then we can head down the coast again.'

I smile. 'Back to St Aidan?'

He looks at his watch, then back at me. 'It's barely afternoon, Betsy Bets. I've got two more shops to show you, then I'll take you somewhere to help you make up your mind.' He cocks his head. 'If that's okay with you?'

'Fine.' I say it like it means nothing at all, but I'm not telling the truth.

None of this is okay. The whole day has felt as if I were walking over tectonic plates that are shifting underneath my feet as I move. Every new step feels like it's taking me further away from the person I am, from the things I know. It's as if I'm crossing a metaphorical bridge and that when I get to the other side there will be no going back.

None of this is comfortable, none of it is what I'd have chosen even this morning, but I'm still here. I can stop it at any moment. I can walk away. But for some reason I'm not. It's terrifying, and it's entirely not me. But I'm here, and a tiny voice inside me is telling me I'm going to follow this all the way to the end. Wherever that might be.

And even stranger still – as we walk back towards the market, it feels like I'm walking with a friend not an enemy.

42

The Walled Garden, Abbots Sands
Life on Mars
Friday

'Four shops would mean industrial quantities of pastries, Miles. How would you handle all that baking?'

It's six on Friday evening, the sun has begun to lose its heat, and we're in a walled garden in a tiny hamlet a couple of miles inland from the village where we saw the last available shop, spreading out travelling rugs on the neatly cut grass square at the centre of an outdoor wildflower meadow restaurant, where Miles has said we'll be the only diners.

My question isn't the kind that's waiting for an answer. It's designed more as a sign off, a full stop to finish the day, to say it's been lovely to dream, but as what he's suggesting is actually not feasible, let's leave it there.

The stress of tearing from town to town with Miles, visiting three potential shops and a market was pushed up a notch when it was all done with the big unanswered question hanging in the air between us – am I about to get on board for the ride of my life, or am I going to follow every natural instinct in my body and run as fast as I can in the opposite direction? The surer he became that he was winning his argument, the more I felt like I had a helicopter in my chest that was about to lift off. Add to that the growing warmth between us now he's opening up and sharing, there's no wonder I'm dazed.

Miles had every reason to feel proud of what he'd lined up. For the second shop he'd used his fashion industry contacts to pull out the most unbelievable newly vacant place on Falmouth High Street. As we left the final shop in Abbots Sands, which was as bijou and hidden away as the second was impressive and out there, my insides felt like a tightly stretched rubber band.

If we'd spent the afternoon at Boathouse Cottage and come straight to the walled garden from there, we would only be missing the rush of the waves. But after the throb of the traffic in Falmouth, this meadow with the swish of the long grass against a backdrop of birdsong feels like an idyll. When the owner comes out and brings us a large picnic tray, some flutes, and two bottles of fizz each in their own ice bucket, I lie on my back, watch the cotton-white twists of the clouds against the deep blue beyond, and decide I've landed in heaven.

I talk to the sky as much as to Miles. 'Are champagne buckets like buses? I've barely met one in my life, and now two come together!'

Miles laughs. 'One is Prosecco, the other is zero alcohol for drivers.'

I push myself up, take the full flute he passes me, and enjoy the prick of bubbles on my nose as I sip. Then, as the feel-good wave of the alcohol seeps all the way to my toes, I help myself to a sandwich.

I look more closely at the wicker platter beside me. 'Avocado toasties, teensy tomatoes and mint salad, apricots with dill seed, hummus, coriander and carrot wraps, peach and mozzarella with croutons, sourdough bread, cheese pastry triangles, courgette and viola flowers! It's literally like eating my magazine pieces.'

I take another swig of bubbly. 'I'm sorry, Fudge, but if this is the treat, I may ask you to eat my shoes more often.'

Miles laughs. 'This isn't only about that. I wanted to bring you to a place where you'd have space to reflect.'

I'm biting into a gruyere twist that's so delectable I take another straight away, then I mumble through the crumbs, 'Before I think, you have to answer my question. You can't duck the production issue when the pastries are why people come into the shops to start with.'

He's stretched out on his side with his chin propped up by his elbow, smiling the kind of slow smile that makes my insides smoulder. 'You're the one with all the good suggestions, B B. Having had all day to ponder, I assumed you'd have worked out an answer to this by now.'

I take a slice of peach and a cube of roasted halloumi. 'You agree you can't make them all?'

'Not unless I work day and night.'

I have no idea why he thinks I'm going to give him his answer when I know next to no one, and then I have a thought. The more I think of it, the more it makes me smile.

I start with the disclaimer. 'You're not going to like this, but...'

'What?'

I smile more. 'We've already had an offer of help today.'

Miles looks horror-struck. 'Not my mum!'

'There's no one better than family.' I keep my eyes on his face. 'You said yourself she has spare capacity and excess energy. If we brought in some of her friends to make a team, they could cover for each other and help with large capacity for busy days. If we played our cards right, they might bake first thing, then tie in deliveries with their usual market and garden centre visits.'

He's looking doubtful. 'I'm not sure it's fair to ask old people.'

I let out a cry. 'They're not old, Miles! They're young and active, a pool of willing, untapped labour, and it would enrich their lives if we involved them.'

He blows out his cheeks. 'This is still hypothetical, but talk me through it.'

I grin. 'We'll invite any who are interested to the cottage tomorrow night and you can show them the techniques at the same time as you teach me. You may well find they're really good bakers already, a lot of their generation are.'

He frowns. 'I thought you wanted to go dancing at the Surf Shack?'

I wave that away. 'This is way more important than a disco – hypothetically obviously.'

Miles rolls his eyes. 'Knowing what the over-sixties social calendar is like, they'll probably be busy.'

I'm very confident. 'Your mum would drop everything for this. I *know* she would.'

'We'll revisit this once you've decided.' He stares at his sandwich for a long time, then he looks at me again. 'My mum and Harry are the reason I'm at the cottage. So you know.'

I'm blinking at him. 'But I thought...?' Now I come to think of it, this is another of Miles's explanations that has never been clear.

He pulls a face. 'Things moved very fast for them when they met. The last thing I wanted to do was to get in the way, but as it was so new I also wanted to stay around in case there were pieces to pick up.'

I'm amused and incredulous. 'You took refuge at the cottage so you didn't have to play gooseberry with your mum and her new boyfriend?'

He closes his eyes. 'Tate found it hilarious too, but thankfully he took pity on me. They never usually let people stay unless they're there.'

I'm nodding. 'I know, Miles. You don't have to tell me that.'

He shakes his head. 'I thought it might fizzle, and I'd be back at Mum's within the week, but it seems to be going well. Then, once Tate and Scarlett started World War 3 Tate was anxious for me to stay on anyway.'

I'm puzzled. 'So why are you telling me this now?'

He raises his eyebrows. 'In the interests of openness and honesty, in case you decide to take the business further.' He shrugs. 'With my last start-up I saw a gap in the market, and my business partner and I saw we could fill it. After that it all happened very quickly.'

I'm remembering what Scarlett told me. 'Was that the one you sold?'

He hesitates. 'I still have an interest in Dedication, but I work from here not Manchester. Betsy & Milo couldn't be more different, but it has a similar buzz. That same potential to go exponential.'

I watch the bubbles rising in my glass. 'As you're the one who hangs out in boardrooms, I'll take your word on that.'

He's looking at me very intensely. 'I know it's all accidental, but we can't ignore it. Anything this exceptional, we have to push it to see where it goes.'

I pull a face. 'Like I said last time, you're the expert.'

His face softens. 'If we were walking on the beach and found a dinosaur's egg hatching, we wouldn't walk past and leave it. We'd take that baby dinosaur, and no matter how strange and unexpected it was, we'd care for it and help it grow.'

I'm right there with him. 'And what would we do when it got bigger?' I grin at him. 'You're so commercial, you'd sell it, wouldn't you?'

He looks like he's biting back his smile. 'That might be one option, but we'd look at rehoming first.'

I'm feeling anxious. 'Most rescues don't take dangerous breeds. I'm not sure I'd want it to live in captivity – definitely not in a cage.'

He's shaking his head. 'It's not real, Betsy! It was an analogy to explain why we should carry on.'

'It also highlights how differently we approach everything in life.' I give him time to take that in, then carry on. 'Anyway, dinosaurs are huge. You really think Betsy & Milo will grow *that* gigantic?'

His smile breaks free. 'I can't make promises, but if we walk past that egg without stopping, we'll never know.' He laughs. 'As for our differences, I don't see that as a negative. This is yours as much as mine – I wouldn't be here if it weren't for you.'

What a difference a day makes.

I lean forward and let him fill up my glass again. Then I sit back and look at him again too. The man I'm seeing here is generous and honest, funny and sensitive, open and vulnerable. So what the hell happened?

I'm only halfway down the bottle so it can't all be down to the Prosecco goggles. It's like the woman who's walked through today all the way to the exclusive venue and the fancy sandwiches has lost the ability to think clearly. If that's what swanning around in a flash car pretending to hang with the rich kids does, I can't wait to get back to being the me I used to be.

One more thing. In my current state, if I were vertical rather than lounging, I might well be tempted to launch myself. Fully, unequivocally and without holding back. Which has to be the final proof that I have totally lost it, when that's everything I've vowed I'd never do again.

I jump when Miles's hand lands on my arm.

He looks concerned. 'Are you okay? You're not cold?'

I suppress my shiver and smile. 'Sorry. What were you saying?'

He laughs. 'So much for my big speech. I was about to say, as what we've found is so special, shall we go for it?'

'Just to check – we're talking about a handful of shops here? To the end of the summer.' No idea why I need to verify.

The corners of his eyes crinkle when he smiles. 'That's the one, Betsy Bets. Maybe a van or two too, for roving sales. Are we in?'

This is the first I've heard about vehicles. That's the thing about Miles. However far you go, he's always one step further.

I open my mouth to say yes, but all that comes out is a squeak.

I gulp down my fizz and slam my hand down on the blanket. 'Rugs. We must have rugs. *In all our shops*. How did we overlook *them*? Everyone needs a picnic blanket.'

As I look at Miles his eyes are fixed on me. 'Nice one, Betty B. *Love you to the beach and back?*'

As if I'd let him have the last word. I open my mouth and begin, '*Life is better in flipflop...*'

But before I can finish his face is there in front of me, so close I can see the individual lashes on his eyelids. For a second it's as if the whole world stops and as I freeze in mid-air all I want to do is to slide my fingers around his head, pull him towards me and kiss the bejesus out of him.

Then, like a bolt out of nowhere, a flash of lucidity saves me. What the hell am I thinking? We're working together, we're house mates, I'm incapable of relationships, I had a dreadful experience with my last man, his mum is going to be baking with us in our kitchen. I come to my senses and the world starts turning again. I dive sideways into my rucksack, pull out a mirror and my barely-there lippy and start to put it on.

Fancying the arse off Miles Appleton has always been a mistake. I've always known it was the kind of hopeless mission that was doomed from inception for all the reasons. If I saw a glimmer of something in his eyes just now to suggest anything to the contrary, it was without a doubt gratitude that I'm doing what he wants with this business. If I'm moving into a whole new unfamiliar territory I need to keep my wits about me, especially when it comes to misreading signals – I need to quit while I'm ahead, starting with the unrequited lust.

It's also ridiculous that my tummy is filled with a fluttering sensation. If this is what dill seeds do, I must remember to avoid them in future.

I swallow hard, and smile back at Miles. 'The picnic has been amazing, thank you for bringing me.'

His eyes narrow. 'We're not finished yet. Are you ready to move to the sweets?'

I take a deep breath. 'Before we do, there's one more thing to clear up. Now you've got your own way with shops, can I take it that I get mine with the baking team?'

Miles looks at me like I'm bananas. 'You know the landlord of the Yellow Canary has a top-flight Range Rover entirely funded by the over-sixties?'

'What's that got to do with anything?'

Miles winces. 'My mum and her friends aren't as sweet as you think. Those market trips are where they nurse their hangovers because they drink for England, and party for the world. But if you're up for a wild night tomorrow, we'll certainly have that try-out, and let you see for yourself why it can't possibly work.'

'Great.'

He pulls a face. 'I just hope you know what you're letting yourself in for.'

I laugh. 'Bring it on.'

Obviously I'm bluffing.

43

Boathouse Cottage, St Aidan
Scaling up and winding down
Saturday evening

If someone had told me seven weeks ago that I'd be hosting an evening for twelve in Scarlett's kitchen, I wouldn't have believed them either, but it's all because I'm proving my point with Miles. When we're fighting, I take risks that I'd never have dreamed of doing otherwise. Worst of all, what happens with tonight's baking evening proves Miles right before we even begin. I'm thinking of a quiet night in for six, and within seconds of me mentioning it to his mum and her friends it's doubled in size. I've never seen a clearer sign of impending disaster.

It began with Miles's mum who added in Harry, then grew to include Martin and Carol too. Then Malcolm, and Edie's Aunty Jo jumped in, and Angela and Barry. Once it was obvious it was getting party-sized, Zofia wouldn't think of staying away and brought Aleksy too. I only managed a size limit because of the seating plan. If the island had been bigger, we'd have had every pensioner in town.

Once I'd committed, there was no point panicking. I took inspiration from last night's dining out and threw together some platters of colourful chopped vegetables and dips to nibble in the gaps between rolling sessions. Miles made bite-sized versions of his savoury croissant curls when he'd finished his massive Saturday shop bake, and everyone came with the promise of a box of boathouse buns they'd baked, to take away.

Miles maintains one of the major problems is what he refers to as his mum's friends' 'hollow legs', so he called in Huntley and Handsome wine merchants. When I saw the delivery more than filled one of the mud room fridges with beers and bottles of pink fizz I was glad Miles was the one covering the bill.

There was so little time between closing the shop and the guests arriving, I only had a second to slip on a new frock or two before we were popping the corks and handing out the Betsy & Milo aprons along with the drinks. Zofia threw herself into organising an over-sixties playlist and I can already hear Ed Sheeran singing about kissing under the light of a thousand stars.

Miles managed a dash to Falmouth to stock up on rolling pins, knives and extra baking trays, and while the more reluctant pastry chefs like Aleksy hover at the end of the island, the rest of us spread out around the remaining three sides.

Jackie has taken the place next to Miles and she pulls him into a hug. 'When your curly croissants take off big time, Boathouse Cottage cookery courses would be a great natural next step.'

I'm starting to see where Miles gets his drive from.

Carol waves her glass. 'If the fizz is always this good, you can count us in for those too!'

Zofia pulls her apron ties tight and brushes an invisible spec off the knee of her white jeans. 'Once Betsy & Milo takes off these two will be moving so fast, they will just be a blur.'

As it's my fault they're all here tonight, however shy I feel I owe it to them all to do a little welcome speech. As they finally put their glasses down for long enough to climb up onto their stools, I give a little cough.

'Welcome to Boathouse Cottage everyone. I need to start with a big thank you to my sister Scarlett and her husband for letting us use their kitchen and for having the forethought to buy enough stools to seat us all when the place was really designed for two.'

Had I known this evening was going to get *this* out of hand, I'd never have brought them here, so this is my way of apologising to Scarlett in advance.

Miles laughs. 'We all know Tate and Scarlett by reputation if not in person, they always think big.'

I overcome the twang in my chest when I think that they might never be here together again, and smile round at everyone. 'I'm also truly grateful to you all for missing the Over Sixties Gardening Group and coming here instead.'

I take another deep breath. 'As I mentioned to you when I asked you all here yesterday evening, Miles and I are hoping to open three more "pop up" shops very soon, which means we'll need a lot more boathouse buns than Miles can make on his own. As we're trying to keep everything local and fresh, my idea is to recruit a team of bakers to help us with supplies over the summer. The search is on to find versatile people with energy, knowledge and life experience, who may have a few hours to spare in the mornings a couple of days a week – so we naturally thought of you.'

Malcolm nods. 'You've come to the right place.'

Jackie's eyes are shining. 'It's going to be just like a baking version of *The Thursday Murder Club!*'

Harry nods. 'With pastries instead of corpses.'

Martin grins. 'And rolling pins instead of revolvers.'

Carol beams. 'And pink champagne instead of Kopparberg.'

As I look round the table every person is watching me. 'I take it you're all interested, and fully committed to keeping this project secret?' Not that we're paranoid, but I've already explained that due to industrial espionage we wouldn't want them chatting about this to just anyone.

There's a huge chorus of 'You bet we are!' and 'Count us in!'

I beam at them. 'In that case I'll hand over to Miles, who is master, creator and *the* boathouse bun baker. He'll be making all the dough in advance, and this evening he's going to show us how to roll it out to make perfect pastries. Tonight is simply a taster to let you decide if you'd like to take this further.'

Miles grins at me. 'Thanks for bigging me up there, Betsy Beth.' He holds up his flour sifter. 'You probably already know that if we shake flour on the board before rolling out it stops the dough sticking, but in case you don't, this is how we do it.'

It's useful that I have a valid excuse to watch him, because when he's swinging around with his bare forearms, alternately concentrating on the square of pastry in front of him then looking up to interact with the people around the island unit, he's so compelling to watch I literally can't look away.

Eventually Zofia gives me a nudge in the ribs. 'Come on

Mrs, we know those are quality pecs, but if you don't do your own pastry you won't get your buns done.'

I vow to concentrate more so I don't look like a ditz in front of Miles's mum, but before I do a vibration in my apron pocket takes my attention away again. I slide out my phone, and murmur to Zofia. 'It's Scarlett, she's FaceTiming. If she's phoning with an update on her sex life, I'd better take it.'

I step back towards the sofa area and Zofia steps into my place. 'No worries, I'll keep your pastry up to speed while you talk.'

I dive behind my clothes screen and ignore that with the music and the rising background noise it sounds more like a party for a hundred than twelve, and make a mental note to take control before she does, to tell her what I've been meaning to tell her for weeks now.

'Scarlett!' I beam back as her face fills my screen, and wave wildly. 'So pleased you rang, I have exciting news – Miles and I have opened a shop. Down on the quayside.'

I need to get her used to the idea of a St Aidan branch before she finds out for herself that we have a chain of the damn things.

'You've got what?' Her voice and her lips are slightly out of sync. 'Whatever it is, I hope you know what you're doing. Miles can be very persuasive.'

I give a sniff. 'Which is why it's a good thing I've had practice at resisting.' If she calls me out on this, I have no idea what I'll say when my whole brain is suddenly filled with the image of his lips coming towards mine in the walled garden yesterday.

'There's a lot of noise, have you got the TV on?' The way she's peering at me out of the phone and over my shoulder reminds me why I avoid FaceTiming, but at least I'm off the last hook.

As I hear Olly Alexander's 'Dizzy' blasting out of the kitchen I'm guessing they've turned up the volume possibly to do a dance-routine break, which Zofia tells me is another thing this group are big on.

'Miles's mum, Jackie, and her friends dropped round to do some baking.' I'm trying to hide one shock with another. 'They're funny, one of them is so into Harry Styles she talks about him as her boyfriend!'

Scarlett's staring past my head. 'Show me, without being obvious.'

In spite of all my misgivings I spin round to give her a long view behind me, and regret it immediately when she lets out a shout.

'Why is the kitchen full of flowers?'

I walked into that one. 'They're from Zofia's garden, her plants do better when they're pruned, these are the clippings.' I've got so used to the place bursting with more vases than a florist, I've almost forgotten how it looked when it was sad and empty.

Scarlett's voice goes up a key. 'Are they *dancing? Is Zofia there too?*'

'And Aleksy. If anything untoward happens it's good we have a cleaner and a builder in the house.'

'A baking evening shouldn't get out of hand – *should it?*'

I turn so she can't see how many empty fizz bottles are already lined up next to the sink, but she's onto me again.

'What was *that?*'

Damn. I move so there's a patch of bare wall behind me. 'Probably my four-panel screen, with a few dresses draped over.'

She isn't hiding her shock. 'It sounds like you've done a complete makeover. Did I see cushions?'

My stomach drops. 'Only a couple.'

'Jeez, Bets.'

I'm trying for my soothing voice. 'Don't worry. It'll all disappear when I do.'

She sniffs. 'Tate would have a fit.'

I blow out a breath. 'That's the whole point – I thought you'd *enjoy* that.' I move onto safer ground. 'How about you? Are your evenings still fully booked and fabulous?'

The beat of silence is the giveaway.

She sighs. 'None of them want to see me again. I didn't want to be left hanging so before each date ended I gave them a list of future activities and time slots to choose from, and every single one politely passed up the offer.'

'Oh Scarlett.' My heart is breaking for her for all the reasons.

She's shaking her head. 'I can't understand it. You'd think they'd put a value on outstanding organisational ability in a partner.'

I hold in my dismay. 'Have you thought that guys may find it easier to commit to showing up for a coffee?'

Her lips are pursed. 'I'm worth a lot more than ten minutes in Starbucks.'

I'm taking on board what Miles hinted at last time he spoke about her and Tate's relationship. 'You don't think you're being too prescriptive? People at the start of a relationship might warm to someone more collaborative?'

I'm not sure how much of this she's taking on board.

She thinks for a moment. 'Making decisions for other people is what I'm good at.'

I should be supporting Miles and spreading jam on my rolled-out pastry strips by now, but having told Scarlett *some* hard truths, I can't stop halfway.

I screw up my courage and launch. 'But you could be waving a lot of red flags here?'

She looks horrified. '*Excuse me?* Which would they be?'

'Pretty much all of it – when you stop to think.' I ponder how best to carry on. 'No one likes being told what to do, people prefer to give and take.'

She gives a defiant toss of her head. 'Tate *liked* me to choose.'

I'm hitting the hard balls here. 'Are you sure?'

She wrinkles her nose. 'Maybe not at first. But he did eventually. It wasn't always me dictating, it was *his* choice for us to come to New York.'

I've got an answer to that. 'New York was different. That was *his* work trip that you jumped in on.'

Her voice rises. 'What are you saying here, Betsy?'

I'm holding my ground. 'I'm simply suggesting it's good to examine what might have led to your break-up, so you don't make the same mistakes again.'

Her face is filled with horror. 'If you're saying Tate and I separated because I told him what to do, that's not true. *We broke up because he had the hots for Virginia bloody Kemp!*'

This is one of the hardest conversations of my life. 'If Tate was truly happy and fulfilled with the life you shared, *would he have left?*'

'You mean, this is more about me than her?' Her eyes are

wide. 'Shit, Betty, if I'd become *that much* of a nightmare why didn't you tell me?'

I'm backing off. 'I wasn't living with you. But even as an outsider, you were very decided and hard to challenge.'

'Well, thank you, Betsy, I appreciate your honesty. I'll give it some thought.' She sounds completely deflated, then she tenses again. '*Was that a dog?*'

As a volley of barks bounces off the walls there's nowhere to hide. I run across the lounge and push my way out into the field.

Then I close the French window firmly behind me and try to explain what should have been dealt with weeks ago. 'That was Fudge, he belongs to Miles's mum. He sometimes comes along the beach with Pumpkin and me.'

'I've met Fudge.' Scarlett looks dreamy. 'Tate and I talked about getting a dog when we got back from New York. That won't be happening now.'

At least I can commiserate with that. 'Dogs aren't all a walk in the park. Recall can be a nightmare, and they eat footwear.'

'They eat *what?*'

'Shoes. Pumps. Anything with a sole that's chewy.'

She lets out a cry. 'Shit, Betsy, don't let him *anywhere* near my wardrobe, it's stuffed with Manolo Blahniks.'

My jaw drops. 'You wear those *to the beach?*'

'No, Bets. I put my favourites there for safekeeping.' There's a pause. 'So let's make sure they stay that way.'

She stops and smiles. 'Miles's mum is lovely, she found us Boathouse Cottage.' Scarlett's tone hardens. 'Let's make sure her son shows you respect. I don't want Miles pushing you into things you're not comfortable with. You're keen to please and easily convinced, I don't want him taking advantage.'

I grin. 'I'll certainly pass that on to him.' Then I stop and think. 'I've learned a lot since I got here, Scarlett. I'm less of a pushover than I was.'

If nothing else, sharing a cottage with a horror like Miles forced me to stand up for myself. I might have been easy at the start, but I seriously doubt he'd describe me as that now.

'Would you like to say hello to Pumpkin?' I hold up my phone so she gets a view of him silhouetted against the sunset.

Scarlett sighs. 'I miss it all a lot more than I thought I would.'

I smile. 'With constant crowds to make a fuss of him and a field of his own, Pumpkin would stay forever.'

Scarlett laughs. 'How about you? Has St Aidan won your heart yet?'

Ever since I arrived I've tried to only think of the day we're in, and even that small reference of the future is enough to remind me that the bit beyond October is stretching like one big empty, scary void. I've never minded living day to day before, so I don't know why it should feel so uncomfortable now.

I smile at Scarlett. 'You know me, I go where the wind blows. I can't afford to form attachments.' I might also need to remind myself of my own mantra about not getting attached. If I'm feeling settled and making friends, I have to remember it can't last. As for me feeling like I might need a plan for the winter – *when did I ever have one of those?*

I turn to give Scarlett a view across the bay behind me, and glance back towards the cottage. If the bakers are on their feet I need to get Scarlett off the line before she spots the party through the window.

'I'd better go and get my pastry rolled out.'

'You can't talk for longer?'

I have one chance to get these over-sixties on the baking team. 'Honestly, I'd better go.'

It's odd that I'm the one ending the conversation. It's odd that Scarlett's still on the line when she used to make the world's briefest calls. It's even odder that I just managed to say 'no' to her.

Scarlett bites her thumbnail. 'Thank you, Bets. For all of this. Talk soon.'

Scarlett taking time to say thank you? That's the strangest of all.

44

Boathouse Cottage, St Aidan
Rocks and rolling pins
Saturday

'Did you know they were going to stay this late?'

When I finally get a moment to look at my phone, hours into tidying after the last of the guests have left, I can't believe the festivities went on so long.

Miles has an armful of bottles and is heading for his umpteenth trip to the recycling bin. 'Midnight is the last pick-up time for the over sixties minibus.' He gives a shamefaced grin. 'After that they turn into pumpkins. No disrespect to our pony friend outside.'

I'm happy to own up to my mistake. I spent so long talking to Scarlett that the rest of the evening I was running to catch up.

Miles frowns. 'You do think he counts as my friend now?'

I pull a face. 'As I got this evening so wrong, and you got it so right, I'm prepared to give you that one.'

Miles didn't let Zofia do any more for me than my rolling, so I was busy cutting strips and scattering chocolate chips and missed a lot of the socialising. Zofia and Aleksy had offered to help, but from where I was standing spreading apricot jam at the island, it mostly looked like everyone helped themselves. Also Miles had the idea of making the most of the calm dry evening by having the cooling trays outside and boxing up from there, I missed that part too.

All I can say is that last Saturday must have been beginner's luck, because this time around my sixteen buns took me an age. I can only assume the crowd around the table didn't give a damn due to the amount of alcohol they'd drunk before they'd even sat down, and had rushed the pastry part so they could move on to the dancing and drinking and visiting Pumpkin and lying in the field looking up at the stars and more dancing – all of which they threw themselves into with the kind of energy levels I last had when I was twelve and running on Fanta.

Fast forward to the end of the evening, and the only finished buns I've inspected are mine, which I'd rate a four out of ten, and Angela's, which came out so badly that she didn't want to take them home.

Miles comes back in while I'm putting the last of the plates into the dishwasher.

He looks at me. 'What bit of tonight do you feel didn't work?'

I nod at the tray, which I've left as an admission of my defeat. 'Angela's snake pit?'

He laughs. 'Angela prides herself on not having visited their kitchen since she married Barry thirty-five years ago. Considering she won't even stab and zap, that was a good first effort.'

I look around. 'If you want more reasons, they drank the entire contents of the mudroom, three people passed out, and it took Zofia an hour to vacuum after they left.' Being Zofia, she said there was no point me doing it, because she'd only have to do it again.

Miles laughs. 'We must never have another party where everyone eats pastries and walks round grinding the flakes into the floor.'

We must never have another party, full stop. Just saying. I understand why he's smiling and I'm happy to concede defeat. 'Well done, Milo, you proved my idea was rubbish. We're back to zero in our search for bakers.'

He frowns. 'Excuse me?'

I pull a face. 'Other than me learning the true meaning of "Party like it's 1999" and finally seeing there was a use for Scarlett's bank of four ovens, it was a complete wipe out.'

His eyes narrow. 'I don't know how you missed it, but if you'd come outside you'd have seen. They don't even need training, we had eight sets of perfect buns. Once their hangovers clear, we have our baking team.'

'We do?' I'm staring at him in disbelief.

'Now that's sorted we can put all our energy into getting the new shops ready.' His eyes are shining, then his face relaxes. 'That's why I didn't mind when they went over the top with the dancing. Yet again, you were right. Your instincts are spot on. I like having you on my team.'

As he tilts his head, I'm close enough to count every eyelash again, and when I see the hollows in his cheeks etched in shadow and watch his lips slide into an even wider smile, that familiar eruption of bird wings flapping in my stomach tells me I have to save myself.

Two leaps puts the island unit between us. 'With so much extra work coming our way, we need to get some sleep.' Another three jumps and I'm well on my way out of the kitchen. 'I'll take first turn in the bathroom, if that's okay with you?'

I don't wait around for his answer. I just hope he isn't anywhere around when I come out.

As for three new shops, I'm too terrified to even go there. For now, all I can think is that anything that keeps him far away from where I am has to be a good thing – because the more time I spend near him, the harder I'm finding it to keep my distance and my resolutions.

JULY

45

Boathouse Cottage, St Aidan
When is a cupboard not a cupboard?
Thursday

New shops keeping Miles and I apart? So much for my unswerving instincts, I got that bit entirely wrong, but the last few days have been so full-on that I gave up worrying.

Sunday is St Aidan's busiest day, which means I carried on as normal at the shop. Once Miles had finished cooking at the Net Loft, he went off to Jackie's to do an afternoon of additional training with the more eager members of the new team. Apparently he's been building up frozen dough stocks ever since he sorted the method, which proves he's had his eye on expansion long before I accidentally showed him a way to do it. Not that I'm questioning him, but he's confident that he can keep the supply going to the end of the season, so at least that's one less thing to worry about.

Zofia looked after the St Aidan end again on Monday while

Miles and I did another tour of the new places. When you're only popping up for a few weeks, it's all about minimal input and quick decisions. By the end of Wednesday Aleksy's painting teams have white-washed every shop inside, and painted over any outside signage, Edie has made us six Betsy & Milo signs, which are quickly hung up, and Harry and Miles have raided Jackie's garage, Zofia's outbuildings and Edie's barns for suitable tables, shelving, hat stands and postcard racks, which get dropped off by Malcolm and Harry in Plum's gallery van.

The shops already have fridges, so we fill those up with vanilla cola and our most popular organic sparkling waters. Miles hits his catering suppliers for his usual pastry storage domes, fruit teas and Betsy & Milo mugs. I put in a large postcard order and then Plum gives me the numbers of the barnyard makers, and I also ring the ones from the market to see what stock is available immediately.

As someone who has lived so minimally, this sudden explosion of spending is hard to reconcile. Miles seems to be better with figures than he is with his reading, and he assures me that this initial outlay is normal and that I'm the only one who's finding it mind-blowing. I'm happy to take his word on that, but I still look over his shoulder as he fills in his spreadsheets every evening. When I offer to type in the entries for him, it's more to distract myself from staring at the curve of his thighs and the way he rubs his thumb along the stubble on his jaw when he's concentrating, than because of his erratic spelling.

Not that I'm wishing my summer away, because I really wouldn't do that with anything so precious, but it'll be a relief when this week is over, and we can go back to having separate areas of responsibility.

Considering what I've added to my remit since Friday when we first visited Stoneybridge, by the next Thursday I'm astonished at how far we've come. We're having the same *SAND, SEA, SALT, SURF* pictures as at the Net Loft, but adding others to give each shop its own identity. So I've done one-word ones for the Falmouth shop saying SURF, SAND and SALT with one letter in each rectangle of the frame, Stoneybridge gets *Meet me at the beach*, and Abbots Sands gets *Wild and free, just like the sea*. When the delivery driver drops a roll of the large prints off at Boathouse Cottage on Thursday tea time I take Fudge for his evening walk along the beach and call in the Net Loft to slip them into the frames we have there and get another item ticked off the to-do list.

I let myself into the shop, flick on the switches, and smile when the soft light illuminates the ceiling all the way to the roof. Then I grab a stack of frames from the kitchen, and unhook the rope on the stairs.

I call to Fudge. 'Come this way. I know it's strictly out of bounds and so secret your dad hasn't even seen it, but if we work up here we'll save mess down below.'

He skips up the stairs ahead of me, and by the time I reach the top he's sniffed around and curled himself up in the armchair to watch me.

I laugh, turn on the extra lights and flick the music on my phone. 'Don't get too comfy, Fudge, we won't be here long.'

I rest the frames on the bed, pull off the first of the packaging, ease off the back of the frame, unroll the print, centre it, and put the backing on again. Half an hour later I'm all done, bundling the wrappers into a bag, still bouncing around to

Queen's Greatest Hits when the click of the shop door opening down below makes me freeze.

A moment later I hear Miles shout. 'There's only one person I know who plays "I Want To Break Free" *this* loud. Do you need a hand up there, Betsy B?'

I don't bother to reply, because I can already hear the creak of the bottom step.

He takes the stairs two at a time, and as he arrives beside me his beam turns to a look of bewilderment. He stares around.

'There's a bed.'

'There is.' There's a nano second where I imagine pushing him down on it, jumping on top of him and snogging his face off, then I see his smile's disappeared and he's looking all superior and sarcastic.

'Has the loft cupboard always been this sensational?'

I wither under his gaze. 'It's a live/work unit; it was my emergency accommodation. In case sleeping on the sofa got too much.'

His face is white. 'You're not seriously thinking of moving here?'

I shrug. 'Not since Scarlett ordered me to guard the cottage.'

His features relax. 'Thank Christmas for that. I like you being there. It wouldn't be the same if you weren't.' He hesitates. 'I mean, it's more practical, with Fudge and the business and Pumpkin.' His eyes are wide and anxious. 'Any time you want the bed...'

I blow out a breath. 'I know – I only have to ask, but I'm okay as I am. And you're right, it is easier.' I feel he's put himself out on a limb, and I want to do the same. 'I wouldn't stay if I didn't want to be there.'

He comes in and grasps me by the shoulder. 'Great, so we're good. Life *is* better in flip flops. Shall we go to Jaggers and drink to that?'

I'm staring up at him, working out how to take this, when I'm saved by the vibration in my pocket.

'That will be Scarlett. She's phoned me every night since Saturday.'

Miles takes the bin bag from me. 'I'll clear up while you talk.' He tilts his head. 'Unless you'd like privacy?'

I shake my head. 'Carry on tidying, then Fudge and I will grab a lift home.'

The moment I press accept, Scarlett launches. 'I've worked out why I've been so single-minded and impossible. After Mum died, I was so afraid of losing control. It was such a shock, our lives disintegrated overnight, everything felt so fragile. When I held on to everything so tight, it wasn't me being a diva. It was because if I let go, it felt like I'd lose everything else too. Making everything perfect and doing everything the way I wanted it was my way of guarding against chaos. It was my way of making myself feel better, my way of coping. And now instead of holding everything together, I've held on so tight it's all spun out of control and crashed and I've lost it anyway.'

My heart goes out to her. 'I'm so sorry, Scarlie. You were always so busy being strong for both of us. I need to hug you.'

She sniffs. 'I really haven't been fair to Tate.' She gives a long sigh. 'I've been very hard to live with and he was too nice to tell me.' There's another pause. 'People dying is supposed to make you want to procreate, but I couldn't bear to have sex for months. I had too much to deal with to even think about it.'

I let out a sigh. 'You really have made Tate do it tough.'

'I think I believed he loved me so much that he'd do anything for me. In the end I pushed him too far ... and I never gave enough back.'

So much reflection is making me think. 'In a funny way Mum shaped my relationships too. Whenever she had a guy around – can you remember? – the moment it was about to get serious she'd start finding fault with them for the most ridiculous reasons. That's why I was determined never to be picky.'

Scarlett's voice rises. 'How did you not know? That was to protect *us*. She'd always think she could do it, then when it came to it, she could never bear the thought of imposing a stepdad on us. I suppose she thought she'd have her time after we'd left home.'

I've trained myself to talk about Mum without sobbing my heart out, but my mouth is filling with the taste of tears. 'It's all so sad.'

I can feel Scarlett pursing her lips. 'If she saw either of us as we are with our relationships now, I don't think she'd feel we've done her justice.'

That makes me even more sad, because from my side it's definitely true. And Scarlett's said that without knowing the part about Mason. As my sister she might have been the natural person to share that with, but even a lot later, when she was back from her spectacular Ice Hotel and Northern Light honeymoon, I couldn't even begin to find the words. And if ever I had found words, I'd never have found the courage to say them out loud. It was easier to keep everything hermetically sealed, rather than shattering someone else's peace and risking all the ripples through other people's lives as well as mine that would result from that.

'So what are you going to do?'

I can hear her mind working. 'I'm going to ease off on the dates until I take it all in.' Her voice hardens. 'Don't get me wrong, however much responsibility I'm taking, Tate's still behaved like a prize bastard. We'll still fight to the death over the assets.'

I'm blinking. 'So you still need me at the cottage?'

'Hell yes.' Her voice softens. 'How about you? You made a big impression on the guy from Ground Force.'

I wrinkle my nose. 'You mean Zach who brings the hay bales?'

She laughs. 'He rang me to ask why you weren't at the Surf Shack on Saturday.'

I roll my eyes. 'Something came up.'

'He wanted your number, but I told him to ask you himself.' She's laughing more. 'Expect another hay delivery any day. And make sure you keep this Saturday free.'

I'm shaking my head. 'I'm flat out here. I can't see I'll make the Surf Shack any time before September.'

Her voice rises. 'Flat out with what? That doesn't sound like you.'

It isn't like me. Since I came to St Aidan it's like someone else has taken over my body. But I can't get into that now, and by the time she comes back it'll all be over anyway.

'It's nothing important. Talk to you tomorrow?'

I end the call and slide my phone back in my pocket, and turn back to Miles who's got his incredulous face on.

'Zach rang New York to ask for your number?'

I look at the ceiling. 'I should have put her on speakerphone then you could have joined in properly.'

He gives a guilty shrug. 'No need, even when Scarlett's channelling her softer side she still shouts.' He looks thoughtful. 'I may have misjudged her – she's more self-aware than I realised.'

It's funny that I've got so old before it's hit me. 'Scarlett's always been the strong one. She's been the parent, and I've acted like the child. It's sad that it's taken her split to make her vulnerable, but it's more balanced now. She's leaning on me rather than always being the other way around. And it's great that we're talking more.'

'But not sharing so much that you've told her about the business.'

I pull a face. 'I'm working *towards* growing up. I didn't say I'm already there.'

Miles smiles back. 'I know you've thrown yourself into getting the shops ready, but you owe it to Scarlett and your mum. Saturday night, we're going to the Surf Shack.'

Just when I think the worst it gets is Miles finding my secret bedroom, it goes downhill a whole lot further.

46

The Surf Shack, St Aidan
Dancers with bruised knees
Saturday

'Do Saturday nights in summer come any better?'

You guessed it. We're at the Surf Shack, Miles is bigging up the evening he pushed me into, but to be fair I couldn't have asked for a better companion. He's danced without a thought every time I've asked, he's just fought his way to the bar with me for the fourth time and now he's lounging on the sand under the light strands that are swinging above us on the edge of the Surf Shack deck, drinking craft bitter from the bottle and getting more snoggable with every wave that comes up the beach.

As I watch the wind tangling his hair and the crowds of lively revellers melt out of focus in the half-light beyond him it's almost as if we were the only people here. 'A Sea Breeze cocktail in one hand, a Beachcomber in the other, "Flowers in the Rain" belting out across the sand dunes, the whole beach erupting every time Abba sing "Waterloo".' I take a sip through my straw. 'What's not to like?

'You know the only downside?' I don't think I'm slurring, but I've lost count of how many Strawberry Daiquiris I've had from Zach. He refuses to take no for an answer, and drops them into my hand in return for the briefest word in my ear before he disappears into the crowd again. Me being about to tell Miles about tonight's wardrobe disaster is a definite sign they're going to my head. 'I was in such a rush, I came out in two dresses rather than four, so I'm only half dressed.'

Miles's eyes narrow as he holds my gaze. 'Am I allowed to say you look great in your underwear?'

Questions like that are why I should never have started this. 'Two months ago you wouldn't have been. This once, I'll let it go.' I'd usually be appalled by the electric tingles that are zinging up and down my spine, but the sea and the tiredness from a full-on week mean for once I give in and enjoy the shivers.

Miles gives me that look where he seems to be peering right inside my head. 'You know that Zach's going to ask you to go home with him?'

I bite my lip and consider. 'If you're talking about the drinks he's been bringing over, I tried to refuse them, but the price he charges for those bales, Scarlett's paid for them three times over.' I'm being true to myself here. 'I might have been tempted once, but I'm not going to go now. Shall we dance again?'

Spot the deliberate mistake. As Miles stands up I'm still holding two full glasses, but I'm happy to say I've not lost my ability to down drinks. A few moments later I've pushed my empty glasses onto the Surf Shack deck and he's reaching out to pull me to my feet.

I smile up at him as he tugs on my hand. 'That's another thing I've learned in St Aidan. It's okay to say "no". And careful selection isn't necessarily a bad thing. I might even have discovered why I always ended up with the wrong people.'

As I join him jumping around to the music I'm shouting at him. 'For someone so up themselves you're surprisingly willing to dance.'

He bends and yells back into my ear. 'I can't be that aloof and distant, Bets. I'm pogo-ing to Plastique Bertrand here.'

It's not a great time to start an interrogation, but in the dusk, on the beach, with the wind whipping away the answers it's somehow easier to ask. 'All those hoops a woman has to jump through to get a date with you. What's that about?'

He calls back. 'Every requirement is a no-brainer. Do they support themselves? Do they know their own mind? Can they create a spreadsheet, host a party, make a playlist, drive a car...'

I cup my hand around his ear. 'You're effing unbelievable, Milo.'

He's still bouncing on the spot. 'It was my mum's contribution that held me back. *Must be able to sing along to Abba.* If only I'd come to a St Aidan disco earlier, I'd have known the whole town would qualify for that.'

'The sheer arrogance...'

He actually sounds pleased with himself. 'It's a comprehensive list. It certainly saved me a lot of wasted time.'

'Me showing an interest doesn't mean I condone it.' I'm shaking my head. 'What happens once some poor woman satisfies all your ridiculous conditions?' Enquiring for a friend here, obviously not for myself.

'If you're wondering how you're doing, you'd ticked every box but one, and you've nailed the final one this evening.' He shrugs. 'Anyone else, I'd go ahead and ask them out. But you're a special case, so you've got to ask me.'

I'm not even trying to hide my incredulity. 'That's it?'

His voice is very low. 'Try me and see?'

I'm right back at him. 'You don't mean that. If we're in another one of those head-to-head situations, you know better than to challenge me. I'm very stubborn. I won't rise.'

As ever, it's three steps forwards two steps back with Milo-pie. Just when I think I'm uncovering his warmer, softer, approachable side, he comes out with this!

I'm reeling at the audacity. The assumptions. The whole overblown confidence that I'll fall at his feet. The more infuriating he is, the more I want to grind my body against his. At the same time, it's comforting to think it's only *this* extreme because I'm on my seventh drink.

As Zofia comes into view her arm linked through Zach's, we ease off on the dancing and suspend the argument.

'Excuse us interrupting, but can you clear something up for lovely Zach here please.'

As Zach steps forward his eyes are less intensely blue than they were last week. 'Are you two an item? Zofia's insisting you are, but I'd heard you weren't.'

I'm quick to confirm. 'We're definitely just housemates.'

Miles holds up a finger. 'Let's quantify that. We're the kind of housemates who opted to stay together when we could have moved on. Who got on so well we became business partners and who are now working with a multi-outlet operation.'

Zofia jumps in. 'If they were one of those surveys where they tell you your progress, they would be ninety-five percent through to becoming a couple.'

It's not lost on me. There's this eager, hunky, Greek god of a guy who I'd once have gone for like a shot, but now he leaves me cold. Then right next to him there's the one-time awful, arrogant, arseholey Miles, and he's the one I'm struggling to keep my hands off. Worse still, since he's become all caring and kind and considerate, he's ten times more irresistible. All I can say is, with this much confusion it's a damn good thing I gave up on men for good.

When I smile at Zach, it's genuine. 'It's a shame we didn't meet in the days when I had a different bad boy every night, Zach. We'd have had a lot of fun.'

Zach holds up another glass full to the brim of red liquid. 'I was going to give you this and offer to drive you home, Betty, but it looks like it's just the drink after all.'

I shake my head at the glass. 'Thanks for the drinks, but give that one to someone more deserving.'

Zofia turns back to Miles and me. 'Well, now we've settled that so successfully, we'll head off and leave you two to the rest of your evening.'

As we watch them walk away across the soft sand, I blow out my cheeks and turn to Miles. 'I'm sorry if that ruined the mood.'

Miles gives a shrug. 'Not at all. Well done for putting that one to bed without ending up in it.'

Now that I'm standing still rather than dancing, the wind is slicing through the fabric of my dresses, and I hug my chest. 'Have you danced enough? Are we done here?'

Miles nods. 'I'm good to go if you are.' His voice is full of concern. 'You're cold. Here, take my jacket.'

I'm actually freezing, but with my head as it is, if I engulf myself in Miles's scent, I may just explode. 'It's no distance to the cottage, you stay cosy.'

It shows you how much notice he takes of me. A moment later he strips off his jacket. Another second and he's sliding it across my shoulders and with the soft denim wrapped around me a delicious scent fills my nose and his heat permeates through to my bones. For the first time all evening I'm truly warm. I'm not sure what happens next, but as my muscles relax, I must drop my guard because one moment we're side by side, and the next he's turned to face me and he's looking down at me.

I'm staring up at the shadows of his cheekbones, his ruffled curls silhouetted against the night clouds and the stars between them.

As he pulls the jacket close around me I step forward, press my body against the planes of his chest, slide my hand upwards over the curve of his biceps and up to his face. I feel the prickle of stubble on my palm, spread my fingers across his cheek, listen to the thud of my heart as it bangs hard enough to leap out of my chest. Then, I stop and tug my own long, floaty scarf until it's free. When I reach up and wrap it around his neck it feels strangely as if I'm marking him as mine.

'There you go, now you look like Harry Styles.'

His laugh is a low rumble. 'I can live with that.'

Then I grab both ends of the scarf and pull him towards me,

push my hip hard against his, move my right hand to bury my fingers in his hair, clear my throat, and whisper, 'Okay. You win. I'm asking. Dates, drinks, nights in your bed, days in your bed, business opportunities, roller coasters, pony rides, picnics, takeaway pizzas. I'll do any or all of it, so long as you kiss me now...'

I watch the hollow at the base of his neck, his Adam's apple moving as he swallows.

I pull back an inch. 'It's got to be now, Miles. If you mess about, it's not going to work.'

He pushes my hair out of my eyes, untangles his fingers and stares down into my face.

'There's nothing I'd like more in the world, Betsy B. But I can't do it now, not when you're like this.'

I let out a shout. 'WHEN I'M LIKE WHAT?' I stagger backwards, he catches my arm and it hits me. 'You're refusing to kiss me because I'm off my face! That's it, isn't it?'

He winces. 'You've had a lot more drinks than me. We wouldn't be equal.'

My voice rises. 'You're so bloody chivalrous! What about what *I* want?'

His voice is level as he pulls me to him. 'I want to kiss you all the time, I've always wanted to kiss you. *You* only want to kiss *me* when you've had a bottle of fizz. If you need ten cocktails before it feels right, that's never going to work.'

My chest is so full of anger I feel like I might burst.

I push him away hard. 'Jeez, Miles, how uptight can you get? If that's your attitude I won't be asking at all. Thank goodness I dodged that bullet.' I take another step back. 'I don't know about you, but I'm going home now.'

I turn and run across the sand and in through Pumpkin's field. I get as far as the sofa before I realise, I'm still wearing his jacket. But by that time, I'm too far gone to take it off.

47

Boathouse Cottage, St Aidan
The wrong trousers
Sunday

As I pull on my clothes and come out from behind my screen on Sunday morning, my head is banging, I feel like I've been awake for hours, and Miles appears from the mud room, his arms full of boxes.

'I'm sorry for the way things ended last night, Betsy Eliza. The last thing I intended was to upset you.'

I blink at the morning sunlight that splashes through the roof windows. 'Upset? *Why would I be upset?*' I hear my shriek, give a cough and lower my voice. 'If you're heading out, you might like to take my scarf off before you go?'

'Damn.' He stares down at his clean T-shirt. 'I don't have any spare hands. I'm off to do some baking tuition at Carol's. I'll do it in the car and return it later.' His eyes pull in to focus on my own top and he frowns at me. 'Did you sleep in your clothes? Because you're still wearing my jacket.'

Crap. There's no way I'm telling him that I slept in it. Or that I couldn't bear to be without it and pulled it straight back on again when I put some different layers on just now.

I pull a face. 'Blame it on the hangover, I picked it up by mistake getting dressed. Just taking Fudge out. I'll swap it when I come back.'

It's crazy that every pore of my body is desperate to soak up the scent from his clothes when the man himself is right in front of me, making me furious. I'm not sure I've ever been turned down by a guy, let alone knocked back so spectacularly I'm still smarting hours later. I refuse to admit the bitter pangs I'm feeling in my chest have anything to do with disappointment.

I give a sniff. 'You made the right call last night, Miles. Now I've lost my booze goggles, there's no attraction at all.'

Perhaps I'm not being one hundred percent straight about that, because in spite of everything that's happened, my body is still screaming out for him. But the good news is, the fury at being rejected means it has cancelled out a bit.

He raises his eyebrows. 'I'm not interested in one-night stands, I'm afraid I want more. You have to ask me when you haven't had a drink. I have to be a rational, well-considered decision, not a reckless lunge that you regret in the morning.'

I make my smile very bright. 'Great we've cleared that one up. It's fabulous we both know where we stand.' If he were the last guy in the world begging to save the human race, I would not be saying yes.

He takes two strides to the door, and when he gets there he

turns round. 'And we're all good to go ahead with the phased opening of the new shops next week?'

Why else would he be smoothing this over? 'No worries on that front, Miles. It'll be business as usual.'

Why did I ever think his apology was about anything else? I grab Fudge's lead, whistle, and we head out to the field to pick up Pumpkin for a walk along the beach.

Boathouse Cottage, St Aidan
Sharp dressing and world domination
Saturday

The good thing about Betsy & Milo is that after a full-on ten days of intensive collaboration setting up the new shops, the time when Miles and I need to be joined at the hip is at an end. The new shops look lovely. We have phased openings, in Falmouth on Tuesday, Stoneybridge on Thursday and Abbots Sands on Saturday, with me taking Pumpkin in his trailer so he can stand outside each shop in turn and do his usual crowd-pulling beach walks.

With four shops ticking over nicely, Milo and I go back to our own areas. He oversees the baking team, and is in charge of the staffing, and he also takes care of the business and money bits, because that's his area of expertise.

When I'm not walking Pumpkin along various beaches selling buns, I'm in the St Aidan shop serving customers and sourcing beautiful things to sell, or tearing around afterhours adding stock and tweaking the layouts. As the word gets around the local makers, sourcing stock gets easier too.

Other than that, I've taken responsibility for Fudge's walks, which means I can do them without having to contend with Miles and his incessant remarks about my quirks. We have a sweet two weeks of tiptoeing around each other, keeping our distance, which actually makes me wonder why it wasn't like this all along. I even have time to pull in some in-depth interviews with local makers that Fenna is interested in for future magazine editions. I also put together a simple Betsy & Milo website and start adding content every day like videos of bits of swirling sea foam, and stay on top of the other socials, and Pumpkin gets his own Insta page too.

As the holiday season approaches there are more and more jobs to fit in for the shops. I've never worked so many hours, never been as tired or slept so well. Some days I'm in such a rush to get dressed I only have time to pull on my cut-off shorts and a T-shirt, but it's only for a short time, so no one seems to mind.

The days pass in a blur, with the only surprise being a lot of thunderstorms, but as they're mostly in the night, apart from the field having puddles in places, they don't impact us a lot. Two Saturdays later I'm on my way out to the beach when I literally collide with Miles in the kitchen. I have to say, my entire body feeling like a champagne bottle with a cork that's about to pop every time I see Miles in person is still a problem, which is why it's great I'm keeping my distance. Today is way worse, because he's wearing a grey suit, which is crazy for a sweltering day in July, but gives him a kind of sexual supercharge that makes me go rigid when I stare at him.

He starts with his usual update. 'The baking is all done, Zofia is helping at the Net Loft, there are pastries here for you to sell on the beach with Pumpkin, and I'm off out for a meeting in Falmouth.'

'Still hell-bent on taking over the world?'

He pulls a face. 'Something like that.' And then he's gone.

I can already see people settling in on the beach with their wind breaks, so as Pumpkin has taken to standing so close to the French windows you can see every whisker, I grab his bunting and head straight out with the buns.

I'm talking to him as we walk. 'It's your favourite kind of day, Pumpkin. The holidays have started and Scarlett says there will soon be so many visitors we won't be able to see the sand. If it's going to be like this for the next six weeks, your Insta followers will be off the scale.'

It's one of those times when the buns fly out of the saddle-bags so fast that before we know it all we have left are a handful of flyers for the shops, which we give out in return for a head scratch all the way back. I turn him out into the field, kiss his velvety nose, and then Fudge and I rush off to fill up the Net Loft postcard racks.

Thanks to all the visitors we take record amounts at the shop and stay open an extra couple of hours. While Fudge and I walk back to the cottage I'm thinking so hard about how I'm going to keep my stock supplies going that I turn up off the beach without scanning the field as I usually do. It's only when I get to the gate and there's no wicker of welcome that it hits me that Pumpkin isn't there.

My heart misses a beat, but I carry on, muttering to Fudge as we head up the slope towards the outbuilding. 'What a pony!

It's taken ten weeks for him to visit that stable and find the shade.'

It's only when I get to the outbuilding doorway and look past the slanting beams of sunlight coming through the dusty window, that I get that the place is completely empty.

My stomach drops through the floor and I scan the boundary. 'There's no sign of a pony crashing through the fence.'

Scarlett is my first thought, but she's too far away to bother her. When it hits me that my next closest person is Miles, for a nanosecond I curse silently. Then I remember there's no time to lose and hit call on my phone. He answers on the second ring.

'Pumpkin's gone!' My mouth is dry as I say the words. 'The gate to the field was bolted. Someone must have taken him! They couldn't have squeezed a horse box down the lane. They must have walked him off along the beach.' I let out a wail as my panic rises. 'I don't know why I've called when you're in Falmouth!'

Miles's voice is calm and level. 'I'm twenty minutes away. You walk towards the harbour and ask everyone you see if they saw him passing. If you get as far as the quayside and haven't had any sightings, work your way back along the beach. I'll drive straight to Cockleshell Castle. By the time I meet you there you'll have checked out the beach that far.' Miles's voice is low. 'We'll work out how to spread the word wider once we meet up.' There's a beat of silence. 'I'm so sorry, Betsy Beth. Now go! Quick as you can.'

As Fudge and I head towards the harbour it's such a different walk from when we were out this morning with Pumpkin. The tide has been all the way up the beach and is on its way out again, but a lot of the same people are still here. It takes me fifteen minutes to get far enough to know Pumpkin hasn't come this way, and another five to pelt back to where I began. Then I begin again heading out towards Comet Cove, but this time it's quicker because the crowds thin out along this end of the beach. Long before I get to Cockleshell Castle, I can see a figure in a suit hurrying towards me.

Miles turns as I arrive, and I give him the worst news yet. 'No one has seen him. Sophie's daughter Milla and her friends were playing by the Little Cornish Kitchen beach hut all afternoon, and none of them saw him either.'

He hurries me along. 'Once we get back to the car you can put it up on the local Facebook groups and ring the police.'

The tears are clumping on my lashes as we pass the castle with its towers etched against the sky. 'There's a stolen pony group I'm in too.' My voice cracks. 'Pumpkin's just so cute and so portable. What was I thinking, parading him round the coast at holiday time when I don't even have a lock on the gate?'

'You mustn't beat yourself up about this. We'll do everything we can to get him back.' Miles puts his arm around my waist and guides me across the side of the lawns, where people are standing with drinks. 'We can cut through the castle grounds. I left the car in the field opposite. There must be some kind of event on.'

We're reaching the lane, when we see a group of very dirty people staggering towards us and Miles springs out to stop them. 'Have you come from the Mud Run centre?'

The guy laughs. 'Is it that obvious? We hired Tough Muckers for the whole day, conditions have been perfect.'

It's a long shot, but I'll take it. 'We've lost a small chestnut brown pony. I don't suppose you've seen him?'

The guys crowd in. 'There *was* a pony in a field.'

Someone puts out their hand to show a height. 'Definitely brown, so small he could barely see over the gate.'

I don't give him time to finish. 'Where?'

They turn and point. 'If you join the Mucker course beyond the cars, it's about two fields up. It'll be a lot quicker than driving if you're in a hurry.'

I push Fudge's lead into Miles's hand and start to run. 'I'll ring you the second I get there.'

He's already jogging beside me. 'We're in this together, Bets.'

I dip under the 'finish' banner. 'What about your clothes?'

He pulls a face. 'How bad can it be?' He answers his own question when he jumps to avoid a puddle then looks down at his splattered trousers. 'No suit could ever be more important than finding Pumpkin.'

We're on a track designed to cover people in mud, and it does its job within the first five seconds. As a measure of how fancy his suit is, five seconds after that Miles takes my phone and puts it with his in his waterproof inside pocket. After that all we can do is suspend our disbelief and go with it. It's one of those times where we lose all track of speed and distance. In the end we're so wet and muddy that there are no shits left to give.

One field in, Miles stops and looks at me. 'If we ever do bonding exercises at Betsy & Milo, remind me to choose an escape room.'

Halfway across the next, I stop and peel my skirt off my legs so I can move them. 'It's so good Scarlett gets special rates at Iron Maidens Cleaners.' Then I stiffen. 'There's an empty hay net on that fence, this could be it.'

We leave the mud track, clamber through a hedge and out onto a lane. When I see the small dark brown pony standing by the gate I flop.

'It's not his fault he's not Pumpkin. It sounded *so* hopeful, we had to follow the lead.'

As Miles blows out his cheeks he looks beaten. 'Come on. Let's go home, clean up and regroup.'

I give a shiver. 'Not that I'm big on short cuts, but if we take that lane, we should be able to pick up the main road.'

It's gently downhill and a whole lot faster when we're not sliding through mud, and ten minutes later we're going through the gate at Boathouse Cottage.

Miles hands me my phone then opens the kitchen door. 'If you want to contact the lost pony groups I'll grab some towels.'

'It feels so unreal.' I sink down onto the bench by the table and wrench off my Converse hi tops which are like mud balls. 'How am I ever going to tell Scarlett?'

'Betsy…' Miles's voice is urgent. 'Come here, there's something you need to see…'

I look down at Fudge who has flopped in his own little mud puddle on the pavers. 'I can't imagine anything in the kitchen worth rushing for. Wait here, I won't be long.'

Even though I tiptoe past the mudroom, I'm still leaving footprints on the polished limestone. As I reach Miles he puts a finger to his lips. 'We have a visitor in the living room…'

My mind races. 'Tate? Scarlett? Zofia? *Your mum?*'

'Much better than that.'

I peer past the sofa to a long ginger tail and a very orange pony rump, and I let out a whoop. 'Pumpkin! You're here! I thought you'd gone forever! What are you doing in the house?'

He turns to look at me and I throw my arms around his neck then bury my face in his mane. 'I left the door off the latch and you pushed your way in. Nice job, Pumpkin. Remind me to always give you your carrots over the fence in future, not in the doorway.' I smile at Miles. 'He's been obsessed with getting into the cottage since he stole your buns through the window that first afternoon.'

Miles laughs. 'He's had his nose pressed against that French window for weeks. It was bound to open one day.'

I can't help scolding him. 'Look at the state of Miles and I, Pumpkin, and you've been here all the time, swishing your tail.' I shake my head at Miles. 'He looks so comical next to the high-end coffee table, we have to take photos before we put him back in the field again.'

Miles frowns at his mud-caked legs. 'If Tate or Scarlett saw this it would blow their minds.'

I grin at him. 'Selfie by the sofa, for you, me, Fudge and Pumpkin only.' I bury my face in Pumpkin's mane one last time. 'And after that, ponies stay strictly in their fields.'

49

Boathouse Cottage, St Aidan
Home truths and antique road shows
Saturday

Pumpkin is safely back in his field, with the addition of one of Tate's bicycle locks on the gate. I climb the stile, turn to watch him standing and swallow hard.

'He's so very precious because he was Mum's.' I've stayed so detached and calm, but now my emotions flood over me and my voice wavers. 'I always try to be bright, but sometimes I can't.' A tear rolls down my cheek and off my chin, and Miles jumps down next to me by the fence.

'Losing Pumpkin then finding him again – days don't come any bigger than this.' His voice is soft as he slips his arms around me. 'It's okay to cry.'

The folds of his shirt are streaked with mud, but I bury my cheek in them all the same. Then as I close my eyes tight and listen to the repeating thud of his heart a reassuring sense of comfort spreads through me.

I shudder. 'Often when Pumpkin and I are walking along the water's edge on the empty beach it's like my mum's there with us. You probably think I'm weird to say that.'

He sighs. 'Not at all. My mum said the same when she lost my stepfather.' He pauses for a moment. 'If I died, I know I'd do my damndest not to leave – to stay close to the people I cared for.'

My cheek is still pressed against his chest. 'Sometimes, just for a moment, I forget that she's gone. I wish you'd met her. She was exacting with her partners, but she was so warm and wonderful and caring and creative and alive.'

'She sounds a lot like you.'

The way his empathy and kindness and warmth seep through me makes me wish I could stay here forever. Wrapped in the lapels of his muddy suit jacket, for the first time since forever I feel safe and calm and whole, and without really thinking I'm speaking.

'You were right. The other day.'

He's talking over the top of my head. 'Keep going.'

'Things weren't okay at Scarlett's wedding. With Mason, it was a lot more than an argument.' I take a breath. 'When I went up to the room, he'd been drinking more, and when I wouldn't have sex with him he threw me against the wall.'

'Jeez, Betsy.'

'It came out of nowhere. I wasn't ready, I fell really hard and smashed my face and hurt my wrist where I put out my hand to break the fall.

'I was so ashamed. All I could think was how awful it would

be for Scarlett if there was a fuss, how catastrophic it would be for their wedding night if anyone heard or knew. How appalled everyone would be to think it had happened, at a wedding reception of all places.'

He's stroking the top of my head. 'I'm so sorry, Betsy. It's unthinkable that we were all there, and no one came to help you.'

'You knew things weren't right, didn't you?'

He sighs. 'I was worried, I felt something must have been wrong when you left so suddenly.'

'I've never told anyone before. My face swelled up like a balloon. I woke to Mason telling me we needed to leave. At six in the morning I took some painkillers, sneaked to the car with my hoodie over my head, and Mason drove us back to Somerset. My friends at the sanctuary assumed I'd fallen doing the conga and they took me off to A&E.'

'What an awful thing for you to go through.'

'The nurses knew, but when I told them that Mason had gone for good they mentioned where to get support and left it at that.

'To begin with I was in shock. I got home running on adrenalin, then I hid myself away. The longer I kept it secret the harder it became to say anything. Even with my closest friends, I kept opening my mouth to tell them the truth, and then pulling back. And then I was scared they'd judge me. The worst thing was, the more I thought about it, the more I blamed myself. For such a big event, I should have been more careful with my choice of plus one. The more I replayed it in my head, the more it felt as if I'd brought it on myself. That if I'd done things differently it wouldn't have happened. That it was my fault for making Mason angry.'

Miles is looking down at me, shaking his head. 'Nothing you did could have made it your fault. It's always okay to say "no". Whatever you do, no one ever has the right to hurt you.'

I let out a long sigh. 'Then I thought, if it came out of nowhere once, it could happen again. But it wasn't a problem, because I didn't want to go out. If I ever did go down the local pub, I spent all my time thinking how fast I could leave.'

'Did you see Mason again?'

I shake my head. 'Even on the journey home he didn't acknowledge he'd had any part in it, and I wanted to get back without annoying him so I left it. Later in the week he sent three dozen roses and a get-well-soon card, but he disappeared completely after. A while later I heard he'd gone to Newcastle.

'I thought once I got the plaster off my wrist, I'd be fine, but it changed who I was. I've carried it with me like a weight that's got heavier and heavier. I didn't plan to share this, but I already feel better. It's just a relief that it's not a secret anymore.'

Miles is rubbing the back my head. 'Thank you for trusting me enough to tell me.'

I'm biting my lip. 'Thank you for listening.' I look up at him, my stomach does another somersault, then I look back to my mud-covered clothes. 'I'm so sorry for the last hour. Why didn't I look inside?'

'Truly, there's nothing to apologise for.' His eyes are soft as he looks down at me. 'I'm more than happy with the outcome from all sides.'

I finally take a step backwards. The more I look at Miles, the muddier he is. 'I suppose we'd better go and hose ourselves down.'

He laughs. 'If we don't go soon the mud will dry.'

I laugh too. 'This'll be a true test of Scarlett's outdoor shower.'

After everything we've been through, and how generous and selfless Miles has been, once we get to the shower terrace I turn on both shower heads. Then I step under the drench, and call to him through my own personal rainstorm. 'We have to shower in our clothes, that way they'll get washed down when we do.'

Miles slides his neatly folded jacket onto the table. 'If these trousers go under a hot shower they'll shrink to the size of doll's clothes.'

I give in. 'Okay. Take them off so long as you're wearing boxers.'

He's hopping round the courtyard, peeling off his socks and kicking them away.

'If you have any ambitions to become a Chippendale, you'll have to improve your undressing technique.' When he picks his mud-covered trousers up by the ankles and lines up the creases I bite back my smile. 'The Chippendales don't do "hospital corners" either. They toss their trousers up stage.'

Miles gives me an eye roll, delivers his own to the table, steps into his side of the shower, rubs himself vigorously, then stops to look at me. 'In the interest of full disclosure, I have to say your four dresses weren't see through when they were mud-covered, but they are now.' He pauses to give me a slow smile. 'In case you want to turn around.'

I don't move. I simply stare at him. 'Back at you. Your formerly white cotton shirt is fully transparent, and never swim in those pants, because now they're soaked they're completely indecent.' I take a step towards him and rub his cheek. 'And your face is covered in soil.'

He rubs his thumb across my chin. 'Did I mention you're even more beautiful with wet hair and tide marks?'

How did I ever think I could get under a shower with Miles and not be in big trouble? I bite my lip, stare past his wet lashes into the deepest, darkest brown eyes, and I know it's time to be honest with him.

'So, Miles – I haven't had a drink, but I'm ecstatic we found Pumpkin, and I'm extremely grateful to you for helping and listening to me talking about my darkest times. So I'm not sure how this fits with your conditions, because I'm not asking – I'm telling you. First I'm going to snog your face off and then I'm going to have to lie you down and bonk you senseless. Are you going to be okay with that?'

Miles looks like he's biting back his smile. 'That's definitely something I could work with.' One eyebrow goes up. 'But only if you're sure.'

I grin at him. 'I've never been more certain about anything ever.' Now that's out of the way, I'm all about the practicalities. 'Probably not right here, because that would be disrespectful to Scarlett and Tate...'

Miles lets his full grin go. 'We might be overthinking this? If they had a pony in their tranquility zone earlier, sex in their shower might matter less.'

I need to cover all bases. 'And I haven't slept with anyone for two years, so I might have forgotten how to do it.'

'Same here.' Miles laughs. 'If we've both got that much catching up to do, this could be a long night.'

I shake my head. 'Can you just stop talking and let me kiss you?'

'Of course. Don't let me hold you up. I'm ready whenever you are…'

He smiles down at me, and as I move towards him, he stands still and carries on smiling and my heart feels like it's going to jump out of my chest. Then I graze his lips with my tongue, run my fingers through his hair, and pull his head down so I can reach him. Then my mouth is on his, and when he parts his lips and lets me in, he tastes of coffee and toffee pecans and raspberries and apple crumble. And then he starts to kiss me back. I arch myself against him and as my whole body explodes I'm hit by a tidal wave of need that makes me forget anything else exists.

50

Boathouse Cottage, St Aidan
Back to front and inside out
Sunday

When I woke early on Sunday morning, I was upside down on Scarlett's immense natural-wool super-king mattress, my legs draped over Miles's, which meant I was looking up at a whole new section of sky. Because he was asleep and naked except for one strand of quilt draped across his ankle, I was actually looking anywhere but at the clouds.

We came to bed yesterday evening via the shower, then most places in the cottage. Then we got up again, had supper, went to bed on the sofa, got up again, had another indoor shower, then lay in the field watching the stars until they faded into dawn. And then we came back to Miles's bed, had a couple of hours sleep, and now Miles has gone to make us what he called a 'wake-up-gently' coffee before we get ready to leave for work.

He strolls across the bedroom, puts the tray on the bed, and passes me a mug.

I pull the quilt around my shoulders, and take a sip. 'It was nice of your mum to cover this morning's baking.'

Miles laughs. 'I'll have to do it tomorrow and every day after that, but I didn't want to rush today.'

He's pulled on some boxers, and however irresistible he's looking, there's something I need to sort out.

'You said you'd always wanted to kiss me. The other day.'

He nods. 'I have.'

I have to deal with this. 'How does that fit with you wrecking Scarlett's wedding album because you refused to be near me?'

He pulls a face. 'It was all down to the stalking thing I told you about. Obviously I fancied you like crazy, but I knew how I felt would show on my face in the photos, especially if we spent all day together, so I tried to avert the problem.'

He takes a breath. 'My partner at Dedication had pulled his influencer sister in to help run our ad campaigns. She was great at her job, but she was also determined to sleep with me. I didn't feel the same, she wouldn't take no for an answer, and it all came to a head around the time of the wedding.'

'Poor woman, poor you – it sounds awful.'

Miles bites his lip. 'It wasn't really stalking to begin with, because it was all very public, but she was quite full on and not always rational. If I'd been all over Facebook in the wedding photos standing next to a bridesmaid as attractive as you, I was worried the whole thing would get out of hand. I didn't want to inadvertently drag you into it either.' He blows out a breath. 'I'm very sorry for messing up Scarlett's pictures, but partnering the very married, very pregnant bridesmaid felt like the safest bet. And I didn't explain on the day, because it wasn't something I wanted everyone to know.'

He frowns. 'That's why I searched high and low for you next morning to apologise properly.'

'It must have got worse if you ended up here?'

He sighs. 'It was all very delicate; we were worried about workplace harassment claims. With her social media experience, it could easily have spiralled out of control, which would have been disastrous for the company. In the end me withdrawing without loss of income was the workable solution we decided on.' He sighs again. 'Not long after the wedding, I stopped going to the office and sold my place in Manchester. And Mum needed me here, so it fitted in.'

I'm shocked. 'That doesn't seem fair.'

He blows out a breath. 'This is how I recognise your feeling of doubting yourself. At the time I was certain I hadn't done anything to suggest any interest other than in our working relationship. But when someone else sees it so differently, you end up questioning every nuance. In a strange way it shattered my professional confidence too.'

I'm smiling. 'And that's why you were desperate to find a new project?'

Miles pulls a face. 'I hate not working. But quite apart from not coming across anything suitable, it was very hard to trust new people and situations. Until you came along, that is.'

I can't help smiling. 'I'm very honoured you looked at me twice.'

He grins. 'I wanted to spend time with you, because I wanted to get to know you better, and when I did your whirlwind approach to life woke me up like a blast of sea spray in my face. You turned my ideas upside down, and reignited my enthusiasm for work.' His smile gets wider. 'You being scorching hot might have had something to do with it too.'

I laugh as I remember. 'You looked very hot at the wedding. And I fancied you so much when you walked in from the beach, I've been dreaming about getting you in that shower most days since then. Last night wasn't an accident – when I stepped onto that terrace, I made a very conscious decision.'

'I'm very pleased you did.' He turns to me and smiles. 'Would you like to do this again?'

I laugh again. 'I'd never meant to, but as we've got this far it seems a shame not to enjoy it while it lasts … if that's okay with you?'

He puts down our mugs and pulls me against him. 'That's good by me, Betsy.' He cocks his head. 'Is that the doorbell?'

'It's the end gate.' I jump off the bed, step over Fudge, and pull on a shirt. 'It could be Zofia dropping plants off.'

As I leave the kitchen and cross the gravel I'm readjusting my expression so Zofia doesn't guess what's happened, but when I open the gate, I'm staring at a guy in a navy suit.

He holds out his hand. 'Mark Osbourne, surveyor.' He takes in my blank look. 'Here for a valuation – a Sunday morning special, booked yesterday. This *is* Boathouse Cottage?'

My blood runs cold. 'That's right. I'm house-sitting for my sister Scarlett, but she didn't say you were coming.'

The guy frowns. 'I spoke to your sister's husband, Tate.'

'Of course.' I do a quick mental tour and take in devastation in every area. 'I'd appreciate a few minutes to tidy so you see the place at its best. You could try the café a few minutes along the beach?'

Mr Osbourne nods. 'I'll grab a coffee and see you in half an hour.'

I watch him head off down the lane, then hurtle inside to Miles who's standing by the bed stretching. 'Do you know anything about a survey appointment?'

Miles smacks his palm to his head. 'How did I forget?'

I laugh. 'Maybe because you've been up all night having super-hot sex?'

He looks at me. 'You *did* like it?'

'Do it to me ten more times, and I'll let you know.' I laugh. 'In the meantime, we have thirty minutes to make the place spotless.'

'Damn.' He pulls me into the kind of slow delicious kiss that makes my head spin.

I finally break away. 'You do the bedroom, kitchen, mudroom and terraces, I'll take the bathroom, sofa area and field?'

And just like that we're back to our day.

51

The Net Loft, St Aidan
South poles and stormy weather
Friday

When I was actively staying away from Miles we barely coincided, but since we slept together, we're drawn to each other like magnets. We walk together on the beach, do our visits to the shops at the same time, and lounge on the sofa with our legs entwined. After months of keeping my hands off, now I can touch, I can't let go. When I'm with him I want to take him to bed and annihilate him. When I'm without him I ache to see him again.

For someone like me, who's used to drifting through life, it's all-engulfing. The sex is the kind of explosive that makes me see stars and immediately want to do it again. The man simply turning up makes my knees give way. I have so much adrenalin coursing around my body, I feel shaky to the point of throwing up. When I've always been able to take or leave guys in the past, the alarm bells are deafening, but I can't think of stopping.

If Scarlett were ringing every day, I'd have to dodge her calls rather than admit any of this, but she's gone strangely silent.

I told her about Tate's valuer coming when she rang on Sunday afternoon and the sound she made was a lot like that time when we were kids when an ember landed in a box of fireworks on bonfire night and they all went off together. Then she said, 'My one-time partner is a prize arsehole. I *will* deal with this.' Then she ended the call and that was the last I've heard.

By Friday, when I close the shop at half past six and walk back to the cottage with Fudge, as most of St Aidan have seen me with my arm draped around Miles this week, I decide it's time to tell Scarlett the news before she accidentally hears it from anyone else.

I fire down two cans of full-sugar vanilla cola, find a comfy place on the dunes to sit for a moment and call her.

She picks up fast and launches. 'Betty, what a surprise. I ran into Tate, and now I'm desperate to have sex with him. I haven't felt like that for years.'

'Shit, Scarlett, talk about bad timing!'

'I went to tackle him about the surveyor. Kiera says it's a normal expression of emotional transfer, and if I do enough affirmations, it'll go away.'

I'm struggling to keep up. 'I thought she was a lawyer?'

'She is. Apparently divorce work is seventy percent counselling.' Scarlett laughs. 'My trouble is, when I should be seeing the decree absolute, all I can visualise is ex-sex.'

I give a cough. 'Well, my news is ... Miles and I are sleeping together.'

Scarlett gives a shout. 'Tate thought you were – he said he talked to Miles on Zoom, and he couldn't stop smiling.' She pauses. 'Are *you* smiling too?'

I try to sum up. 'It's amazing, but awful. I feel sick when I see him and dizzy when I don't. And before you ask, I'm not pregnant, because it only happened a few days ago.'

Scarlett's straight back with her reply. 'You're in love.'

'I'm *what?*'

Her voice is soft. 'That's what it feels like when you truly fall for someone. It's unmistakable.'

'I can't be. If it's that, I'll have to stop it. Immediately.'

Scarlett's talking quietly. 'It happens to everyone in the end, sweetie.' She pauses. 'Don't think he's too fancy and ostentatious for you, because he's really not. He has money, and the confidence that goes with it, but beyond that he's very down to earth.'

'I haven't thought about that for weeks.'

Scarlett laughs. 'Of course you haven't. Love is blind, that's why they talk about chemistry. For the first few months the dopamine and adrenalin alter your perception and you won't see any negatives at all. You'll be completely out of control, and you'll lose the ability to think critically.'

My whole body freezes. After what happened with Mason, I need to be fully aware at all times. Every atom of my being tells me I'm safe with Miles, but if my brain is fogged by chemicals I can't rely on any of it. I might be about to replay the worst mistake of my life.

'I need to stop this now.'

'You've always been strangely reluctant to let go of your childhood. Now might be the time.' Scarlett sounds frustrated.

I protest. 'That's not fair. Lots of people like fairy dresses.'

Her voice rises. 'You're twenty-eight, Betty, grown up things are going to happen. You've managed to get four retail outlets and a brand that's put Miles back in the game in two and a half months. However much you protest, you're already adulting.'

I let out a groan. 'How do you know about the other shops?'

She gives a sharp intake of breath. 'Tate may have mentioned. If you can handle big stuff like that, being head-over-heels will be like falling off a log.'

I have more important things to do than sit on the beach arguing with Scarlett. 'It's out of the question. I can't be in love! Thanks for telling me, I'll deal with it straight away.'

I know what I have to do. I end the call, and two minutes later I'm in the tranquillity zone, stuffing my clothes and laptop into a rucksack.

When I arrive upstairs at the Net Loft I throw my bag on the bed, take Fudge's lead off, then I go out onto the back terrace and phone Scarlett.

'Two calls in as many hours!'

I've decided what I have to say, and I launch. 'You need to sort yourself out, Scarlett. Stop messing Tate around. Just decide what you want to do with the cottage and your relationship, and tell him. Then hope to hell you're lucky enough to get it.'

There's a gasp, then a gap.

I carry on before I lose my nerve. 'I won't be staying at the cottage again until Miles leaves. I'm very grateful for everything you've done for me, but this once I can't do what *you* want. I have to do what's good for *me*.'

I hear her reel, then she gives a cough. 'Well done with that, it's great practice for me not always getting my own way.' She pauses for a second. 'I heard from Kiera. That valuation was because Miles is offering to buy the cottage.'

I'm caught off guard again. 'Why would he do that?'

Scarlett sniffs. 'I was hoping you could tell me that.'

As there's nothing more to say, we end the call together.

AUGUST

52

The Net Loft, St Aidan
Hot house plants and herbaceous borders
Friday

It's Friday, and a week since I started staying here at the Net Loft instead of the cottage. It's been a thousand times more unbearable than the week before that, when Miles and I were all over each other – for all the opposite reasons. Seeing Miles even less – i.e. not even bumping into him in the mud room – has been horrible, but this is the only way I can deal with it, and I'm hoping I'll get used to it eventually. In the meantime, I'm still dashing backwards and forwards along the beach with Fudge to sort out Pumpkin and sell Miles's buns.

When I come back into the shop after this afternoon's beach sales there are crowds of visitors milling on the harbourside. Zofia is serving drinks at the pastry table, but there's no danger of meeting Miles, because he's now baking at Jackie's or the cottage. Even though I've just spent my seventh night here, Zofia is still protesting.

'You do know you and Miles are the most stop-go couple in St Aidan?'

I know Zofia too well now. 'Why not skip the preamble and tell me where you're going with this?'

'I've promised Miles I'll deliver you to my house at four.'

Jackie steps out from behind the postcard rack. 'I'm here to cover while you go.' She fingers the silk scarf that's knotted around her neck. 'Whatever he's done, Betty, please give him another chance. He's never been as happy as he has since you guys got together at the cottage. Or as miserable as he's been the last few days.'

I shake my head. 'I'm sorry, Jackie. It's not him, it's me.' I'm not going to get out of this, but at least I can do it my way. 'It's busy so there's no need for you to deliver me. I'll leave you two here and drive myself.'

Zofia squeezes my fingers as I pass, and whispers. 'He'll be in the gazebo in the second walled garden.'

Then Clemmie and Plum burst through from the kitchen, pull me into a hug, and say, 'Go get him, girl!' which somewhat blows the secrecy vibe out of the water. The whole village knows about this, but whatever.

I'm heading out of town against the traffic, then I hit the single-track lanes, but thirty minutes later I'm padding across the soft green lawn of Zofia's vegetable garden, past the vibrant orange and pinks of the marigolds and cosmos, and the lavender that is buzzing with the sound of bees. The trellis structure where Miles is waiting is like a mini version of the bandstand on the *Neighbours* TV show where so many crucial plot moments happen.

I step under the shingled roof and get in first. 'If you're about to propose to me, Milo, please don't.'

'I'm not.'

I'm relieved he's got that right. 'Great. How can I help?'

He's resting his bum on the table. 'I've waited my whole life to feel like this, Betsy – you can't tell me to go away.'

My chest constricts because he sounds so broken. I owe it to him to explain. 'I was fine when we first got together. Then it hit me that the reason I want to throw up every time I see you is because I'm in love with you. And now I know I can't cope with any of it.'

'So you feel it too?'

'The vomiting?'

He shakes his head. 'No, Betsy, the love.'

'That's the bit I can't do.' My mouth fills with so much sour saliva, I wince. 'It all goes back to what happened with Mason.'

Miles winces. 'Something like that is bound to stay with you. Which part are you struggling with especially?'

I take a deep breath. 'I can't help the feeling that if I'd been more aware, I could have averted it.'

Miles blows out his cheeks. 'I don't know.'

'I should have seen the signs. It stood out a mile Mason had a problem with alcohol, but I missed that because I didn't think past how well his sharp suits would go down with Scarlett. When I found out the state he was in, I should have taken more care to protect myself.'

His voice is low. 'You're being very hard on yourself, Betsy.'

I shake my head. 'Part of moving forward was me facing up to the truth. I made bad calls that night, and I had to learn from that.' I cross the grass and pick an African marigold, then sit on the step with Fudge at my feet, crush the leaves with my nail and breath in the sharp smell. 'For two whole years I've honed my instincts, and kept myself safe and I've grown able to trust myself again.'

As I say the words out loud, I can't believe how far I'd come. 'I actually felt safe enough with you to try to kiss you. Then all hell broke loose, because I like you too much.' Even as I say it, I know it's impossible. 'How can I call anything at all, when my mind is blown because of how much I care about you, and I'm completely dizzy because I'm desperate to have sex with you?'

Miles pushes himself off the table and comes and sits down next to me. 'If you stop to think about it, you'll find you have made good calls. We're not strangers. You've had three months seeing me twenty-four-seven; you already know my worst bits.'

I'm shaking my head. 'All the bits I used to find impossible have grown on me. Beethoven symphonies, folding up dishcloths like origami, car washing every other day.'

'The dust on that lane is a nightmare with dark paint.'

I look at the sky. 'Okay, I'll let you off that one.'

He relaxes again. 'I've never felt anything like this either. It's very powerful.' He looks at me sideways and smiles. 'I've never met anyone I liked as much as you before. You have integrity, you live what you believe, you are quirky and funny and full of surprises, you call me out on every single thing, and you're unbelievably sexy. I've loved you since the day I walked in off the beach. I'll do whatever I can to find a way to make this work. Do you think you might be up for that?'

I bite my lip. 'That first week we were together was so incredible I felt like I'd been knocked over by a tidal wave. But if I think of never seeing you again, that's impossible to imagine too.'

Miles narrows his eyes. 'Maybe we could tone it down by limiting how much we see each other?'

I'm talking and thinking at the same time. 'Meet for small amounts of time. Hold off on the touching. Don't sleep together every night.' I purse my lips. 'Even as I say the words, I know I want all of you, all of the time.'

His smile widens. 'Whatever makes it comfortable for you, I'm happy to try it.' He stops. 'You have your own space at the Net Loft. From now on you decide how little or how much we see each other.'

I smile. 'That sounds good to me. I'd like to order one small kiss to test myself out.'

I reach across and graze his lips with mine, then go in for a whole lot more.

As I pull away I shake my head. 'There you go, I'm spinning again. Maybe what I need is *more* practice, not less.' I stop for a second. 'Scarlett said you're buying Boathouse Cottage, is that right?'

He gives a guilty shrug. 'I've been looking for somewhere since I sold my last place, and I hoped it would help them out, but please don't think I'm pushing you into anything with that.' Then he shakes his head again. 'Okay, I'll come clean – the real reason is I was worried someone else would buy it and leave Pumpkin without his field.'

I look at him hard. 'You're buying it for Pumpkin?'

'That's it.' He looks at me again. 'You must have seen the way he turns his head to listen to the waves? And puts up his nose and sniffs the salt in the air? And you're both devoted to each other.'

I get up and pull on Miles's hand so he's standing in front of me. 'A man who will buy a house so my pony can keep his favourite field – there isn't really a question mark is there?' I laugh. 'If you're hoping to avoid his side eye forever, this will only take you so far. You'll have to stay on top of your game in every area.'

He grins at me. 'I'll do everything I can to achieve that.' Then he squeezes my hand. 'I won't let you down, Betsy B.'

I put my hands around his neck. 'Do you think Zofia would mind if we borrowed her greenhouse?'

He laughs. 'We can't go near her seedlings. But I'm sure she won't mind if we have a quiet half hour in her arbor before we head back to the shop.'

And with that promise he leads me off across the garden.

53

St Aidan Beach
Meet me at the beach
Friday

It's close to five by the time we leave Zofia's swing seat. We have a very long goodbye kiss, and head back towards St Aidan in our own cars, but as the roads are clogged, we divert to Boathouse Cottage, double park, and then walk the rest of the way. It's almost time to close up, so we pick up Pumpkin from his field and lead him over the dune path at the top of the beach where it's quieter.

As we pass the Surf Shack my phone starts to vibrate.

'Scarlett!'

'Tate and I are back together. We've both agreed to give it another go.'

I smile. 'Are you going to tell me how?'

She snorts. 'I went to his with that list of requirements you told me to give him, and we ended up in bed.' There's a beat of silence. 'I apologised, too.'

'I'm pleased you got your happy ending.' I hesitate. 'I asked Miles about the cottage. Apparently it's for Pumpkin.' I flash a grin at Miles. 'And I'll join him there too. Unless you've changed your mind about selling?'

Scarlett is straight back. 'You know Tate and his projects. He's already looking for another Cornish wreck to transform.'

I shake my head. 'We'll look forward to seeing you in October.'

And then she ends the call and we walk on. When we come off the sands and onto the quayside, I can see the Betsy & Milo shop front is crisscrossed with bunting that's flapping in the breeze.

As we get closer, I squint to see. 'What's going on at the Net Loft? There are tables with ice buckets...' My stomach drops, and as I turn to look at Miles he gets in first.

'Still not proposing.'

'Phew.' I fan my face. 'Right answer.'

He laughs. 'I knew I wanted to marry you that first day at Scarlett's wedding, but last summer, a guy sent a plane across St Aidan bay pulling a "Marry me!" sign. If I've got to top that, you're safe for a while yet.' His smile widens. 'It's a birthday party for Pumpkin.'

My heart skips again. 'Pumpkin! How did I forget? It's the first of August!'

Miles grins. 'It's fine. His fan club is huge! Carol was in charge of cupcakes, Mum baked the main cake, Cressie's brought muffins, the Yellow Canary lent glasses. The whole village is joining in.'

I'm frowning. 'But how did you know?'

He laughs. 'The week you got here you told me he shared it with Yves St Laurent. I found out when it was, then logged it in my reminders.'

'Milo Appleton, what are you like?' I pull him into a kiss. 'I'm so glad I love you.'

He kisses me again. 'You know I love you too?'

I squeeze his hand. 'I do. Now I've had an hour to get used to it, I'm surprisingly okay with that.' I smile more. 'It couldn't be any other way, could it?'

He pulls me into a hug. 'It feels very right. And like it's what I've waited for my whole life.'

He calls across the cobbles to the group in front of the open shop door. 'Bring out the carrot cake, Mother, the guest of honour is arriving!'

Jackie and Zofia rush towards us with their arms outstretched and pull us into a big hug. 'We're very happy to see you holding hands again.'

Miles looks at the clouds. 'I'm with you on that.'

Then Fudge launches himself at Jackie and as Pumpkin gives Zofia's hip a nudge she scolds him. 'Sorry, boy, I don't have your home-grown carrot in my pocket today, but there's a bucket of your favourite herbs waiting by the tables.'

Miles laughs. 'A promise like that, Pumpkin, what are we waiting for? Let's pop those corks!'

When Miles said *everyone* in St Aidan, he wasn't exaggerating. We reach the Net Loft and find the whole of this end of the harbourside filled with people I recognise from the beach and the town, all here to join in the party. Clemmie's there, with Bud and Arnie; Plum and Nell are there; Sophie's kids and their friends are darting between the crowds, handing out crisps and veggie sausage rolls; Edie and Aunty Jo have big platters of cupcakes to give out. Lots of the makers are here waving their glasses, and the baking team have brought most of the over-sixties along too.

Aunty Jo has made Pumpkin a special strand of pink and orange gingham bunting which she drapes over him, and everyone is coming up to ruffle his mane and wish him 'happy birthday'.

A few glasses of fizz later Zofia comes across and pulls me into another hug. 'All thanks to you, Betsy Beth, my summer projects are going very well.' She grins. 'First my plant sales, now my matchmaking.'

I'm talking through a mouthful of buttercream. 'You were right when you said, "never say never".' I hug her back hard. 'Thank you for helping.'

I smile at Clemmie, who's holding Bud up to pat Pumpkin. 'We couldn't have done it without you and your friends at the barnyard.'

She beams back. 'You're very welcome. And it's the best news about you and Milo. Now you've put your fruit bowl issues behind you, there'll be no stopping you!'

Malcolm wanders over, waving a muffin. 'Any time you want to extend the lease on the studio, just let me know.'

Miles is standing with his arm draped over my shoulder. 'Betsy's more comfortable living in the moment, so it might be best to ask again later.'

I'm shaking my head. 'Actually, I'm good. Once I wouldn't have been, now I am. However long you want, Malcolm, this is us – Betsy and Milo are here to stay.'

When I look up at Miles, I know the reason there isn't any doubt. 'Are you okay with forever too?'

'I am.' He grins. 'Forever will be perfect.' His eyes are shining as he looks down at me. 'I promise we're going have the best adventures.'

Then he pulls me into another kiss and we only stop when Pumpkin lunges to take a bite of geraniums out of the window box he's been eyeing up since the day we arrived.

PS

I've often heard people say that life is full of surprises, but until this summer I was the kind of person who preferred things to be easy and consistent. Calm and uneventful. Then one day in May, Pumpkin and I drove into St Aidan, and since then nothing has ever been quiet again.

For the rest of the summer Miles and I have 'his place' and 'her place', and move freely between the Net Loft and the cottage spending nights in both places. Then, as winter draws in and the wind howls through the lobster pots on the quayside, we spend more time in the cottage, which is sheltered from the westerly gales. When the Boathouse Cottage conveyance finally goes through in December, we have a proper housewarming with all our friends clustered around the long deal table, which also quietly marks that Miles and I are properly living together too.

When Tate and Scarlett come back in autumn, they have a shortlist of properties to visit. They settle on a faded Customs House at the back of St Aidan harbour. Tate and Aleksy are busy making plans for that, and it definitely won't be faded when they've finished with it.

With Scarlett and I she had always been in charge; our whole life she was the strong one, while I was happy to lean on her. The way things panned out this summer flipped that relationship and shook up those lifelong habits, and we're both better for that.

Scarlett and Tate's astonishing news is that she is expecting a baby in June, which is going to mean big changes for them, but with their newly shaped partnership I'm sure they'll cope. And Miles and I can't wait to do the 'uncle and aunty' thing.

And what about Betsy & Milo? With Miles, it was never going to stand still. We now have Betsy & Milo postcards, and cards with all Milo's croissant flavours. By the end of summer we've added two more shops, three beach huts and a handful of those vintage vans he'd promised. Our mission statement always begins with me saying 'Small is amazing...' and Miles's inevitably adds '...and bigger is even better.' We'll always find something to argue about, but we'll find our own way forward that's comfortable for both of us.

At Malcolm and Aunty Jo's suggestion, I got in touch with all the local gardening clubs in the area, so in future when there are gluts of produce, we can sell that on from our shops to the visitors. Miles has set up the new business to include an element of profit sharing for all the helpers. For now he's agreed to stay in the southwest, but everyone knows he's looking further away too, and we're all excited about that.

Sometimes the way to slay your dragons is to talk about them and that's certainly proved true for me. Two years on, bringing my worst night ever out into the open has helped me face up to it. As long as I kept it buried, the shame, and the guilt, and the fear it could happen again defined my life. Sharing has helped me to understand that it wasn't my fault, and Miles has given me confidence and the will to try again.

Miles has also come clean about the cottage. He said he could easily have stayed somewhere else when I first turned up, but he liked me too much – and as things have turned out, I'm grateful he made that call. We couldn't be any more in love. Below the whoosh of excitement there's a solid and reassuring certainty that this is going to work for us.

As for how much the world has opened up for me since Pumpkin and I arrived in St Aidan – a wise woman once said, life shrinks or expands according to one's courage. Don't get the wrong impression – I haven't grown up entirely. I still dance on the beach, and I'll always enjoy looking like a jumble sale, but I'm strong enough to make my own choices and have the confidence to know that I'm good at what I do. If this is what being brave does, I'm very happy I tried it.

RECIPES

Sadly Miles's recipe for croissant dough is top-secret, but a St Aidan book wouldn't be complete without a recipe or two so I've chosen other bakes instead.

Betty's Scones

As Betty found when she visited the garden gate jam shop, warm home-baked scones are wonderful to eat outside on a summer's day, but they're just as delicious on a winter's afternoon by the fire, and very easy to make. Fabulous with or without sultanas, I love mine with Bonne Maman strawberry jam.

Ingredients:

- 1 lb plain flour
- 2 heaped teaspoonfuls of baking powder
- 2 oz caster sugar

4 oz cool butter or baking margarine cut into small pieces
2 free-range eggs
A little milk
A handful of sultanas for fruit scones

Jam and butter to serve (or clotted cream if you're really spoiling yourself!)

Method:
Pre-heat the oven to 220°C/200°C fan/Gas 7. Lightly grease two baking trays.

Sift the flour, baking powder and sugar into a bowl and mix together. Add the butter/margarine pieces, and lightly rub into the dry ingredients with your fingertips until the mixture is the texture of fine breadcrumbs. Add the sultanas here if you're including them.

Crack the eggs into a measuring jug and whisk lightly. Top up with milk to 10 fl oz. Gradually add the liquid to the dry ingredients and mix with a blunt knife and stop when you have made a soft sticky dough. (You may not need all the liquid.)

Lift the dough to a floured board, kneed lightly, then gently roll to a rectangle 3/4 inch thick. Cut into rounds with a fluted 2 inch cutter, reshaping and rolling the left-over dough until it's all used up.

Place the rounds on the greased baking sheets. If you want a glossy finish, brush with the remaining egg and milk mixture, then put in the oven. Cook for twelve to fifteen minutes, when the scones should be well risen and golden brown.

Transfer to a wire cooling rack, and eat as soon after baking as you can. To serve, split each scone in half and spread with butter or clotted cream and jam.

For extra light scones use milk, eggs and butter straight from the fridge. Keep your touch light when handling the dough. For bigger scones, use a larger cutter and roll the dough slightly thicker.

Pumpkin's Carrot Cake

This is a smaller version of the one baked by Miles's mum Jackie for Pumpkin's birthday celebrations – definitely for humans not ponies.

Ingredients:
For the cake:

- 225g self-raising flour
- 1 level teaspoon of baking powder
- 150g soft brown sugar
- 50g chopped walnuts
- 100g peeled carrots, coarsely grated

2 large eggs
150ml sunflower oil

For the topping:

50g butter (softened)
50g full fat cream cheese
150g sifted icing sugar
1/2 teaspoon vanilla extract
Chopped walnuts to decorate

Method:

Pre-heat oven to 180°C/160°C fan/Gas 4. Line a deep 20 cm round cake tin with grease proof paper.

Sieve flour and baking powder into a large mixing bowl. Stir in the sugar, then add the chopped nuts and grated carrots and mix lightly.

Make a well in the centre of the mixture, add the eggs and the oil to this, mix and then beat until it's mixed thoroughly.

Pour the beaten mixture into the prepared tin, then put into the oven and cook for one and a quarter hours, or until golden brown and the cake is coming away from the sides of the tin. (The cake is baked when you push a skewer into the centre of the cake and it comes out clean.)

Once baked, turn the cake out of the tin, remove the baking paper and place on a wire rack to cool.

For the topping:

Place the topping ingredients into a bowl and beat well with a hand mixer until smooth and creamy.

Once the cake has cooled, spread the topping evenly over the cake with a palette knife and decorate with chopped walnuts. (For a truly luxurious version make extra topping and split the cake and add a layer of topping in the centre too.)

Leave the topping to harden slightly, then serve in slices.

Betty's Chocolate Brownies

In case all the mentions of Betty sinking her teeth into chocolate muffins has made you crave cocoa, here's her favourite brownie recipe. As it's a tray bake, you can make the pieces as small or as large as you like!

Betty's tried many brownie recipes, but this St Aidan one is a favourite. She makes it in a tin that's 13 inches by 8 inches and 2 and a half inches deep. Some days she lines the tin with parchment, but if she's in a hurry she wings it and cooks without. Again, temperatures of different ovens may vary, and you may want to alter the cooking time to get a stickier brownie too. Remember the brownies will carry on cooking as they cool.

Ingredients:

- 375g butter at room temperature
- 375g dark chocolate if you're feeling posh (cocoa is fine if you don't have that)
- 6 large eggs
- 1 tablespoon vanilla extract
- 500g caster sugar
- 225g plain flour
- 1 teaspoon salt

Method:

Preheat the oven to 180°C/160°C fan/Gas 4.

Grease the tin or line with parchment.

Melt the chocolate and butter together in a heavy based saucepan and put aside to cool.

In a bowl, beat the eggs with the sugar and add the vanilla extract.

Sieve the flour into another bowl and mix in the salt.

When the chocolate mixture is cool, beat in the eggs and sugar.

Stir in the flour and beat until the mixture is smooth.

Transfer to the baking tin and bake for about 25 mins. Check often at the end to make sure not to cook it for too long.

When it's ready the top will have a paler brown crust, but the inside will still be dark and sticky.

Leave to cool and then slice into pieces.

Love, Jane xx

AUTHOR'S NOTE

To my readers,

St Aidan is a fictitious place, but I spend so much time walking around it in my head I feel as if I live there. In case you're wondering, all my St Aidan stories are standalone reads. The books run chronologically, some characters appear in several books, but not everyone is in every story. If you've enjoyed your time in St Aidan and would like to visit again, for anyone who'd rather avoid accidental spoilers, this is the order in which they were written:

The Little Wedding Shop by the Sea
Christmas at the Little Wedding Shop
Summer at the Little Wedding Shop
Christmas Promises at the Little Wedding Shop
The Little Cornish Kitchen
A Cornish Cottage by the Sea (aka Edie Browne's Cottage by the Sea)
A Cosy Christmas in Cornwall
Love at the Little Wedding Shop by the Sea
Tea for Two at the Little Cornish Kitchen
A Winter Warmer at the Little Cornish Kitchen
The Cornish Beach Hut Café

And lastly... *The Cosy Croissant Café*.

Happy reading and lots of love,
Jane xx

ACKNOWLEDGMENTS

Thank you to all my readers. These stories come to life when you turn the pages, and I love that you've chosen to escape for a few happy hours in St Aidan.

Thanks also to Charlotte Ledger for being the most wonderful friend, editor and publisher. And thanks to lovely, amazing Amanda Preston, my friend and dream agent. However many books we three create together, the magic and excitement never get any less.

Thanks to the One More Chapter family who get more incredible every year, and the wider HarperCollins team too.

Huge hugs to my Facebook friends, bloggers, Insta people and the social media book community – you are stars; I'm so grateful for your unstinting and generous support. My stand-out moment this year was when the lovely Wendy McLaren and her fab husband, Mike, travelled all the way from Moss Vale, NSW, Australia and came to see us in (very rainy) Derbyshire. Please come back again soon, Wendy and Mike, we promise to make the sun shine for you next time!

All the love to my children, Anna, Indi and Max, and their partners, Aladdin, Richard and Izzy. To Eric, Theo, Dahlia and Lyla-Rose too.

Saving the last hugs for Phil. And of course, Herbie and Bear. xx

Escape to Cornwall with the most heartwarming, feel-good romcom!

Florence May never expected to trade the high life of London for the cosy comfort of a beach hut in her Cornish hometown, but the moment she steps inside she knows it was the best choice she ever made. The fact that it comes with a requirement that she sets up a business on site? A minor setback that's easily fixed by opening up a surfside outpost of her friend Clemmie's Little Cornish Kitchen ... where Floss finds herself unexpectedly flourishing.

And when the hotel owner next door sets out to buy the land out from under her? Floss calls on her loyal friends to help her save her little slice of heaven. Because if there's one thing the community of St Aidan does well, it's banding together to make the most of every second, whatever life throws at you.

Available now in paperback, eBook and audio!

THE LITTLE CORNISH KITCHEN

**Have you discovered the
Little Cornish Kitchen series?**

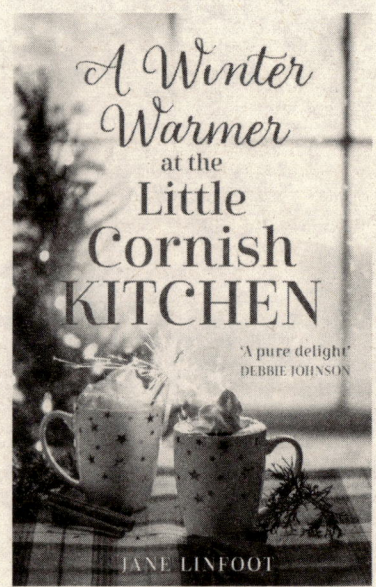

Tea for Two at the Little Cornish KITCHEN
JANE LINFOOT

'A pure delight'
DEBBIE JOHNSON

A Winter Warmer at the Little Cornish KITCHEN

'A pure delight'
DEBBIE JOHNSON

JANE LINFOOT

ONE MORE CHAPTER
YOUR NUMBER ONE STOP FOR PAGETURNING BOOKS

The author and One More Chapter would like to thank everyone who contributed to the publication of this story...

Analytics
James Brackin
Abigail Fryer

Audio
Fionnuala Barrett
Ciara Briggs

Contracts
Laura Amos
Laura Evans

Design
Lucy Bennett
Fiona Greenway
Liane Payne
Dean Russell

Digital Sales
Laura Daley
Lydia Grainge
Hannah Lismore

eCommerce
Laura Carpenter
Madeline ODonovan
Charlotte Stevens
Christina Storey
Jo Surman
Rachel Ward

Editorial
Kara Daniel
Charlotte Ledger
Federica Leonardis
Ajebowale Roberts
Jennie Rothwell
Caroline Scott-Bowden
Helen Williams

Harper360
Jennifer Dee
Emily Gerbner
Ariana Juarez
Jean Marie Kelly
emma sullivan
Sophia Wilhelm

International Sales
Peter Borcsok
Ruth Burrow
Colleen Simpson
Ben Wright

Inventory
Sarah Callaghan
Kirsty Norman

Marketing & Publicity
Chloe Cummings
Grace Edwards
Emma Petfield

Operations
Melissa Okusanya
Hannah Stamp

Production
Denis Manson
Simon Moore
Francesca Tuzzeo

Rights
Helena Font Brillas
Ashton Mucha
Zoe Shine
Aisling Smyth
Lucy Vanderbilt

Trade Marketing
Ben Hurd
Eleanor Slater

The HarperCollins Distribution Team

The HarperCollins Finance & Royalties Team

The HarperCollins Legal Team

The HarperCollins Technology Team

UK Sales
Isabel Coburn
Jay Cochrane
Sabina Lewis
Holly Martin
Harriet Williams
Leah Woods

And every other essential link in the chain from delivery drivers to booksellers to librarians and beyond!

ONE MORE CHAPTER

YOUR NUMBER ONE STOP FOR PAGETURNING BOOKS

One More Chapter is an award-winning global division of HarperCollins.

Subscribe to our newsletter to get our latest eBook deals and stay up to date with all our new releases!

signup.harpercollins.co.uk/join/signup-omc

Meet the team at
www.onemorechapter.com

Follow us!
- @OneMoreChapter_
- @onemorechapterhc
- @onemorechapterhc
- @onemorechapterhc

Do you write unputdownable fiction?
We love to hear from new voices.
Find out how to submit your novel at
www.onemorechapter.com/submissions